London Rain

NICOLA UPSON

FABER & FABER

First published in this edition in 2015
by Faber & Faber Ltd
Bloomsbury House
74–77 Great Russell Street
London WC1B 3DA

This paperback edition published in 2016

Typeset by Faber & Faber Ltd
Printed and bound by CPI Group (UK) Ltd, Croydon CR0 4YY

A CIP record for this book
is available from the British Library

ISBN 978-0-571-28776-5

2 4 6 8 10 9 7 5 3 1

For Mandy, and for my Mum and Dad, with all my love.
And for Phyllis. Friend and inspiration, still.

Part One

At Broadcasting House

There had never been a finer time to see London, Josephine thought as she strolled down Cavendish Place, enjoying the way in which the early summer sun seemed to welcome her back to the city. With only a few days to go before the Coronation, it would have been hard to say which had done more to put a spring in England's step: the sudden, unexpected heatwave, softening the disappointment of a lacklustre April; or the months of work that had gone on behind the scenes as the nation looked forward to crowning a new king. Everywhere she looked, those quiet preparations had come magically to fruition: government buildings encrusted with the soot of ages were given a new lease of life by vigorous cleaning; stands of tiered seating sprang up in front of churches; poles and planks now obscured famous statues, caring little for the celebrity of history when there was a sparkling new future ahead; and the West End took on the appearance of a colourful, streamered fairground, with decorated masts standing proudly in main streets and marquees beginning to dot the parks.

The air of celebration was infectious, and had spread like a tide of goodwill through the country. Yesterday, as the train from Scotland brought Josephine south, she had stared in amazement at suburbs dressed from top to toe in red, white and blue, their narrow streets a tunnel of ribbons and paper crowns. It could have been garish, but Josephine – who was inclined to mistrust public displays of any emotion – found it strangely touching, a rare declaration of unity after the uncertainty of the abdication. Businesses everywhere were shrewdly taking advantage of the nation's excitement: no one could compete with the vast golden crowns and specially commissioned sculpture that had won Selfridges every front page, but even more modest shop windows were crammed with coronation souvenirs to suit most pockets – embroidered silk sheets and engraved cigarette lighters sat alongside sponge bags, playing cards and flower pots, and it was impossible now to buy anything remotely necessary for daily life without its being adorned by a royal motif: as she brushed her teeth each morning, Their Majesties stared up at her from a bar of Yardley's soap, and even the label on her face powder advised her – with a shameless lack of irony – to begin a reign of personal loveliness.

The latest bus strike had entered its second week and the pavements were crowded with reluctant pedestrians, a mixture of tourists in town for the special occasion and seasoned Londoners trying to go about their business. At the junction with Regent Street, Josephine glanced to her right and saw the hordes of people spilling slowly from Oxford Circus; their stilted, shuffling progress was so different to the normal bustle of the capital that it gave her the peculiar sense of watching a newsreel played at the wrong speed, and she was glad that her club was only a short walk from Portland Place and her afternoon appointment.

Broadcasting House was an austere, modern building in a stripped classical style, which dwarfed its Georgian neighbours and seemed itself to be torn between past and future. In its five years of operation, it had set critic against critic on every subject from architecture to programming, with an admiration for one often encouraging a tolerance for the other. Josephine had never really liked the building, but it interested her to note that today – when she was more than just a passer-by – it looked finer than she remembered it; like most clubs, it seemed, the British Broadcasting Corporation was best viewed from the inside. The long approach from Oxford Street showed the building's design off to its greatest advantage, curved and streamlined like the bow of a ship, the masts and flags on its rooftop lending further touches to the nautical feel.

Window boxes on three of the eight floors provided a welcome splash of colour, relieving an otherwise stern and unforgiving exterior, and Josephine wondered if the multitude of tulips in red and yellow – recently announced as the official coronation colours – had been a lucky guess, or if someone with good connections had been given a helpful hint.

Taxis paused one after another outside the entrance, and she noticed a group of young girls with autograph books waiting hopefully at a discreet distance to see who might be delivered or collected from the studios. She was obviously not at all what they were hoping for: even if they had known her name, writers here were the poor relations of announcers and variety stars, and her approach barely warranted a second glance. It suited her that way: she felt more comfortable as a fan than as a star, and had Bing Crosby suddenly alighted from a black cab, her own fame would not have prevented her from rummaging in her handbag for a scrap of paper and entering wholeheartedly into the scrum. Still, as she paused under Eric Gill's hauntingly beautiful statue of Prospero and Ariel, she realised that she had not felt this excited since the opening night of her play, *Richard of Bordeaux*. She was still astonished that another of her West End hits – *Queen of Scots* – had been included in a cycle of royal radio dramas to celebrate the Coronation, taking her work into thousands of homes throughout the country. The choice amused her: Mary Stuart was hardly a good advertisement for a long and happy reign, but if the irony had escaped the BBC, she wasn't about to point it out.

The entrance hall – semicircular in form and lined with English marble – gave the immediate impression of a much older organisation, solid and established, and more like a bank than a state-of-the-art home for a pioneering venture. It was a beautiful space, softened by the grace of natural curves, and the only extravagance was a show-stealing arrangement of gladioli in a brilliant white vase. The display would have held its own in the grandest of churches, and the comparison was an apt one: a second Gill sculpture, this time of a figure sowing wheat, occupied an altar-like position opposite the main door, looking down on everything with a calm, almost spiritual benevolence. Above it was a chiselled inscription in Latin, and Josephine recognised enough of the words – temple, wisdom, Reith and Director General – to understand why the statement of intent had inspired some of the more cynical newspapers to new heights of sarcasm.

Reception was flanked by an information desk and a bookstall selling various BBC publications. She announced herself, then took a seat as directed on one of the leather benches and watched the Corporation go about its daily business. Pageboys hurried through the building in smart blue uniforms, collecting and delivering letters; men of all ages went up and down stairs, some wearing suits, others more casually dressed in roll-neck jumpers and corduroy trousers, and Josephine wondered if she was making assumptions by dividing them into 'management' and 'creative' accordingly. There were very few women, but, on the dot of two o'clock, the front door gave way to a surge of chatter and perfume, and Josephine smiled as a battalion of secretaries walked across the glossy entrance hall in high heels and sheer stockings, beautifully made up and talking disdainfully in high, clear voices: the hub of the organisation had obviously just returned from lunch. As the army disappeared up the stairs, she was reminded of a scene from the film *Metropolis*. How many people worked here, she wondered. Five or six hundred? More? The organisation was its own small town, broadcasting *to* the world from a world of its own, and Josephine envied the sense of communal endeavour. It was so different to her own work, and she could only imagine how exhilarating it must feel to be part of it.

After a few minutes, she saw a distinctive figure with small, round glasses and a goatee beard bound down the stairs. She had known Julian Terry for several years, but as a fellow detective novelist rather than the BBC's Director of Features and Drama. His younger brother, John, was a celebrated classical actor who had starred in or produced two of the West End productions of Josephine's plays, including *Queen of Scots*, and Julian dabbled with minor parts on stage and screen, most recently in a film based on his own novel, a murder mystery set at Broadcasting House. He shared his brother's lean, graceful figure and sharply chiselled features, and the similarity was even more remarkable when he opened his mouth: the voice – a milder version of his brother's – would have justified a performing role in the plays he produced. 'Josephine, how nice to see you,' he said, with a warmth and charm that explained how he had reached his third marriage before his fortieth birthday. 'I hope I haven't kept you waiting.'

'Not at all, but I wouldn't mind if you had. I could sit here for days without getting bored.'

'It is impressive, isn't it? You only start to see the drawbacks when you work here.' He kissed her and led her over to the lifts. 'It's stupid of me, but I still miss our old offices at Savoy Hill. They were chaotic and inadequate and falling down around our ears, but it was all an adventure. This feels very grown-up, and I'm not sure some of us are ready for that yet.' Josephine did know what he meant. Even to someone visiting Broadcasting House for the first time, it felt as though the organisation had made a conscious decision to shake off the old world of cosy amateurism and start again, free from the clutter of those first faltering steps. As the lift made its flawlessly smooth ascent to the seventh floor, Terry continued: 'I'm the last person who should complain, of course – being here has revolutionised what we can do in the drama department. We've got a suite of studios now, all with different acoustics, and you'll be astonished when you hear your play next week.' He grinned. 'In a positive way, I hope. But first things first. I thought we'd have a quick chat about the rehearsals before we go down for the read-through? The cast has been called for two o'clock to do some photos for the *Radio Times*, then we can crack on. It'll make a nice change for us to have the author there – anything to make them eager to please . . .'

Josephine laughed. 'The next time I have that effect will be the first. In my experience, being present at any sort of rehearsal just makes an actor more determined to prove that the character he wants to play is so much more interesting than the one you've actually written.'

'Even my brother?'

'*Especially* your brother. The irritating thing about him, though, is that he's invariably spot on. *Richard of Bordeaux* was a much better play for the suggestions he made.'

'Yes, Johnny was *born* right, but I've learned to live with it.' The remark was made without a hint of bitterness and, in any case, Josephine knew that there was a genuine affection between the brothers, each successful enough in his own right to admire the achievements of the other. 'I wish we could have included *Bordeaux* as well,' Terry added as the lift opened its doors onto a labyrinthine series of carpeted corridors, 'but the schedules were too tight and the powers that be felt we needed a queen.' He offered a conspiratorial grin. 'Believe me, you've no idea what a novelty *that* is in this organisation.'

'Yes, I'm sure. Actually it's nice for Mary to get her day in the sun. She's always lived in Richard's shadow.'

'Exactly. And let's hope our new Scottish queen will prove more popular with the English public than yours was.'

'I suppose being called Elizabeth is a good start. Actually, though, *Queen of Scots* does seem rather a backhanded coronation tribute. Is there a republican working secretly in the Drama Department?'

'Several, probably, but I think it's got more to do with available material. How many plays about happy kings can you name?' Josephine gave it a moment's thought as Terry led her past a bewildering number of offices and studios, but eventually had to admit defeat. 'Anyway, there's nothing wrong with celebrating a deposed monarch as long as you don't mention the one who went of his own accord.' He stopped suddenly and showed her into a pleasant room on the eastern side of the building, overlooking Langham Street. 'They're not making any announcements about the wedding until after the Coronation, you know.'

'You sound disappointed.'

'I make my living out of drama, Josephine, not tact.' He pushed a glass cigarette box across the desk and leaned forward expectantly, a child waiting for a story. 'Lydia tells me you've met Wallis Simpson.'

Josephine smiled. 'To be taken with a pinch of salt, of course. Our paths crossed in Suffolk while she was waiting for her divorce, and Archie was looking after her. I was much more aware of her than she was of me, though. I doubt I'll be on the guest list for the wedding, whenever it is.'

Terry looked so crestfallen that she felt half obliged to make something up simply to please him. Instead, she changed the subject and asked cautiously: 'How is Lydia?'

'You mean how is she taking her demotion from Queen of Scots to lady-in-waiting?'

'Something like that, yes.' Josephine had originally written the play for her friend Lydia Beaumont, who had starred in its West End run and made the part of Mary Stuart her own. Lydia was considered too inexperienced in radio drama to take the lead in this production, though, and was instead playing one of the minor characters.

'With her usual grace and charm, which is much appreciated. Not everyone understands what a different medium this is. I've had actors in here who hold packed houses spellbound every night in the West End but they can't utter a word the minute you stick them in front of a microphone. Even Johnny, the first time he came in.

Made quite a change for me to have the upper hand, and I probably enjoyed it more than I should have. I don't doubt that Lydia will be excellent, and I'm hoping to work with her more often, but she's got to be broken in gently. And we're lucky to have Millicent Gray on board. She's not the easiest person to deal with and there's always a bit of tension when she's in the building – for obvious reasons – but she's one of the most brilliant radio voices we've got and she'll give a good performance.' Before Josephine could ask him what he meant by 'obvious reasons', Terry moved on. 'Now, if you really don't like any of the changes I've made, let me know after the run-through and we'll talk about it then. A certain amount of butchery is always involved, but I like the author to have a say in where the knife falls – as long as it's not in my back.'

'I'm sure everything will be fine,' Josephine said with more confidence than she felt. 'As you say, it's a very different medium from anything I'm used to, and nothing could be as drastic as what Alfred Hitchcock is doing to my novel as we speak.'

'Yes, I heard he was filming one of yours. Lucky devil! *A Shilling for Candles*, isn't it?'

'It is at the moment.'

Terry threw back his head and laughed. 'I suppose there is a good chance that you won't recognise it when he's finished. But you can't lose with Hitchcock's name on it. I took the coward's way out and did my own adaptation, but I think *Death at Broadcasting House* suffered from—' The telephone rang, preventing Josephine from discovering what Terry disliked about his own film. He lifted the receiver and she was amused by the expression of disdain on his face. 'What? You mean he's actually in reception? Good God, no, I can't see him now. Make any excuse – tell him I'm dead if you want to – just get rid of him. And no more calls now, Stan. I'll be busy for the rest of the day.' He turned back to Josephine. 'That's the great thing about this building. No one can touch you if you don't want them to – not even actors who think you owe them a part. Shall we go down and meet the cast?'

Josephine nodded and picked up her bag, but before they could leave there was a knock at the door and an attractive woman in her late thirties came into the room without waiting for an invitation. She glanced apologetically at Josephine. 'Sorry to interrupt. Is there any point in my asking you for some copy for next week's issue, Julian?'

The words were spoken with a weary resignation that suggested the conversation took place on a regular basis. Terry had the decency to look sheepish, but hid behind formalities. 'Do you two know each other? Viv, this is Josephine Tey. She's in this afternoon for the read-through of *Queen of Scots*. Josephine, I'd like you to meet Vivienne Beresford. She's holding the fort at the *Radio Times* while Gorham's off on grace term, and doing a better bloody job of it than he ever did, if I may say so.'

'You mean I'll write your copy for you if you make me wait long enough. Well, not this time, Julian. I've got enough on my plate. No one can decide whether Cicely Courtneidge is taking part in the coronation revue, Irene Veal has threatened to resign if I cut her copy to make room for the crossword, and someone from the Co-op just telephoned with a small change to the colour advertisement that went to press three weeks ago. So flattery will get you another few hours, but nothing more and don't try palming me off with the cast list again, because it won't work.' She smiled sweetly at Terry, then turned to Josephine for the first time and held out her hand. 'I'm sorry, but I had to get that off my chest. Bloody producers. They all want the publicity for their plays but they won't give a column inch to get it. It's lovely to meet you.'

'And you.'

'I don't know how you've got the cheek to complain about producers.' Terry drew breath to retaliate, and Josephine sensed that both he and Vivienne Beresford relished the sparring. There seemed to be an easy affection between them, and she wondered how long they had known each other. 'You editors – you swan round the building, getting everyone else to do your job for you, while you play with pretty pictures and take the credit when the issue sells well. It certainly wasn't like that in my day.'

'The issue *didn't* sell well in your day – that's the point. And at least I don't have to make my own letters up. When he was Assistant Editor, Miss Tey, he spent most of his time churning out fake correspondence about the drama department. Now they've let him run the damned thing.'

'I didn't know you worked on the *Radio Times*, Julian,' Josephine said.

'Yes, back in twenty-nine – it's how I started at the BBC. Viv and I shared a desk. I taught her all she knows.'

'God help me if that were true.' Ignoring Terry's next move, she turned to Josephine and said: 'I don't suppose you'd do me an enormous favour? We've got a photographer downstairs, taking some rehearsal pictures of your play. Would you have one taken with them? Readers love to see who's behind the broadcast, and we don't get the chance to do it very often.'

'Will that hold you up?' Josephine asked hopefully, but Terry shook his head.

'No, of course not. You go down with Viv and I'll join you in a few minutes.' He glared at his colleague. 'It'll give me time to cobble a few words together. Unless, of course . . . now that *would* be a splendid idea.' There was an impatient sigh from the door as he kept them in suspense. 'Why don't we ask the author to do it? Get Josephine to write something for you, Viv. "The drama of kingship" by the author of *Richard of Bordeaux*. That would be quite a coup. You two can work out the details between you.'

He ushered them out of his office, leaving Josephine unsure as to whether it had been a serious suggestion or merely a ploy to get rid of them. Hoping to discourage the idea, she changed the subject. 'Julian said the editor was on grace term – what's that?'

'It's like time off for good behaviour. If you've been at the BBC for ten years in what they call – and I quote – "a creative and responsible role", you get three months off and a grant to expand your horizons in a way which will benefit both you and the Corporation. Maurice Gorham's spending the summer in America.'

'Leaving you in charge?' The surprise in her voice must have been obvious because the other woman gave a wry smile, and Josephine felt obliged to explain her lack of tact. 'Sorry, that didn't sound quite right. I just meant that a woman in such a senior position must be unusual here.'

'I suppose they wondered what harm I could do in three months, and it would have taken them that long to break someone else in. I've worked with Maurice for years, and the job's not as lofty as you might think. Everyone at the top is a bit sniffy about the *Radio Times*, even if it does make thousands of pounds a year. But it keeps you in touch with everything – drama, talks, outside broadcasts – and that's what I love about it. Do you mind if we go via my office? I need to drop these notes off.' Josephine shook her head and followed Vivienne Beresford down yet another flight of stairs. She was fascinated by the vast array of functions stacked one on top of another within the building, from general offices, restaurants and post rooms to libraries, council chambers and the different-sized studios that Julian had mentioned; it was surprising that anyone who had to move around the departments got any work done at all.

The *Radio Times* offices were away from the main building in one of the adjoining houses on Portland Place. 'You're right about the women, though,' Vivienne continued, opening the door onto a small courtyard that functioned as a shortcut. 'It took them ten years to trust the British public with a female announcer, and even then I swear they half-believed the building would crumble to the ground in protest as soon as Sheila opened her mouth. On the other hand, I believe the waiting list of charwomen currently stands at around three thousand. Right, these are our offices – cramped, chaotic and friendly, but give me that any day. The other place is far too anonymous for my liking.'

Josephine assumed that Vivienne had not bothered to move for her brief tenure in charge: the office she headed for was shared with a kindly faced, grey-haired typist, so elderly that the room might well have been built around her, and her desk had nothing temporary about it; letters and proof pages for the new issue sat happily alongside personal photographs, postcards and well-thumbed reference books. Directly opposite, a framed *Radio Times* cover from 1929 stood on the floor against a filing cabinet, and Josephine's attention was drawn immediately to the painting that had replaced it on the wall. 'Is that the Coronation cover?' she asked.

'Yes, it's the original artwork. Stunning, isn't it? Maurice did so well in persuading Nevinson to do it for us. I must remember to return it to his office before he gets back from the States – it's his pride and joy.'

Josephine smiled and walked over to take a closer look. 'I'm not surprised. It's lovely.' The artist, more famous for his harrowing war images than his royal tributes, had chosen an unusual perspective for this particular cover design, looking down into Whitehall from a top floor window. The pavements were packed with cheering crowds, while hundreds more gathered to watch the procession from every vantage point afforded by the buildings on either side, their faces just visible through the flags and bunting that all but obscured the sober grey stone of London's governmental heart. Sunlight – it was, of course, a fine, dry day – glinted on the polished helmets of the guards below, echoing the ceremonial red-and-yellow masts that lined the street and bringing a feeling of warmth and celebration to the image as a whole. And in the foreground, resting on the window ledge at which the viewer sat, was a microphone, poised and ready to broadcast the BBC's coronation commentary to the world. The design was a masterful combination of symbolism and atmosphere, worthy of the history being made. In fact, it was so convincing that Josephine half-believed she could hear the horses' hooves and the cheers of the crowd as she looked at it, that she could – if she wished – throw open the window and feel the rough cloth of the flag between her fingers.

'I think that will knock everything else on the bookstands into a cocked hat, don't you?' Vivienne said, joining her by the painting. 'We shouldn't be smug, but we are.'

'You've every right to be. I'm surprised your boss didn't hang around to enjoy his moment of glory, though. Won't he be lonely in America? Most of them are over here.'

'I think Maurice has lived with the build-up for so long that he feels as if he's seen the event already – we all do. Because there's such a large print-order for this issue, the cover and the colour supplement had to go to press a while ago. Look, this is it.' She showed Josephine what she meant, opening the supplement to reveal a double-page map of the coronation procession. 'We knew the important stuff weeks ago – the route, the order of service, the street layout – so everything that should be so exciting is actually old news.' She pointed to Nevinson's painting again. 'Actually, it was this that gave us the biggest headache of all. Before he could finish it, he had to know how the city would be decorated, but nothing had been announced. Poor Maurice ended up at the Privy Council, only to be told that they couldn't possibly say anything but if we made it red and yellow we wouldn't be far wrong. I half think he left the country just in case they were lying.' Josephine laughed and handed the map back, but Vivienne shook her head. 'I'll have thousands of the damned things on Friday, so you might as well keep it and plot your position. It's going to be chaos out there. I assume you're staying on for it?'

'Yes, but I have a good friend at Scotland Yard. He's organised some seating for us near the Abbey.'

'Very handy.'

'What about you?'

'Oh, equally nepotistic. My husband's a broadcaster here . . .'

'Anthony Beresford?' Josephine felt slow for not having made the connection earlier: Beresford was one of the best-known voices at the BBC.

'That's right. He's one of the observers on the day, so I'll probably be with him during the commentary.' She picked up a sheaf of papers from her desk and opened the door. 'Right, I'd better not make you late for the read-through or Julian will regain the moral high ground. They're in the concert-hall green room.'

'What about *your* grace term?' Josephine asked as they walked through the courtyard and back into Broadcasting House. 'I imagine some time off would be welcome after this.'

'Not really. I'd rather be at work, if I'm honest. Maurice is off for another two months and I'm enjoying myself – not that anything's *particularly* different. The workload seems remarkably similar whether he's here or not.' Josephine had already learned that Vivienne Beresford used a smile when it counted, not when it was expected, and it came now, warm and conspiratorial. 'Anyway, when my time comes to spend the Corporation's money, I'll do it somewhere much closer to home. Anthony was a foreign correspondent for a while after we were married, so I've had enough of moving around. I'm happiest on English soil – always have been.'

Thankfully, the BBC's concert hall was on the lower ground floor and comparatively easy to navigate. 'I'll apologise in advance for putting you through this,' Vivienne said as she opened the outer door to the green room. 'The shots aren't always flattering – less action than actionable, if you know what I mean – but it does help the magazine.'

The space designed for artists using the concert hall could not have been more different from the public areas of Broadcasting House – as vibrant and modern as the entrance hall was classic and restrained, with a chocolate-brown carpet and pale-green walls, offset by beautiful art-deco chairs upholstered in a Chelsea stripe. The room had the potential to be divided into two by central curtains which were currently drawn back, and the photographer had placed his tripod at the far end, where a large mirror brought light and the illusion of space to the room. He had his back to the door and the session was in full swing, with all but a handful of the cast oblivious to the women's entrance. Standing script in hand by another striking flower arrangement, they waited as the photographer tried to tease what he wanted from the most prominent actress, an auburn-haired woman with the look of a worldly Betty Balfour, whom Josephine recognised as her queen. 'Come on, Millie darling,' he said impatiently, and his voice was high-pitched and regrettably clear. 'At least try to smile. Just remember you're knocking off the acting editor's husband.'

Josephine could not decide if she had actually heard herself gasp or had simply imagined it, but she saw her own embarrassment reflected in the faces looking back at her. The murmur of conversation in the room stopped instantly, as if an imaginary director had said 'cut', and she looked pleadingly at Lydia, who responded with one of the finest performances she had ever given. 'Josephine, darling – how wonderful to see you. Everyone's been longing to meet you. We're all so excited about this.' She wrapped Josephine in an enormous hug and dragged her over to the rest of the cast, whose relief made each and every one of them far more amenable to the presence of an author than they might otherwise have been. As she was introduced to Darnley, Bothwell and Rizzio in turn, she glanced quickly at Vivienne Beresford, who stood still and impassive, her humiliation acknowledged only by the tide of crimson rising slowly from her neck; before she could think of something – anything – to say which might involve the editor in the conversation and make the situation easier for her, Millicent Gray dropped her script onto the coffee table, glared at the camera and walked over to the door. For a moment, Josephine thought she was going to bring the confrontation out into the open, but she left the room without meeting the other woman's eye. A few seconds later, Vivienne Beresford turned and followed her out into the corridor.

'I think we might be looking for a new queen,' the photographer said, apparently unruffled by the damage he had done. 'Could be your moment after all, Lydia darling, although I wouldn't bet against Millicent in a fight.'

Lydia chose not to rise to the bait, but the actor playing Bothwell – introduced to Josephine as Douglas Graham – was not quite so restrained. 'Don't be so bloody stupid, Leaman,' he said. 'It's about time you learned to keep your mouth shut. In fact, I'm surprised someone didn't do it for you years ago.'

'Are you offering, Dougie? No? Then I'd save your histrionics for the broadcast. Anyway, it's not as if I've let the cat out of the bag, is it? Vivienne knows perfectly well what's going on. We all do, so I don't quite see what the fuss is about.' The words were defiant, but Leaman sounded rather less sure of himself as he turned to Josephine. 'And last but not least, the author. Then I'll leave you all to it.'

By now, he seemed to have lost heart for anything creative, and Josephine's ordeal consisted of nothing more arduous than a few perfunctory portrait shots. When it was over, she sat down gratefully next to Lydia. 'Now I know what Julian meant by Millicent Gray and tension in the building. I wanted the ground to swallow me up, so God knows how Vivienne Beresford felt. You were marvellous, by the way.'

'Thank you. It's nice to be appreciated. I think Viv's used to it, though. Gerard Leaman may be a troublemaking little shit, but he's right about the affair being the worst kept secret at the BBC. And regardless of her marriage, Viv's no stranger to gossip. Her maiden name was Hanlon.'

Josephine looked blank. 'Should that mean something to me?'

'Yes. She's *Olivia* Hanlon's sister.' When the explanation failed to bring the moment of clarity that Lydia expected, she added impatiently: 'You must have heard of Olivia Hanlon! The night-club hostess? She owned the Golden Hat in Soho. It was legendary back in the twenties.'

'Yes, I remember it, but I couldn't have told you who owned it.'

'Well, discretion was her middle name, I suppose. Then she drowned in a swimming pool about ten years ago and discretion went out the window. There was quite a fuss about it at the time.'

'Not in Inverness, there wasn't. Must have clashed with a flower show.' Josephine thought about the intelligent, no-nonsense woman she had just met, trying – and failing – to see her as the unhappy victim of a bad marriage, whose past refused to lie down. 'Vivienne didn't strike me as the type to be made a fool of. Why doesn't she divorce him?'

Lydia shrugged. 'Who knows what goes on in a marriage? And there are two sides to every story, aren't there?'

It was an innocent observation, but they were straying into territory that made Josephine uncomfortable. Her deepening rela-tionship with Lydia's lover carried with it a complex blend of joy and soul-searching, and – while she suspected that Lydia was per-fectly aware of the situation and had her own reasons for tolerating it – the subject remained an unspoken source of friction between them, threatening their friendship but never quite derailing it. Re-luctant now to continue a conversation that could have any kind of subtext, she steered it carefully back to Vivienne Beresford. 'When you say there was a fuss about her sister's death, do you mean it was suspicious or just scandalous?'

'Both. There was talk of debts and suicide, and some of the papers hinted that she was bumped off because of something she knew, but I suppose that was inevitable with what she did for a liv-ing. Nothing was ever proved, though. The verdict was death by misadventure, and that was that.'

Josephine was prevented from asking anything else by the

arrival of Julian Terry and the return of a noticeably subdued Millicent Gray. The producer was accompanied by a young woman with a notebook and stopwatch whom Josephine took to be his assistant, and another man who was introduced to the cast as a studio technician. 'Right everyone,' he said when the formalities were dispensed with, 'we'll read straight through from the top and I'll try to keep any interventions to a minimum so we get a rough idea of the timing. Obviously the pace will be different when we're working in the studios, but this will tell us if any major cuts are needed.' Glancing apologetically at Josephine, he continued: 'For that reason, if you have any questions about your characterisation, I'll ask you to save them until the end, when there'll be plenty of time to discuss it. We're lucky enough to have the author here with us, so we might as well use her – and I want you all to be completely comfortable with your characters before we address any additional problems thrown up by working with the microphone. Is that all clear?' Terry's ignorance of any unpleasantness helped to defuse the remaining tension in the room, and everyone nodded, keen to get on. 'Right then, Beatrix – kick us off when you're ready.'

Josephine listened intently to the opening scenes of her play, noting where changes had been made and enjoying the way in which the cast grew in confidence as they lost their initial nerves and began to enjoy the story. On reflection, *Queen of Scots* was a shrewd choice for radio: writers like her, who had cut their teeth in the theatre, found it hard to think about a play as something whose magic was not in part visual; much of the success of *Richard of Bordeaux* lay in its seductive sets and costumes, and many critics had blamed the comparative failure of *Queen of Scots* on a lack of appeal to the eye; here, freed of any visual expectations, Josephine's words took on a new intensity and their impact thrilled her. Fascinated, she watched Terry as he worked, making notes on the strengths and weaknesses of each actor, and deciding whether persuasion, encouragement or bullying would best get him what he wanted. He was a benevolent dictator, working always for the good of the play, instilling trust in the cast by his own confidence, and Josephine found herself wondering if he manipulated people so effortlessly in all areas of his life.

Time flew, and before she knew it the actress who had opened the play was speaking its final words. Terry held up his hand for silence. 'And then we'll have the closing song . . .Thank you, everybody. That was wonderful.' He led a round of applause and looked across at Josephine. 'Happy?'

With twenty people staring back at her, she was relieved not to have to lie. '*Very* happy. Honestly – I couldn't be more pleased. It was like coming to the play for the first time.'

'Excellent. Let's go through the scenes one by one and I'll give you my thoughts, but any questions first?'

They spent another couple of hours with the script, then Terry called it a day and scheduled the next rehearsal, this time in the studios. The cast drifted out in twos and threes, and Lydia took Josephine's arm. 'Fancy a drink? I don't have to be at the Criterion till eight.'

'I'd love one. I don't know why, but there's something about Mary Stuart that always drives me to gin.' Lydia laughed and led the way up the steps to the ground floor. As they were leaving, Josephine noticed Vivienne Beresford in the foyer with an ordinary-looking silver-haired man in his late forties. 'Is that her husband?' she asked in surprise. 'I suppose it's superficial of me, but I expected the fuss to be over something more memorable.'

'I've never met him, but I suppose so. If we get a move on, we might find out.'

Before Josephine could stop her, Lydia walked briskly across the entrance hall, timing her ploy to perfection. Vivienne greeted her warmly, enquiring how rehearsals had gone with a dignity that Josephine doubted she could have mustered under similar circumstances. Any introductions were superfluous as soon as Anthony

Beresford opened his mouth; the voice that drifted so often into thousands of homes, including her own, was instantly recognisable – soft, authoritative and somehow reassuring – and Josephine found herself transfixed by it, in spite of her misgivings about the man's character. After a polite interval, Beresford looked at his watch and gently touched his wife's arm. 'Come along, darling,' he said, 'I've got an early start in the morning and the Tube's bound to be hell.'

She nodded, but refused to be rushed. Instead, she turned to Josephine. 'If I said eight hundred words by Friday afternoon, would that be all right?'

'I'm sorry?'

'The article you promised me. Normally I'd give you longer, but the printers are closed over the coronation holiday.' She smiled and joined her husband before Josephine could argue, then called back over her shoulder. 'I'd never admit it to his face, of course, but Julian does have some very good ideas. It'll sit perfectly with next week's *Richard III*.'

Lydia watched them go, looking apologetic. 'That was my fault, wasn't it? The gin's on me.'

'Damned right, it is. We'd better make it a quick one, though. I seem to have a deadline.'

2

Anthony was right about the journey home. Commuters poured like lost souls into the station at Oxford Circus, and the mood on the platform was brittle and confrontational as the familiar stoicism of Londoners on the move fell victim to the noise and the crush. Vivienne Beresford watched two trains arrive and depart before the natural momentum of the crowd carried her and her husband into another packed and stifling carriage. There was nowhere to sit, but she rarely relaxed on the twenty-minute journey home and the snippets of conversation that carried on around her were a welcome distraction from her own thoughts. She felt Anthony's arm at her back as the train jolted into life, a gesture both protective and habitual, and glanced at his face while he stared absent-mindedly into the blackness beyond the window. Even in the early days, before their marriage became a wary, prolonged game of chess, she had never been able to guess what he was thinking, and once upon a time that had bothered her; now, she counted it as a blessing. In the dusty, smoke-stained glass, he noticed her reflection looking up at him and smiled. 'I'll be glad when this is over and we can all go back to normal.'

His voice distinguished him suddenly from the other solid, reliable-looking men on the train; it drew the usual glance of curiosity and recognition from one or two of the women closest to them, and Vivienne wondered when the pride she used to feel had changed to resentment. 'Not wishing away your chance to shine, surely?' The response was more aggressive than she had intended and she bit her lip, hating the petulant note in her voice but unable to do anything about it. 'I sometimes wonder whose coronation this really is.'

Anthony could reasonably have argued that the occasion was benefiting her career as much as it was his but, as usual, he refused to rise to the bait. The tunnel widened for a moment and another train appeared alongside theirs, pulling ahead and falling back, the carriages offering a mirror image of randomly gathered lives until the tracks diverged again. It was how they existed, she thought sadly – always a little apart, one moving forward at the expense of the other, and it amazed her that the charade could have gone on for so long. Every evening, they picked at the trivialities of their day with a tedious thoroughness, but what really mattered – the slow and inevitable disintegration of their marriage – sat mute and un-acknowledged between them. To begin with, she had tried to fight the silence, driven by anger and disbelief at the first of Anthony's many infidelities, but she had never been a match for him: the voice, the control, the diplomacy – all the tricks of his professional trade – were used to devastating effect on the domestic front, and she had no defence when such apparently inoffensive weapons were turned against her. He had perfected the art of never allowing a row to surface; as soon as she opened her mouth, he would adopt a look of weary concern and shake his head, as if it were up to him to weigh the value of her accusation, and if she continued what she had started, it was her behaviour which seemed foolish and unreasonable.

The lights flickered as the train pulled into Marble Arch with a groan of brakes, and Vivienne shuffled her position slightly to accommodate the influx of parcels and shopping from a busy Oxford Street. 'They should get to Constitution Hill just after two,' Anthony said, as if continuing a conversation that had been going for some time. 'It'll take three quarters of an hour for the whole procession to come through, so the trick will be to let the bands and the marching do some of the talking.' She nodded, wondering why he hadn't yet asked about her day as he always did before mulling over his own. Did he know already what had happened at the read-through this afternoon? It wouldn't surprise her; gossip spread through Broadcasting House at a breathtaking speed, remarkable even for an organisation devoted to communication, and it was one of many things that she hated about the building.

She remembered how hopeful it had all seemed when they first moved in – a new start, to which she had perhaps given more significance than she should have. Anthony's office was panelled in English walnut, free of unnecessary decoration like the rest of the building but sparse and unwelcoming after the homeliness of Savoy Hill that he professed to miss. She had bought things for it to surprise him – a painting for the wall, a clock for his desk – but the gesture had simply embarrassed him, and when she tackled him about it, he said that they made the space look cheap and frivolous. The gifts, chosen with such care, were gone within a week. Thinking about it, that was probably the moment that she had begun to hate her husband, or at least the moment that she *realised* she hated him. To her surprise, she found that she was as good at hate as she must have been deficient at love, and she knew now, as the train stopped at Notting Hill Gate and he stood aside to allow her out of the carriage, that she hated him still, that there was no way back for either of them.

By mutual consent, they finished their journey on foot rather than change lines for the station closest to home. Vivienne never tired of walking the streets of Kensington, which – in small, precious corners – could still pass for a large country town, offering the flurry of Oxford Street without its brashness. The air – a bracing reminder that summer was still in its infancy – felt fresh and invigorating against her face after the staleness of the Tube, and she could happily have wandered for miles, but the lofty Gothic spire of St Mary Abbot's appeared on the horizon all too soon. Reluctantly, she followed Anthony across the High Street and into

Young Street and home. The house, which they had bought when Anthony returned to London for good at the end of the twenties, wrapped itself around her like a vice as soon as she closed the front door. Their evening routines were as precise and as ordered as the pattern on the carpet, and the predictability with which he went through to the sitting room to switch on the wireless and pour them both a drink might have been laughable had it not seemed suddenly so pointless. There was a time when she had comforted herself with the thought that she still had this, the right to their shared, familiar rituals. His company at the dinner table, the sound of his footsteps on the stairs, belonged to her and to her alone – but what were those footsteps really worth when they were always coming and going from someone else? Night after night she lay awake, wondering what made him stay? He wasn't a coward, so why didn't he simply pack the battered brown suitcase that had seen Paris and Vienna and Tangier, and leave? Was it just the knowledge that any sort of scandal would ruin his career, or had he never found anyone worth the effort? It was true that his affections seemed to die, in time, with each affair, but they always grew again somewhere new – and Vivienne could never decide if that was a mark for or against the possibilities of love.

She moved his macintosh from the banister to the coat stand, automatically going through its pockets, disgusted at the cliché that her life had become. He had only been careless once, but the shock of that crumpled piece of paper with its hastily scribbled number still had the power to knot her stomach whenever she thought of it. The hotel was in Pimlico, a scruffy, tawdry affair called the Tivoli, and she had paced up and down outside for half an hour before finding the courage to go inside. The woman on the desk had the look of someone whom nothing could surprise, certainly not the appearance of another curious wife, and Vivienne blushed even now at how naive she must have seemed; it had never occurred to her that rooms could be booked by the hour, but she

26

had handed over her fifteen shillings and sat for as long as she could bear behind a grubby net curtain looking down into Belgrave Road. Quite what she had hoped to achieve by her visit was still a mystery, but all she could remember now was the smell of cheap perfume in the hallways and the aching sense of betrayal. A picture hung over the bed, she recalled, a poor reproduction of Monet's 'Woman with a Parasol'; it had been one of her favourite paintings but she had not been able to look at it since, and it occurred to her now, as then, how easily beauty could be destroyed. As she left the hotel room and walked out into the street, no wiser than she had been before, she wondered why history and literature were always on the side of the lover, and had vowed then and there to play Anthony at his own game, testing the water with someone at work who had always admired her. To her horror, Anthony had encouraged the attachment, finding ever more ingenious ways to throw them together and seizing the opportunity with such obvious relief that any words of passion intended for her would-be lover had died in her throat.

But he had never humiliated her in public, not until today. In that split second, when she had seen herself through the mocking, pitying eyes of others, everything had changed. The charade was over, and it was impossible to pretend any longer, even behind closed doors. Suddenly, she couldn't stand the house for a minute longer. It should be Anthony who felt trapped by these walls, Anthony who needed to be free, but she was the one suffocating, and she had to get away. She took her coat from the rack and picked up her bag, then stopped as she saw her husband in the doorway, their drinks redundantly in his hands. 'Whatever's the matter?' he asked, looking at her in surprise.

Vivienne felt a hollow sense of victory in the knowledge that she could in some small way bewilder him as he bewildered her, but it faded as her words betrayed the courage of her convictions. 'I need to go out again. I forgot your cigarettes.'

'Don't worry, darling. I'll pop out later if I need to. You've had enough for one day.'

'It's all right. I won't be long.' Ignoring any further arguments, she slammed the door behind her and walked out into the street, heading away from the shops to the peace of Kensington Square. At the corner, she turned to glance back at the house, afraid that Anthony might sense the crisis and come after her, but the door stayed firmly closed. It was raining now and she had come out without an umbrella, but she pulled her coat around her and walked to the far side of the gardens, taking what shelter she could from a line of young trees. Still the rain stung her eyes, bringing with it a clarity that she had rarely experienced. She knew what she was capable of, and understood, too, that her resolve wasn't simply a response to what had happened today; it came from a thousand incidents and emotions, some from the past, some more recent, most from imagining a future in which nothing ever changed – and despair was more powerful even than hate. One day, if her life carried on as it was, she would kill her husband. As she waited for the rain to stop, she wondered how and when she would find the courage.

3

Two martinis later, Josephine left Lydia at the Criterion Theatre, wondering what the cocktails would add to Coward's beautifully crafted script. The evening had settled into a half-hearted drizzle, and the roar of daytime Piccadilly died a little as the centre of the West End made its transition from a life of work to a life of pleasure. Even the most dogged of flower sellers – who seemed to Josephine now to have a fancy-dress air about them, left over from a different age and strangely out of place against advertisements for Brylcreem and chewing gum – had moved away, leaving the fountain steps vacant for tourists to gaze at the lights and the traffic. It was still the middle of the evening and Piccadilly had not yet come into its own; later, when the theatres poured themselves into the streets and the clubs opened their doors, this small but iconic part of London would become all things to all people, as if the coloured signs and extravagant promises could drain the life from the rest of the city; now, it was a compromise, whose maze of entrances and exits underlined its lack of purpose. Even Eros – it defeated Josephine why the statue should be so famous – seemed unusually diffident, pointing his arrow vaguely towards a short, elderly man who was too busy struggling with an umbrella to notice. He seemed an unlikely candidate for romantic intrigue, she thought, but so did Anthony Beresford; no doubt the small metal god knew more about love than she did.

On a whim, she crossed the street to a telephone box and asked the operator to put her through to Scotland Yard. It took Archie several minutes to come to the phone, but it was worth the wait to hear the pleasure in his voice. 'Josephine! I wasn't expecting to hear from you tonight. How was the read-through?'

'Fascinating, but not necessarily for the right reasons. Have you eaten yet?'

'After a fashion. I had a sandwich a couple of hours ago on the way to a briefing. With everything that's going on here, I'm not sure I can remember the last time I sat down to a meal. Mrs Snipe's threatening to hand in her notice if I leave one more breakfast untouched.'

'So could you spare an hour for dinner? It's my shout. Timber won last week at Newmarket.' For her fortieth birthday, Archie had bought Josephine a half-share in a racehorse and the colt was proving a particularly shrewd investment, securing a place in each of his first three outings.

Archie laughed. 'I know he did. I backed him, so we'll go Dutch. Are you at the Cowdray Club?'

'No, in Piccadilly. I've just left Lydia at the theatre. We both needed a drink after the BBC.'

'Is everything all right for the broadcast?'

'Oh yes. The action was all off-mic. I'll tell you about it when I see you. Would it be easier if I came to you? I'm not sure I fancy the Yard's canteen, but we could find somewhere nearby if you're pressed for time.'

'Actually, I could do with seeing another part of London. Let's go to the Criterion Restaurant. I could meet you there in about half an hour?'

'Perfect. Do you want to call Bridget? I haven't seen her for ages and it sounds like you're a stranger, too, if you're living at work.'

'That would have been nice but she's in Cambridge until the weekend. She's the only person I know who genuinely doesn't give a damn about the bloody Coronation.' Although she liked Bridget, Josephine breathed a sigh of relief; she and Archie were always more relaxed on their own and she was pleased to have him to herself. 'I'll be as quick as I can,' he promised. 'See you at the restaurant.'

Josephine walked back to the Criterion to wait, touched by the way that Archie always found time for her, no matter how busy he was, and looking forward to seeing him. Their friendship – love would not have been an exaggeration, although she would have found it hard to place that love in any of the conventional categories – had survived twenty years of distance, jealousies and misunderstandings on either side, and was the stronger for it; more recently, as each of them found happiness with someone else, Josephine had waited anxiously for things to change between them, but by some miracle the awkwardness had never come. If anything, they were closer than ever.

The restaurant was crowded and there was no point in trying to talk her way to a table when Archie would manage it effortlessly, so she took shelter from the rain under the front canopy and watched the audience arrive for the 8.30 performance of *Private Lives*. The Criterion was often overshadowed by its grander neighbours in Shaftesbury Avenue and St Martin's Lane, but she had a great affection for London's intimate basement theatre. In the bustle of Piccadilly, very few people gave the building a second glance and the delicate classical stone seemed almost shy about its beauty – but there was something very special in the way it refused to shout to make itself heard, looking out over the madness but never rising to it. The theatre's restrained frontage gave no indication of the foyer beyond, but those who walked through its doors were well-rewarded: large mirrors alternated with exquisite decorative tile-work, and Josephine passed a pleasant few minutes in contemplation of the foyer's lurid but magnificent coved ceiling, where threatening cherubs danced round an impossibly muscular musician and a maiden whose innocence was scarcely more convincing. As she waited, the last few stragglers drifted down into the beautiful horseshoe auditorium, and she imagined Lydia in her dressing room, preparing for her first scene. The whole afternoon had left her feeling guilty and unsettled, and – although her own situation was different – she found it impossible not to refashion the eternal triangle in her mind and see herself in Millicent Gray's corner. Once or twice, as she sat across the table from Lydia, talking idly about theatre and the BBC, she had come close to broaching the subject of Marta – but each time she had stopped herself, partly from an absurd reluctance to upset her friend so close to a performance, partly because of her own inexcusable cowardice. And perhaps it was her imagination, but Lydia seemed to sense the danger, skilfully directing Josephine down other paths until neither of them was sure who had more to fear from the truth.

Archie was better than his word. In less than twenty minutes, Josephine saw his car enter Piccadilly from Haymarket, although it would have been more accurate to say that she recognised his sergeant's driving rather than the vehicle itself. She waved and walked over to meet them, wincing as the Daimler pulled in to the kerb, utterly oblivious to the fury of several drivers who had hurriedly readjusted their course into Regent Street to avoid an accident. Archie jumped out, tall and bare-headed despite the rain, and she noticed that his good looks and vitality distracted some of the passing women from their more ordinary companions for a moment. He lifted her off her feet, and Josephine smelt the tobacco on his clothes as she always did when he came to meet her straight from Scotland Yard. Bending to speak to Bill Fallowfield through the fug of cigarette smoke in the car, she caught the expression of wry amusement on the sergeant's face as he watched his superior shake off the mantle of Detective Chief Inspector as easily as if it were an unwanted item of clothing; it was a remarkable transition, and Josephine wished she knew Archie better at work to appreciate its full impact. 'Thanks for getting him here so quickly, Bill,' she said. 'I know how busy you are.'

'It's a pleasure, Miss Tey. It's about time he left that desk and . . .'

The rest of Sergeant Fallowfield's thoughts on Archie's welfare were lost in a barrage of hooting and swearing as a line of cars built steadily behind him; reluctantly, he rejoined the traffic with a gesture which might have been a wave of farewell or something rather more obscene, and Archie smiled. 'That's two favours he's done me. I've sent him on to Maiden Lane with a hearty appetite to get me back into Mrs Snipe's good books.' Josephine knew Archie's formidable housekeeper well enough to realise that he wasn't joking. 'It's lovely to see you.'

'You too. I half thought I'd have more luck if I asked the King out to dinner.'

'It's not quite that bad but it will be by next week. You made the right choice, though – I'm much better company.' And almost as well-connected, Josephine thought, as she watched him charm the head waiter into realising that one of the coveted recessed tables was available after all. 'That was lucky, wasn't it?' Archie said with a wink as someone took their coats.

Josephine shook her head in admiration, tempted to ask what he had said but – like a child who finds sixpence in an empty hand – loath to spoil the magic. In any case, the restaurant offered an atmosphere which made it easy to believe in miracles: gold and marble surfaces glinted everywhere she looked, and the room's beautiful gilded ceiling, grand windows and imposing arches seemed to transport its diners back to a glorious Byzantine past. It always took her breath away, no matter how often she visited. Like every other couple in the room, they chatted about the Coronation while waiting for the menus, and she noticed how tired he looked. 'I'm guessing that all these celebrations aren't quite as exciting for you as they are for the rest of us.'

'Honestly? The whole thing's a bloody nightmare. Twenty-two thousand men in uniform to look after three million people – and that's a guess – not to mention the entire royal family. Give me a good honest murder any day.'

'Be careful what you wish for. I thought I was going to witness one of those at the BBC today. It was daggers drawn at the read-through.'

Archie seemed grateful for the change of subject. 'What happened?' he asked, as soon as they each had a glass of Chablis in front of them.

'Well, it's probably only interesting if you're in those circles,' Josephine said, suddenly doubtful that her gossip could compete with the event that had the world's attention, 'but it certainly brought the green room to a standstill. You know Julian Terry, don't you?'

'I've met him at a party or two. He seems nice enough – a bit more down-to-earth than his brother.'

'Yes, he is. I like him very much, and it was fascinating to watch him work. He was brilliant with the cast and I love what he's done with *Queen of Scots*. It didn't sound anywhere near as half-hearted as it looked onstage.'

'You've always been over-critical of that play.'

'I know I have, but it's strange when you don't like something you've created. You feel that it's betrayed you somehow, even though the faults are entirely yours. Must be what it's like to have a disappointing child.'

'Fortunately we'll never know.'

'Quite. Anyway, before the read-through, Julian introduced me to a woman called Vivienne Beresford – she's editing the *Radio Times* at the moment. I didn't place the name straight away, but she's married to Anthony Beresford, the broadcaster.' The first course arrived and, as they ate their way through beautifully cooked scallops, Josephine told Archie how impressed she had been by Vivienne Beresford, and how unwittingly she had walked into the scene downstairs. 'It was absolutely excruciating,' she admitted. 'Lydia did a sterling job, but there was no saving anyone. The poor woman was mortified.'

'I can imagine,' Archie said. 'It doesn't surprise me about Beresford, though. There's something in his voice that tells you he thinks he's God's gift.'

Josephine laughed, and waited discreetly while the waiter refilled her glass. 'Nine out of ten women in this country will tell you that what you see as smugness is actually a reassuring and very attractive strength.'

'You're not defending him, surely?'

'Of course not. I'm merely pointing out that it's easy to be wise after the event.'

Archie grinned. 'Fair point. I met him a while ago, you know – when Mrs Beresford's sister died. I didn't know she worked for the Corporation as well, though.'

'No, I don't suppose you did,' Josephine said wryly. 'The women don't seem to have quite such a high profile. So were you involved in the case?' Archie nodded. 'What happened? Lydia said something about a scandal.'

'That's right. A death like Olivia Hanlon's was always going to keep the papers going for weeks. You know she owned the Golden Hat in Soho? We went there once in the twenties.'

'Did we? I don't remember. Are you sure you're not confusing me with someone else?'

He laughed. 'Hardly. When have I ever made that mistake? I'm not surprised *you're* a little hazy about the evening, though. You had to be all but carried home.'

'Don't be ridiculous,' Josephine said, ready to argue. 'I've never been . . .' She stopped, then flushed with embarrassment as a half-formed memory began to niggle at her. 'Oh God, it was my birthday, wasn't it? We went to that terrible *Twelfth Night*, and it was so awful that I challenged you to take me somewhere exciting. Was that the Golden Hat?'

Archie nodded, trying to keep a straight face. 'As I recall, I had to sleep on the floor because you were too worried about going back to the Cowdray Club. You'd only just been elected, and you thought they'd cancel your membership if you turned up worse for wear.' He paused as the waiter brought their main course, but the respite was only brief. 'It was an excellent night all round,' he added with a twinkle. 'You were particularly taken with the dance floor.'

Josephine thought back to the evening, feeling betrayed by a memory which was obliging enough to embarrass her but far too vague to offer any coherent line of defence. 'You're absolutely right,' she admitted, recalling now how beautiful that glass floor had looked, illuminated from below by hundreds of tiny coloured lights that rippled and shone like sunlight on the sea. 'God, Archie, it seems like a different life. Who were we?'

'Exactly the same people we are now, just a little younger and a little drunker.'

'It's not just us, though, is it? London's aged. Who'd have thought a change of decade would make everywhere so different?' She looked round the room, taking in the restrained elegance and quiet buzz of conversation. 'Don't get me wrong – this is lovely, but everything was so intense in those years after the war. Then the thirties arrived and we all grew up. You can just tell that the most daring thing any of us will do tonight is have another brandy.' It was Josephine's turn to be self-conscious now, and she smiled, surprised at her own nostalgia. 'But you were telling me about Olivia Hanlon. What happened to her?'

His grin acknowledged the swift change of subject, but he let her get away with it. 'She was found dead in her swimming pool after a party. Well – no one ever really admitted there'd been a party and they'd done their best to clear up, but it was obvious what had been going on.'

'When you say "they", who do you mean?'

'Good question. Beresford was there, and Olivia Hanlon's housekeeper, but it was impossible to get to the bottom of who else had passed through that evening. You could make an educated guess from the normal run of things – actors and musicians, one or two high-profile politicians, a handful of people from the BBC. There were rumours about Tallulah Bankhead and even the Prince of

Wales, but that's probably all they were – rumours. Nobody was going to step forward after such an unfortunate accident.'

His tone managed to put the last word in inverted commas.

'Didn't you question them?' Josephine asked.

'Not with any great vigour. Olivia Hanlon had friends in high places.'

'All the more reason to get to the bottom of her death.'

The comment sounded naive, but Archie took it seriously. 'You and I might see it that way, but we're not protecting our reputations. For a while, the Golden Hat was legendary. Olivia Hanlon was one of Mrs Meyrick's girls originally . . .'

'The 43 Club?' Kate Meyrick's name had been synonymous with London nightlife when Josephine first began to spend time in the city on a regular basis. Although she had never met the club hostess in person, many of her friends in the world of theatre and cabaret still spoke of her with great affection, and it was said that all the dance bands in London had fallen silent at the news of her death. 'She was supposed to be quite special.'

Archie looked sceptical. 'Yes, in the way that Dick Turpin's quite special, or Robin Hood. It's easy to get romantic about people who live on the edge of the law, but there's always another side to it. Kate Meyrick kept a gun in her drawer and was on friendly terms with more gangs than I'm likely to meet in my entire career. She could break up a fight as easily as any policeman I know, and she did three stretches in Holloway for a reason – most notably for bribing a policeman called Goddard. But she *was* very good to the girls who worked for her. She encouraged a lot of them to set up on their own, and Miss Hanlon was one of her more successful protégées. The Golden Hat was a victim of its own success, really – a little more risqué than the others, with what you might call more adventurous pleasures.'

'Now I'm even more embarrassed that I can't remember much about it.'

'Don't be. It was still quite ordinary when we went. The interesting times came later, just before Miss Hanlon's death.'

'What happened?'

'Oh, one raid too many. One bribe too many. She got into debt, and the club was in dire straits by the time she died.'

'So did she take the easy way out? Was it suicide?'

'Who knows? As I said, it wasn't a very thorough investigation. A few people much higher up the chain than I was were far too familiar with Olivia Hanlon, either because they frequented the club or because they took bribes to protect her. As I recall, the path to death by misadventure was cleared very quickly.'

'What do *you* think happened?'

'I'm not sure we'll ever really know. My guess is that the drugs or the sex got out of hand, and when they came up for air, someone noticed that their hostess had stopped breathing. After that, the party disappeared into the night and the Beresfords were left to mourn a tragic accident at a private gathering.'

'It must have been awful for Vivienne, though – to lose a sister *and* be tarred with scandal.'

'Yes, although they tried to play the scandal down. There was much talk of an asthma attack while swimming and no medical evidence to disprove that. Unwittingly, the press encouraged the verdict by indulging in so much ludicrous speculation that it would have been impossible to sift out the truth, even if there had been something more sinister in it.'

A waiter took their plates, and Josephine refused dessert in favour of coffee and brandy. 'No wonder Beresford left the country,' she said. 'Vivienne told me that he worked abroad for a while when they were first married. I imagine he was keen to put some distance between himself and the gossip he'd married into before coming back to claim his glittering career.'

'Yes, that sounds about right. From what I've heard, Reith takes a very dim view of the slightest misdemeanour. The BBC is an extremely moral outfit.' He smiled. 'At least as far as the general public is concerned.'

'Well, I shall look at them all in a new light now I know what went on,' Josephine said.

'Do you have to go to all the rehearsals?'

'No, thank God. Julian extended what might best be described as a polite invitation, but they'll get on much better without the author breathing down their necks and I'm happy to leave them to it. I've decided to go to the cottage for the weekend. I haven't had a chance to spend any time there since February, so I want to make sure that everything's all right while I'm down here. Marta's supposed to be joining me on Saturday if she can get back from Cornwall in time.'

It might have been her face or her voice that gave her away, but Archie was quick to pick up on her concern. 'Is everything all right with Marta?'

'Yes, it's wonderful. That's the trouble.'

'Now you've lost me.'

She told him about the uneasiness she felt with Lydia. 'I suppose it was worse because of the Beresfords, but I just know that all this is about to blow up in my face and it terrifies me.'

'Would that really be so awful, though? It's time, Josephine. You know by now that this isn't a whim or a cheap infatuation. You and Marta love each other. Don't let guilt rule you forever. You're braver than that.'

'I'm not so sure. My star sign should be Cancer, not Leo – I can crawl sideways round any confrontation.' She took a cigarette and leaned forward to let him light it. 'You're right, though. I'll talk to Marta about it while we're at the cottage. It's always easier there.'

'Good. And you'll be back in London in time for the party?'

'Oh yes. I don't suppose I need to ask what you're doing?'

'No. I've got a bit of time off at the weekend. Bridget's involved in a group exhibition in Bond Street, so we're going to the opening on Saturday.'

'Are you seeing much of her, or is she in Cambridge a lot?'

'She's here more than there.' He grinned. 'Well, she has been lately, so I must be doing something right. And we spend time together when we can, in between my work and hers.'

'Is that all right with you?'

'Surprisingly, yes. I keep waiting for the excitement to wear off, but it hasn't yet.'

'Must be that Irish charm of hers working its magic.'

'Something like that.' He paused, looking for the right words, and Josephine sensed that his relationship with Bridget was something that he had not yet managed to explain to himself. 'When we first met, all those years ago, it was very brief and very intense.'

'That's war for you. No time to notice the imperfections.'

'Exactly. But there's plenty of time now and I still haven't found them.'

She smiled, pleased that Archie was happy. He signalled to the waiter and they argued over the bill before Josephine got her way, claiming the meal as a thank-you for her coronation ticket. 'What will it be now?' Archie asked as they walked back out into the street. 'A nightcap or a taxi back to the Cowdray Club?'

The rain had stopped and the air was fresh and invigorating, encouraging crowds of people to drift in and out of the invisible streets around Piccadilly. Josephine loved moments like this, when the true fabric of London touched her soul, and she was reluctant to go back indoors. 'Neither,' she said. 'We're not far from Soho. Why don't you jog my memory and show me where this club was? If I'm not going to live it down, I should at least be able to picture the scene of my disgrace.'

They struck out towards Leicester Square, and the night-time bustle made rural names like Haymarket and Windmill Street seem even more incongruous. Josephine followed Archie into the maze of roads which ran behind Shaftesbury Avenue, noticing how suddenly and completely the character of the area changed. Soho was dominated these days by foreign restaurants and exotic grocers' shops, and the smells that drifted up from basement kitchens blended with the faded, shabby architecture to give the streets a faint but melancholy air of exile. In Gerrard Street, Archie stopped outside a nondescript red-brick building that now housed an Italian cafe on the ground floor and offices above. 'This is it, I'm afraid. The Golden Hat was in the cellar.'

Josephine stared in disappointment. She didn't know quite what she had expected, but the grime-ridden steps down to a dingy basement flat and the smell of garlic and fish failed to recreate the atmosphere of faded decadence for which she was hoping. 'You certainly knew how to show a girl a good time, didn't you?' she said eventually. 'No wonder I've done my best to forget it.'

'It was rather different then, I promise.' He drew her closer to the railings to allow a group of passing Italians more room to gesticulate. 'Have you seen enough?'

'Yes, I suppose so.' Still, she lingered a moment, trying in vain to reconcile past and present, disorientated by the familiarity of Archie's arm in hers and the strangeness of the building in front of her. 'We really can't go back, can we?'

'No, we can't,' he said softly, turning towards Charing Cross Road. 'The trick is not to want to.'

4

Josephine delivered her article to Broadcasting House on Friday afternoon, just in time to receive a late lunch invitation from Julian, who was holding court in the foyer. 'Go on,' he said persuasively as she looked at her watch. 'Give me an excuse not to go back upstairs yet. Our sound-effects department has got thirty-seven different engine noises waiting for me in the library, and they expect me to listen to the lot. I only want the sound of a bloody car driving away.'

She laughed. 'All right, when you put it like that. I have to get the Ipswich train at five, though. Can we go somewhere nearby?'

'Oh, I can do better than that. I'll introduce you to the BBC canteen. If you haven't eaten there, you really haven't lived.'

Intrigued, Josephine followed him downstairs to the basement, which was a mixture of communal spaces and smaller studios. It seemed an odd place for a restaurant, surrounded by politely phrased signs requesting silence, but when they left the functional rooms behind in favour of the buzz of conversation and chink of crockery, Josephine was glad she had come. It was as if all the excitement and camaraderie of the organisation had been distilled into this one room; like many areas of Broadcasting House, the canteen was stark and modern in design, with long glass tables and tubular steel chairs, but it was saved from its own formality by the people who used it – a glorious mix of staff, performers and visitors, universally attracted to the offer of three courses for sixpence. Now and again, the columns which punctuated the room lit up, calling people away from the groups they were gossiping in and back to work. 'This is lovely,' Josephine said, watching a row of women behind the counter dish up plate after plate of delicious-looking food. 'I'm surprised you get anything done at all.'

'It is hard, I admit, especially now it's open into the early hours. If it were licensed, I suspect most of the output would be run from here. As it is, that honour goes to the George in Mortimer Street.' They took their place in the queue behind two variety performers dressed in sailor suits. 'What will you have?' Julian asked. 'I should tell you that steak and chips is customary if rehearsals have gone well, but there's salad if you're feeling miserable.'

'I'll have whatever you think we deserve.'

'Steak and chips it is, then.' They took their plates and found a space on the table farthest from the counter. 'How's everything going with the film?' he asked, pouring them each a glass of water.

'I have no idea and no wish to find out,' Josephine said firmly. 'A friend of mine is with the Hitchcocks in Cornwall at the moment, filming the opening scenes, and I've told her I don't want to hear a word about it. The very fact that they're in Cornwall when the book's set in Kent tells me everything I need to know.'

Julian smiled at her indignation. 'Who's in it?'

'Derrick de Marney's playing Tisdall and Nova Pilbeam is Erica.'

'Clever casting. Nova did *Dear Brutus* here for me recently – she was Margaret. It's a strange part, but she did it brilliantly.'

'Yes, I heard her. Millicent was excellent, too.'

'She always is. I find I take that for granted these days.'

'It was so exciting to hear her read Mary on Wednesday. I thought the awkwardness of what had just happened might put her off, but it seemed to have the opposite effect.' Julian hardly ever needed an excuse to gossip, but this time he remained uncharacteristically reticent. 'How long has the affair been going on?' she asked, abandoning any pretence at subtlety.

'A couple of months or so, but there have been others before Millicent. I don't know why Viv puts up with it.' He smiled at someone over Josephine's shoulder, and suddenly spoke more loudly. 'Anyway, all that wide-eyed innocence is wasted on radio.'

The sudden change of subject confused Josephine until Vivienne Beresford sat down next to him, holding a copy of the brand new *Radio Times*. 'Whose career are you trashing now, Julian?' she asked, taking a chip from his plate and smiling at Josephine. 'I suppose I should be able to guess – wide-eyed innocence rather narrows it down.'

'Nova Pilbeam. She's in Josephine's film, and I was just saying how good she'd be.'

'Oh? What film is this?'

'Well, it's not exactly mine. The Hitchcocks are adapting a book I've just published.'

'How exciting! Have you met them?' Josephine nodded. 'What are they like?'

'Surprising, and very, very memorable,' she said, well practised by now at telling people what she thought of Britain's favourite film director. 'Actually, the two of them make quite a team. He's a genius, but I don't think he'd have achieved half as much without Alma. No matter what people say, they have a genuinely creative partnership and a really strong marriage.'

'Lucky them,' Vivienne said caustically, and Josephine wished she had chosen her words more diplomatically. 'What's the book about? I hope it's more uplifting than *Dear* bloody *Brutus*.'

It wasn't hard to see why a wistful play about second chances and lives as they might have been lived would not be to Vivienne Beresford's taste, and Josephine tried to think of something less inflammatory to say. 'It's about the triumph of good over evil,' Julian explained before she could answer, 'like all good detective stories.'

'Or in your case, a shoot-out on the roof when you run out of ideas.'

'Harsh, but fair. She hides it well, Josephine, but Viv's not a fan of crime fiction.'

'Let's just say I grew out of it.' She smiled and turned back to Josephine. 'Is he right?'

'Yes and no. The book's about a man accused of murder who tries to prove his innocence.'

'That rings a bell. I've just read your article on Richard III and it's very interesting – thank you. Justice is obviously important to you.'

'I'm not sure it's quite as laudable as you make it sound,' Josephine admitted. 'I'm just a coward where *in*justice is concerned. I've always thought it must be so much worse to be accused of something you haven't done than to be caught for something you have.'

'Yes, I suppose that's true.' She moved her chair along to make room for half a dozen members of the Henry Hall Orchestra at the other end of the table. 'But he's vindicated, the character in your book?'

'Yes, he is. I don't agree with Julian that good should always triumph in a detective novel – life's not like that – but this one *does* have a happy ending. Not because of the justice system, though – he's only cleared because someone else believes in him. That's the point.'

'I bet that went down well with your friend at Scotland Yard.'

Josephine looked at her, surprised that she should have remembered such a fleeting piece of information; no wonder she excelled in a job which relied on attention to detail. 'We agree to differ,' she said. 'And he'd be the first to admit that real life isn't always perfect.'

Vivienne nodded but said nothing, and Josephine wondered if she was thinking about the unanswered questions surrounding her own sister's death. She longed to ask what had happened, but it would have been tactless to mention the scandal even if she had known Vivienne well enough to venture into personal territory. A column to her left was suddenly illuminated and Julian stood up.

'That's me, I'm afraid,' he said. 'Back to work. I'll see you next week, Josephine. Have a lovely time in Suffolk.'

He kissed them both and left. 'I have no idea how they know which light is for whom,' Vivienne said, anticipating Josephine's next question. 'I've spent years trying to work it out. I'm glad he's gone, though. There's something I'd like to ask you – in confidence, if I may?'

'Yes, of course.'

Vivienne hesitated, and Josephine noticed how tired she looked around the eyes. 'What's she like?' she asked eventually.

'Who?'

'My husband's mistress. I can't ask anyone here – my pride won't let me. But you must know her from the theatre, and I couldn't be more embarrassed in front of you than I was the other day in the green room.'

'I'm not sure I can answer that,' Josephine said truthfully. 'I've only met her once or twice at after-show parties, and no one behaves normally at those.'

'Even so, you must have formed some sort of impression of her and you strike me as a good judge of character. Please tell me, Josephine. Is he just flattered because she's young and pretty? Should I be more worried than I was last time?' She looked down, embarrassed by her own behaviour but committed now to the conversation. 'God, this is so bloody demeaning. I've always been able to rise above it before, but there's something different about him lately and I don't know what to do.'

Josephine exchanged her seat for the one next to Vivienne so that they no longer had to talk across the table. 'Different in what way?'

'It's hard to explain. More settled, perhaps. Less angry. It's as if he's arrived at some sort of resolution, some sort of peace with himself, and that frightens me. It feels too much like the calm before the storm.'

Josephine considered her own impressions of Millicent Gray and found little there which might be of reassurance to Vivienne. 'As I said, I really don't know her, but from what I've seen, she's very talented and very ambitious.'

'So she wouldn't think twice about breaking up a marriage?'

'Probably not, but that's just my opinion.'

'Do you think these women have any idea of the pain they cause?' Josephine said nothing, and Vivienne misread her hesitation. 'I'm sorry. I've put you in an impossible position. You might not know her very well, but you don't know me any better and there's no obligation to be on my side just because I've asked you to be.'

'It's not that. It's a perfectly valid question, but my house isn't quite sturdy enough for me to be throwing stones at other people's.' Vivienne looked at her curiously, but was too discreet to take advantage of her honesty. 'I understand what you're saying and I agree with you,' Josephine added, 'but I also know that people do things out of character because it's hard not to be selfish. I can't tell you what Millicent Gray is like, but I'm not even sure that matters. Your answer doesn't lie with her, it lies with your husband – what he wants and what he's capable of. Does he know how you feel?'

'I'm not sure Anthony's ever known that.'

'And you can't talk to him about it?'

She shook her head. 'We're beyond that.'

'Then can I ask *you* something?'

'I'm hardly in a position to refuse.'

'Wouldn't you be better off without him?'

'It's funny,' Vivienne said after a long pause, 'but I was just beginning to wonder that myself.'

Part Two

Private Lives

It was funny, Josephine thought: all the elaborate preparations that London had made, only to be eclipsed by a small corner of a Suffolk woodland. Everywhere she looked, swathes of violets, wood anemones and luminous pink campion offered their own patriotic tributes, and if their shades were not quite the true colours of pageantry, their subtle, nonchalant beauty was a more authentic celebration of Englishness than anything she had seen in the city's streets. Since she was last here, the tentative spikes of bluebell leaf had been replaced by a vein-blue tide that spread through the woods as if spilt from a glass, and the flowers filled the air with their strong, green scent. She moved the picnic rug to follow the dance of sunlight, softly filtered by the youthful foliage of early summer, and wondered how many more surprises this newly dis-covered landscape would give her.

Larkspur Cottage, which she had inherited out of the blue from a godmother she barely knew, had arrived as a gift of fate when she most needed freedom and peace. The time she had spent there – sometimes with Marta, mostly alone – had given her the chance to find out who she really was and what she wanted from her life. The knowledge had grown hand in hand with the joys of each new season, until the cottage and everything it stood for became inex-plicably bound up with her own sense of being. Summer was new to her here, and it was as if the countryside had saved its most precious promise until last. The pure, melodious song of a skylark drifted across from the neighbouring field, sweeter and more ju-bilant than anything composed for the new king, and Josephine made a vow to herself there and then that – no matter how busy or complicated her life became – she would always find time to see Suffolk in May.

'We could just listen to it on the wireless,' Marta suggested, sharing her thoughts.

'The play or the whole Coronation?'

'Both. Why would we want to leave this?'

Josephine smiled, pleased that Marta loved the life they were building here as much as she did. 'That suits me. I'll make sure the battery's charged.'

Marta sat down and looked for the corkscrew. 'It's a lovely idea. I wish we meant it. Arranging a party with the rest of the country wasn't the best way of finding some time for ourselves, was it?'

'It's not the rest of the country that bothers me.' Josephine had hedged round the subject of Lydia ever since Marta's arrival. It would not have been her choice to threaten the beauty of the afternoon with a row, but she had put off the conversation with a cowardice that was typical of her when it came to talking about her feelings, and now she was running out of time before they headed back to London. 'Are you happy the way we are?' she asked.

It was an ambiguous question, clumsily introduced, and no one would have guessed that she had spent days mulling over the best way to broach the subject. Marta sighed and Josephine knew that she was irritated by how much of their precious time was spent in analysing their situation – as yet, without any hint of resolution. 'How many times have we been through this? Look at me, Josephine. Think about the day we've had and the night we spent together. Is that really such a hard question to answer?'

'I don't just mean here and now. This is the easy part.'

'So what *do* you mean?'

There was an edge to her voice, but it was eagerness rather than anger and Josephine sensed with relief that the conversation might not be as unwelcome to Marta as she had feared. The thought gave her strength. 'I want you to tell Lydia about us,' she said. 'Perhaps it's because you and I are getting closer, perhaps it's because I've seen more of her than usual over the last few days, but we can't go on like this.' She thought of the expression on Vivienne Beresford's face that day in the green room and imagined Lydia in a similar situation because of her – then, more selfishly, she considered how *she* would feel if she were the subject of the sort of gossip that had followed. 'I won't take part in one of those charades where everyone puts their head in the sand until it all comes tumbling out in the most destructive way possible. It's cheap and it's shabby, and we're better than that.' Marta nodded and started to speak, but Josephine knew herself well enough to finish what she had started before the moment was lost. 'And apart from anything else, I'm tired of having to be so bloody careful all the time. Lydia might still have her own digs but she always seems to be at Holly Place whenever I'm in town, so I have to stay at the club when I want to be with you. I don't even feel that I can phone you in case she answers and I have to pretend that it's both of you I'm interested in seeing – then we have one of those excruciating evenings where we all try to be normal. And I want to surprise you, Marta – I want to turn up at your door and see the joy on your face because you weren't expecting it. How can I do that? Even when we're here, it's always at the back of my mind that Lydia has a cottage half an hour down the road. Jesus, I wouldn't put it past her to appear over the horizon at any minute.' Marta laughed, and Josephine felt suddenly vulnerable. 'Don't laugh at me,' she said. 'I'm sick of pretending. I know it's unreasonable, and I'm not the one who has the right to be angry here, but . . .'

'Why not? I wish you'd be angry more often, so don't stop on my account.' Marta put a hand to Josephine's cheek, forcing her to look up, and the touch was enough to dispel her fear instantly. 'I'm not laughing at you, Josephine. I'm laughing because that long and very eloquent speech has just said everything I've been longing to hear for months. I know I've let things with Lydia get out of hand

and I'm sorry, but you asked me to wait. You told me not to rock the boat.'

'I know I did. But the more I have of you, the more I want.'

'I'll take that as a compliment.' Marta leaned forward to kiss her. 'You know what you're asking, though, and how difficult it might be for you? It will probably cost you your friendship with Lydia.'

'I don't think "probably" comes into it.'

'And we can't rely on her to be discreet. I'm not sure I'd be gracious in her position, and if she wants to lash out, your reputation will be first in line. Mine's shot to hell already.' Josephine hesitated. The shame of being publicly linked with another woman – at home in Inverness, even in the more liberal but still competitive world of theatre – terrified her, and there was no point in pretending otherwise. 'You once told me you weren't brave enough to face that,' Marta said gently.

'I know I did, and I'm not sure I am now, but there's only one way to find out. And anyway, it might not come to that.'

Marta looked unconvinced, but let it go. Eventually, the afternoon grew chilly and they walked home across fields strewn with thistles and buttercups. 'It's almost the anniversary of Maria Marten's murder,' Josephine said, thinking about the infamous crime that had taken place in the village a century before. Her own cottage was closely linked to the story, and she often felt the ghosts of the past there, the happiness and tragedy of other lives engrained into old iron door handles or well-worn floorboards. 'These fields can't have changed much since she walked across them. It's easy to imagine her still here.'

'First Lydia, now Maria – it's all starting to sound a bit crowded.' Josephine laughed, but Marta stopped walking and took her hand. 'Listen, Josephine – promise me this won't change anything. You won't do anything ridiculous like sacrifice us when it's all out in the open because Lydia's been hurt? I know you, and I know what guilt can do after the fact in a relationship. It can destroy the very thing you're trying to protect, and if you let that happen, I will kill you.'

'You've tried that before and I'm still standing. But no, Marta, I won't,' she added more seriously, understanding that it was her turn to allay some fears. 'I've thought long and hard about this, and I wouldn't ask you to do it if I couldn't face the consequences – I love you, and I'm sure.'

The cottage closed in around them as it always did, gracing their life there with an unquestioning, everyday reality that made it possible to believe in its permanence. Josephine stayed awake for a long time after they made love, wanting to hold on to the illusion of safety and peace before the morning came and she had to face her fears.

2

The magazine proofs were in unusually good shape for a Monday afternoon, which was just as well: the earlier deadline, forced by the coronation holiday, allowed no leeway for page after page marked 'details to come', or ominous white spaces where instructions to leave four inches were followed by the delivery of two lines. Vivienne glanced through the mock-up of the next issue, noting the final changes and choosing one or two replacement pictures for programmes which had changed at the last minute. She paused at Josephine's article – a provocative, engaging refutation of Shakespeare's villainous Richard – and allowed her eye to fall on the author's photograph and the credit next to it; the name brought back all the shame and humiliation of the previous week, intensified by sleepless nights spent dwelling on it, and she moved quickly on through the rest of the issue. She knew it was petty to take her anger out on someone two or three steps removed from its real source, but pain brought value to the smallest of victories, and Gerard Leaman would never work for her in this building again.

She gathered the artwork together, ready to take to the printer, and collected her coat and hat from the rack. Her assistant looked at the clock and raised an eyebrow. 'Half past four? That must be a record. Maurice is in for the shock of his life when he gets back from America.'

Vivienne gave her a wry smile. 'That's what I'm hoping for. I don't know why these men make it look so difficult. Left to you and me, Danny, the job would be done in half the time.'

'And on half the salary.'

'That will be why, then.' They both laughed, and Vivienne

realised how much she had cherished the easy camaraderie of the office over the last few weeks, doing a job she loved without constantly having to defend her ideas or prove her ability. 'Let's just enjoy it while it lasts, shall we?' She fastened her coat and checked through the pages one last time. 'I'll go straight home from Waterlow's, so I'll see you in the morning.'

'Do you need to come in tomorrow? Next week's issue is in good shape already, and I can take care of anything that comes up here until after the holiday. Wouldn't you rather get ready for the big day?'

The offer was well-intentioned, but Vivienne could think of few things less appealing than rattling round the house on her own, with nothing to distract her from herself. 'It's kind of you,' she said, 'but I'll only sit about if I stay at home, and I'd rather be working.'

It was the phrase of a bereaved or jilted woman and it made her sound more vulnerable than she had intended. 'Are you sure you're all right, Viv?' Danny asked, looking at her with genuine concern.

'Perfectly all right. Is there anything else before I go? Shall I drop those articles off to be typed on my way out?'

'Yes, if you've got time.' She held out the envelope, forcing Vivienne to meet her eye. 'Don't let it get to you, Viv. You're worth ten of him.'

Verity Daniels had demonstrated her loyalty in every conceivable way over the years, but never so outspokenly, and Vivienne didn't trust herself to reply. She smiled weakly and walked out into the courtyard, taking time to compose herself before facing the thinly disguised curiosity of the general office. The light, airy room on the first floor of Broadcasting House was packed with about forty typists, working on everything from transcripts of talks to general correspondence. The office prided itself on an air of happy efficiency, and the insistent clatter of typewriters greeted her as she opened the door. Afternoon tea had just been served at the desks and she thought she caught some of the girls glancing at each other as she put her envelope into one of the vast in-trays, but Danny, it seemed, had done her a favour: pity from someone who had always looked up to her put the idle gossip of strangers into perspective, and she walked back through the aisles of desks with her head held high.

Of all the temporary responsibilities she had taken on, passing the pages of each new issue was the one she valued most: there was something supremely satisfying about watching her ideas become a reality, and the moment when her signature sent the magazine on its way through the presses – when it was too late to change her mind – came with a sense of finality that was both frightening and exhilarating. The *Radio Times* had recently changed its printer and the new firm was based in north London, several miles further out than the original contractor, so a car was provided each week to take her there; privately, Vivienne thought that the service had less to do with her convenience than with the fact that a former editor had once lost an entire set of proofs on the Underground, but she appreciated it anyway. The car was waiting for her in Langham Place and she acknowledged the driver with a wave. 'You did well to get here on time, Billy,' she said, looking at the traffic snaking back towards Oxford Street. 'I thought I might be in for a long wait.'

'It's not too bad away from the centre, Mrs Beresford. Just as well we're not doing this tomorrow, though – it'll be hard to go anywhere once the road closures start.'

Billy Whiting had worked for the BBC for years and Vivienne knew him well. They chatted easily as the car inched forward through the familiar streets, and it was a relief to be with someone who seemed genuinely oblivious to her private life, although Billy – a royal chauffeur, too, in his time, and the soul of professional discretion – would never have indulged in gossip, despite being privy to more secrets than anyone else she knew. As the traffic thinned out a little and they picked up speed through Edgware, he turned the wireless on and smiled at her in the rear-view mirror. 'You won't want to miss this.'

Preoccupied by the business of the afternoon, Vivienne had quite forgotten that Anthony was giving a five o'clock talk on the *National Programme*. The subject was free entertainment in the city, and she listened as he described the colour of a London street market, picturing him in front of the microphone, his notes carefully laid out in front of him, a glass of water close to hand. His voice was so well-known in every home that people who had never met him could judge his mood as well as she could; if he had the slightest cold, packages would arrive at Broadcasting House with cough tablets or obscure family remedies, and she had lost count of the cufflinks and white silk scarves that she had sent to charity, anonymous gifts from women who thought his voice was 'simply marvellous'. The talk, as always, was perfectly judged and flawlessly executed. Each week, as Vivienne prepared the copy for the *Radio Times*, her heart sank at some of the more obscure subject matter, and it often occurred to her that before broadcasting was invented, nobody had ever had such opportunities for boring so many people simultaneously – but Anthony was never dull. His voice gathered pace slightly as he described the thrill of a fire engine dashing through the West End, then slowed as he recalled the joy of Regent's Park on a sunny afternoon, and Vivienne marvelled at the natural way in which he felt about for his words, for all the world as if he were having a conversation with the listener rather than reading a script which had taken him hours to prepare. And most valuable of all, he had that rare ability to make you think that he was talking just to you. That was the quality she had fallen in love with, and the quality that so many other women had found attractive since. She wondered if all those listeners, hanging on Anthony's every word by their firesides or in their kitchens, would feel betrayed if they knew that he was as flawed as they were, that the honour and integrity they so admired was merely a professional skill? It was the hypocrisy of it all that Vivienne hated most, but hypocrisy was fostered by the world they moved in: to be involved in a divorce was the quickest way out of the Corporation, yet sex and adultery were the staple fare of office life; and while Anthony did as he pleased, she and other married women had to fight tooth and nail for the right to work at all. Her husband and her employer had both assumed that she would resign as soon as she walked down the aisle, and it would have been hard to say which of them was more rankled by her decision to stay.

The calm, confident voice pecked away at her mood, and she was glad when the signal crackled and faded, defying Billy's best efforts to revive it. He turned the wireless off with an apologetic shrug, and Vivienne settled into the silence, wishing it was as easy to remove her husband from her thoughts. The car wound through the suburbs of Acton, past alternating rows of factories and terraced houses, and every now and then she caught a glimpse of children playing in the streets, solemnly acting out their own improvised version of Wednesday's ceremony with crowns cut from cereal packets and mud-stained red cushions. Would children have made a difference, she wondered? If she had agreed to give Anthony the son she knew he wanted, would he have been less inclined to stray? It was a futile line of thought, but one that she had often tormented herself with, and she was glad when their arrival at Twyford Abbey Road prevented her from taking it any further. She gathered her things together as Billy turned into Park Royal and pulled up outside a handsome, purpose-built construction of brick and steel. The *Radio Times* was a difficult contract with a large print-run and a high proportion of last-minute changes, but Waterlows was more than equipped to meet those demands: as well as being a pleasure to deal with, the firm offered the last word in modern printing, and Vivienne would never forget how exciting it had been to walk onto the factory floor for the first time when the presses – the largest in the world – were working at full speed. It was a thrill she would greatly miss when she relinquished the reins in a few weeks' time.

She left Billy to wait with the car and made her way through to the office at the back of the building, breathing in the smell of ink and rubber that filled the corridors. Even here, as far from the vast machine-room as it was possible to get, the roar of the presses was barely muffled and she had to knock twice on the glass door before Philip Berkeley looked up from his work. 'Sorry, Mrs Beresford,' he said, moving a stack of paper samples off a chair so that Vivienne could sit down. 'I thought I'd be ready for you, but it's been a busy day. Is everything all right with the proofs?'

'Yes, there's nothing major to change. A couple of replacement programmes, some better photographs – the usual stuff, really.'

'Well, anything would be a breeze compared to last week. That one pushed us to our limits, and I'm not ashamed to admit it.'

'You and me both, Mr Berkeley. It was worth it, though. We've sold three and a half million so far – that's a record for a weekly. Even the Director General is pleased – or so I'm told.'

'So he bloody should be. You worked your socks off to get it done on time. We all did.'

He looked genuinely pleased, and his words reminded Vivienne of the two things she liked most about Waterlow's general manager: his pride in his work, and the fact that he had never once felt the need to adjust his behaviour because he was dealing with a woman. 'And this is from Richard Nevinson,' she said. 'High praise indeed.'

Berkeley read the card she had passed to him, a thank-you from the artist for the careful reproduction of his cover painting. 'That's nice. We don't often get fan mail. It does look good on the stands, though, doesn't it? This one will, too.' He nodded approvingly at the design for the following week, a striking image by John Gilroy – simple but eye-catching, and easily recognisable as the work of a man who had made his name in advertising, most famously for

Guinness. 'Right – let's go through it page by page.'

It took a couple of hours to finalise everything to their mutual satisfaction. Pleased to have another issue under her belt, Vivienne signed off the final proofs and stood to leave. 'Will you print it overnight?'

'First thing in the morning, all being well, but don't worry – we won't pack up for the holidays until it's done.'

'I know you won't. Then you're closed until Friday?'

He nodded, and held her coat for her. 'That's right. It's more than my life's worth not to take a couple of days off. I don't know who's more excited – Angie or the kids. Wild horses wouldn't keep them away.' He smiled, and she was touched by the affection in his voice. 'I expect you'll be in the posh seats?'

'Something like that.'

'Well, think of us while you're there – six rows back and soaked to the skin. We probably won't see a thing.'

But you'll be happy, Vivienne thought, wondering if Philip Berkeley had any idea how much she envied his ordinary, family coronation. She thanked him and walked back to her car, apologising to Billy for keeping him waiting, even though it was his job and something he never minded. The skies were heavy and overcast, inviting darkness to close in quickly, and the first drops of rain fell as the car reached the outskirts of the city. She looked at Billy's profile in the half-light, oblivious now to everything but the road ahead, and thought back to the night of her sister's death, when, at Anthony's request, Billy had driven her out of London to avoid the press and the scandal. She would never forget how surprisingly kind Anthony had been in those dark, difficult days – so attentive and protective as she struggled with her regrets and her guilt, quietly handling everything to shield her from the mess that Olivia's life had created, even though the scandal was as big a risk to his career as it was to her family name. At the time, she thought that they had come through the crisis unscathed – stronger, even

– but of course she was wrong. She didn't blame the circumstances of Olivia's death for their problems, but she realised now that her behaviour in those early days had set the tone for their marriage: a little too grateful, perhaps, always feeling to some extent in his debt, encouraging him to believe that she would put up with things that made her unhappy. But she had not imagined his kindness to her, of that she was sure, so where had *that* Anthony gone? Looking out at the rain, she understood now that what she felt for her husband was a form of grief, far deeper than she had ever felt for her sister. Over the last few days, when this crisis of shame had driven her to consider the most drastic of solutions to her sadness, she had begun to imagine the practicalities of a world without Anthony – where she might live if she kept her freedom, how she would feel if she were made to pay for what she had done – but in hindsight they were small considerations: the real mourning, for the man she married, had been going on for years.

Now, as it had back then, the car felt safe and warm, an interlude from the cold reality that awaited her when the journey was over, and she was sorry to leave it. She watched as Billy drove away, turning towards home only when his tail lights blended into the rubies and pearls of Kensington High Street, and reluctantly put her key in the lock. The hallway was in darkness and Vivienne knew she was wasting her breath, but she called Anthony's name out of habit and walked through the silence to the sitting room; in her heart, she had known he would be out, celebrating the success of his talk in Millicent Gray's bed. The decanter on the side was nearly empty, so she went upstairs to the study to find the quantity of whisky she needed and sat down at the desk to drink it. The desk was as tidy as usual, but Anthony's passport was caught in one of the drawers, as if it had been hurriedly put away. Vivienne stared at it, suddenly fearful of what she might find if she didn't get up now and leave the room, but her curiosity was too strong. She opened the drawer and took out the passport and some travel tickets, trying to work out what they meant: two passages to Canada, booked in her husband's name for the following month, and with no mention of a return journey. At first, the discovery bewildered her: Anthony never left his desk unlocked – God knows she had checked often enough – and for the briefest of moments she dared to hope that he had placed the tickets there deliberately as a surprise for her to find, a declaration of a new start for them both. It took just a single sheet of paper to dispel the illusion: a letter from John Reith, reluctantly accepting Anthony's resignation on the grounds of an impending divorce.

In that split second, Vivienne realised that she had never truly known the meaning of anger until now. Her rage disorientated her, refusing to take any of the forms that she might have expected; there were no tears, no sudden outbursts of violence, no urge to hurt the woman who had replaced her – just a cold conviction that Anthony would pay. She sat there for a long time, afraid that the anger would give way to a sense of loss and betrayal, but it didn't; if anything, it grew stronger with each passing moment, until she knew exactly what she was going to do. Calmly, she put everything back exactly as she had found it and went downstairs to the telephone. 'Danny? Sorry to bother you at home, but I've changed my mind about coming in tomorrow, if you're sure you can manage? No, nothing's wrong, but Wednesday's going to be such a big day for Anthony. I need to make sure that he's ready for it.'

3

By Tuesday evening, Detective Chief Inspector Archie Penrose was heartily sick of the Coronation. He sat in the sprawling organisation room on the third floor of Scotland Yard, and did his best to concentrate on the final briefing before the ceremony the following day – the culmination of months of work, during which plans had been made, scrapped and remade until they were as perfect as humanly possible. Detailed models of the processional route, all carefully built to scale, took up most of the available desk space, and one enormous map stood on an easel at the far end of the room, dotted with hundreds of flags to identify areas of potential danger. The room was brightly lit, as if to bring a freshness and excitement to information which everyone present had heard a dozen times before, but he saw his own weary impatience to get to the real thing reflected in the faces of his colleagues. The forthcoming week of coronation events was the largest operation that any of them had ever been involved in, and if everything went smoothly there would be plenty to be proud of; right now, if someone were to grant Archie a wish, he would have had no hesitation in asking that kings might be made more quietly.

Nothing had been left to chance. He thought back to those meticulous rehearsals, held over the last three Sundays; to the strange sight of khaki-clad mountain troops moving through the streets at dawn and the empty carriages with their skeleton escorts – ageless silhouettes that seemed to stand for all the monarchs whom history had honoured in this way. Every movement was choreographed with the precision of the finest ballet, and even the King and Queen had been put through their paces, riding the grand coronation coach within the palace grounds to get used to its idiosyncrasies. Once word got out, the early morning starts had not deterred the crowds from taking part wholeheartedly, and half a million people had witnessed the final rehearsal, many of them paying threepence to watch the shadow show from the covered stands erected in the Mall and Parliament Square. The atmosphere had been both moving and a little dreamlike, and Archie wondered how many of the observers had, like him, felt the shadow of an uncrowned king hovering over the proceedings.

The Assistant Commissioner – a grey-haired, quietly spoken man who had grown up on London's streets and had the respect of the entire force – finished his speech on crowd psychology, and Superintendent Day stood to run through the travel restrictions one last time. Like everyone else in the room, Archie could easily have done the job for him: central tube stations would be partially closed from nine o'clock that evening, allowing exit only and no admission from the streets; in the morning, a private tube would run from Kensington High Street to Westminster, taking peers and MPs to their coveted seats in the Abbey; taxis could drop people within walking distance of the route but were not allowed to loiter for return fares; and streets would be closed to pedestrians as well as traffic when their safety limits had been reached, and opened again only in an emergency. 'Right, that's it,' Day said, smiling as he sensed the collective sigh of relief in the room. 'Go home and get your heads down for a few hours. I want you back here bright and early in the morning. And good luck, everyone – let's make it a day to remember.'

They could do no more now than sleep on it and hope for the best, and Archie went back to his office to collect his things. The wireless, which had been his constant companion for the last few days, giving him a valuable insight into celebrations all over the country, continued its murmured countdown in the background. At the moment, *In Town Tonight* was coming live from the steps of St Martin-in-the-Fields, broadcasting to the crowds in Trafalgar Square. Archie stood by the window and looked out over the Thames, listening as Freddie Grisewood interviewed a patissier who had fashioned the crown jewels from sugar and a society girl who was to be waitress for a day at Westminster Hall. Darkness had come early, the natural successor to a dull afternoon, and the evening had an unseasonal, autumnal feel. Across the river, the buildings illuminated for the celebrations were already making their mark, casting greens and golds into the steel-grey canopy of the sky; and down below, the water moved peaceful and oblivious towards the sea, its blackness more mysterious than ever when contrasted with the myriad lights mirrored in its depths. There was a break in the showers, but Archie didn't envy the crowds who would be sleeping on the streets or camping on rain-soaked grass in the parks. The city had made up its mind to enjoy every moment of the coronation holiday: restaurants would be open all night and cinemas until the early hours of the morning, but nothing seemed more enticing to him now than his own bed.

The Embankment was quieter than much of the city, with pavements reserved for thousands of school children – girls on the north side and boys on the south. It amused Archie that he could no longer bring any part of London to mind without mentally running through the arrangements that had been made for it, and he plotted his journey back to the Strand with an emphasis on peace rather than distance.

'I knew if I waited long enough I'd be lucky.'

The soft, Donegal accent came out of the shadows to meet him, and he turned in surprise and delight. 'Bridget! What on earth are you doing here? I thought you had plans for tonight.'

'I wasn't really in a Savoy mood. Richard was there, celebrating his bloody *Radio Times* cover, and I couldn't stand it for longer than the first course. It's not a bad effort, but I'd have done it better. God forbid they should give the commission to a woman, though.'

Archie smiled at the familiar tirade; Richard Nevinson was one of Bridget's closest friends, but as artists they were bitter rivals. 'So as I was just up the road, I thought I might as well come and look for you.'

'How long have you been standing out here?'

'Oh, a while, but the view's nice and you're worth it. How long have I got you for?'

'A few hours. I'm needed back here at five. Until then, they've told us to go home and go to bed.'

Bridget laughed and took his arm, and he wondered for the thousandth time why it didn't bother him more that he never knew where he stood with her. 'Funny,' she said, 'that's exactly what I had in mind. Let's go to yours – it's closer.'

They walked along the Embankment, pausing at Richmond Terrace to look back down the river. County Hall was bathed in green light now, and across the bridge St Thomas' Hospital offered proud horizontal bands of red, white and blue. 'I'll be pleased when we get back to normal,' Bridget said.

'We've gone to all this trouble and you're not impressed? People have come for miles to see those lights.'

'It's pretty, I suppose, but it was perfect as it was. I love the way the night takes all the muddle out of it. Tell me, Archie, what could be more beautiful than the south of the river when it's getting dark?' Archie looked again and saw that she was right: on the distant horizon, beyond the reach of civic pride, the jumble of smaller buildings blended into one exquisite pattern whose jagged outline against the fading sky was both simple and dramatic. It reminded him of how much he loved the way she looked at the world, through an artist's eyes – and of how she encouraged him to see things differently, too. So much of his work was brutal and bleak – the violence that erupted on the surface, the motivating darkness that lay beneath – but with Bridget he saw beauty more often. Just as she had once helped him face the horror of war, she now made the everyday violence of peacetime – more dreadful because it had no armistice – somehow easier to live with. He turned to kiss her, feeling her body move eagerly towards his own. 'What was that for?' Bridget asked.

'It would take too long to explain. Come on.'

The comparative quiet of the Embankment was a luxury which they soon left behind. A vigil had begun in Whitehall: the crowds lining the street were already four or five deep, well-prepared with coats and blankets, knitting or playing cards to pass the time; in the distance, Archie could hear a rousing version of 'Land of Hope and Glory' performed by the unlikely pairing of kettle drums and accordion. Trafalgar Square always seemed bigger to him at night, but this evening there was barely an inch of space to spare on its pavements. The BBC had done its best, but no broadcast could do justice to the atmosphere of celebration and revelry under Nelson's watchful eye as the illuminated fountains flung sprays of colour into the air and queues snaked from telephone kiosks, chains of happy people trying to make a rendezvous in the chaos or describing the scene to those left behind at home.

At last, they got to Maiden Lane, where Archie had a top floor flat in the same building as his cousins, Lettice and Ronnie Motley, and their long-suffering housekeeper, Dora Snipe. His heart sank when he saw the lights blazing from every window but his own. 'Are you sure you wouldn't rather go back to yours?' he asked, looking hopefully at Bridget. 'Coronation fever struck here weeks ago and it looks like it's about to peak.'

'It'll take us hours to get to Hampstead in these crowds. Then you'll be panicking about getting to work on time in the morning and I'll have you to myself for twenty minutes if I'm lucky.' She rifled through his pockets for the keys and smiled mischievously. 'We can sneak up the stairs. If they're that excited, they probably won't even notice.'

Archie admired her optimism but had little faith in her plan.

Ronnie, in particular, had an almost psychic ability to scupper any plans he made for an anonymous entrance or a fast exit, and he failed to see why tonight should be any different. He opened the front door as quietly as he could and ushered Bridget through, hoping that the dance music blaring from the gramophone downstairs would continue long enough to see them to safety. In the end, it was more than Jack Hylton could do to help him. 'Archie! Perfect timing,' Ronnie called, as a shaft of light from the ground-floor flat stopped him in his tracks. She beamed at him through a haze of Gauloises, and Archie knew he was lost. 'Lettice and I can't remember what you said about tomorrow morning. Do we have to be in the stand by six o'clock or seven?'

'Seven,' he said, relieved to escape with such a straightforward question. 'All the instructions are with the ticket.'

His cousin looked a little awkward. 'Yes, that's what the Snipe said. The thing is, we can't seem to find our tickets at the moment.'

'What do you mean?' he asked in exasperation, forgetting all his good intentions not to be sidetracked. 'Do you have any idea how precious those tickets are? If they get into the wrong hands and someone traces them back to me . . .'

'We'll all be fucked – yes, I know, but I'm sure they'll turn up. It's just a bit of a mess in here at the moment and we can't quite remember who had them last.' Ronnie looked past him up the stairs and saw the figure skulking in the shadows. 'Bridget! How nice to see you. Come in for a moment, both of you, I've just made another round of drinks.'

Archie glanced through the open door into the chaos beyond. The ground-floor apartment actually belonged to Lettice, but tonight it could easily have been mistaken for the backstage area of *HMS Pinafore*: every surface was covered in colour-coded dresses; the rug in front of the fire seemed to have had Selfridges' entire shoe department emptied onto it; and even Chaplin, Mrs Snipe's Jack Russell, whom Archie had inherited from a past case, sported a hand-knitted coat of red, white and blue. But it was the human statue in the middle of it all that caught Archie's attention: perched precariously on a footstool while Lettice pinned her hem, Dora Snipe was the very image of a modern-day Britannia, head held high and one arm raised in front of her. Her cheeks were slightly flushed and she wobbled a little as she nodded to him, and Archie decided that it really was time to go. 'We'll leave you to it,' he said, leading Bridget firmly up the stairs. 'I've got an early start in the morning.'

4

The vaudeville studio was in the basement of Broadcasting House, an imaginative foundation stone for the tower of recording rooms which rose up through the centre of the building. It was an unusual theatre in miniature, modern in style and intimate in scale, and had been designed specifically for the BBC's popular programmes of comedy and revue. The audience – a select gathering of about sixty – sat on tubular metal chairs covered with an orange worsted fabric, and the walls were an unsettled mix of grey and tangerine, accentuated by lemon, blue and pale red stripes. Josephine couldn't quite envisage the sort of person who had ever thought the colour scheme a good idea, but she admired their spirit.

The initial impact was soon dulled by the silky glow of stage lighting, and if the decor was a far cry from the West End, the entertainment onstage could hardly have been more traditional. The BBC's coronation revue had been perfectly designed to reflect the party atmosphere of the streets outside, with a bill that featured the cream of the country's most experienced variety stars. The spotlight fell on Cicely Courtneidge, and a huge cheer went up as she launched into her signature comic sketch, a complex, fast-paced series of elaborate tongue-twisters. The piece – so well-known that Josephine could see one or two members of the audience mouthing the lines almost as smoothly as the star herself – was delivered with charm and perfect timing, and it brought the house down; even Marta – the only person Josephine knew who actually meant it when she said she hated music hall – had tears streaming down her face. After an ensemble closing piece, where Courtneidge was rejoined onstage by George Robey, Frank Lawton and a full supporting cast, the audience had recovered sufficiently to join in a rendition of the national anthem, so rousing that it barely needed the resources of the BBC to carry to the listeners at home.

The on-air lights went out and the applause faded, and Josephine and Marta made their way back up to the entrance hall with the rest of the crowd. 'Half past nine,' Marta said, looking at her watch. 'When are you due upstairs?'

'Oh, any time now. Julian asked me to be there at the end of the final rehearsal in case they had any questions. We can hang around and listen if they haven't quite finished.'

'Are you sure I won't be in the way?'

'Of course not. It won't take long, then we can go for dinner.'

Marta hesitated. 'Or we could forget about dinner, and I could go back to Holly Place with Lydia and get it over with.'

Josephine looked at her in surprise. 'We were going to wait until after the play,' she said, her doubts obvious in her voice.

'I know, but why? Are you worried she'll say something indiscreet in the middle of a live broadcast?' Josephine's horror must have been written all over her face because Marta smiled. 'That *was* a joke.'

'Perhaps it was, but it would be a bloody good way of getting her own back.'

'Lydia's not like that. I don't mean she wouldn't be tempted to insult us to an audience of millions, but she'd never jeopardise her chances of regular work here by being unprofessional.'

That was true, but the familiarity which it implied and the speed with which Marta had jumped to Lydia's defence grated on Josephine. 'Are you having second thoughts about this, Marta? Is that why you want it over with – so you can't change your mind?'

'No, of course not. I just don't like living a lie, even if it's only for a few more days.'

Get used to it, Josephine felt like retorting, but she kept her silence. Marta's uncompromising honesty about the way she chose to live her life impressed and frightened Josephine in equal measure; occasionally, she found herself craving a more human chink of cowardice or shame in the woman she loved, but it never came – and while she told herself that Marta's attitude was unrealistic, sanctimonious even, when so many women of their generation felt compelled to hide or make excuses for their choices, really that was envy on her part; if she could choose to be more like Marta, she would. 'Promise me you'll wait,' she asked, trying not to sound too anxious.

'Of course, if that's what you want.'

'It is,' Josephine said, bewildered as to how being together had so easily become a divisive issue, 'but I don't mind if you want to call it a night now. I'm not sure I'm in the mood for dinner with three place settings, either. Would you rather go home and I'll see you tomorrow?'

Marta didn't answer, and Josephine followed her gaze to the artists' reception desk, where a tall, distinguished-looking woman was obviously waiting to be collected. 'Look!' Marta whispered. 'You must know who that is?'

Josephine glanced at the noticeboard opposite the lifts which detailed the day's programme schedules together with the studios from which they were to be broadcast. 'Vita Sackville-West, at a guess. She's giving a talk on the last Coronation in about twenty minutes. So what?'

'So what? You're staring at Orlando in the flesh and that's all you can say?'

'I'm not staring at anyone – you are. And it wasn't one of my favourite books, if you remember. Hardly a great advert for historical accuracy.' She smiled, amused to see that Marta – who was *never* star-struck – had a weakness after all, and some of the tension between them fell away. 'Why don't you go and say hello?'

'Don't be silly. I couldn't possibly just go up and speak to her.'

'Why on earth not? She looks almost human. Go on – I dare

you,' she added as Marta hesitated. 'No? Well, I'll leave you fearless lovers together while I freshen up.' She headed for the ladies' cloak-room, glad that something could shake Marta's confidence, even if it wasn't the thought of their future together. 'I won't be long.'

The cloakroom was a study in chic, art deco perfection, with walls of blackened mirror glass and a silky white Lincrusta ceiling that caught and played with the light. Josephine put her bag down by the sink and reapplied her lipstick, wondering if she should, after all, have let Marta do as she wished. It was a cliché, perhaps, but only eighteen months ago mirrors had held no fear for her because her conscience was clear; now, she could barely meet her own eye. Millicent Gray and Vivienne Beresford had never been far from her thoughts over the last few days, and she realised now how unconsciously she had divided other women into the sort who had affairs and the sort who were betrayed, always assuming that she had no place in either category. Unsettled by how wrong she was, she looked at her reflection in the glass, resenting the overly critic-al comparisons with Lydia but unable to stop herself making them; when the door of the cubicle behind her opened and her friend emerged as something more tangible than conscience, it was as if she had been summoned by guilt, and Josephine blushed with em-barrassment.

'Josephine! What are you looking so shifty about? Have I caught you stealing the towels?' Lydia smiled and walked over to the sink to wash her hands. 'There's no need to be so surprised – we're having dinner, aren't we?'

'Yes, of course. It's just that I thought you'd still be in the studio.'

'You should know as well as I do – there's plenty of time to go walkabout in that part.' She meant no malice by the remark, but Josephine felt it as another rebuke. 'Where's Marta?'

'In the foyer, plucking up the courage to speak to Vita Sackville-West.'

'Ah – so we have competition.' For a moment, Josephine

thought she had imagined the 'we', but the illusion was short-lived. 'Listen, darling – whatever it is that Marta's building up to telling me, I know already.' Lydia turned to face her, and the challenging expression in her eyes belied the casualness of her voice. 'You forget how well I know her, Josephine. Better than you do.' Josephine opened her mouth to disagree, but the words died in her throat and she could think of nothing to replace them with; it would be pointless to deny the conversation that Lydia had prophesied, but the subject had been introduced too suddenly for her to have any clear idea of how to tackle it head on. 'You see, Marta's always nice when she's about to tell me something I don't want to hear, and these last few days she's been *very* nice. So what is it?'

'If Marta's so transparent, I shouldn't need to tell you.'

'Humour me.'

'We've fallen in love,' Josephine said, scarcely needing Lydia's laughter to tell her that the declaration sounded like something out of a bad first novel. 'I'm sorry, Lydia. We never meant it to happen. You weren't together when it started, but since then we've seen a lot of each other and it's grown into something that neither of us wants to give up.' The apology was instinctive, rooted in her surprise at having to be the one who broke the news, but still she resented it. She tried to remind herself of how selfish Lydia had been in the early days of her relationship with Marta, obsessed with work and caring little about anyone else's happiness, but self-justification was beyond her now that it mattered, and she realised that Lydia was waiting for her to say more.

'And?' she prompted.

'And what?'

'And what are you and Marta going to do about it? Is she throwing me out? Breaking off all contact?' Josephine hesitated, suddenly aware that they had never actually discussed what Lydia was to be told beyond a declaration of their feelings for one another; her uncertainty over what she could and could not promise on Marta's behalf made her angry and vulnerable, and Lydia hammered home her advantage. 'Are you moving to London to be with her?'

'You know I can't do that.'

'So she's going to Scotland?'

'Of course not, but . . .'

'Then I don't quite see what's changed. The two of you might be in love, but you're apart more often than you're together and that makes people very vulnerable. Don't think I'm giving her up.'

'She's not yours to give up, Lydia – not in the way that matters.'

'Really? So why do we still have a life together? Why are you and I even having this conversation? As you very kindly explained, Josephine, back when this little affair of yours started – and yes, I know perfectly well when that was – Marta and I were finished. She could have just left it that way and made a new start with you, but she didn't – she picked up the telephone and invited me back into her life because this halfway house you offer her wasn't enough.'

'That was a long time ago. Things are different now – Marta's different, and so am I. Stronger, more certain of what we want.'

'Yes and no. But that's what I mean about knowing her – you have to be with someone for a long time before you can say that. I see Marta's moods when her work doesn't go well and her highs when it does. I know when she cries in the night because she can't quite leave her past behind and you're not there to help her. Those precious weekends you snatch here and there are all very lovely, I'm sure, but they're not real, Josephine – and in your heart you know that.'

The depth of Lydia's understanding floored Josephine, and for the first time in her life, she genuinely understood what it meant to have to fight for someone. 'I love her, Lydia. That feels real enough.'

'Oh, we all love her, darling. The question is – what are we going to do about it?' It took Josephine a second or two to realise that it was a genuine question, requiring an answer. 'I suggest we carry on exactly as we are if you've nothing more concrete to offer.'

'You can't care about Marta if you're prepared to do that.'

'This streak of romance you cling to really isn't very modern, Josephine. Look around you – we all make do, we all make compromises. That's the world we live in now. I know how much Marta loves you, and I know that the love she has for me is companionship – but I'll settle for it. I don't want to be on my own, and I have very little pride left to speak of.'

'You think Marta will agree to that out of pity?'

'Not pity, no – but the trouble with Marta is that she's fundamentally decent. She'll tell me about you because it's the right thing to do, and the knife will go in – but she hasn't got the heart to twist it, and you're not in a position to force her to.' Josephine turned to go before her doubts conspired to defeat her, but Lydia caught her hand. 'I was so relieved when I knew it was you,' she said.

'Am I supposed to take that as a compliment?'

'If you like. But I just meant that someone else might have offered her everything, and you have too many other concerns to do that. Even if you didn't, we've been friends long enough for me to know that you'll never give yourself completely to another person, no matter how much you care. As long as Marta loves you, there'll always be a part of her that comes running back to me.'

For a moment, Josephine was too shocked by Lydia's words to register that they were no longer alone. Millicent Gray stood awkwardly in the doorway, and Josephine wondered how much she had heard of the conversation. In the end, it was Lydia who left first. 'I'll see you upstairs,' she said, as if nothing had happened between them.

Josephine picked up her bag to follow, wishing that she could recover as quickly. She had no idea how she was going to face anyone when she was so upset; if Lydia's intention had been to fill her full of doubts, then she had succeeded – and that in itself felt like a betrayal of her own love for Marta. She made for the door, reluctant to show any more of her emotions in front of Millicent Gray, but the stranger stopped her in her tracks. 'She's right, you know. Don't fool yourself.'

Josephine turned to her, surprised. 'What do you mean?' she asked. 'Right about what?'

'All the hope and all the pain – and to get where? You put up with it because you think you're going to be enough for them – one day. But you never will be.'

Part Three

London Rain

I

She must have walked for miles, drifting with little sense of purpose through a London she had never seen before and would never see again, a strange, nocturnal world of the dispossessed. People lay on pavements under rugs or curled tightly in doorways, while thousands more had given up on sleep altogether and were content simply to squat on the kerb with their feet wrapped in newspaper, refugees by choice, waiting for the day to reward their patience. Josephine wandered among them, having slipped from her club in the early hours to seek the peace and clarity that had eluded her since her conversation with Lydia. It was an unlikely place to find refuge: the streets were full of voices and a commotion that jarred with the time of night, and only in the still, bare mystery of the area around Buckingham Palace – cleared of revellers by police just after midnight – did she find anything resembling genuine silence. Yet the anonymity of the crowd soothed her, and the air – chilly and bracing as patches of cold, thick fog drifted up from the river – cleared her mind.

After the shock of the night before, Josephine was thankful that she and Marta had not made plans to watch the coronation procession together. Keeping her temper with Lettice and Ronnie and the inevitable enthusiasm of the day was challenge enough, but sharing Marta's company without being able to talk properly would have been impossible. She had left Broadcasting House as soon as the rehearsal was over, claiming a headache which quickly obliged her by becoming a reality, and had ignored all subsequent messages from Marta to ask if she was all right. Tonight, she would have no choice but to face up to what had happened, and their evening would be very different from the one they had envisaged. She had no idea how Marta would react to the decision she had made, or even if she would be capable of standing by it, but she had to try while her resolve was still strong. She had turned things over and over in her mind, trying to think of an alternative, but there was none – or at least none that she could live with. Her conscience dogged her as she walked, stronger even than her desolation at the thought of walking away from a love she had neither looked for nor expected, but had gradually come to depend on. Whether she knew it or not, Lydia had delivered the performance of a lifetime; her words seared into Josephine's consciousness, and there was no escaping the truth of them.

She retraced her footsteps towards Oxford Street, noticing that Hyde Park was by far the city's most popular sleeping place. Daylight promised an end to the long vigil, but there was still a heavy mist that limited Josephine's horizon to twenty or thirty yards. Through the railings, she could just make out a series of shadowy, indistinct figures moving across the grass, some carrying sleeping bags or folding up blankets, others trying to rub some life back into stiffened limbs, and she felt a pang of guilt for voluntarily leaving the bed that any one of them would have paid handsomely for. In the space of a few hours, she had relived her whole relationship with Marta, tormenting herself with thoughts of how she might have done things differently. It would have been so much easier if their initial reaction to one another – wariness, fed by strong opinions that were not always in harmony – had lasted, but was she fooling herself now to think that the tension between Marta and Lydia was already there by the time she appeared on the scene? Marta was the first genuine love that Lydia had known after a series of fickle if passionate affairs, but even she could not compete with the actress's obsession for her work. And Marta had had her own agenda for getting close to Lydia, driven by demons of which only she was aware.

For Lydia's sake, Josephine had tried to steer them through their problems, but – perhaps selfishly – she had obviously not tried hard enough. Then Marta had chosen to confide in her rather than in Lydia, and the jealousies that friendship had barely managed to keep in check spilled over irrevocably. Looking back now to that brief but intense bond, Josephine saw all too clearly the beginnings of a strong mutual attraction, but she had been blissfully ignorant of it at the time. Marta had left – for good, as far as Josephine was concerned – and Lydia waved a tentative white flag of truce which Josephine was happy to accept. It was funny how much and how little had changed, she thought, remembering the fights and awkward conversations that she had tried to mediate in those early days; she had always been caught in the middle of Marta and Lydia, and still it was no different.

A few rough notes of 'Pack Up Your Troubles' drifted out from the mist, picked up and amplified by voices in other areas of the park. Each section of town, it seemed, favoured a different style of entertainment; over in Piccadilly and Regent Street, where the revelry was at its most raucous, musicians were treating the crowds to dance songs of the day; here, closer to the military side of the pageant, with small camps of soldiers dotted all over the park, the mood harked back to the war. It reminded her of Armistice night in London, not least because she had felt as detached from the air of celebration then as she did now; to her, and to many others for whom peace had come two years or three months or five days too late, the triumph stood shakily on foundations of grief. The war had changed all their lives in one way or another, and perhaps Marta's most of all; the loss of a husband and a lover had taken its toll years later with the most tragic of consequences, and Josephine still felt the urgency of those conversations, still admired the courage with which Marta had claimed and paid for her past. They had grown close in exceptional circumstances, but it remained a feature of their love that it never dealt in trivialities. What Lydia had rightly referred to as snatched weekends also carried an obligation to make things count. Not a moment of their time together had been wasted.

It was ironic that the fear she felt now at the prospect of losing Marta should resemble so closely the fear of loving her. She remembered how Marta had returned out of the blue, not for Lydia but for her, and how she had tried to persuade Josephine that they had a future together. At first, Josephine had resisted – partly from a reluctance to betray Lydia, partly because her own feelings terrified her. Until then, she had never taken risks with her emotions, and she knew that her desire for Marta threatened the easy, unruffled life she had chosen. The first time they made love, she had felt an intensity that left her more vulnerable than she could ever have imagined, and she had dealt with it by running away, by making more of her responsibilities in Inverness than she needed to and demonstrating through her cowardice that there would be long absences to fill, that the all-consuming commitment in which Marta needed to trust was impossible. Marta responded by turning to Lydia for the security that Josephine could not give, and the compromise became a way of life. Josephine was as much to blame as anyone, but now it was she who felt betrayed by it.

At dawn, the bugles sounded a reveille from the camps in the park and Josephine took it as her signal to face the day. By the time she reached Marble Arch, men and women from the St John Ambulance brigade had begun to line the processional route, bringing the first note of order to the day in disciplined lines of black and white. In Oxford Street, alarm clocks tied incongruously to lampposts had served their purpose and people were beginning to stir: rugs, boxes and mattresses of infinite variety were packed neatly away, while women did what they could to restore their make-up after the long night-time vigil. Some still slept, wrapped head to toe in newspaper, but most sat hunched over a flask of tea or a nip of something stronger to keep out the cold, reluctant to move about for warmth in case they lost their place. Every so often, the smell of bacon rose up from a tiny camp stove, and those who had not been so well-prepared looked on in envy. There was an air of expectation now: most people had grown impatient with any entertainments brought for their own amusement, and the ground was littered with discarded books and knitting; instead, they talked to their neighbours or passed round early editions of the morning papers, keen to share what information they could about the forth-coming spectacle. It was an extraordinary scene, and it reminded Josephine of one long theatre queue snaking all around the city – peaceful, good-natured and stoic, a moment of history in itself.

The entrances to the side streets were packed as well now, and Josephine saw her own weariness reflected in the faces of those who still had twelve cramped hours of waiting ahead; in fact, the only people not to look tired were the hawkers of food and souvenirs who would live for weeks on what they had taken during the night, and had no intention of stopping until every opportunity was exploited. She looked at her watch; it was long before the allotted time of seven o'clock, but many of the wooden barriers had already been put in place and the crowd seemed to swell as she looked at it. Gritting her teeth, and trying in vain to think of something which would make her queue all night in such a determined fashion, Josephine fought her way back to Cavendish Square to dress for the King.

2

Vivienne woke early, just as it was getting light. She left their bed, conscious that this was the last time she would ever think of it as theirs, and pulled the curtains back quietly so as not to wake Anthony. It was a lacklustre, depressing day which should have belonged to the dark months of winter. A damp, insistent mist hung over the trees, utterly at odds with the celebrations on the city's streets, but so in tune with her own mood that it could have been designed especially for her. She watched as yellow squares of light began to appear one by one in the windows opposite, a checkerboard of anticipation, and wondered what it would be like to wake to the ordinary excitement of a historic day, shared with thousands, rather than to this lonely, personal sense of change. As it was, she was amazed by how calm she felt.

Leaving Anthony to sleep until the alarm did its work, she went downstairs to the kitchen. There was some ham in the pantry, left over from the supper that he had been too late home to eat the night before, and she got it out, together with a fresh loaf and some pickles. She cut the bread carefully while she waited for the kettle to boil, listening to Anthony moving about in the rooms above, struck more forcefully than usual by the familiar noises of their marriage. Eventually, he joined her in the kitchen, immaculately dressed and wearing an aftershave that seemed absurdly extravagant for the time of day. 'What are you doing?' he asked.

'Making you some sandwiches.'

'What's brought that on? You don't usually bother.'

'It's not usually the Coronation. You've got a long day ahead.'

'But I can't mess around with sandwiches. I've got enough to take as it is.'

'Then I'll bring them to you. I'm not sitting far away, and I hate waiting around. I'll keep you company during the dull bits – God knows there'll be a few of those.' She finished what she was doing and wrapped the food in greaseproof paper.

'Don't overdo it, though, Viv. I need to concentrate on what I'm going to say.'

'There'll be plenty of time for that. Sit down and have some breakfast – there's fresh tea in the pot.' She pushed the toast rack towards him and took a slice herself. 'It's a ten fifteen start, isn't it?'

'That's right. Snagge's getting us underway – the crowds and the foreign dignitaries, that sort of thing, all building to the first glimpse of the King. I'm not sure that wasn't the plum job, in hindsight – or Howard in the Abbey, of course.' She watched as he poured his tea, intensely aware now of the way he held his cup and the movement of his lips as he talked; the thought of Anthony's absence, it seemed, had magnified his presence in the room, and had made her more sensitive to all the physical things he would take with him when he left. 'I'm not so sure that Constitution Hill was the best choice after all.'

'Don't be silly. The return to the palace of a newly crowned king? It's what the whole day's about. And your commentary is by far the longest section – they're not going to waste you on anything less than the most crucial moments.'

'I only hope those bloody television cameras don't get in the way. It's just my luck to have to compete with the novelty value and stand by while Freddie Grisewood steals the show. It's going to be quite something, you know – the first glimpse of the carriage and the close-ups as it goes through Apsley Gate.'

'But what's left for Freddie to do? The pictures are already there for everyone to see. There's no magic about television.' Suddenly, Vivienne realised how tired she was of boosting her husband's confidence all these years, of picking him up every time his ego received a knock from new developments at the BBC or the threat of a new voice on the scene. It would be nice to have some peace.

'Yes, you're right. Actually, it'll be handy to have you nearby just in case I need something. You can tell me what the mood is among the crowd and I can build that into the commentary. You've got your ticket?'

'Yes, of course. Have some more tea.'

'It seems funny to start such a momentous day in such an ordinary way.'

Doesn't it just, Vivienne thought. 'The king's probably saying the very same thing. How must they feel, I wonder – looking out at all those people in the Mall over their toast and eggs? It's not even as if he was born to it. I imagine his brother's ears are burning this morning, even if he is in France.'

'Bloody stupid to give your life up for a woman, though.'

Vivienne looked at him sharply but there was absolutely no hint of irony in the remark; she thought about the letter in the drawer upstairs, the sacrifice of his own career, and wondered why it had taken so long for her to realise that there was a fundamentally stupid streak in her husband. Not that she could talk; she had been aware of all his infidelities, but she had never dreamt that he would leave her – or that Millicent Gray would be the one to tempt him away. She could have understood it with some of the others, some of the women at work who had an intelligence to match their glamour – but not this one. She realised that Anthony was waiting for her to comment on something he had said. 'I'm sorry, darling – I just remembered something that needs to be added to the new issue. What did you say?'

'Just that we've come on so far in the last few years that it's hard to believe this is the very first coronation broadcast. The whole world will be waiting to hear what we do today.'

'Are you nervous?'

'Not really. I just keep telling myself that it's what we do all the time. Poor old Woody was beside himself, though – and I can't say I'd want to trade places with him. If anything goes wrong in that control room at the Abbey, it's not just our broadcast that's at risk – it's all the microphones along the route and the loudspeakers in the Abbey, not to mention the foreign broadcasts. If I were him, I'd be ill and take the day off.'

'There must be a backup, surely?'

'There's a transmitter on the Abbey roof with a wireless link to BH, but even so.'

'And what about you? What help will you have?'

'I'll have an engineer with me, but only while I'm broadcasting live.'

'So you'll have plenty of peace and quiet to prepare?'

'I hope so.'

Vivienne hesitated, knowing it was futile but wanting to give Anthony one last chance to save himself. 'We should book a holiday when this is all over and Maurice is back. Somewhere nice, just the two of us. We haven't been away for ages.'

'Yes, well, I can't think about that now. And you needn't wait for me later. I'll have to go back to the office for a debrief afterwards, and discuss the schedule for the rest of the week. Then there's the King's broadcast. I might be late.' How easily the lies tumbled out of his mouth, she thought; she knew exactly where her husband planned to be later, and it had nothing to do with the King's speech. 'So I'll see you back here?' She caught her breath, struck for the first time by the finality of what she was about to do. 'Viv? Are you all right?'

'Yes, perfectly all right. I'll go and get changed.'

'Well, don't take too long about it. I don't want to be late. You can always come on later if you need more time.'

'No, I want to collect something from Danny while you're at the office. You're leaving for the observation point at twelve, aren't you?' Anthony nodded. 'Good. Give me five minutes.'

She ran up the two flights of stairs to her dressing room and slipped into the outfit she had laid out the night before – a sober two-piece suit in an unmemorable dark blue, chosen specifically to blend easily into the crowd. She heard a car draw up outside and looked down into the street, where Billy was waiting in his usual place. Anthony's voice drifted up to her, impatient now, and with a sharpness that revealed the lie in his denial of nerves. 'The car's here, Viv. I'm going to have to go without you if you're not ready now.'

'Coming, darling.' She joined him in the hall, hoping that he wouldn't comment on the lack of effort she had made with her clothes, but he barely looked at her. With a final glance back at the ordinariness she was leaving behind, Vivienne picked up the handbag which she had packed so carefully the day before and left the house with her husband for the very last time.

3

A temporary annexe had been built onto the front of Westminster Abbey, blending beautifully with the older fabric of the building. The doors, carved in light oak and reserved for members of the royal family, stood expectantly open and a scarlet-and-gold canopy added a touch of extravagance to an otherwise understated facade. The colours were mirrored in the Royal Standard which fluttered gently in the breeze above this new addition to the city's architecture, and the skyline beyond was broken by tiny figures moving across the rooftops, keen to take advantage of their privileged view. Down below, cars bringing guests to the Abbey flowed in and out efficiently, and the handful of guests who had arrived in state coaches were welcomed by the crowd as an early piece of pageantry in what had so far been a very dull morning of forgettable comings and goings.

Josephine looked at her watch and stifled a yawn. It was already ten minutes to seven, and the Motleys were pushing the strict rules of admittance to their limit. If they didn't arrive soon, she would be tempted to stretch out on the three spare seats next to her and sleep through the whole damned thing. She listened idly to the conversations going on around her, most of which seemed to be about the weather, and wondered if her inability to share a fascination with the subtlest change of cloud-colour revealed something lacking in her or in everyone else. Just as she had given up hope of more stimulating company, Lettice appeared at the entrance to the stand, dressed in a beautiful off-white suit which would have been the height of elegance had it not been unsettled by the weight of a large picnic hamper. The empty seats – a rarity now in the stand

– drew her eye quickly to Josephine and she waved, then beckoned impatiently to the stragglers in her party. When Ronnie emerged in peacock-blue silk, Josephine would happily have bet all she had on the colour of Mrs Snipe's outfit, and she wasn't disappointed: the housekeeper brought up the rear in a triumphant red, which made her already majestic stature even more impressive. Josephine counted at least four more variously sized baskets as the trio made its stately progress up the steps towards her, and she did not have to be an expert in lip-reading to know that Ronnie's reaction to being seated in the middle of a full row was less than gracious. In the end, Mrs Snipe took charge, positioning Ronnie and Lettice at intervals down the line and passing the baskets over the heads of those already seated. Realising that she was expected to act as the final link in the chain, and conscious of providing a welcome interlude for the crowd, Josephine stood to receive each basket in turn and somehow managed to wrestle them all into the space by her feet.

'We haven't missed anything, I hope,' Lettice whispered, sitting down next to her.

'On the contrary. Your entrance has been the only thing worth getting up for so far.'

'Oh good. We were all ready to go, but Ronnie toyed with a last-minute change of colour.'

'Not green, I hope. That would have given the wrong impression entirely.'

'No, just a different shade of blue, something closer to the proper flag. Then she decided that was far too dull, so back we went to the peacock. By that time, it was gone six and the Snipe was beside herself.' She redistributed the baskets along the row and glanced round at the crowd. 'Haven't they gone to a lot of trouble?' she added, gesturing towards the plush red fabric on the chairs and the white-and-gold valances that draped each stand. 'I wonder what they're doing with the decorations when it's all over? We've got a *Henry V* coming up at the New, and this would be perfect.'

'Bugger *Henry V*. For God's sake, get the flask out,' Ronnie urged. 'The early start I've had today will kill me.' She peered at Josephine, who suddenly felt the inadequacies of her own makeup. 'And you look awful. Has Marta kept you up all night?'

'Yes, but not in the way you mean.'

'Is everything all right?' Lettice asked.

Josephine glanced at Mrs Snipe, who sat at the other end of their quartet. The housekeeper was the soul of discretion and they had shared confidences in the past, but Josephine still did not feel quite liberated enough to discuss her love life openly in front of her. Fortunately, the housekeeper was engaged in fishing out a round of bacon sandwiches which seemed miraculously to have stayed warm in spite of Ronnie's prevarications. 'Not really,' she said. 'It's my fault. I wanted things to change, but I think it might rather have backfired on me. Now isn't the time to talk about it, though. I'll tell you later.' It was hard to say how much of the conversation Mrs Snipe had heard, but she smiled at Josephine and passed her a steaming cup of coffee laced heavily with brown sugar, just the way she liked it. Josephine took it gratefully, feeling as wretched as she looked, then changed her mind about the sandwich; she had skipped dinner the night before and left herself no time for breakfast, and the smell of bacon made her realise how hungry she was.

Ronnie took the programme out of her bag. 'Bloody long day, isn't it?' she said, flicking through the pages. 'What are we all supposed to do while he's in there being anointed? And how can it take three hours? It's not as if he's got anything to think about – he's stuck with it now, whether he likes it or not.' She looked apprehensively up at the sky. 'Then there's the weather to worry about. I'm beginning to think that Bridget was right, you know – we'd get all the good bits on the wireless.'

'The weather will clear up soon, you mark my words,' Mrs Snipe said confidently, and it amused Josephine to see that her down-to-earth attitude to life could cut through the Motley sisters' nonsense as effectively now as it had when they were younger. Very few people could keep Ronnie in line, but the Snipe – who had virtually raised Lettice and Ronnie after their mother's early death – managed to keep their love and respect while allowing them to get away with nothing.

Her optimism about the day seemed justified, too; by the time the bacon had been followed by cheese scones, sausage rolls and another round of coffees, the skies had brightened a little and the crowd was in cheerful mood. Throughout the morning, police had allowed more people to filter through to different vantage points, and paper caps of red, white and blue began to appear in all directions; vendors selling cardboard periscopes seemed to be doing a particularly good trade, while others chose to gain their extra inches by paying sixpence for stilts – short lengths of sawn wood that said much about the British public's eye for an opportunity but offered little practical benefit. The atmosphere inside the Abbey seemed relaxed; peers wandered in and out in their robes, exchanging a word or two with spectators, and shadowy figures moved around just inside the doors, checking small details that had, no doubt, been checked a hundred times before.

'So what *is* wrong?' Lettice asked, ignoring Josephine's preference not to talk. 'Can we help?'

Josephine hesitated. Ronnie and Lettice were friends with Lydia as well as with her, but she trusted them to be impartial, even if that meant dishing out a few home truths that she didn't want to hear. The person she longed to talk to was Archie, but there was no chance of getting him on his own for the next couple of days and this couldn't wait. 'Oh, it's just Lydia,' she said, trying not to speak too loudly over the hubbub of the crowd. 'To quite frank, I'm sick to death of her.'

'No surprise there,' Ronnie said, with an irritating retrospective wisdom. 'I don't know how you ever thought that little arrangement was going to work, darling.' She drained her coffee and smiled provocatively. 'But if it's any consolation, I'm sure the feeling's mutual.'

'It's certainly that,' Josephine agreed, and told them what had happened at Broadcasting House, relieved to share the conversation after a long night of soul-searching.

'So Lydia saw what was coming and got in first,' Lettice said. 'That's tricky.'

'I know, and it's my fault as well. Marta wanted to talk to her as soon as we got back from Suffolk, but I made her wait.'

'So what do you actually *want*?' Ronnie asked. 'I'm not sure I quite understand.'

'I just want it to be simple,' Josephine said, and cut Ronnie off before she had time to argue. 'All right, I know it never will be and there are a thousand and one things that make it complicated, but I can live with all the distance and the secrecy and the pretence because we deal with those together. Lydia's different, though. She divides us, and she always will.' She sighed, wishing that everything she was trying to explain did not boil down quite so transparently to a straightforward case of jealousy. 'I thought it was enough to know that Marta loves me and that what we have comes first, even if we can't be together as often as we'd like to be. But it isn't. In the early days, whenever I had to go back to Scotland, I missed Marta dreadfully and that was hard, but it was all part of the love. Now when we're apart, I spend as much time thinking about Lydia and what she's getting up to as I do about Marta, and that's got nothing to do with love. Resentment and suspicion and paranoia, perhaps, but not love. And it's not like me. It's not who I thought I was.'

'You mean you've become someone you don't even recognise, and you hate yourself for it.'

Josephine looked at Lettice, surprised by how much feeling she had put into the observation, but something in her friend's expression told her not to probe any further. 'Yes,' she said curiously, 'that's exactly it. And something's changed. I can't put my finger on it, but I know Lydia's suddenly making more effort with Marta. Perhaps it's the cottage. At last, we've got somewhere to go that Lydia doesn't feel she can just walk into at any time, and perhaps that's made her more vulnerable. I know she never entirely forgave Marta for leaving her at Christmas.'

'The trouble with you, Josephine, is that you're just not pushy enough,' Ronnie said, with sufficient exasperation in her voice to suggest that the problem was obvious to the point of banality. 'Say what you like about Lydia, but she doesn't give up. You need to fight much harder and much dirtier if you want Marta to yourself.'

'I didn't know it was a military operation,' Josephine said huffily.

'Of course it's a military operation. Sex always is.'

'She's right, you know,' Mrs Snipe said, and all three of them turned to stare at her in surprise. The housekeeper carried on looking through her binoculars, apparently finding a particular fascination in the pigeons on the roof of the annexe. 'You need to put your back into it, Miss Tey. No woman likes to be messed about. If Miss Fox thinks you're not bothered, then why should she be?'

The Snipe's wisdom silenced everyone for a few moments. 'Well, that's me told,' Josephine muttered eventually. 'Now can we please change the subject?'

Lettice squeezed her hand in solidarity. 'We won't say another word about it. Does anybody fancy something sweet?'

The first procession of royal cars arrived just after nine, carrying relatives of the royal family and heads of state from across the Empire. Then, at last, some picturesque carriages came into view, headed by the prime minister and Mrs Baldwin who received the first truly rousing cheer of the morning. Their escort of mounted police was a restrained introduction to the day's pageantry, but the familiarity of the uniform did nothing to diminish its impact; in fact, its ordinariness brought a human touch to the ceremony, making it easier for people to believe that the moment belonged to them as well as to history. A whisper passed through the crowd, hints of something more significant at last, and when the head of a longer, more colourful procession appeared in the distance, the sudden, collective elevation of periscopes suggested a Wellsian fantasy of another world. As if in response, a shaft of light broke free from a sullen sky and the sun shook off the clouds for the first time, coaxing a new and indefinable glory from the polished metals and heraldic colours which suddenly filled the streets. 'See?' Mrs Snipe said, her faith in a benevolent world justified. 'It's kings' weather after all.'

And it was. Sunlight danced and sparkled on a pair of glass coaches, and two small princesses waved exuberantly from the windows of the first. Josephine looked down at the young Elizabeth and wondered if she had any idea yet of what this day meant for her future; there were times when she herself felt as though the path of her life were all too clearly mapped out, but she couldn't begin to imagine how it must feel to have the years laid down for you so publicly and so irrevocably. Would this little girl embrace the responsibilities that had unexpectedly come her way, or would she secretly kick against the loss of her freedom for the rest of her days, envying the sister who seemed so close to her now but whose fate was so very different?

It was amazing what a difference the weather made to the public's mood. Queen Mary's procession followed quickly on the heels of her granddaughters', and she acknowledged her ovation with characteristic dignity and grace, visibly moved by the warmth and respect she had received from everyone over the years – well, almost everyone. 'Third time lucky for her,' Ronnie said irreverently. 'She certainly knows how to see them in and out, doesn't she?' The sun brought a new dimension to the vista of brilliant uniforms and tossing plumes, recreating the movement of the horses and the marching of the bands in an ever-shifting shadow play on the streets and nearby buildings. Even to a nation so confident of its own pageantry, the precision of the spectacle was extraordinary, but it was the noise that struck Josephine most – the clatter of hooves, the jingle of harnesses and the crunch of gun-carriage wheels, distinct even above the roar of the crowds. The procession was relentless as it reached its height: sailors and marines, soldiers and airmen, all interspersed with less-familiar sights; three maharajahs – the King's Honorary Indian Aides-de-Camp – looked splendid in jewelled turbans of blue, cream and gold; and the Yeomen of the Guard, the King's Bargemaster and a dozen Watermen wore uniforms which brought vanished centuries to life. Behind them, massed bands struck up another spirited march, and for a few brief moments, the intensity of the experience silenced everyone. 'There's no finer sight than a country at peace with itself,' Mrs Snipe said eventually, and Josephine had to agree.

Then, at last, the moment that everyone had been waiting for. The breastplates and plumes of the Lifeguards heralded the approach of the King and Queen, and the crowds in this part of the city got their first glimpse of the coronation coach. Looking down the line of stands, Josephine marked its approach by an advancing tide of flags and handkerchiefs, long before the horses came into view – eight Windsor Greys in gold-and-crimson harness, driven by four postilions in red jackets and jockey caps with grooms walking beside them. The sun seemed to increase in strength, repentant for its late arrival, but it had met its match in the gold-encrusted windows and painted panels of the state coach. George VI wore the crimson velvet cap of state, trimmed with ermine; beneath it, his face was pale – he couldn't have had any more sleep than she had, Josephine thought – and he gazed straight ahead, exchanging an occasional word with his wife. 'God, he looks terrified,' she said, borrowing the Snipe's binoculars to get a better view. 'You would be, wouldn't you?'

'Mmm. Look at her, though – you'd never guess who was the commoner if you didn't know.' The Queen sat on crimson cushions, dressed in an ermine cloak, and Ronnie was right about her confidence: she smiled broadly at the crowds, bowing to left and right as the cluster of gold moved forward.

The coach received a tremendous ovation in Parliament Square amid the music of the bands, the pealing of the Abbey bells and the fluttering of handkerchiefs and flags, finally drawing to a halt outside the annexe. Moved as much by the spirit of unity as by the occasion which inspired it, Josephine watched the King step down, followed by his queen. It was ironic, she thought, that of all the people gathered here today, only these two were playing out a different role; the abdication had changed nothing for the crowds or the officials or the guests, all of whom behaved exactly as they would have done had this been Edward VIII's coronation. History rolled on, but there was a personal drama here that Josephine found more poignant, a sacrifice made by one couple because of the love of another. They paused for a moment to acknowledge the appreciation of the crowd, then turned and mounted the blue-carpeted steps to the Abbey. As they disappeared inside, the Royal Standard which flew over the annexe was taken down and another flag raised above the main building to mark the beginning of the ceremony. It was precisely eleven o'clock.

'That's that, then,' Ronnie said, eyeing up one of the baskets that was yet to be opened. 'Is it too early for a gin?'

4

The walls of the Abbey could scarcely keep the noise of the crowds at bay. Ripples of applause grew rhythmically outside, gathering strength like the tide and breaking against the stone, falling away suddenly only to begin again somewhere else. The intrusion felt curious, out of kilter with the quiet mystery of what was happening inside, but far less brazen than the microphones positioned at various points around the building. From his post high up in the triforium, Penrose could count four by the altar, eight around the thrones and chairs of state, and – perhaps most incongruously of all – two hanging down over St Edward's Chair, where the most intimate moments of the ceremony would take place. Apart from one short break during the prayer of consecration, when the broadcast would switch to a hymn from St Margaret's Church, everything that was said or sung today would be heard by millions, and Penrose could not help but feel that the microphones were as symbolic in their way as any of the more ritualistic items laid out on the altar table; they were a reminder that – for the first time ever – the world was present even after the doors were closed, and they stood not for age or for tradition, but for democracy.

When the ceremony began, though, a stillness descended on the Abbey and it was as if all the comings and goings had never happened. The crowds faded, and everywhere Penrose looked the past reclaimed the day – in the quiet strength of the stone, in the diffuse light which fell on the cross, in the echoes of lost centuries and the tombs of the famous dead. He should have been scanning the crowd, but, as the last notes of 'Zadok the Priest' died away, he found it hard to concentrate on anything but the thousand-year-old ceremony unfolding in front of him. For all the secular pomp and military showmanship, the Coronation was first and last a hallowing, a consecration, and its central act was the anointing. Penrose watched, spellbound, as the Lord Chamberlain removed the King's crimson velvet robes, stripping him of the trappings of earthly majesty. Clothed simply now in white shirt and breeches, the King walked slowly towards the altar to sit for the first time on Edward the Confessor's chair, a gothic piece of ancient oak with freshly gilded lions at its feet. Four Knights of the Garter stepped forward to hold a canopy of gold cloth over the monarch, partially concealing him from view, and the Dean poured oil from a golden ampulla, shaped like an eagle, into a spoon. With great solemnity, the Archbishop of Canterbury dipped his fingers in the oil and anointed the King in four places – the palms of both hands, the chest and the crown of his head. The gesture was both earthly and mystical, an acknowledgement of the bond between God and King, and Penrose – who had no religious faith but who sometimes envied those who did – was moved.

He looked back at the congregation and saw his own fascination mirrored there, even in the faces of those who had witnessed the ceremony before. So far, the day had been flawless and he hoped that the street celebrations which followed – a far greater challenge than his duties here – would go as smoothly. His mind wandered during the investiture, and he found himself thinking about the contingency plans that had been made for the afternoon and evening, trying to predict the areas of most concern. Eventually, the ceremony began to move more swiftly, and the anticipation in the Abbey was almost tangible as the Archbishop lifted the crown from its place on the altar. The King bowed his head in reverence during the prayer that followed, and the crown was carried towards him, past the Queen and her entourage and below the Royal Gallery where his mother and daughters sat expectantly. Then the Archbishop held the crown aloft with both hands and lowered it slowly until it rested on George VI's head.

A cheer rang out through the Abbey, and the triumphant notes of silver trumpets rose up to greet them. As the tumult died down, the pealing of the bells could be heard, faint and muffled through the stone walls. In the distance, Penrose thought he detected the booming note of a gun salute from the Tower of London, but it was soon eclipsed by a repeated, staccato chant that came from all directions, uniting those inside and out. 'God save the King! God save the King! God save the King!'

5

The wireless was on in the background and Marta half-listened as she worked, still in her pyjamas and conscious of being the least appropriately dressed woman in London, but too engrossed in what she was doing to care. Yet another trumpet fanfare marked the latest significant moment in an otherwise obscure ceremony, and she thought again about Josephine; a day of waiting and cheering and crowds would not be doing much for her headache. It was odd that none of her calls had been returned, but Josephine had had an early start and Marta knew by now that she was always anxious and short-tempered when something important was happening with her work – and the situation with Lydia was preying on both their minds. In hindsight, she wished she had ignored Josephine's protestations and talked to Lydia as soon as they got back from Suffolk. The waiting wasn't good for any of them; even Lydia had been quiet and distracted over dinner last night, and that wasn't like her at all.

She lit another cigarette and read back over the script she was working on, an early draft of a screenplay for Alfred Hitchcock and Alma Reville. *The Lost Lady* was an adaptation of a recent novel, and Hitchcock – looking for a follow-up to *Young and Innocent*, the film he was currently making of Josephine's book – had inherited the project from another director as a way of fulfilling his contract before moving to America. It was Marta's job to add some dialogue to the original script, working with the new scenarios that Hitch and Alma had developed, and she enjoyed it as she enjoyed all the work she did for them. It was well-paid if not well-credited – Hitchcock's attitude to dialogue writers was less than complimentary – and she found it easy as well as satisfying; she had held imaginary conversations in her head for most of her life, so putting words into the mouths of other people came as second nature – and the beauty of a script was that they only answered back if she let them.

The first, uplifting notes of the *Te Deum* drifted across the room and Marta turned the wireless up to listen to the closing part of the ceremony. She had always loved choral music and the voices soothed her while she worked, reminding her of when she was young and lived in Cambridge, and often went to Evensong at King's. It had been a sanctuary of sorts from a bad marriage, not in the religious sense, but because it offered more precious gifts of beauty, peace and hope, the very things that her husband had taken from her. The bell that sounded the call to prayer each day had been just audible from where she lived, and she remembered how desperately she had left the house when she heard it, not to find God but to find herself. It was funny, but Cambridge had been on her mind more often of late, and she couldn't decide if that was because her life in London was beginning to crowd in on her, or because she was finally ready to face her past.

She put her source material down, imagining how shocked Hitch and Alma would be by the idea that Ethel Lina White's original novel might have any relevance to what she was doing, and went to make more coffee, looking out across the garden as she waited for the kettle to boil. She had sat by this window for hours after the first night that she and Josephine spent together, and she could still recall the devastating sense of loss she felt when Josephine left her alone in the house. It was as far from the euphoria with which she might have hoped to greet a new love as it was possible to get, but, in her heart, she had never expected her to return. The intensity of Josephine's feelings had surprised Marta more than her own: once the love was there and acknowledged between them, there was an innocence to Josephine's trust in it;

she worried too much about the outside world, but not once when they were alone had Marta sensed anything but a fundamental faith in the beauty of what they shared, and she realised now that the assurance of that had healed her. Once or twice in her life she had considered ending everything, and she wondered if Josephine would ever know how many times she had saved her from the darkness of her own soul – by a look or by a kiss, by the passion and tenderness of her touch, by loving her in spite of the risks. And it was stupid or selfish of her – she wasn't sure which was worse – to forget that Josephine *also* needed something more to live for. She was just as self-destructive in her way, and although she might baulk at leaving the world altogether, she would deny herself what she loved if she felt it was the right thing to do, no matter how much pain it brought her. Marta had made too many sacrifices in her life already to add their love to the list.

Outside, the weather had lost its patience with the day and rain poured down into the garden, soaking the deckchairs that she had forgotten to bring in and laying low the early summer irises. Even so, she was pleased with how the garden had come on in the two years she had been there, and satisfied that it was in good shape for the next custodian along. She would miss it, but selling the house was the right thing to do. Although she hadn't yet discussed it with Josephine, she knew that it would take more than one conversation to unravel her life with Lydia, and broaching the subject was just the beginning. If her intentions were to be taken seriously, she needed to find somewhere new that Lydia didn't regard as a second home, somewhere out of London and less convenient for the theatre, somewhere she could be alone, and where Josephine could turn up unannounced whenever she liked without having to look over her shoulder. There would be somewhere that made them both happy. Cambridge might be the answer or it might not, but there would be somewhere.

6

'Their Majesties appear in the doorway and the people get a first glimpse of their crowned monarch. The Queen – sceptre and rod in hand – is the first to enter the state coach, and the national anthem crashes out as they drive away, drowned in mighty waves of cheering...'

Vivienne sat in the broadcast cubicle on Constitution Hill, listening as Anthony's colleagues described the royal couple's departure from Westminster Abbey. The commentary so far had been flawless, the pictures both vivid and dignified, and she could only imagine the self-congratulation that would go on later: there was no organisation more practised than the Corporation at taking credit where credit was due. Every moment that passed according to plan put more pressure on Anthony not to drop the baton once it was handed to him, and she watched as he fidgeted in his chair, adjusting the microphone for the hundredth time and reading through some notes without taking any of them in. Her husband was more nervous than she had ever seen him. At breakfast, he had been irritable and self-absorbed, as he always was before a broadcast, but his mood had changed over the course of the morning to something approaching panic, and she watched him curiously, interested in a vulnerability that she had never seen before. 'Look, it's raining,' she said, trying to distract him from his nerves. 'What a shame.'

'I can see it's bloody raining, Viv. There wouldn't be much point in my being here if I'd missed that.'

'Sorry, darling.' She poured a coffee from the flask and put the cup on the desk next to him. 'Have some of this.' He ignored it, and she knew that what he wanted most was for her to leave him alone, but his discomfort gave her an obstinate desire to linger.

'Don't you want to go and soak up the atmosphere?' he asked eventually, when she refused to get the message.

'I think those crowds are soaking up a bit more than atmosphere.' She stood beside him and looked out of the small oblong window, which offered a prime view over the solid bank of faces on Constitution Hill. The hill was a splendid setting for pageantry at any time, but today, at intervals of fifty feet or so, tall masts flew white-and-gold banners emblazoned with the royal arms, offsetting the soft green plane trees that lined the avenue and leading the eye gently down to the Victoria Memorial and the beginning of the Mall. A bird's-eye view of the procession from here would indeed be an unforgettable sight, and Vivienne did not doubt that Anthony would do it justice for the millions listening at home. 'I'll wait until your engineer gets here,' she added, 'just in case you need anything.'

'If you must, but don't keep talking to me. I can't have any distractions while I'm working.'

She could have retorted that the next time he let her interrupt his work would be the first, but she didn't waste her breath. They were long past the pettiness of squabbles. It was after two o'clock and the head of the procession was approaching Hyde Park Corner; it could only be a matter of minutes now before Anthony's turn came. 'The skies have been ominously grey for some time, and now the first drops of rain are falling,' said the voice over the airwaves – a little behind events, Vivienne thought. 'The King and Queen – showing some understandable weariness now – pass through Marble Arch, where the crowds remain undaunted by the weather. The state coach begins its long progression down East Carriage Drive, where – as you will shortly hear – members of the British Legion stand proudly ready to greet Their Majesties with song, and then to Hyde Park Corner, where television cameras will for the first time transmit an historic event, taking our viewers to within a few feet of the coach as it passes through Apsley Gate.'

Behind her, Vivienne heard the door open and the engineer nodded to Anthony as he sat down by the control desk and put on his headphones. She stood to go, but paused as the red light came on, genuinely curious to see what Anthony's first words would be. They set the tone of his commentary – warm, authoritative, and with a richness of understanding that lifted his remarks to a different level from the more matter-of-fact observations which had preceded them. 'And so, the King and Queen – *our* king and queen – begin the last leg of a triumphant journey which will bring them home to Buckingham Palace almost six hours after they left it.' His voice danced in and out of the scene in front of her, never eclipsing the natural atmosphere of the day, and she remembered how good he was, with a strange mixture of resentment and regret. 'They have, in a sense, travelled through many centuries between their departure and their return,' he continued, 'and the people – *their* people – acknowledge that now with the warmest cheers of the day so far.'

Vivienne slipped from the cubicle and walked carefully down the rain-soaked wooden steps and out into the throng. Still it poured and still the crowds cheered, waving hats and flags with an exuberance that was almost frenzied. Ignoring the seat with her colleagues in the stand, she took her chances out in the open, enjoying the sting of the water against her face after the claustrophobic tension of the broadcast room. The crowd was eight or nine deep, and she peered through the heads in front of her as troops moved by in a steady stream, separated from the spectators by a double line of steel rails but still quite breathtakingly close. Even from where she stood, the sight of the Guards – bayonets silver against the solid black mass of bearskins, arms moving in a synchronised swathe of scarlet – was exhilarating. The rain gathered the intensity of a storm, as if determined to compete with the climax of the day, and for the first time the loyalty of the crowds was tested. Disciplined and obliging until now, the downpour proved too severe a test and hundreds of people broke ranks to run for shelter, creating a chaos which suited her purpose. Those who remained lined the route with a forest of black umbrellas, an incongruous replacement for the red, white and blue, and she thought how fitting it was that – in the midst of the celebrations – there should also be a sense of mourning.

In the distance, troops marched round the Victoria Memorial and away down Birdcage Walk, and the royal coach entered the palace under a sky the colour of stone. After a wait that seemed longer than it was, the mass movement of people told Vivienne that soldiers and police had been withdrawn from the palace railings, and the crowds surged forward for the balcony appearance, demanding to see their king. She stood to the side to let them pass, anxious not to be carried away in the wrong direction; Anthony would, by now, have handed over the commentary to his colleague inside the Palace grounds, and she waited impatiently for the engineer to leave her husband on his own. When she saw him come out, the collar of his mackintosh turned up against the weather, hat pulled low over his eyes, she fought her way as quickly as she could back to the broadcast cubicle. 'Congratulations, darling,' she said, shutting the door behind her. 'How do you think it went?'

He stared at her rain-drenched clothes in astonishment and she could hardly hear his response over the roar of noise outside. The chants for the King grew louder, making everything else inaudible, but Vivienne did not need to listen to the broadcast coming through the wires to be sure that the King had stepped out onto the balcony. The cheers were deafening, and she knew that it was time; no one would hear anything in this noise. 'It was a fitting swansong for you, then,' she said, and he stared at her in confusion, either because he had not heard or did not understand. Quickly, Vivienne took the gun out of her bag – her sister's gun, the one that Anthony had removed from Olivia's house on the day she died – and turned it on her husband with a deadly accuracy, pulling the trigger before he could stop her, and before she could change her mind.

7

By late afternoon, a taxi was as rare as a glimpse of the King, and just as coveted. Josephine waited impatiently in the entrance hall of the Cowdray Club, looking out across Cavendish Square. Here, the buildings remained more immune to decoration than most, and – at this stage in the celebrations – there was something restful about their plain, beautifully proportioned elegance. The city's illuminations would stay up for another week to give as many people as possible a chance to see them; perhaps it was her mood, but to Josephine they had already begun to feel as depressing as a Christmas tree in January.

Strains of a carnival atmosphere drifted over from Oxford Street, but the club itself was peculiarly quiet. The public rooms off the foyer were usually buzzing with conversation around now, with nurses coming off duty and taking tea or an early evening drink, but today they all stood empty; and even the wireless, given temporary pride of place by the door for the coronation coverage, had a sense of anticlimax about it, as commentators tried to fill a fifteen-minute slot with the news that play at Lords had been rained off. 'Are you sure it's on its way?' Josephine asked the receptionist, more snappily than she had intended.

The girl looked at her in surprise, either because she wasn't usually one of the club's more demanding members and rarely caused a fuss, or because it smacked of insanity to request a taxi at all. 'I'll check for you,' she said, and the weary note in her voice implied that if Josephine was really so indifferent to the day's celebrations, she would happily trade places with her. 'It won't be long,' was the best she had to offer when she replaced the receiver. 'He'll be as quick as he can.'

Josephine sighed and returned to the table of newspapers, unable to concentrate on anything but Marta. She was heartily sick of the advice she had received sporadically throughout the day, well-intentioned as it had been, and none of it had changed her mind. What she had to say to Marta might not constitute 'putting her back into it', to use Mrs Snipe's expression, but there was no other way – God knows she had tried hard enough to find one. Just as she was considering doing battle with the Underground, a taxi drew up by the kerb and she hurried out into the rain to claim her prize. The route north from the centre was necessarily circuitous to avoid the endless street parties, and Josephine wondered if a crowded tube would have been quicker after all. She gazed out of the window at tables of food covered in tarpaulins, admiring the stoicism with which the English made the best of the weather. Some roads had had the sense to hang their decorations so thickly that the rain barely got through; most had put their faith in a fairytale day of sunshine, and could only look on as the flags began to surrender their dye to the weather and the gutters ran with red, white and blue.

To her relief, Hampstead seemed to have confined its celebrations to the High Street, and the approach to Holly Place – a quiet byway on the south side of Hampstead Hill – was almost as tranquil as usual. Somehow, without any sense of compromise, the area managed to combine the excitement and stimulus of London with a quiet, rural feel, and she could understand why Marta loved living here. A thin plume of smoke rose bravely from the chimney, unseasonal but welcome against the rain; the ground-floor windows glowed cheerfully, and a softer, understated light was just discernible in the bedroom upstairs. The whole house seemed to await her arrival, and, just for a moment, Josephine was defenceless against images of the evening as it should have been. She paid the taxi driver and said goodbye, then thought better of it and asked him to wait.

Marta opened the door before she had a chance to knock. 'It's lovely to see you,' she said, giving Josephine a hug. 'I was worried when you didn't call last night.'

'I'm sorry.'

'But you're all right?' Josephine nodded. 'Good. Come into the kitchen for a minute. I'm running behind with dinner, but you can tell me all about the Coronation while we wait. It sounded extraordinary on the wireless.'

Josephine followed her down the hallway, trying not to notice how many of the coats on the rack were Lydia's. In spite of Marta's protestations, the house smelt enticingly of lamb and rosemary, and the kitchen testified to a meal being well on its way. Marta was the only person Josephine knew who could use half a dozen pans to make an omelette, and the scope offered by three courses had obviously driven her to explore the darkest corners of her cupboards; pots, utensils and a bewildering amount of ingredients were strewn across every surface. 'It looks worse than it is,' Marta grinned, handing her a corkscrew and a bottle of wine, ice-cold from the refrigerator. 'Here – do your worst with this while I rationalise things a bit.' Josephine did as she was asked, her heart in her mouth at the thought of what she had come to say, knowing that the longer she waited, the more painful it would be. She felt Marta's hand brush her back whenever she walked past, and already her resolve began to weaken. In the end, it was Marta who gave her the prompt she needed. 'Why is your taxi still here?' she asked, looking out of the window. 'Didn't you tip him?'

'I'm not staying, Marta. I can't stay.'

Her smile faded when she realised that Josephine wasn't joking. 'What do you mean? Of course you're staying. We've been looking forward to this for ages.'

'I know we have, but that was before Lydia cornered me and shared a few home truths.'

'Oh God, Josephine, I'm sorry. When?'

'Last night at Broadcasting House, just before we went up for the rehearsal. She was in the cloakroom when I walked in, and let's just say she seized her moment.'

'So that's why you left? You didn't really have a headache?'

'Oh, I had a headache by the time she'd finished.'

'Why didn't you tell me?'

Josephine paused, wondering how to explain to Marta what she had felt the night before. 'I wanted to,' she said eventually, 'but I was too ashamed. When I walked away from you last night, I felt as though I were crawling on my hands and knees.'

'You have *nothing* to be ashamed of. God, I could kill Lydia for this.'

'It's not Lydia's fault, though, is it? I spent all last night trying to blame her, but she's right.'

'Why? What did she say?'

Josephine heard the fear in Marta's voice as she began to understand the damage that Lydia had done. 'She said that whatever you're building up to telling her, she knows already. She knows when this started, she knows when we're together, and she knows how we feel about each other. In fact, she went to great pains to point out to me that she knows everything, especially *you* – and far better than I ever will.'

'That simply isn't true, Josephine. Lydia knows things *about* me, but that's not the same thing at all.' She took Josephine's hand. 'I'm sorry. I should have sorted this out ages ago whether you wanted me to or not. I could have spared you all this anguish if I'd only talked to her sooner.'

'It's not about that, Marta. None of this is about *when* you tell Lydia, or even what you tell her.'

'Then what is it about?'

Marta's apparent inability to understand why she was so upset bewildered Josephine. 'It's about there even *being* a Lydia,' she said, her frustration getting the better of her. 'It's about walking in here and feeling like your mistress, which is exactly what I am.'

'Of course you're not.'

'No? Look around you, Marta. You're so used to it that you don't even see it anymore.' She grabbed Marta's arm and led her through to the sitting room. 'You want to know what it's about? This room is what it's about. You hate Thomas Hardy, and yet your shelves are full of his books. I've never seen you drink sherry, but you've got three different types on the drinks tray. And as for this.' She picked up an ornament from the mantelpiece and threw it scornfully down onto the sofa. 'Never in a million years would you have bought *that*, thank God.' Marta opened her mouth to speak, but Josephine was no longer in the mood to be reasoned with. 'Shall we go and look in the bedroom now? See how much of Lydia you've moved in there? How can you say I'm not your mistress, Marta? Jesus, I bet when I leave you even wash the sheets.'

The slap came from nowhere and it was hard to say which of them was more shocked. 'Christ, Josephine, I'm sorry. I didn't mean to do that.'

She put a hand gently to Josephine's cheek, and Josephine covered it with her own. 'I don't blame you,' she said quietly, more surprised by her own outburst than by Marta's. 'I probably deserved it. But how was I to know you felt so strongly about the ornament?'

It was a weak attempt to claw back some normality, and Marta didn't even smile. 'You don't really think that's what you are to me, do you?'

'No, of course not. I'm not explaining myself very well.' She walked over to the window and looked out across the garden that Marta had transformed from a wasteland to something beautiful, something hopeful for the years ahead; it was, she noticed now, the only part of the house that had remained uniquely hers, without a hint of compromise. 'When I first came here, you'd only just moved in, but everywhere I looked told me a bit more about who you were. It was a sanctuary after what you'd been through, and you only let in the things that were important to you. The fact that you allowed me in, that you wanted me here – well, that felt special. But all that's gone. Now when I come here, I feel like an intruder.' Josephine had dreaded this conversation but, to her surprise, she found it a relief to give voice to things she had felt for a long time but kept to herself. 'How would you feel if you came to the cottage and it was full of someone else? We chose everything there together, and it's as much yours as it's mine, but this isn't. I'm not blaming you, Marta. If anything, I blame myself for not being here more. But you asked me how I felt and it's time for me to be honest. Last night, Lydia told me that whatever you and I say, whatever we decide among ourselves, nothing will really change, and she's right. This house is living proof of that.'

'And that's exactly why I've decided to—'

'She also told me that I'm never there when you really need me. Is that true?' Marta's hesitation was as much as Josephine could take. 'See?' she said sadly. 'None of us is happy with the way things are. I can't do this any more, Marta. It's just not right. Something's got to change.'

She turned to go but Marta caught her hand. 'You can't leave like this, Josephine – there's no need. Everything's out in the open now. Let's talk about what we're going to do.'

'We're beyond talking, Marta. I'm exhausted with it.'

'So you just walk away? That's your answer?'

'No, it's not an answer, it's a question. Only you know what the answer is.' She took Marta's face in her hands and kissed her, feeling a mixture of sadness and desire that seemed to express more eloquently than any words the risk she was taking by asking Marta to choose. 'I love you. Come back to me when you're free.'

She pulled away while she still could and walked out into the street. The taxi driver glanced curiously at her in the rear-view mirror, and Josephine could only imagine how he was accounting for her tears; a quarrel, perhaps, or a death – and in that he might not be far wrong. She had said everything she wanted to say and more, but the confrontation hadn't had the cathartic effect she was hoping for. Instead, with all the contrariness of someone in love, she wondered what she should make of Marta's willingness to let her go.

8

Vivienne remembered very little of the journey home – just a sea of faces, their smiles grotesque and distorted, and a suffocating tide of bodies that threatened to overwhelm her as she fought her way through. The noise in the streets was deafening and panic played tricks with her mind, transforming the harmless shouts of the crowd into an angry, collective cry for justice, the beginning of a nightmare from which she would never wake. Anthony's face haunted her, and she saw again and again the horror in his eyes as he realised what was happening. In that split second of clarity, he had seemed to understand her as he never had before, and she wondered what his greatest regret had been. That he hadn't achieved all he wanted to? That he hadn't been more careful to protect his other life? That he hadn't loved her more?

To Vivienne's relief, the crowds melted away as she left the heart of the city behind, and Young Street itself was eerily deserted. The slam of the front door echoed through the empty house, and in the stillness and solitude, the shock of what she had done finally caught up with her. Bile rose in her throat and she got to the cloakroom just in time, bending low over the sink as the sharp, acrid smell filled the air. The memory of Anthony hit her again – slumped in his chair, a wound in his head – and the finality of her actions shook her body with all the force of the gunshot. She retched again, as if the guilt and disgust she felt could somehow be dispelled by another physical act, but they remained now as part of who she was – permanent, inevitable, damning. She splashed her face with cold water and stared at her reflection in the mirror, wondering how she could possibly look like the same woman who had left the house this morning.

And then she heard his voice. She shook her head, trying to clear her mind of what must surely be a figment of her imagination, but there it was again – coming from the sitting room, low and insistent. Panic seized her as she remembered how quickly she had fled the scene, so horrified by what she had done that she had not even stopped to check that Anthony was dead, but it was soon replaced by relief; if her husband had survived, she could put things right after all – she would explain and he would understand, and there would be a second chance for them both. In her desperation to believe in a miracle, Vivienne did not stop to ask herself how Anthony had got home ahead of her; she ran across the hall to his voice, and it took her a few seconds to register that the sitting room was empty after all. The wireless had been left on in the hurry of their early morning departure, and what she had believed to be her salvation was merely a recording of her husband's coronation commentary, now taking pride of place on the six o'clock news. As the illusion left her, relief gave way to an emotion which she had never expected to feel. Her loss overwhelmed her, and she sank to her knees and wept.

It was a long time before she could even stand. When she had finally run out of tears, she forced herself to go upstairs to change, feeling Anthony always at her shoulder. She thought back to the countless long nights when she had lain awake in their bed, picturing him with another woman, and realised how strange it was that she had ever believed him to be absent. He was everywhere, filling the house with his tastes and his opinions and his routines – the half-drunk cup of tea from breakfast, the gloves he had changed his mind about wearing, the book on the bedside table that he would never finish. She had always struggled to find him in their marriage; now, she couldn't get away, and perhaps that was her punishment; perhaps that was what people meant when they talked about grief.

Vivienne stood on the stairs by the door to her husband's study, unable to go any further. Already, the room seemed to be gathering dust. She would pay for what she had done, she knew that now: Anthony's death was an end for her, not a beginning. She had told herself that she cared little about being caught; a trial, if it came to that, would only expose her husband's hypocrisy and leave her exonerated – but that was a fantasy, and the rope was as good as round her neck. The fear, when it came, was like nothing she had ever known, and there was no escaping it. She sat on the stairs in the deepening darkness, listening to the rain and waiting for someone to come.

9

Penrose watched as the man was led away to the police car, saddened by how quickly two lives could be destroyed. It was the first serious incident of the Coronation, a fight in the crowds at Piccadilly which had left one man critically ill and another arrested for his assault. The ambulance men had done their best, but no one believed that the victim would survive the night, and there was every chance that the charge would be manslaughter – or worse – by the morning. Penrose thought about the two men, strangers when they left their homes this morning, now inextricably linked by a moment of madness, and couldn't decide which of them he felt more sympathy for. Eighteen or nineteen was no age to lose your life, but a single punch in a drunken brawl didn't make you a criminal, either, and he wished for the thousandth time that the law he was asked to uphold had room for a few more shades of grey.

A temporary ambulance station stood opposite the London Pavilion, and the crew's cheerful, efficient treatment of various minor injuries had provided a different sort of entertainment during the long periods of waiting. The faces of the men and women on duty wore a graver expression now, though, and Penrose left them to it, fighting his way back through the crowd to one of the wireless vans that Scotland Yard had positioned at key points throughout the city. Piccadilly Circus had proved a popular vantage point, offering the lucky few a chance to watch the procession move up one street and down another, and most of the revellers were mercifully oblivious to the tragedy that had taken place a few yards away. The pomp and spectacle was over, and the streets belonged to the people again: Eros was under siege and seemed ill-equipped to cope with the offensive, and in the rare spaces that allowed it, pretty young girls grabbed perfectly complicit policemen and fox-trotted gaily in the rain; children leapfrogged down pavements, overexcited at the prospect of another late night; and outside cinemas, long queues were already forming to see the first newsreels of the ceremony. Young men with an eye for a good time were turning the merriment to their own advantage, trying their luck with any girl who took their fancy, and Penrose smiled as he passed, wondering how many marriages would owe their existence – for better or for worse – to the high spirits of coronation night.

The smile faded as he saw his sergeant coming to meet him with a face like thunder. 'The incidents are coming in thick and fast now, sir,' he shouted above the crowd. 'Which do you want first – the tragedy or the bloody nightmare?'

'I don't really want either, Bill, but I'll take them as they come.'

'All right. A little girl's had an accident at a house over in Carlton Gardens. Fell sixty feet down a lift shaft – God knows how.'

'Did she survive?'

Fallowfield shook his head. 'No, poor little devil. They rushed her to Westminster Hospital, but she died soon afterwards. Charmian Hamilton-Russell, her name is – daughter of Viscount Boyne.'

'How old was she?'

'Four.' Penrose closed his eyes. 'Her parents were at the Abbey when it happened, waiting on the Princess Royal. I don't know why that makes it worse, but it does.'

'Have you sent someone to see them?'

'Yes, sir – WPC Wyles. She'll be good with them, and she'll find out how it happened without making a fuss.'

'Well, that's not going to stay out of the papers, so what have you got that's even more newsworthy?'

'It's Anthony Beresford, sir.'

'What about him?'

'He's been shot. His chauffeur went to collect him from the observation point at Constitution Hill and found his body inside the cubicle.'

'Jesus, Bill – when was this?'

'He was found over an hour ago.' Fallowfield held up his hand, anticipating Penrose's fury at not having been told sooner. 'The chauffeur telephoned the BBC first, sir. It seems that he who pays the piper gets the condolence call.'

'And have they any idea what happened?'

'Absolutely none, or so they say. We're trying to get a car through for you as quickly as possible.'

Penrose looked doubtfully at the mass of people in every direction. 'It'll be quicker to walk, even in this,' he said. 'What about Spilsbury? Have you managed to get hold of him?'

'He's on his way, sir, but he's coming from Maida Vale so it could take a while.'

'All right. Let's go.' They set off down Piccadilly, trying to keep sight of each other in the good-natured chaos. 'I don't understand how someone could just go in and shoot him,' Penrose said during one of the rare moments that found them side by side. 'Was he on his own? Don't they have any form of security?'

'Whatever they have, it's obviously not very effective. There was another incident at Green Park – harmless enough this time, but someone got into the cubicle and started to broadcast to the world. It was a few minutes before an engineer back at base noticed the voice wasn't one of theirs and cut him off. And in these crowds...'

They were separated again, but Penrose didn't need to hear the rest of Fallowfield's sentence to know that he was right. It would be nigh on impossible to keep track of anyone's comings and goings on a day like today, and the continual movement of people meant that they could never be sure of tracking down all potential witnesses. Whoever did this had chosen the moment well. He thought back to his conversation with Josephine the week before, and caught up with Fallowfield again. 'Beresford had a very colourful private life, I believe – and it doesn't seem to have been *that* private. Do you know if his wife's been told yet?'

'Not to my knowledge. I can't say for certain, but I rather got the impression that everyone at the BBC is very keen to keep this quiet, at least until after the King's speech.'

'I bet they are. I imagine Reith's gone up in the air and stayed there.' He frowned, frustrated by how slow their progress was. It seemed incredible that London could accommodate more people, but trains were still running from the provinces and thousands were forcing their way to the Mall for the evening balcony appearances. A quarter of an inch of rain must have fallen in the last couple of hours, and it was impossible to avoid the puddles in the road; already, his shoes and the turn-ups of his trousers were soaked through, conspiring with the noise and the purpose of their mission to make the journey as unpleasant as it could possibly be. After what felt like an age, they arrived at Constitution Hill and Penrose looked at the broadcast cubicle in front of him – a small, temporary affair, built for purpose rather than aesthetic appeal and not unlike their own portable wireless points.

A police constable had been stationed at the bottom of the steps to the door, and two men stood slightly apart from him, talking quietly among themselves. Penrose didn't recognise the shorter of the two, but his uniform marked him out as the chauffeur who had discovered Beresford's body; the other – so impeccably dressed that even the rain seemed reluctant to touch him – was Bill Murray, the BBC's Director of Public Relations. His presence here was no surprise: the BBC was itself news these days, and the press was notoriously anti-Corporation and anti-Reith; Murray was in charge of a valuable but delicate reputation, and Penrose knew him to be a highly influential figure, likeable and known for his tact and discretion – although he would have challenged anyone to know what he really thought about anything. They had met several times, most recently in connection with a young woman who had died at a medical specialist's house while receiving treatment. The woman was a BBC secretary, her husband a senior BBC official, but somehow that had never reached the newspapers, even when her death became the focus of a trial for manslaughter. Thanks to Murray's skilful handling of events, the husband had been described simply as a 'wireless expert' and the BBC was kept out of it altogether; to this day, Penrose didn't know how he had managed to pull it off, but even Bill Murray would have his work cut out with this case. Once it was made public, Anthony Beresford's death and the speculation around it would fill the papers for weeks.

Murray greeted him with a wary respect. 'Good to see you again, Chief Inspector. I'm sure you understand that this needs to be handled correctly, and with as much discretion as possible. The reputation of the BBC is at stake here, and that must be our priority.'

Nothing like getting down to business, Penrose thought. Murray's lack of any obvious grief for his colleague interested him, and he wondered how popular Beresford had been with his peers. He smiled, and shook the hand that was offered. 'I'm sure you understand that *my* priority is to find out who did this, and why, as quickly as possible. I hope I can rely on your co-operation in that? Yours, and the Corporation's?' As if they were separable, he added under his breath. Murray nodded, but offered nothing further in response and Penrose turned to the other man, whose emotions were more readily on show – shock, certainly, and a sadness which was only just kept in check. 'I'm sorry, sir – I don't know your name,' Penrose said when it became clear that Murray wasn't going to introduce them.

'Whiting. Billy Whiting.'

'And you found Mr Beresford's body?'

'That's right.'

'When was that?'

'Quarter past five.'

'You can be that precise?'

'Yes.' He nodded towards the broadcast unit. 'The wireless is still on in there. The cricket news was just finishing and I remember thinking . . .' He tailed off, apparently embarrassed, and Penrose encouraged him to continue. 'It's stupid, really, the things that go through your mind at a time like that, but I remember thinking it was a shame that Mr Beresford would miss the end of the test match. He loved his cricket.'

'Could you describe exactly what you were doing here this afternoon and what you found when you went inside? Please be as specific as you can – even the smallest details are helpful.'

'I came to collect him as planned,' Whiting said. 'He was due to go back to BH for a debrief on the day, then he was going to stay on for the King's broadcast and the coronation news at ten. I was a bit early, but no harm in that on a day like this. I knocked on the door and called his name, but there was no answer and I thought he must have his headphones on while he listened to the wireless, so I just went in. That's when I saw him, and I knew right away that there was nothing I could do for him. You know, don't you, when you've seen dead bodies before?' Penrose nodded, understanding immediately what he meant. Billy Whiting was of an age to have fought, and, like many men at all levels of the BBC, had probably joined the Corporation after serving in the army or navy. 'I didn't touch anything except the telephone on the desk, and I used that to call Mr Murray.'

'Not the police?'

'I assured Billy that I'd take care of speaking to the police,' Murray said quickly. 'He was upset, naturally.'

'Naturally,' Penrose said sweetly, and turned back to the chauffeur, effectively excluding Murray from the conversation. 'What did you do then, Mr Whiting?'

'I stayed with Mr Beresford until the constable here arrived, then he asked me to wait outside with him. I've been here ever since.'

'Did you notice anyone else near the unit? Either someone you recognised from the BBC, or a stranger hanging round?'

'No, not especially. There were loads of people around, but no one close by and no one who seemed interested in the unit.'

'What about Mrs Beresford? Has she been here with her husband today?'

'She was here for the procession, I think, but he told her not to wait for him afterwards.'

'How do you know that?'

'I drove them to work this morning, and they were discussing it in the back of the car. Mrs Beresford was planning on going home after the procession, and I assume she did because I haven't seen her since I got here. Mr Beresford wanted to get on with his work. He always does, and she's used to it by now.'

Penrose was surprised by Whiting's familiarity with the Beresfords' routine. 'Do you know them well?' he asked.

'I wouldn't say I know them, but I've driven both of them for years now, and people tend to talk in the back of a car.'

'And how did they get on?'

Out of the corner of his eye, Penrose saw Murray glance sharply across at him, but Whiting answered the question without any hint of suspicion. 'Like most married couples, I suppose.'

He was about to ask the chauffeur what he meant by that when Murray interrupted him. 'Someone from the Corporation should go and see Mrs Beresford,' he said. 'She'll need our support at a difficult time. You've no objection to that, I assume?'

Resisting the temptation to respond in similar textbook style, Penrose said: 'Actually, I do, sir. I'll be going to see Mrs Beresford myself immediately after I've finished here, and I'd be grateful if no one else tried to contact her before then.'

'But they are both employees . . .'

'I understand that, Mr Murray, but they are also at the heart of a murder enquiry and I'm afraid that takes precedence over any other concern.' It was strange, he thought; he always insisted on keeping an open mind in every case, at least until he had viewed the body, but not for an instant here had he considered suicide as a possibility. Unprofessional as it was of him, something about Anthony Beresford made Penrose assume that he valued his own life far too greatly to take it, and Murray didn't seem inclined to argue.

Leaving the two men together, he went to find Fallowfield, who was attempting to clear a path for the arrival of the pathologist and police photographers. 'Bring Spilsbury in as soon as he gets here,' he said. 'And keep an eye on Murray. I don't trust him to play by the rules on this one.' The sergeant nodded and Penrose took his gloves out of his pocket, ready to examine the room where Beresford had died.

Inside, the broadcast cubicle was small and claustrophobic, although it was hard to say if death had made it so. Conscious that his shoes were wet and dirty from the walk, and reluctant to contaminate the scene until it had been properly examined and photographed, Penrose stood quietly at the door and took everything in from there. A bank of dials, panels and wires ran along one side of the room – a miniature, less sophisticated version of the control room that he had seen in Westminster Abbey this morning. There was an empty chair next to the controls, presumably where the engineer had sat, and a pair of headphones discarded on the seat. As Whiting had said, the wireless was still on, and the unfamiliar, disembodied voice struck Penrose as an unwelcome intrusion into the stillness. It was obviously Children's Hour, and he recognised the story as Hans Andersen's 'The Happy Family'; the irony seemed disrespectful, and he reached over to turn the volume down.

Anthony Beresford was still sitting in the chair that he had broadcast from, his body slumped awkwardly to one side, a briefcase open at his feet. From where he stood, Penrose could see a small, circular hole in his forehead, a wound as neat and as efficient as the most professional of executions. A thin trickle of blood ran down his face and onto the collar of his white shirt, deceptively innocent in its restraint and hardly more serious than if he had cut himself shaving. The true extent of the damage – where the bullet had passed through Beresford's skull and exited the other side – was hidden from Penrose's view, but it revealed itself in the crimson pool which soaked the floorboards, thick and viscous and dark, and in the bloodstains on the wall behind his chair. His headphones were still round his neck, and Penrose wondered if that meant he had been shot soon after his broadcast was finished, before he had had the chance to get up and walk about – but it was pointless to speculate on exactly what had happened until he had Spilsbury's careful analysis down in black and white. There was, he noticed, no weapon left at the scene, and again he would have to depend on experts to tell him what sort of gun had been used.

He looked long and hard at the murdered man's face, pale in the fading light, the eyes that had once been so watchful now glazed and dull. It was nearly ten years since they had met at Olivia Hanlon's house on the night of her death, and Penrose knew that his dislike of the broadcaster originated in a feeling of being deliberately obstructed back then, in a lingering conviction that Beresford was somehow managing her death in the way that Murray was now attempting to manage his. A glass of water stood on the desk by the telephone, next to a Thermos flask and a packet of sandwiches, wrapped in greaseproof paper and apparently untouched, and this small hint of domesticity moved Penrose. Could Vivienne Beresford have done this, he wondered? Her husband's infidelity was undisputed, and betrayal was a powerful motive, particularly when coupled with the sort of public humiliation that Josephine had described – but was it enough? Then there was Beresford's mistress to consider – an actress, Josephine had said; if those small domestic touches hinted at a reconciliation in the marriage, the motive passed immediately to another point in the triangle. Penrose sighed, depressed at the prospect of an investigation which would ask him to use a woman's deepest shame against her, exposing what should remain private, destroying her self-respect and exploiting her fears and her weaknesses, whether or not she was guilty. And the alternative was scarcely more appealing: if a political motive was involved in Beresford's murder – a strike against the BBC, perhaps, or against the country on a day when the scandal of a high-profile death would make such an impact – the task ahead of him was so enormous that he could hardly bear to think of it.

A glance around the rest of the room told him very little. The boarded floor was scuffed and dirty, and mud and grass had been brought in from outside, mostly by Billy Whiting, Penrose suspected, although they might be lucky with some of the other partial footprints. The side wall opposite the radio controls had been turned into an information board and was covered in maps of the processional route, lists of telephone numbers and a schedule of the day's broadcast, taken from the *Radio Times*. He looked at his watch: nearly a quarter to seven, and there was still no sign of Spilsbury. There was nothing else he could do here for the time being, so rather than waste time by waiting, he decided to catch up with the pathologist later and get on with what he needed to do.

Outside, Murray had barely moved from the spot and Penrose wondered if he was going to insist on shadowing him throughout the entire investigation. 'I'll need to talk to the engineer who assisted Mr Beresford with his commentary this afternoon,' he said. 'Perhaps you'd be kind enough to give his name and address to my sergeant?'

'Yes, of course.'

'Is there a recording of the broadcast?'

'Yes – why?'

'We need to build up a picture of the hours before Mr Beresford's death, and anything that can help us do that would be most appreciated.'

'It seems a little extreme. I don't quite see how Anthony's thoughts on the Queen's dress are relevant to his death.'

'Even so. Who knew he was going to be here? His immediate colleagues and his wife, obviously, but who else?'

'Christ, Penrose – anybody who read the *Radio Times* knew. We published the whole bloody schedule, map and all, so the world and his wife knew exactly where Anthony Beresford would be this afternoon.' Penrose felt a little stupid for the question, but it was worth the rebuke to see Murray lose his composure for once. 'We were very proud of our plans for the day,' the diplomat added more calmly, 'so naturally we outlined them at great length. As for Anthony's colleagues knowing his whereabouts, I'm not sure I like what you're implying.'

'I'm really not implying anything,' Penrose said with what he hoped was an irritating civility.

'Can I see him?' Murray asked.

'No, I'm afraid that's out of the question. The pathologist needs to do his work at the scene, and then the body will be removed for a post-mortem.'

'Not publicly, I hope. We've still got to get through the King's broadcast, and this isn't the sort of tarnish we want on the day.'

He gestured towards the broadcast unit and Penrose was astonished at his lack of concern for all that had been lost with Anthony Beresford's death. Whatever he thought of the dead man's morality, he had admired the broadcaster professionally and, as a human being, respected his right to live out his life to the last natural moment. 'Your colleague's body will be removed quietly and discreetly,' he said, making no effort now to hide his anger, 'but we'll do it for the sake of *his* dignity, not yours.'

The raised voices threatened to draw the attention of passers-by. Murray took Penrose's arm and led him further into the shadows. 'You know what the score is, Penrose,' he said. 'I don't need to tell you how potentially explosive this is. We're going to be faced with extremely difficult questions when the news gets out, and the Corporation will be subjected to some very unwelcome publicity. I need to be in a position to manage that.'

Penrose thought of the other lives that had been lost that night, of the families whose world had been destroyed in a second because of carelessness or rashness or simple bad luck. He thought of the boy who had died in a fight and the man who might hang for it, and of the four-year-old girl who was a victim of her own child-like curiosity; messy deaths, all of them – unexpected, random and cruelly juxtaposed against a backdrop of joy and celebration. And the more he remembered of the day's sadness the more sickened he was by the idea that death and loss and grief could be 'managed', even by the BBC.

'You'll be told the results of the post-mortem in due course,' he said, 'and I give you my word that you'll be kept up to date with all non-confidential aspects of the investigation. In the meantime, if you have any ideas at all about what happened today, I suggest you share them with me now.' He stared directly at Murray, daring him to confide the dirty little scandal that he seemed so afraid of. 'Is there anything you know of in Anthony Beresford's life that might have brought us here? Any professional jealousies? Any private indiscretions?' Murray was silent, and Penrose watched him trying to gauge how much the police already knew. 'No? Then if you'll excuse me, I have to go and break the news to Mrs Beresford.'

10

The chime of the doorbell rang through the house even sooner than she had expected. Vivienne looked at her watch, surprised to find that it was already after eight o'clock. She hadn't moved for the best part of two hours and the house had grown melancholy around her, nurturing its shadows to match her mood. Reluctantly, she forced herself to stand and look down into the street from the window in Anthony's study. There it was, the police car she had been waiting for, its engine still running, the light from its head-lamps falling softly on the puddles in the road. She looked round, conscious that all the rooms were in darkness, and wondered what would happen if she simply didn't answer? Would he assume that she was out and leave? Could she suspend the nightmare by ignoring it, at least for a few precious hours?

The bell sounded again, more persistent this time, and Vivienne realised that it was futile to delay the inevitable. She went down-stairs, marking her progress through the house by switching lights on in the rooms she passed, fooling herself that she had nothing to hide. By the time she opened the front door, he was already walking away, but he turned back as soon as he heard her. 'Mrs Beresford?' She nodded, surprised because he was not at all what she had expected – an expensively tailored suit rather than a uni-form, a sensitive face and intelligent eyes that looked at her without judgement. 'I'm Detective Chief Inspector Penrose from Scotland Yard. I'm afraid I have some distressing news about your husband. May I come in?'

His voice was gentle, sympathetic, and she stood aside to let him pass, confused by how quickly reality had departed from the scenario she had imagined – in her mind, the moment of her arrest had been brusque and detached, with no room for civility or discussion. They stood awkwardly in the hall, and Vivienne realised how peculiar she must look, her eyes swollen from crying, her clothes still damp from the rain. 'Can I get you a drink?' she asked, as if this were some sort of twisted romantic encounter. Her voice sounded strained and nervous, like a bad actress making the best of a terrible play.

'No, thank you. Is there somewhere we can sit down?'

She led him through to the sitting room and saw him glance round appraisingly, taking in everything from the expensive art to the conventional furniture. Her lack of curiosity must have roused his suspicions already; shock affected people in different ways, but an innocent woman would surely by now have asked him what he meant. She should have mentioned Anthony as soon as she opened the door, but it was too late now and she cursed herself for not thinking more carefully about what would happen afterwards. Why hadn't she made plans or considered possible options? The answer was simple: she had never truly believed that she would go through with it until it was too late to change her mind. The detective – she hadn't been listening when he told her his name – waited for her to sit down, then took the seat opposite. 'I'm sorry to tell you that your husband was killed this afternoon,' he said, and although the words themselves were brutally blunt, his regret seemed genuine. She wondered how many times he had delivered news like this, and if any reaction would surprise him. 'His body was found just after five o'clock in the broadcast unit on Constitution Hill, and we have reason to believe that he was shot shortly after finishing his commentary. I realise that this will be a very difficult time for you, but I must ask you to help with the police enquiries into Mr Beresford's death.'

It was impossible to tell from the careful phrasing how much he already knew, but Vivienne found that she was too tired and too frightened to string the conversation along. 'You don't need to look any further for your killer, Inspector,' she said. 'I can tell you exactly what happened to Anthony, and why. Where would you like me to start?'

He was taken aback – less, she suspected, by the admission than by the readiness with which it was offered. 'Mrs Beresford, I must ask you to think very carefully about what you've just said. Are you confessing to your husband's murder?'

She got up and left the room, feeling his eyes in her back, knowing that he was trying to gauge whether or not to follow. Her handbag lay discarded on the hall floor and she felt inside to locate the gun, but the cold, heavy weight of the metal in her hand brought back all the revulsion of that moment and she had to fight not to gag again. Unable to take the weapon out, she took the bag through to the sitting room as it was and handed the whole thing over; the policeman looked down at the revolver, but didn't remove it. 'It was my sister's,' Vivienne said redundantly, just to fill the silence. 'She was in a line of work where guns come in handy.' He nodded, and she realised that he knew exactly who her sister was. 'Anthony removed it from her house when she died, just to avoid any trouble. It's ironic, I suppose, but how could he have known what he was doing?' She tried to laugh, but the noise that came out was more of a strangled sob. Horrified, she put her hands over her mouth, desperate to stem the tide of emotion that threatened to overwhelm her, but still the noise carried on. What on earth was she doing? She, who never showed her feelings in public, falling to pieces in front of a stranger? He got up, and she thought he was going to leave her to pull herself together as Anthony had always done on the rare occasions that she cried in front of him, unable to cope with any ripples on the even surface of their marriage. But she had underestimated this quiet, unusual policeman. He put a glass of whisky in her hand and sat down next to her, unembarrassed by the outburst and waiting patiently for it to pass.

'Why did you do it, Mrs Beresford?' he asked eventually.

She wished that he would stop using her married name. She had no right to it now, and anyway, that person no longer existed. But he seemed sincere in his desire to understand, and she did her best to explain. 'He was going to leave me,' she said, knowing how pathetic that sounded.

'He told you that?'

She shook her head, and held the whisky in her mouth for a moment, allowing its smoke to burn and focus her. 'No, I found out. There are some travel tickets upstairs in his desk and a letter from Mr Reith acknowledging his resignation.'

'He'd resigned from the BBC?'

'Yes. He had no choice if he was going to end his marriage. We don't do divorce at the BBC – although it's preferable to murder, I suppose.'

'When did you discover all this?'

'The day before yesterday. I found the tickets by accident while I was tidying his study.' She had just shot a man, and her need to justify the smaller crime of rummaging through his desk made no sense, but she had already accepted that her world now functioned without logic.

'And that's when you made your decision?'

'Yes.' The cause and effect which that implied wasn't strictly accurate but it seemed easier than the truth. How could she possibly explain the years of never quite being good enough, the sense of waste as she watched her life tick by in the shadow of his, the shame of that moment in the green room when even her dignity was taken from her? He might be understanding, but he would never know what that felt like, and she hadn't the words to tell him.

'Can I ask you to tell me exactly what happened today? And take your time. Please include everything, even if it seems unimportant.'

Vivienne went through most of the day's events, sticking to

the facts but avoiding how she felt about them, and he listened carefully without interrupting. 'What will happen to me?' she asked, when he seemed satisfied with the details.

'When you're ready, I'll take you to Scotland Yard, where you will be asked to make a formal statement. If you repeat there under caution what you've just told me, you will be charged with your husband's murder and held in police custody until your first appearance at a magistrate's court. That will be in the next day or two. After that, you'll be remanded in custody, awaiting your trial.' He didn't waste a single word, she noticed; his speech was succinct but everything was made to count, and she admired that. Suddenly, she was all too aware of how many words she and Anthony had squandered in their lives – all the lies and the tricks and the meaningless conversations, all the times he had asked her how she was and never really cared, all the breath she had wasted in telling him. 'You are, of course, entitled to legal representation throughout. Do you have a solicitor?'

'Yes, but he's Anthony's solicitor. They've been friends since Oxford, so I hardly think he'll be rushing to my defence, do you?'

'Then someone independent. We can provide a lawyer for you, if you prefer.'

'Is there really any point, Inspector?'

'There's always a point in having your side of the story represented truthfully and effectively.'

For a moment, she almost believed him. 'And after the trial?'

It was the first time that he had let her down. His eyes left hers for the briefest of moments, but it was enough to tell her what he thought of her chances against a jury; after all, everyone adored Anthony Beresford. 'First things first,' he said. 'It's best not to look too far ahead. The tickets and the letter – do you still have them?'

'They're upstairs where I found them.'

'Will you show me?'

She took him up to the study and opened the drawer, but the paperwork was gone. 'That's funny,' she said, closing it again and opening the next drawer down in case she had been mistaken. 'I don't understand. They were all here together.'

'Perhaps Mr Beresford took them with him?'

'Why would he do that? He kept all his paperwork here.'

'Well, don't worry about it now. We'll check his briefcase and his office to see if they're there.' Was it her imagination, or was there suddenly an edge to his voice? 'If you're ready to leave?'

Vivienne looked down at her dishevelled clothes and mud-splattered stockings. 'Can I change first?'

'I'm afraid not, but you're very welcome to take a change of clothes with you, and to pack a few things that you think you might need. And are you sure you won't reconsider hiring a solicitor? I'm very happy to wait while you telephone from here.'

'I'm sure.'

'Then what about someone else? Is there a friend or a family member you'd like to call, just to let them know where you are?'

He was doing all he could to be kind, but he could have no idea of how alone, how isolated, his words made her feel. She realised as he spoke that there was no one in the world she wanted with her, and no one she could trust to be entirely on her side. For a second, she toyed with the idea of calling Danny, but she couldn't stand to see the look of disappointment in her eyes; it was too big a risk to her already crumbling self-respect. She turned to go upstairs and pack, but something occurred to her at the door. 'Does she know?' she asked.

'Who?'

'Millicent Gray. My husband's mistress.'

'No, Mrs Beresford. Nobody else has been told yet.'

She nodded, absurdly comforted by this sliver of protocol, a small nod of recognition which put her first. When she was ready, he cautioned her and led her out to the waiting car, and she resisted the temptation to glance up at the neighbouring windows to see if anyone was watching; the shame of last week was nothing compared to what she felt now, and what was still to come. The silence in the car depressed her. She would have been grateful for conversation, but it was not his job to distract her from herself and she looked out of the rain-streaked window, wondering if she would ever see the familiar landmarks of home again.

It took the car some time to force its way along Victoria Embankment, through the crowds that had flocked to see the lights of the Thames at dusk. The calm orderliness of Scotland Yard was almost a relief by comparison. Vivienne was led through a maze of corridors and asked to wait on a hard wooden bench by some sort of reception desk while the detective – Penrose, she was reminded by one of his colleagues – went to talk to his superiors. She was sorry to see him go and the loneliness hit her again, more intense now because her surroundings were suddenly so alien. A blur of faces passed her, glancing curiously in her direction before fading away into distant, unseen offices, and she imagined that the low murmur of conversation was all about her, spreading through the building, leaving her exposed and vulnerable. The atmosphere was uncompromisingly male and she supposed she should be used to that after Broadcasting House, but this was different somehow. No matter how far the BBC had progressed, and how respected it was around the world, she would always see an element of 'boys and toys' in its ambitions, probably because she had been there since the early days. But there was an earnestness about Scotland Yard, a sense of real power in the men who moved through its corridors – an institutionalised power over freedom and confinement, life and death, and it terrified her.

When a woman came to fetch her she could have cried with relief, but there was no sense of solidarity; if anything her demeanour was even stonier than her colleagues', and Vivienne didn't blame her; her own struggles to be taken seriously in the profession she had chosen must surely pale into insignificance compared to those of a female police constable. She allowed herself to be led quietly away down a corridor which seemed to stretch the length of the building, past miles and miles of dove-grey doors and polished wood, until her guide turned apparently at random into a small, airless room with no windows. The only furniture was a desk with two chairs on either side, and Vivienne sat where she was told to, painfully conscious of the chaperone at her shoulder, wishing she could just be left alone. After a long, uncomfortable silence, Penrose joined them, accompanied by another man in uniform, and their presence in the room made its confined space almost unbearably claustrophobic. She smiled, but his response lacked its former warmth and she realised her mistake in regarding him as an ally. He took her meticulously back through everything she had told him, forcing her to relive the horror of every moment, and she was astonished by how much he had remembered without the aid of notes. When they were done, the uniformed man read the statement back to her and she listened, bewildered; the words were hers, of course they were, but she felt as detached from them as if she were listening to a story from a newspaper, sitting in judgement on the irrational behaviour of a woman who had nothing whatsoever to do with her.

She signed where she was asked to, wondering why Penrose felt the need to thank her for something which she had had no choice but to give. Then he excused himself, and left her in the charge of her mute, inscrutable shadow, back along the corridors, downstairs this time to an area which was much less designed for public view, the province of the unlucky few. The tiled walls smelt of disinfectant and something far less tangible, something like despair, and Vivienne felt as though she were being taken quite literally to the depths of hell. What little courage she had left deserted her completely at the door to the cell. She stopped, horrified, and stared at the toilet in the corner with the scrubbed wooden seat, the iron bedstead and the coarse grey blanket. For a moment she was physically incapable of stepping inside, because to do so would have been to accept her fate, but the hand on her arm – surprisingly gentle, now it was just the two of them – encouraged her to move forward. 'I'll leave you to change,' the policewoman said, and Vivienne saw that her case stood on the floor waiting for her, a parody of a good hotel. 'Put the clothes you're wearing to one side and I'll collect them in a bit.'

Why on earth did they have to take her clothes, Vivienne wondered. Hadn't she admitted everything? But she agreed willingly, if only to get a few precious minutes to herself. Already, she knew the hell of prison for her would not be the confinement but the lack of privacy. Unlike her sister, who had lived and died as the soul of the party, Vivienne had always kept people at arm's length. When she was a child, she put it down to shyness; as an adult, to shame. The intimacy that came with friendship would only have forced her to admit the essential, humiliating failure of her life – her husband's betrayal – and so she had cultivated a reputation for aloofness that ultimately fooled even her. But here, in this garishly lit room with the square-cut hole in the door, there was nowhere to hide. It came as a surprise to her to realise that she had never truly known helplessness until now. Even with Anthony, in the darkest days of their marriage, there was always something she could do – leave him, change him, kill him – but now she had no choices left to her, no hopes for the future. She sank down on the bed in despair, caring little now who came to stare at her as she opened her mouth and screamed.

Part Four

Vile Bodies

I

After a long night and a busy day, Josephine was sufficiently tired to let sleep get the better of her. It was already after nine when she woke and she dressed hurriedly, conscious that it would take a braver woman than she was to arrive for breakfast outside the Cowdray Club's strictly observed mealtimes. Downstairs, the smell of toast and freshly brewed coffee rewarded her efforts and she noticed that she wasn't alone in enjoying a leisurely start to the day; the dining room was still reasonably full, and the lounge and bar areas buzzed with conversation as people traded their own coronation stories or discussed the coverage in the morning papers. Josephine paused in the entrance hall to see if any messages had been left for her at reception, and tried not to look too disappointed by the answer. In the absence of a note, she picked up a copy of *The Times* to read over breakfast and headed for the nearest free table, but a headline at the bottom of the front page stopped her in her tracks. She read it again in disbelief, attempting to reconcile the discreet size of the type with the sensational news it conveyed, and realised suddenly that the animated conversations taking place around her were not all about the Coronation.

Quickly, she scanned the rest of the column and walked back to reception with all thoughts of breakfast gone. 'I'd like to use the telephone,' she said, 'in private, if that's possible?' The girl behind the desk nodded and led her through to the club office, panelled in oak and contrasting sharply with the ivory-white enamel that reflected light into the rest of the building. The room smelt of polish and old books, and Josephine sat down at a vast desk, opposite a statue of Florence Nightingale placed in a wooden niche like a saint in a church, a permanent reminder of the club's nursing origins. She picked up the telephone, longing to speak to Archie but reluctant to make him choose between a lie to her and professional indiscretion; in any case, if the story were true, he would be anywhere but in his office, so she chose the next best thing and asked for Broadcasting House, confident that she could rely on Julian Terry to be as indiscreet as was humanly possible. She waited a long time for a connection, imagining the pressure that the switchboard was under from press and public alike, and had just begun to wonder if the BBC had shut down communications altogether when a voice answered, unusually terse and wary, and she was put grudgingly through to the Director of Drama.

'Josephine, you beat me to it. I was going to call you but I haven't had a minute. Quite frankly, it's bloody chaos here this morning.'

'Is it true, then?'

'I'm afraid it must be. None of us has been told anything officially yet, but the top brass are running round like headless chickens and there's an emergency meeting of the Board of Governors going on as I speak. Beresford's office has been sealed off, I know that much, and there are police outside to keep the reporters at bay. The whole staff's been summoned to the Concert Hall at midday to be briefed on, I quote, "studio discipline and relations with the press". And there's no work being done, of course. Everyone's in shock.'

'Yes, I can imagine. It's much the same out here, and we only *thought* we knew him. People will be devastated.'

'They are. I can see them all now, gathering in the street outside the Round Church. The response inside the walls is rather more ambivalent, I must say. Most of us are wondering if we should pretend we actually *liked* the man, or if a professional respect will do.'

'And Vivienne? The paper says a woman from the Kensington area has been taken into custody.'

Julian paused and Josephine heard the click of a cigarette lighter and a sharp intake of breath; the air in Broadcasting House would be thick with smoke this morning. 'It must be her, don't you think? Who else could it be? No one's confirmed that here but I've been phoning her all morning and there's no answer. I wondered if you'd heard anything from your contacts on the inside?'

His tone gave the words a tantalising sense of mystery, and under different circumstances Josephine would have smiled. 'No, I haven't spoken to Archie. Is that why you were going to phone? To pump me for information?'

'Not exactly, although it would have been rude not to ask. No, it was more about the play.'

'Why? Is it being cancelled?'

'Good God, no. The golden voice might be lying in the mortuary, but the service of the British Broadcasting Corporation can't be disrupted. I wanted to talk to you about Lydia.'

'Lydia?'

'Yes. It's all a bit awkward, but I can't imagine Millicent Gray putting in a good performance this evening, can you? I wondered how you'd feel if I asked Lydia to step up?'

Josephine wasn't proud of the uncharitable thoughts which ran through her head at the prospect of Lydia's triumph, but it was a sensible suggestion. 'Have you spoken to Millicent Gray?' she asked, remembering the expression on the actress's face when they had met by chance in the cloakroom. Her relationship with Anthony Beresford had obviously had its problems, but they wouldn't shield her from the guilt, grief and anger caused by his death.

'No, she's not answering her phone either, but I'm not sure it would be deemed appropriate to have Beresford's mistress on air, even if she thinks she's up to it. Anyway, I thought you'd be pleased to have Lydia on board. She knows that part better than anyone.'

So much for the gulf between stage and microphone, Josephine thought. She could tell by the impatience in Julian's voice that he hadn't expected to have to argue the point, and that in itself made her more inclined to be stubborn, but she also felt a great sadness for the two women caught up in Anthony Beresford's life – far greater than any sadness she felt at his death, no matter how wrong that might be. She knew how she would feel if something happened to Marta and she was forced to keep her own grief hidden, and she refused to stand by while Millicent Gray was sidelined professionally as well as personally. 'Shouldn't you at least talk to your current leading lady before you move on to the next one? You told me how dedicated she is, regardless of her private life. Perhaps it might help her to keep working.'

'Do you have to be so bloody decent all the time?' The objection was half-hearted, but Josephine's victory was tinged with guilt: decency wasn't the only motive driving her argument. 'You're right, of course,' Terry admitted. 'I honestly can't see Millicent wanting to come in here and face everyone, but we should speak to her first. You'll have to do it, though.'

'Me?' Josephine said, horrified. 'Why on earth would I get involved? I hardly know her and you're the director.'

'Yes, but I can't leave the building. There's no way I can go tramping the streets looking for bereaved actresses when Reith's about to deliver a three-line whip. Anyway, you're just round the corner from her and it'll be better coming from another woman.'

Julian was being deliberately provocative now, but he was also probably right: for reasons unknown to him, Millicent Gray would no doubt find it easier to talk to Josephine. 'All right,' she said reluctantly, wondering if the actress even knew about Beresford's death yet. 'What's the address?'

'Hang on, I've got her contract here somewhere.' He read out the details and she wrote them down in the margin of the newspaper. 'It's the basement flat, I believe. And thank you, Josephine – I really appreciate this. Will you let me know what Millicent would like to do, and I'll speak to Lydia if necessary?'

'Yes, of course. And if you hear anything about Vivienne...'

'You'll be the first to know, I promise. I still can't believe it, you know. We've been friends for years, Viv and I, but I never saw this coming.'

'Did she talk to you about her marriage?'

'Not really. He was a shit to her, we all knew that, but she always seemed to rise above that somehow. And she was a different person when she was away from him – funny, clever, and immensely attractive.' There was a real warmth in his voice as he spoke about his colleague, and Josephine wondered again if there had ever been anything more than friendship between them. 'I can't bear to think of what she'll go through, Josephine. Anthony Beresford was a saint in most people's eyes, and the press will tear her to pieces. Personally, I think he deserved all he got, but I don't suppose a jury will see it that way.'

'No,' said Josephine sadly. 'I don't suppose they will.'

2

The Director General's office was on the third floor of Broadcasting House. Penrose followed a page boy and his own Assistant Commissioner down a long, plushly carpeted corridor, noticing that most of the BBC's senior staff seemed to have rooms in the curved southern prow of the building. Not surprisingly, John Reith's office was the grandest of all, symbolically placed at the head of the ship, with sweeping views down Regent Street to Oxford Circus, but his status was not marked by location alone. The space was beautiful, tastefully decorated with expensive carpets and drapes that added just the right amount of colour to the restrained oak panelling, and far more like a domestic study than an office. Here and there, Penrose noticed some unexpectedly feminine touches – a suite of furniture upholstered in pink satin, a rug resembling a compass rose, even a flower-decked balcony – and he looked with interest at the only personal photograph on display, a woman pictured with two children, presumably the Director General's family. The more obvious focal point was an open fire at the back of the room, crowned with a delicate landscape painting which was remarkable only for its blandness.

Bill Murray was already there, and Reith stood to greet them as his Director of Public Relations made the introductions. He was a dominant figure, tall, with strong, intelligent eyes and an intense gaze, and even in a room full of people Penrose would have known instinctively that he was in charge. The desk was covered in the morning's newspapers and Murray gestured towards them, cutting straight to the point without any social niceties. 'We've just come from the Governors' meeting and no one is very happy about this.

It's rather more coverage than we'd hoped for at this stage. Couldn't you have been more careful?'

The Assistant Commissioner looked at Penrose, somehow managing to distance himself from anything to do with the Metropolitan Police, and Penrose knew that he was on his own; Rygate hadn't risen this far up the force without knowing how to make an awkward situation reflect badly on someone else. 'It would have been impossible to keep this out of the papers altogether, sir,' he said, addressing Reith directly. 'Someone was bound to notice all the activity around the broadcast unit in a crowd that size, and, as Mr Murray has pointed out to me, everybody knew who was there. Add to that the BBC's refusal to comment and the cancellation of a programme in which Anthony Beresford was scheduled to appear, and it's very easy to put two and two together. As it is, I think we're fortunate to have kept the information relatively insubstantial.'

'Insubstantial? What's insubstantial about the murder of our most popular broadcaster? And what about the woman taken into custody? Surely you're not going to put that little snippet down to the keen eyes of the great British public?' Murray was right, of course; there was no explanation for that other than a loose tongue on the inside, and Penrose didn't intend to inflame the situation even further by trying to invent one. 'Well,' Murray continued, 'whatever's happened up to now it's time that we took charge of this story and presented it in the way . . .'

Reith held up his hand and spoke for the first time. 'Perhaps you could tell us exactly where you are with your investigation, Chief Inspector.' His voice carried a calm authority, and Penrose could just detect the traces of a Scottish accent, soft and attractive, and not unlike Josephine's. 'Then we can decide between us how best to proceed.' Penrose nodded and gave a succinct account of Vivienne Beresford's arrest and statement. 'And there's no doubt in your mind that Mrs Beresford is telling the truth?' Reith asked.

'No, none whatsoever. The post-mortem is scheduled for this

afternoon, but I'm confident that its findings will be consistent with her story.'

'Well, that's something, at least,' Murray said. 'It makes things much easier for us if there's a straightforward narrative to work with.' Penrose opened his mouth to comment, but Murray was too self-absorbed to notice and Rygate threw him a warning glance. 'Mr Reith and I would like it to be made very clear in any statement you issue that this is a domestic matter between husband and wife, and nothing whatsoever to do with the BBC.'

Rygate looked doubtful. 'We can certainly make every effort to do that,' he said cautiously, 'but we have no control over how this is perceived by the press. It's unfortunate but inevitable that the Corporation will be involved to some extent.'

'To some extent, yes, but Vivienne Beresford was actually employed by the *Radio Times*, not by the BBC.'

'Is there a difference?' Penrose asked.

'Technically, yes. Moreover, her position as editor was temporary, and that must be emphasised.'

'But she's worked here for years,' Penrose said.

'Only in a minor role.' Murray handed Rygate a piece of paper. 'Here's a copy of the statement we'll be issuing after we've spoken to the staff at midday. As you can see, we've chosen to concentrate on everything that Anthony Beresford achieved in his career. His record is unblemished and it speaks for itself – twelve years of unsurpassed loyalty and dedication.' It was a shame that Beresford hadn't applied himself to his marriage with equal diligence, Penrose thought; if he had, he might have deferred his obituary for a few more years. 'I hope we can rely on you to support the message we're sending out?'

Rygate nodded. 'Yes, of course, and I'd like to give you both my personal assurance that the case against Mrs Beresford will proceed as swiftly and as quietly as possible.'

'Excellent.' Murray paused, as if there were something else that he wanted to say. 'Obviously we have to be careful about how we do this, but it might be worth our while to remind everybody of Vivienne Beresford's maiden name and what happened to her sister. I have some contacts in the press who would be willing to help with that.'

'But this has got nothing to do with her sister,' Penrose objected. 'She did what she did because she was unhappy in her marriage. How can Olivia Hanlon's death possibly have any relevance to that?'

'You don't think a violent past is relevant? You know as well as I do what went on at the Golden Hat, Penrose – drugs, sex, gang wars. Olivia Hanlon had trouble in her genes and why should her sister be any different? She was nothing until she married Anthony, and blood will always out.' The hypocrisy of the conversation infuriated Penrose; Murray and Reith were not involved personally, but they could surely not be ignorant of the fact that many people from the BBC had been very happy to frequent the Golden Hat and other clubs like it. 'Anyway,' Murray continued, 'am I not right in thinking that she shot Anthony with her sister's gun?'

The information in Vivienne Beresford's statement was confidential, and there was only one way that anyone at the BBC could have gained access to it. Penrose glared at his boss, and tried to keep his voice even and measured. 'Let's not fool ourselves about this. Regardless of any efforts we make to contain what has happened, the press will go to town on Vivienne Beresford. If we taint her any further with a scandal that was not of her making, or link her with illegal clubs when she had nothing to do with that lifestyle, it will be impossible for her to get a fair trial. There will be a witch-hunt.' He might have imagined the look of satisfaction that passed across Murray's face, but somehow he doubted it. 'What happened to the path of wisdom and uprightness?' he asked, more sarcastically than he had intended. 'Or is that inscription downstairs out of date now?'

He hadn't meant it as a rhetorical question, but Rygate stepped in before anyone could offer an answer. 'Once again, we will do everything in our power to make it clear that the BBC is not at fault here,' he said. 'Won't we, Penrose?'

Reith got up and walked to the window, absent-mindedly straightening the rug on his way. 'I'm not sure that's entirely true,' he said thoughtfully. 'We are culpable to some extent. We should never have given Mrs Beresford such a demanding and responsible role. It was clearly far too much for her to cope with, on top of her duties at home.'

Penrose looked at the Director General in astonishment, but he was sincere in what he had said. 'Her husband's infidelity drove her to this, sir, not a tight deadline.'

Murray looked at him sharply. 'Surely you're not trying to tell us that Anthony Beresford deserved this, Chief Inspector?'

Penrose felt his superior's eyes drilling into him and knew he had gone too far. 'Of course not,' he said, as contritely as he could manage, and turned back to Reith. 'Anthony Beresford had resigned, hadn't he?' he asked, and Reith nodded. 'Because he was getting a divorce?'

'That's right.'

'You must have been sorry at the prospect of his leaving. Weren't you tempted to make an exception? After all, divorce isn't so unusual these days. People move with the times.'

'We're not here to question the Director General's employment policy, Penrose.'

'It's a reasonable question, Commissioner, and I'm happy to answer it. The BBC isn't obliged to propagate ideas just because they're modern, Chief Inspector. Lots of our listeners don't find it quite so easy to "move with the times", as you put it.'

His tone was patient, but strained, and Penrose sensed in him a weariness that was to do with more than the current situation, almost as if his creation were becoming too much for him. John

Reith was the driving force behind all that the BBC had achieved, steering the Corporation to its position as a public institution and ensuring that the whole nation now turned to its wireless in times of celebration and crisis. The last few years alone had seen some remarkable milestones – the first Empire broadcasts, the Jubilee, the death of the King, which Reith had announced personally – and the coronation broadcasts should have set the seal on a glittering career. Who could blame him if Beresford's death made him question if it was all worthwhile? 'We found some travel tickets and a passport in Mr Beresford's briefcase. Did you know what he was intending to do after he left?'

'No, he didn't discuss his plans with me and I didn't ask,' Reith said. 'But I *was* very sorry to lose a man who had brought so much to the Corporation – and to answer the question you're not asking, I'm also sorry to lose his wife. I respected her achievements and liked her personally, but I'm sure you must understand that my first duty is to protect an organisation which is more important than any one individual.'

Rygate stood up, keen to close the meeting on a note of truce, which was more than he had hoped for. 'We'll keep you fully informed of any developments,' he promised. 'And don't hesitate to contact Penrose if there's anything else we can do.'

'I'd like to see Mr Beresford's office before I leave,' Penrose said, as keen to shake off his boss as he was to learn more about the dead man. 'Don't let me hold you up, though, sir. I'll see you back at the Yard.'

They parted company at the lift, and Penrose followed Murray up another flight of stairs to a smaller office on the Langham Street side of the building. The first thing that struck him was how sparse the room was, almost as if it had been cleared already; the only embellishment he could see was a single vase of flowers, something he had come to recognise as a hallmark of Broadcasting House, and he doubted it was a feature that Beresford had chosen, or even noticed. It was a stark contrast to the tasteful domesticity of the

Director General's office, and, although everyone worked in different ways, the lack of any individual touches surprised Penrose; it wasn't what he expected from someone whose success had depended in part on his personality. 'He didn't believe in making himself at home, did he? Is the office always this bare?'

'Or have we been round with a fine-tooth comb first, you mean?' Murray grinned. 'No, it's been like this since the day we moved in. Anthony hated clutter. I don't ever remember walking in here and finding a thing out of place.' He paused to light a cigarette, more relaxed and open now that he was away from Reith. 'I often thought it had something to do with the way he lived his life, you know. Everything had to be in its box, tidied neatly away. Nothing left open to confusion.'

It was a perceptive comment, and Penrose wondered how well Murray – or anyone else, for that matter – had actually known his colleague. 'Was his affair common knowledge here?' he asked.

'Affairs. Miss Gray was the latest in a healthy line of women, and none of them lasted long. But yes, lots of people knew that he had other interests, and he never went to any great effort to hide it.'

'That must have been hard for his wife.'

'I have no idea how she felt about it, or about Anthony. She's always kept herself to herself here, never really mixed with anyone, and perhaps that's how she coped. But you know what these things are like – it's known, but never spoken about, at least not in front of the people concerned.'

'Until last week.'

'Oh?' Penrose told him about the incident in the green room, grateful to Josephine for supplying him with a piece of information that had somehow escaped Murray's omniscient attention. 'I hadn't heard about that,' he admitted, 'but it was inevitable, I suppose.'

'Could you give me a list of the women he was involved with?'

'I could tell you who some of them were, but you have your killer so I'm not entirely sure why I should.'

Penrose wasn't sure either. Conscious of behaving more like a defence lawyer than a policeman, he accepted defeat graciously and walked over to the desk which dominated the room, a strikingly modern piece of furniture with concealed lighting and a secret swivelling shelf that cleverly hid the telephone. He took some gloves out of his pocket and opened the drawers one by one, finding nothing but a history of Beresford's recent broadcasts in note form, all meticulously dated and filed. Just as he was about to give up hope of anything more interesting, he saw a set of car keys tucked towards the back of the top left-hand drawer; he pulled them out and something else came, too – a small lead soldier, caught up in the key ring. The paint was faded and chipped, but the figure was still recognisable as a Coldstream Guard, identical to one that Penrose had owned himself as a boy. Surprised, he looked up at Murray. 'From what you tell me, Mr Beresford wasn't the sentimental type. Why would he keep an old toy in his drawer?'

Murray shrugged. 'I really don't know, but he didn't drive a car, either, so I don't think any of that can be his.'

The idea of someone else's belongings finding their way into a private office made even less sense to Penrose. 'Then I'll hang onto these, if you don't mind. I'd like to know if Mrs Beresford recognises them.' He took a bag from his pocket and put the keys and toy inside, then stood to leave. 'I've finished here for now, but, as the Assistant Commissioner said, you'll be kept fully up to date with developments.'

His sarcasm wasn't lost on Murray, who gave him a wry smile. 'We're both just doing our jobs, aren't we? None of this is personal.'

'Perhaps not for us,' Penrose said, 'but I'm not sure Vivienne Beresford would agree with you.'

3

Many of London's shops and offices were still closed for the Coronation holiday, and it seemed to Josephine that everyone with leisure time on their hands had chosen to spend it in the streets around Cavendish Square. Wide pavements allowed for two lanes of pedestrians, one close to the shop windows, drifting aimlessly past the goods and mannequins, the other nearer the curb for people who actually had somewhere to go. Still, the crowds were larger than the space allowed and Josephine threaded her way impatiently in and out, keen to get on with the task she had unwittingly set herself.

The address that Julian had given her was in a small quadrangle of four-storey houses tucked behind the smart shopping and elegant facades of Wigmore Street. In other parts of London, buildings of identical size and date would probably be regarded as slums, but these were lovely, a gentle combination of red-and-cream brick with brightly painted front doors and window boxes that hid many of the panes with flowers. Even a basement flat here was an enviable prospect, small but close to Millicent Gray's work at the BBC and just a stone's throw from the West End, and Josephine wondered if Anthony Beresford's salary had contributed to the rent. If so, convenient digs would be one of the more minor casualties of his death.

She opened the iron gate in the railings and walked down the steps, noticing how quickly the noise from the street disappeared as soon as she got below ground level. Shrubs in painted tubs stood at intervals along the path to the door, and there was a tiny table and chairs placed to catch the afternoon sun, but the actress had resisted the bunting and other coronation regalia that embellished windows higher up the building; either she wasn't a royalist, or she had had other things on her mind. Josephine knocked and waited, but there was no answer except for the insistent mewing of a cat from the hallway. The curtains at the window were partially drawn and she peered through the crack, looking into a tiny kitchen. Only the brightest of days would have thrown light into the room, and the heavy grey cloud-cover offered very little help, but she could just make out a set of breakfast things washed up on the draining board and a tray on a small table along the back wall, laid ready with an open tea caddy, a plate of biscuits and three cups. As she peered in, wondering whom Millicent Gray was expecting, the cat – a beautiful, black Persian – jumped up onto the windowsill and stared out at her with beseeching yellow eyes. 'Sorry, puss,' Josephine said, putting her finger to the glass, 'I don't think I can help you.'

The quiet of the flat was beginning to concern her. Anxiously, she retraced her footsteps and tried the other window, but the curtains were pulled tighter here and the glass was so grimy with dust that she could see very little. 'Morning!' called a jovial voice from above and Josephine looked up, embarrassed to find that a girl of about twenty was leaning out of a first-floor window, watching her every move. 'I'll throw the key down if you hang on a minute.' Josephine opened her mouth to argue but the girl had already disappeared back into the room, returning a few seconds later with a key on a piece of red ribbon. She must have seen the hesitation on her caller's face because she smiled reassuringly. 'Millie likes us to keep this so we can let her friends in. It happens all the time, so don't worry about it. You're one of the theatre lot, I suppose?' Josephine nodded, wondering what marked her out so clearly. 'Thought so. She's probably just popped out to get something, so you can wait or leave a note. Here it comes.' Josephine caught the key and thanked her, feeling guilty about the fraudulent way in which she was gaining access to a stranger's life, and torn between curiosity and conscience; either way, if she ever found herself with a neighbour as helpful as this, she really would have to move. 'Just leave it with Millie when you're done, or run it back up. I'll be in all day, recovering from last night. It was quite some party, wasn't it?'

'Yes, it was.' The girl obviously had no idea just how significant the day had been in her neighbour's life, and Josephine wondered how well she actually knew Millicent Gray. 'Have you seen Millie today?' she asked, managing not to stumble over a familiarity she had no claim to.

'No, but I've only just got up. I shouldn't think she'll be long. She always takes a nap when she's got a job in the evenings, and she's been looking forward to this one for ages.'

The girl left her to it and Josephine knocked loudly one more time, just in case it was the nap that was keeping Millicent Gray from her door. When there was still no response, she put the key in the lock and let herself into the hallway. The flat was dark and she switched on the light, noticing that the corridor smelt faintly of a rich, musky perfume. She bent down to stroke the cat, who rubbed round her legs and led her through the nearest door to the kitchen, where two empty bowls sat side by side on the floor by the sink. The first cupboard she tried proved a lucky guess, but the eagerness with which the cat devoured the food concerned Josephine; somehow, she didn't think that Millicent Gray was out shopping, and it seemed unlikely that she had spent the night at home. In a matter of minutes, her dread of coming face to face with the actress had transformed itself into an urgent wish to see her.

There were three more doors off the hallway, and Josephine took the rooms in the order they came. The first was a small but comfortable sitting room, with French doors leading out to a tiny courtyard. Some of the furniture had been painted cream to match the walls, and all the colour in the room came from the fabrics it contained – rugs and oriental cloths, a divan piled high with embroidered cushions. The effect could have been overpowering, but it wasn't; Millicent Gray obviously had the flair for design which comes naturally when things are done for personal taste rather than effect, and Josephine admired its individuality. An incense burner hung from the ceiling, the source of the scent which she had believed to be perfume, and the room was dotted with *objets d'art* that suggested its occupant loved nothing more than poking about in junk shops and flea markets – odd bits of china, a set of very old liqueur glasses, and several shelves of second-hand books. Millicent Gray's identity was stamped all over the room, and it wasn't at all what Josephine had expected: the narcissism of actresses was a cliché, but she knew enough of them personally to understand that it had its basis in fact, and its absence here was striking; there were no playbills or stage shots, and no subtly framed cuttings from the *Radio Times* to highlight the many notable successes she had had. It was unmistakably the room of a woman who felt she had nothing to prove, to herself or to anyone else, and Josephine wondered how that tallied with the emotional vulnerability she had witnessed so briefly just a couple of days before.

The photographs which *had* earned a place here were all natural and informal – varying combinations of family shots, some taken in this country, others obviously abroad. A young man in a wheelchair featured in many of them, often wrapped in a hug and always smiling at the camera, and there was a strong enough resemblance to suggest that he was a younger brother. Unusually, the pictures made no attempt to hide his disability; instead, they seemed to celebrate the obvious bond he shared with his sister – protective, happy, and loving, and Josephine liked Millicent Gray all the more for it. She looked round the room again, surprised by the absence of two things in particular: she would have expected someone who worked in radio drama to own a wireless, but the only form of entertainment was a gramophone and a stack of well-used records; and there was nothing whatsoever to indicate the significance of

Anthony Beresford in Millicent's life. Feeling every bit the intruder she was, Josephine left the sitting room and went next door to the bathroom, but again she found nothing to suggest that Beresford spent any time in the apartment; the toiletries in the cabinet were exclusively feminine – no gentleman's razor, no aftershave, not even a spare toothbrush. Perhaps the actress was simply being discreet, or perhaps all evidence of the affair was confined to the bedroom, the one area of the flat that Josephine had not yet seen.

It was also the only door that was closed. She hesitated outside, aware that to open it would be to overstep the boundaries of privacy and respect that she valued so highly in her own life, but driven now by more than curiosity. The silence of the flat closed in around her, heavy and suggestive, taunting her with a sudden, overwhelming premonition of tragedy. If Millicent Gray had learned of her lover's death, alone and with no one to confide in, what might the shock and the grief and the guilt have led her to do? Josephine knocked twice, then – when there was no response – put her hand on the door and opened it gently, resisting a childish urge to close her eyes as the light from the hallway fell on the carpet, the bedside table, the crumpled sheets.

For once, reality made light of her imagination. The actress lay on the bed, face down with her feet towards the pillows, her right arm outstretched towards the door. Her body was awkwardly con-torted, a parody of the writhing, twisting dragons that covered the oriental bedspread, and her clenched fingers clutched at the sheets as if she could somehow drag herself free from the agony of her death. Her head was turned slightly to the right, and Josephine forced herself to meet the blank, glassy eyes that strained from their sockets, grotesque and doll-like in the carefully made-up face. Two thin trickles of blood, dried black as pitch, ran down from her nose and ear, tracing the contours of a mouth stretched wide in protest, before losing themselves in that final, silent scream.

A man's white evening scarf was still wound tightly around her neck, and Josephine could see deep scratch-marks on the skin where Millicent had clawed in vain at the silk. The air in the room was oppressive, making it an effort to breathe, and now she did close her eyes, fighting the mixture of shock, incredulity and horror that threatened to overwhelm her. When she opened them again, the violence seemed more intense than ever, the colours artificially bright; she stared at the livid dance of blue and purple on Millicent's neck, at her red hair, which now seemed unnatural and vulgar against the pallor of her skin, and wondered if she could really be looking at another human being. She longed to run but the horror of the scene paralysed her, and only when the cat jumped softly onto the bed did she come to her senses. It was a welcome reminder of the everyday, but the tableau of death remained so vivid and so disturbing that it was life which seemed out of place, and Josephine scooped up the animal and left the room, stumbling as if she were drunk.

Ignoring its cries of protest, she shut the cat in the kitchenette and picked up the telephone, but her hands were shaking uncontrollably and it took her three attempts to dial Scotland Yard. Her call was soon answered and she opened her mouth to speak, but her tongue refused to form the words, as if the scarf which had killed Millicent Gray were wrapped around her own throat, too. The voice came again, impatient now, and this time she managed to explain. 'I want to report a murder,' she said. 'The woman's name is Millicent Gray, and she's been strangled in her flat. I've just found her body. Please come quickly.' Try as she might, she couldn't remember the address, but she found it eventually on the newspaper she had brought with her, proof if she needed it of Beresford's death; the moment when her greatest fear had been breaking the news to a distraught mistress seemed a lifetime away, and she reiterated her need for help. 'Will it be Detective Chief Inspector Penrose?' she asked. 'I'm a friend of his.'

The words sounded childish and pathetic in their context. 'I'm afraid I can't say who's available, ma'am,' the desk clerk said, his tone somehow making it clear that policemen couldn't be booked like hairdressers, no matter who she was.

'Of course not. But this might be linked to another case he's working on and I think he'd want to know as soon as possible.' There was a pause on the line, followed by a satisfying change in attitude, and Josephine gave the details and her name. She replaced the receiver, hoping that the promise of immediate assistance would hold good.

There was no way that she could wait in the flat with the body. She took her cigarette case out of her bag and went outside, making sure that the front door was firmly closed behind her. The light summer rain was a relief, and she lifted her face to its cool, gentle solace, inhaling the smoke and trying to rid her mind of the haunting, insidious images that crowded it. Above her, she heard the first-floor window open again and wished after all that she had chosen to stay inside. 'Just pop the key through the letterbox if you've finished,' the girl called, but her cheerfulness subsided when she registered the expression on Josephine's face. 'What's wrong? Didn't Millie come back?' Without waiting for an answer, she disappeared and joined Josephine downstairs. 'Has something happened? Please tell me. You look awful.'

She made a move towards the basement, but Josephine stopped her. 'I'm so sorry. There's no easy way to say this, but Millie's dead.'

The girl gave an odd, high-pitched laugh. 'Dead? Don't be silly, she can't possibly be dead.' She looked at Josephine in disbelief. 'What's happened?' she demanded again. 'What have you done to her?'

'Nothing. I haven't done anything. I just found her in the bedroom. She must have been there a while.' The girl snatched the key from her hand and Josephine could do nothing this time except follow her back into the flat and witness the horror all over again, this time through the eyes of a friend. 'We shouldn't be here,' she said gently, leading the girl back down the hallway. 'The police are on their way and they'll take care of Millie. Perhaps we could wait in your flat? I'll make us some tea.' The girl nodded, too shocked to argue. 'I'm sorry, I don't even know your name. I'm Josephine.'

'Euphemia,' she said, 'but everyone calls me Effie, thank God.' She held out her hand, and the formality of the introduction seemed to steady her, restoring some sort of order to a world that suddenly made no sense. 'Come upstairs. I'm sorry about the mess, but some friends came back with us last night. The others had to work today and I haven't got round to clearing up.'

The first-floor flat did indeed give the impression that the party had merely been suspended. 'How many of you live here?' Josephine asked, looking round at the half-drunk cocktails, cast-off evening wear and ashtrays brimming with cigarette butts.

'There's three of us. Vi makes most of the mess, but her parents are the reason we can afford the rent so we forgive her for it. Then there's Lou – she works at Heal's, so she gets a good deal on furniture. And me. I work evenings at the Hippodrome, so my contribution is to clear up every day. Worth it for the peace and quiet alone.' Her face clouded again as the small-talk faded, and she made no attempt to hide her tears. 'It'll be even quieter now, I suppose. I'll put the kettle on. Sit down, if you can find some-where.' Josephine moved some clothes off a seat by the window, where she could watch for the police car. 'Bugger tea,' Effie said, returning almost immediately with the dregs of a bottle of gin. 'I need something stronger. It's not often there's anything left the morning after, so we might as well make the most of it.' She divided the contents meticulously between two glasses and handed one to Josephine. 'I can't believe we'll never have another drink together,' she said, sitting down on the floor. 'Millie was such a laugh once you got to know her.'

'When did you last see her?' Josephine asked.

'Tuesday afternoon, it must have been. We had a cup of tea be-fore she got ready to go to the BBC, and she helped me put this lot up for the party.' She gestured towards the bunting and souvenir posters that decorated the walls, smiling at the memory. 'Actually, she teased me about it. Said we were crowning the wrong king and people shouldn't be so ridiculous about divorce. She would say that, though, wouldn't she?'

'Yes, I suppose she would.'

'I bet it was that bastard she'd been seeing.'

The accusation was sudden and direct, and it shocked Josephine. She realised now that she had been too sickened by her discovery to give any thought to who might be responsible for it. 'What makes you say that?' she asked, trying to decide if she would have come to the same conclusion herself eventually, and wondering when Millicent Gray had been killed. Even if she had died before Beresford, it was still hard to imagine the broadcaster finding time on the most important day of his professional life to pop round and strangle his mistress. And anyway, why would he want to? If the rumours at the BBC were true, he had never had any trouble before in moving on from a woman he tired of.

'He messed her about right from the start. Far too comfortable at home with his wife, I reckon, but she wouldn't have a word said against him. Not until recently, anyway.'

'Oh?'

'Yes, she said he was making a fool of her, but she'd found a way to get back at him.'

'Do you know what it was?'

Effie shrugged. 'Telling his wife, I suppose. Bursting their little bubble, she called it.'

Whatever motive Beresford might have had, it certainly wasn't that one, but Josephine didn't want to stem the tide of information by arguing. Again, she wondered if the broadcaster could have found time to commit the murder; if he had, that would also have given him the opportunity to remove anything personal that related to him from the flat. 'Was he here a lot?' she asked.

'Hardly ever. I only saw him a couple of times, and then I couldn't understand what the fuss was about. Millie liked him, though. She liked him a lot.' Effie finished her gin in one go, and took the cigarette that Josephine offered. 'Christ, if it *was* him I hope he swings for it. I'll be first in the queue to see the notice go up.'

She obviously didn't know what had happened yesterday, and Josephine doubted if she even knew who Millicent's lover had been. 'Did she have any other visitors in the last couple of days?'

'Only a woman. I saw her going down the steps yesterday as we were leaving. It was about half past nine, I suppose, but I didn't take much notice because we were late and Vi was already cutting up rough about getting a good place in the crowd.'

'What was she like?' The description – a middle-aged woman, dark-haired and smartly dressed – could have fitted thousands of women, but it certainly didn't rule out Vivienne Beresford and Josephine's heart sank. Before she could press for any more details, she heard the sound of a police siren nearby and two cars turned in from Wigmore Street, shattering the quadrangle's mendacious peace. Leaving her gin in good hands, she went down to meet them, more pleased than she would have thought possible to see Archie get out of the second car.

'Josephine! Are you all right?'

He touched her shoulder, oblivious to the curious glances from his colleagues. 'I'm really not sure,' she said honestly. 'It was such a shock.'

'Of course it was. But what on earth were you doing here?' Josephine told him about the conversation she had had with Julian, and gave as succinct an account as she could of what she had found. 'Was there any sign of a break-in?' he asked when she had finished.

'No, nothing. It's all very calm until you get to the bedroom. She must have let whoever it was in, unless he or she had a key.'

'And you've left everything exactly as it was?'

'Yes, except the bedroom door. It was closed when I got there, and I think I've left it open. Oh, and I shut the cat in the kitchen, but you'll find a good home for it on the first floor. One of the girls who lives there is called Effie and she was friendly with Millicent. She's quite shaken up and she's running out of gin, so I think some company will do her good.'

'All right. I'll go and talk to her as soon as I've had a look inside. Did she tell you anything interesting?'

'She thinks Beresford killed Millicent to shut her up before she could tell his wife about their affair. But that hardly makes sense, does it?' Archie shook his head. 'How is Vivienne?' Josephine asked quickly, seeing that he was impatient to leave her and go inside. 'I'm assuming it *is* Vivienne you've got in custody?'

'Yes, it is. She's shattered by what she's done, but the consequences are only just beginning to hit her.'

'I think she was here yesterday,' Josephine said quietly.

'What? How do you know?'

'Effie saw someone going down the steps yesterday morning, and her description could easily have been Vivienne.'

Archie rubbed a hand over his eyes, and Josephine was struck by how concerned he seemed. 'I didn't think it could get any worse for Vivienne Beresford, but this will make my boss's day and the BBC will keep the flags up for another week. They're already intent on throwing her to the wolves.'

'Do you think she might be innocent, then?'

'It depends what you mean by innocent. I've no doubt she shot her husband, but there is such a thing as provocation and I want her to have a fair trial.' Another car drew up and a police photographer got out. 'I'm sorry, I have to go, but I'll telephone you later. Will you be at Marta's?'

She smiled awkwardly. 'A lot's happened since we last spoke. Now isn't the time to explain, though. I'll go back to my club for a bit, and then I'll be at the BBC. Can I tell Julian what's happened?

It seems trivial to worry about the play, but he'll need to ask Lydia to stand in.'

'You can tell him what's happened in the strictest confidence, but only the facts. Don't repeat any of the speculation about who was here or who might have done it. And give me a couple of hours before you say anything. If Julian Terry finds out before Reith knows, I'll be looking for a new job. Right now, I'm not sure I'd mind.' He smiled at her. 'Is that all right? Lydia can step in at the last moment, can't she?'

'Oh yes,' Josephine said, and she wasn't proud of the bitterness in her voice. 'Lydia can fill anyone's shoes at the drop of a hat. It's what she does best.'

4

Penrose sat at his desk and looked through the photographs of Millicent Gray's body. It always astonished him that no matter how meticulous the Yard's photographers were in recording every small detail of a crime scene, these stark black-and-white representations of death never quite did justice to its horror. Had he not been there to experience it for himself, he would never have known the sadness that hung around that room, the sense of despair at another life wasted or the suppressed outrage in the dead woman's ugly, distorted features. Perhaps he carried sorrow with him to every body he viewed, and that was why it remained stubbornly immune to a camera, but somehow he thought not: whenever he was with a murder victim, in those few precious moments before the body was moved and analysed, he felt their anger as a physical force, a tangible presence in the room that demanded a response – and it was that, not duty or abstract notions of justice, which drove him.

The full post-mortem results would not be available for some time, but Spilsbury had been confident in his estimate at the scene: Millicent Gray had died approximately twenty-four hours before she was found – no more than thirty, no less than eighteen. Before bringing Bill Murray up to speed with the latest turn of events, Penrose had asked him for a detailed schedule of Beresford's last day. He didn't want the BBC to construct an alibi around its own reputation rather than the truth, but, as it happened, there seemed to be no need. From the moment he arrived at Broadcasting House, Beresford had been involved in a constant round of meetings and briefings, followed by the broadcast itself. He had had just half an hour alone in his office to go over his notes, and the switchboard confirmed that some of that time had been spent on the telephone. Once he moved to Constitution Hill, he had taken part in hourly soundchecks, and an engineer had confirmed that it was Beresford's voice on the line each time; the hour in between each test was unaccounted for, but it scarcely gave him time to get through the crowds to Wigmore Street and back again. Thinking back, Penrose wasn't sure that he had ever had to construct an alibi for a dead man before, but what he had come up with would have been the envy of most living defendants. Things looked bleak for Vivienne Beresford, and the pressure on him to extract a second confession from her was greater than anything else he had experienced in his entire career.

There was a brisk, familiar knock and Sergeant Fallowfield put his head round the door. 'They're ready for us downstairs, sir.'

'All right, Bill. Let's get on with it.'

Penrose picked up the files he needed and walked with Fallowfield to the interview room, wondering why he was suddenly so reluctant to do his job. He had never been afraid to analyse his own motives, even if they showed him in a poor light, and he knew now that he simply did not want to be wrong. He liked Vivienne Beresford, sympathised with her situation, and admired the way in which she had acknowledged her crime. And he had always despised men like her husband, who took whatever they wanted and moved through life with no awareness of the devastation they left behind. His objection wasn't a moral one. It came from years of clearing up the mess that a combination of selfishness and power created: the suicides of abandoned women; the husbands who killed unfaithful wives in a moment of jealous rage; and occasionally – like now – the wives who fought back. Beresford's death had been swift and functional, almost merciful when compared with the years of pain which his infidelity had inflicted. Millicent Gray's murder was altogether different – spiteful, cruel, and out of proportion to what she had done. If Vivienne Beresford proved to be capable of that, there was a side to her that he had never believed was there.

She looked pale and tired today, and he knew that she had had to be sedated overnight. Tall, and still elegantly dressed, she seemed somehow shrunken against the WPC who sat beside her, as if her flesh were responding instinctively to the emotional turmoil of the last two days. He had seen it before in the accused, this steady disintegration of body and soul, and it had nothing to do with innocence or guilt. He found it hard to put into words, but by the time a court appearance came, it sometimes seemed to Penrose that the prosecution was trying a ghost.

He greeted her and sat down. 'Mrs Beresford, I'd like to run through your movements again for yesterday morning.'

'They haven't changed, Chief Inspector,' she said, more out of weariness than defiance.

'Even so, if you could bear with me. A BBC car collected you and your husband from your home in Kensington at half past seven – is that right?'

'Yes.'

'And after that?'

'Billy drove us both to Broadcasting House and dropped us at the front entrance. That must have been between eight and quarter past.'

'And what did you do then?'

'Anthony had to go straight upstairs for a briefing, so we arranged to meet back in the entrance hall at ten o'clock, ready to go to Constitution Hill. I went through to my office for a while to check on the progress of the next issue. I hadn't been at work the day before, so I wanted to catch up on any copy that had come in and any changes that were due to be made.'

'But you didn't stay there?'

'No, as I told you yesterday, I took my assistant a small present to thank her for everything she's done over the last few weeks. It's been a very busy time and I don't know how I'd have managed without her.'

Penrose looked down at his notes. 'A Miss Daniels, in Great Titchfield Street.'

'That's right.'

'But she was out when you arrived.'

'Yes. I got distracted by the magazine, as I often do, and by the time I got there, Danny had already set out for the Coronation. I left the present on the step and went away.'

'We've spoken to Miss Daniels and there was nothing on her doorstep when she got home.'

'Then someone else must have taken it. I'd buy her a replacement, but that's a little difficult at the moment.'

The small show of spirit pleased Penrose. 'Did anyone else see you there?' he asked.

'I have no idea. You'd have to ask them.'

'And you didn't go anywhere else?'

'No, I didn't.' There was a wariness in her voice now, as she sensed a new purpose to Penrose's questioning. 'By then it was getting late, and I knew I couldn't keep Anthony waiting.'

'So if someone claimed to have seen you in the Wigmore Street area at around half past nine, they'd be mistaken?'

'Quite mistaken.' She recovered quickly, but there had been a flicker of concern in her eyes and Penrose knew that she was lying. He left the next stage of the questioning to his sergeant, and sat back to watch her reactions.

'Do you recognise this, Mrs Beresford?' Fallowfield asked, placing the white silk murder weapon in front of her.

She hesitated, but more out of surprise at the change of tack, Penrose thought, than guilt. 'My husband has several like it,' she said, 'but so do most men. I couldn't say for sure if it was his. Why do you want to know?'

'Because it was used to kill Millicent Gray in her flat off Wigmore Street yesterday morning.'

Penrose watched Vivienne Beresford's face, and if it was a performance put on for their benefit, it was one of the finest he had ever seen. Shock and confusion at the news were swiftly followed by outrage and horror as she realised what they were suggesting. 'My God, you think I did that as well, don't you?'

'Mrs Beresford, you readily admit to killing your husband—' Penrose began, but he was soon interrupted.

'That's different. I had a whole lifetime of reasons to hate Anthony. Millicent Gray was just the latest in a long line of irritations. Why would I risk my life to take hers?'

'Because he was going to leave you. Millicent Gray was more than an irritation, wasn't she? She was the woman who had finally succeeded in destroying your marriage.'

'We were perfectly capable of doing that ourselves, Chief Inspector. We didn't need any help from her.'

'But you must have known you wouldn't get away with killing your husband. You have made no effort whatsoever to lie about it, or to evade arrest. Given those circumstances, perhaps you thought you might as well destroy Millicent Gray's life as well. I can easily understand why you would want to punish them both.'

'No,' she said firmly, but she was growing increasingly agitated. 'Just listen to yourself, Chief Inspector. Do you honestly think I took the decision to kill my husband lightly? Years of pain and rejection led to what I did yesterday, so the idea that I would kill a woman quite simply because I "might as well" is absurd and repellent.'

'I believe you went to see Miss Gray yesterday morning, not Miss Daniels, and once you were there you confronted her about her affair with your husband. Perhaps she taunted you with her happiness and things got out of hand, or perhaps it was always your intention to kill her, but either way you strangled her with your husband's scarf—'

'Why would I go to the effort of strangling her when I had a gun in my bag all day?'

'You're an intelligent woman, Mrs Beresford. You know that it's one thing to fire a shot in a soundproof cubicle among cheering crowds, and quite another to shoot someone in a quiet residential area when you have no idea who might be at home to hear.'

'You've obviously thought of everything, so what is the point of my even being here?'

She shook her head cynically, but Penrose could see how frightened she was, and he knew he would have to exploit that fear to get at the truth. 'Perhaps Miss Gray bought the scarf for your husband, so you decided to teach her a lesson with it. You wanted her to pay for all those years of pain and rejection, didn't you? All those years of knowing you were never quite good enough, of looking at her when she came into the BBC and wondering what it was that made Anthony choose her. Was it her youth or her looks or her independence? Was it the novelty of being with her when your life together was so predictable?' She was crying now and he loathed himself for taunting her with her own darkness when she had done nothing but be honest about it; he criticised the BBC for its lack of sympathy, but was he really any better? Feeling as though he were holding a woman under water long after she had drowned, he hammered home his advantage. 'Or was it simply because she embarrassed you at work? It was the one place where you thought you had some respect, but Millicent Gray walked in there and stripped you of that illusion. She humiliated you in front of your colleagues, so you . . .'

'No.'

' . . . so you went round to show her who really had the power. Perhaps you even told her you were going to kill Anthony. Is that it? If you couldn't have him, she certainly wasn't going to?'

'No, that's not true,' she shouted, standing up and slamming her hand down on the table.

'So you waited for the right moment and you choked the life out of her.'

'I didn't kill her.' From nowhere, she slapped him hard across the face, sobbing uncontrollably now. Fallowfield and the WPC stood as one to restrain her, but Penrose held up his hand and waited for her to calm down. 'I will happily hang for what I did to Anthony,' she said eventually, 'but I will not go to the gallows for his fucking mistress.'

'You were there, though, weren't you, Mrs Beresford?' Penrose said softly. 'We have a witness who saw a woman fitting your description on the steps to Miss Gray's flat at around the time she died.'

'Yes, I was there, but I didn't go inside. I didn't even see her.'

'Why did you go?'

'Because she asked me to. She sent me a note, asking me to go and see her on Wednesday morning at nine. She said it would be worth my while and there was something I should know.'

'Do you still have the note?'

'No, I destroyed it. I had no intention of going at first. I wasn't about to jump to her call, and anyway, I knew what she was going to tell me because I found the travel tickets shortly afterwards.'

'So you think that's what she meant?'

'What else could it be? Mistresses always think the wife doesn't know, but sometimes she simply doesn't care.'

'And why did you change your mind?'

'Because of everything you've just said. I *did* want to stand up to her and tell her that things weren't going to go her way, and for all the reasons you mentioned – the shame and the humiliation, the sense of never quite being good enough. I suppose I wanted to understand what was so special about her, as well. I could never see it myself, but Anthony obviously could. It sounds stupid, but I wanted to understand him before I killed him, and there was a part of me that longed for her to save him.'

'What do you mean?'

'Even though I knew exactly what was going on, I wanted her to tell me that I'd misunderstood, that he wasn't really going to leave. She was his last chance, I suppose, but I never for one moment intended to kill her, and I didn't do it on the spur of the moment, either.'

'Why did you lie about what you did that morning?'

She gave a wry smile. 'Sometimes I make no sense even to myself, Chief Inspector. I can look you in the eye and tell you I shot my husband, but I'm embarrassed to admit to wanting a showdown with his mistress.'

'So you still insist that you have never been inside that flat, then or at any other time?'

'No, I haven't. I knocked several times but there was no answer and that made me angry. I wasn't about to waste more of my time waiting for her, so I left and went back to Broadcasting House.'

'How long were you there?'

'About five minutes, I suppose – if that.'

'Did you see anyone else?'

'No one in particular. A few passers-by, that's all. It seemed very quiet. I suppose most people were at the Coronation.'

'Miss Gray didn't invite your husband at the same time, did she?' Penrose asked, remembering the three cups laid out on the tray.

Vivienne Beresford looked at him in surprise. 'Not to my knowledge. I'm sure she would have known that Anthony couldn't stop for a social call on a day like that.'

Penrose took a small bag from the folder in front of him and pushed it across the table. 'Do you recognise this, Mrs Beresford? Before you say anything, I should tell you that it has your fingerprints on it.'

She looked down at the silver powder compact. 'I'd expect it to. It's mine. Anthony gave it to me for an anniversary, but I lost it recently. Where did you find it?'

'In Millicent Gray's bedroom, near her body.' He let the words sink in, then asked: 'How do you explain that if you've never been inside her flat?'

She had no trouble in meeting his eye. Rather than destroy her, the accusation of a second murder seemed to have given her a new strength, and he was pleased to see her spirit return, even if it was at his own expense. 'What do you think I did? Killed her and powdered my nose? Actually, Chief Inspector, I can think of a number of ways it might have got there. Perhaps my husband had it all along and left it there. Or perhaps it mysteriously appeared while the police were carrying out a search of the premises. As you said earlier, I'm an intelligent woman and I know how convenient it would be for you and for the BBC if I were guilty of two murders. To use your own logic, you've got my confession for Anthony's murder; you might as well try for Millicent Gray's, too. But I'm afraid I can't help you. I wasn't in her flat, and I didn't kill her.'

'And that's your final word?'

'It is, yes.'

He nodded, satisfied with her answer, although he knew his own belief in her innocence would do him no good when he reported back to the Assistant Commissioner. He took the bag with the set of keys out of his pocket, and asked her to look at them. 'Have you ever seen these before? They were found in your husband's desk at Broadcasting House.'

She shook her head. 'No. They're not his.'

'They have his prints on them.'

'Then he must have been looking after them for someone else. We haven't owned a car for several years. It's a nuisance in town, and if we went away it was usually abroad. And those are not our house keys.'

'What about this?' Penrose asked, showing her the toy soldier.

Vivienne Beresford looked at him as if he were mad. 'Is that something else you found lying around in Millicent Gray's apartment?'

Penrose suppressed a smile. 'No. Again, it was in the drawer of your husband's desk.'

'Anthony had long outgrown tin soldiers, Chief Inspector. When he wanted to play, he chose women. If he hadn't, neither of us would be here.' She watched him carefully as he closed the files and gathered up the evidence. 'What happens now?'

'You will shortly be charged with the murder of your husband. After a brief appearance in a magistrate's court, probably tomorrow morning, you will be held in remand at Holloway until your trial.'

She flinched at the name of the prison, and he realised how synonymous it still was with the abortive hanging of Edith Thompson; Thompson's treatment and the publicity around it must strike the fear of God into any woman facing a murder charge. 'And her death?' she asked. 'Will I be charged with that, too?'

'I have to speak to my superiors. They'll look at the evidence and make that decision.'

'You mean they'll look at the newspapers and have a word with the BBC,' she said, her voice more cynical than ever. 'If for some reason my husband killed his lover – he is a logical suspect, after all – that will be very awkward for the Corporation, won't it? With that scenario, you might even call what I did justice.' She paused, waiting to see if Penrose would comment, but he didn't. 'Either way, I want a solicitor now. I presume it's not too late to change my mind?'

'Of course not. You'll be allowed to make the necessary telephone calls.'

'And can I have visitors while I wait for my trial?'

'Visits are always made at the discretion of the Deputy Governor, but I can't see a problem in this case.'

'Thank you.'

He left her with Fallowfield and went upstairs to find Rygate waiting in his office. 'Well?'

'She denies any knowledge of Millicent Gray's murder, sir, and I think she's telling the truth.'

'I'm not interested in your bloody hunches, Penrose. What evidence have you got against her?' He listened as Penrose outlined the facts. 'So she was seen at the flat at the time of death. She admits being there, even though she lied about it. The scarf was probably Beresford's, something she could easily have taken with her from the house. Her powder compact was found in a room she claims never to have seen. And she had every reason in the world to want the woman dead. Oh, and we know she's capable of murder because she happened to shoot her husband six hours later. Quite frankly, Penrose, I don't see what your problem is.'

'Her prints aren't anywhere else in the flat, but—'

'So she wore gloves. And if you're about to tell me that Beresford's prints *are* there, I think we both know why that is. Anyway, there's no point in going down that road – you told me his schedule was too tight.'

'There's nearly an hour between the engineer's soundchecks, and anyway, we haven't had the full reports yet. Spilsbury might revise the time of death.' Rygate gave him a look which was perfectly justified; the pathologist was rarely wrong once he had nailed his colours to the mast. 'Anyway, why are we limiting this enquiry to two suspects? What about the tea tray? Miss Gray was obviously expecting someone else, so couldn't you at least give me some time to find out who? Look into her life a bit more, find out who she was – I can't believe her only purpose on this earth was to be Anthony Beresford's mistress, so perhaps there's another line of enquiry, another grudge we're missing.'

'There's no time for a wild goose chase, Penrose. You seem incapable of understanding what a high-profile case this is – even the Home Secretary's taking an interest in it, for Christ's sake. It's vital that we're seen to have it in hand from the very start.'

'Even if we've got the wrong person? Millicent Gray's parents are on their way up from Kent. They're devastated, naturally. I'd like to be able to offer them a bit more than the most convenient solution.'

Rygate sighed. 'Look, Penrose – you know how much I respect your work and how highly I value your opinion, but in this case I genuinely believe you're wrong. You've got some bee in your bonnet about Vivienne Beresford and I don't know what it is, but it's not doing you or the force any good. Open your eyes and look at the facts. I want you to charge Mrs Beresford with both murders, and then I'm putting you back on royal duties.'

'But sir . . .'

'No buts. As soon as my back's turned, you'll be on this like a terrier unless I find you something else to do. That stubborn streak will be your downfall, and I'm doing this for your career, not mine. The royal couple will be driving through north London later this afternoon. It's supposed to be a surprise but we all know it will leak, so I want you there to make sure there's no trouble. Is that understood?'

'Yes, sir,' Penrose said reluctantly.

'Good. Now, go and get the paperwork sorted and I'll call Broadcasting House.'

5

As it turned out, Josephine was saved the ordeal of telling Julian about Millicent's death. Archie had obviously been swift to alert Broadcasting House because a message was left for her at the Cowdray Club long before her two-hour curfew was up. Apparently, Lydia would be 'delighted' to help them out, and would be at the studio early for a final run-through with the rest of the cast; Josephine was welcome to join them, but if Julian didn't hear from her, he would meet her in the entrance hall at the time previously arranged. It was a relief not to have to go through the experience all over again, and, with a bit of luck, everyone would be far too busy with the broadcast later to make her relive each detail. As time went on and the cushioning effect of shock faded, Josephine became increasingly upset by what she had seen. It wasn't just the horror of being confronted with violence, or the loss of an actress she had respected; as much as she had tried to resist the idea at the time, Millicent's final words to her had created a sympathy between them that made her death – and the obvious sadness of her last few days – all the more tragic, and all the more personal.

For a while, the murder distracted her from Marta, but the contemplation of three lives so easily destroyed soon brought her back to her own situation, and she felt the pain of their separation more intensely than ever. She longed to get a cab to Holly Place and take back every word she had said the night before, but it wasn't fair to keep changing her mind, and, in her heart, she knew that she had done the right thing: if she and Marta were to stand any chance at all, their love had to be built on honesty, and she hadn't needed the last few days to teach her that. To pass the time, she sat in Hyde Park, watching khaki-clad soldiers pat down muddy, foot-wrecked turf. The clean-up operation had begun in earnest, but many of the streets were still covered in litter and parts of London looked like a giant refuse heap, a treasure-trove of opportunity for those with the patience to sort through the rubbish for more valuable items left behind by accident. At five o'clock, she went back to the Cowdray Club, where good-luck flowers from the Motleys awaited her, together with a note to say they hoped 'all was well otherwise' and an invitation to drop by their studio in St Martin's Lane the following day to bring them up to date. As she changed into an evening dress which Ronnie and Lettice had made for her, Josephine wished heartily that she had arranged to listen to the broadcast with them instead.

The grandeur and excitement of Broadcasting House almost made her change her mind, but she had to fight her way through a crowd of scandal-hungry reporters to gain admittance, and it soon became obvious that the BBC was not itself, no matter how hard the staff tried to give the impression of business as usual. Uniformed commissionaires on night duty had replaced daytime receptionists, and Josephine announced herself and waited for Julian to collect her. Two sets of lift doors opened simultaneously and Julian emerged from one of them, spruce and dapper in black tie. She smiled and stood to greet him, but was suddenly aware that everything else had stopped around her as a tall man strode purposefully from the second lift to the front entrance. The lift attendants, commissionaires and pageboys left what they were doing and stood to attention, and even Julian folded his hands meekly in front of him and kept her where she was by a subtle shake of his head. The cause of this extreme reaction looked neither to left nor right as he passed, and when the front doors closed behind him, a collective sigh swept through the entrance hall as everyone breathed out and returned to work. 'Was that the Director General?' Josephine asked, as Julian kissed her on both cheeks.

'How on earth did you guess?'

'I narrowed it down to two and Christ has a beard.'

Julian laughed. 'To be fair, he earns that sort of respect, but there's a hint of fear thrown in after the day we've had. Nobody wants to get in his way at the moment. God help any reporter who dares to speak to him outside.'

He took her across to the reception desk to collect a pass, and the commissionaire gave them a wry smile. 'I see you're using more studios than ever tonight, Mr Terry,' he said cheerfully, nodding to the noticeboard which gave a list of room allocations.

'Yes, Cyril, I am. It's my intention to take over the whole building, as you know, and this is the lady who'll help me to do it.' He winked at Josephine and called back over his shoulder. 'She writes delightfully large casts, keeps actors in work all year round, and single-handedly soaks up my budget for a month.' Once they were alone inside the lift, his demeanour changed completely. 'Josephine, I'm sorry about earlier. I had no idea what I was asking you to do by sending you round to Millicent's. It must have been bloody awful for you.'

'Yes, it was, but how could you have known? Someone had to find her.'

'Even so. The word here is that Viv killed them both, but I find that so hard to believe. Have you heard anything?'

'Not really,' Josephine said diplomatically, remembering Archie's instructions. 'I suppose we'll know more as soon as they're sure.'

'Yes, I suppose so. Whatever happened, it's given me a bloody headache for the next few weeks. Millicent was contracted for five major productions.'

'Really? How selfish of her to let you down.'

He had the decency to look contrite. 'Point taken. I'm excited about tonight, though. I think Lydia's change of role will give the whole thing an edge and a freshness that we didn't have before.'

The lift stopped at the sixth floor and Josephine got out,

depressed by how dispensable everybody seemed to be. Julian showed her into a small green room, where the cast had gathered after the rehearsal. Like its larger counterpart downstairs, the room was elegant and modern, decorated with flowers, art-deco chairs and two abstract sculptures, and Josephine was struck by how different it was from its equivalent in a theatre – probably because actors never had the chance to move in and mess it up. Everyone stood round in black tie and evening dress, honouring the production by behaving as if the audience really could see them. Lydia, in particular, looked stunning in a Vionnet design that emphasised her figure and a beautiful sapphire necklace. Any tension between them was diffused by the crowd, and Josephine comforted herself with the thought that a false kiss never looked out of place in a green room. 'I think these chaps are the only people you haven't met,' Julian said, leading her over to four men who stood slightly apart from the rest of the group. 'Allow me to introduce our musicians for the evening – Charles, Michael, William and Keith.'

Josephine chatted to the quartet for a while, genuinely interested in the music they were going to play. When the dominant black-and-green clock on the wall said a quarter to eight, Julian cleared his throat and held up his hand for attention. 'Right, everyone. Time to take your opening places. Good luck, and remember what I said about atmosphere. I want the audience to *see* the dagger going in when Darnley's killed, and I expect tears running down their cheeks when Mary realises that Bothwell's betrayed her.'

There was a rustling of paper as the actors picked up their scripts and disappeared to separate studios on the sixth and seventh floors. 'It must be odd to take cues from people you can't even see,' Josephine said. 'You mentioned *opening* places – does that mean they have to move studios while the play's going out?'

'Some of them. We need the acoustics to be different between the street scene and the queen's room, but Bothwell has to be in both, so he'll go from 6A to 7B.' He must have seen the concern on her face as she looked down long corridors at identical sets of double doors. 'Don't worry. That's why we have studio managers. It'll be all right, I promise. Come on – we're on the upper deck.' She followed him up a steep, corkscrew staircase, beginning to understand what a clever and complex art form radio drama was. 'I should warn you – I'm sure you're not going to bitch about your cast, but things can easily be overheard through the microphones. One should be gagged all the time in a building like this. Now, here we are . . .'

He opened the door with a flourish, and Josephine could see three chairs lined up alongside a peculiar contraption of battleship grey. A daunting bank of apparatus – two rows of volume-control knobs and a series of tiny windows which, when illuminated, bore the number of a studio – rose up in a sort of elongated hump from the centre of a heavy, cellulosed table. 'My pride and joy,' Julian said, as if he were showing her a new car or his first-born son. 'The dramatic-control panel.' The room had a distinctly futuristic feel, and the only things that Josephine recognised were a telephone, a loudspeaker and a microphone. 'Now you can see why this is so good,' he continued enthusiastically, flicking a couple of switches. 'There are no visual distractions and I don't have to look at Dougie's ugly mug while he's delivering his lines – yes, Dougie, I know you can hear me and you know I'm right – so we're as close as we can possibly be to the position of the listener at home. Have a seat, Josephine – you're on the left. This is Peter – he'll be handling the controls for me while we're on air. Some producers like to do it all themselves, but I find it a distraction from the script and we work well together. He knows the play almost as well as I do, and much, much better than the author.'

He grinned and Josephine sat down, nodding to Peter but making no effort to interrupt the stream of information which Julian seemed determined to share with her before they went on air. His mood was infectious, and when the room eventually fell silent, she followed his example and stared excitedly at the light on the wall until it began to flash red. 'Dry lips and throat-clearing time,' Julian said, pressing a button in response. 'Stand by, everyone.' A second later, the red signal shone again, this time as a steady, unwavering light, and Josephine heard the announcer's voice, rich and clear through the loudspeaker. 'This is the *National Programme*. Ladies and gentlemen, tonight we present to you a broadcast of a radio play entitled *Queen of Scots* by Gordon Daviot, author of *Richard of Bordeaux*. The cast is as follows: Mary Stuart is played by Miss Lydia Beaumont; Hepburn, Earl of Bothwell, by Mr Douglas Graham . . .' The names ran on, and Josephine realised that Julian was right – the cast was considerable, and she wondered how on earth it would all be co-ordinated. 'Incidental music is provided by the Stonehouse Quartet,' the voice concluded eventually, 'and the play is adapted for broadcasting and produced by Julian Terry.'

After just a few lines, Josephine realised how different in timing and atmosphere the broadcast was from its rehearsal. The read-through she had attended could have been for any stage play, but this was unmistakably radio, and not just because of the lights and the controls and the headphone-wearing engineer: the actors took their place alongside audio props – music, sound effects, artificial echo – which were just as important as costumes and stage sets, and the result was a series of mental pictures as vivid and absorbing as anything fashioned below a proscenium arch. Producer and engineer were performers, too, she noticed. In a theatre, once the curtain went up, there was nothing a director could do except bite his fingernails and give notes afterwards, but here he was as involved in the creative pace and the artistic performance as any of the cast. She watched, fascinated, as Peter's fingers played swiftly over the controls like an organist in a cathedral, responding instantly to Julian's instructions and getting maximum impact from every single word she had written. It was a real ensemble effort, and Josephine was thrilled to have found something that she would genuinely like to become more involved with, perhaps to write specifically for.

After a while, she forced herself to close her eyes and just listen. No one would ever know that Lydia was playing a part that hadn't originally been hers. She spoke the lines with such feeling, as if they had been written for her – which, of course, they had – and Josephine was moved to tears by the scene in which Mary finally realises that Bothwell has never loved her, but has always stayed true to his wife. It reminded her of Millicent Gray's disillusionment and of something Effie had said that morning – that Millie intended to 'burst the Beresfords' bubble'. What did that mean? It implied a bond between husband and wife which simply did not exist, and Josephine could make no sense of it. Her thoughts tore at the web of fantasy which the play had convincingly woven and wrenched her back to the present. How odd that they should all be here, absorbed in this play, when two people had been killed and another imprisoned. She could not decide if that was a creditable show of courage and a comforting insistence that the world must go on, or a simple affront to decency.

Either way, the hour was soon over. Most West End producers would be apoplectic at the idea of so much time and effort going into a single performance, but Josephine knew that the pleasure of what she had just heard was worth every minute, and she could tell by the triumph on Julian's face that he felt the same. He hugged her and they went down to the green room, where cast and technical staff were mingling in celebration. She looked round for Lydia, carefully rehearsing what she would say, but the actress beat her to it. 'Congratulations, darling,' Lydia said, coming up behind her and putting a glass of champagne in her hand. 'You must be so pleased.'

'I am, but don't congratulate me. You all did the work, and it was extraordinary. Thank you.'

'Oh, I didn't mean the play. I meant Marta – persuading her to sell the house.'

'What?'

'Surely you knew? Oh dear – I hope I haven't spoilt the surprise. She's putting it on the market as soon as the holiday's over, apparently.'

'When did she tell you that?'

'Last night. She wasn't in the best of moods, but I expect you know that.'

'Where's she going?' Josephine asked. She cursed herself for acknowledging that Lydia knew more than she did, and for the note of panic in her voice, but the question had slipped out automatically and there was nothing she could do now to claim prior knowledge of Marta's plans.

Lydia shrugged. 'I didn't ask. She made it perfectly clear why she was doing it, though, so I suppose we must call that round two to you.' She finished her drink and looked defiantly at Josephine. 'But don't think for a moment that I'm giving up.'

She walked away to join the rest of the cast and Josephine watched her go, trying to rationalise the emotions of the last few minutes. 'A few of us are going out for dinner afterwards,' Julian said, coming over to top up her glass. 'Will you join us?'

'No thank you, not tonight.' The refusal sounded more brusque than she had meant it to. 'There's something I need to do and it can't wait,' she explained. 'In fact, I should be going soon. Will you thank everyone again for me? It really was very special.'

'Of course I will. I'll walk you downstairs, though. Visitors have wandered these corridors for days when left to their own devices.'

They left the party and headed back to the ground floor. Julian was uncharacteristically quiet as they walked, and she noticed how sad he looked now that the adrenaline rush of the broadcast was over. 'Penny for them,' she said, 'although I think I already know.'

He smiled. 'That transparent, eh? She must be so frightened, Josephine. How on earth must it feel to sit in a cell and know that there's nothing you can do? And he bloody asked for it. He treated her abominably.'

'And Millicent Gray?'

'As I said, I don't believe Viv did that for a moment. It could have been anyone.'

'Can I ask you a personal question?'

'They're the only sort worth asking.'

'Were you and Viv ever more than friends?'

He hesitated. 'I'm not sure how to answer that truthfully. I think I've always been a little in love with her, and there was a time when I thought she felt the same, but it was soon over. It's always been Anthony for her. God knows why, but it has. You don't shoot someone out of indifference, do you?'

'No, you don't.' The building was unusually silent now, as if keeping secrets of its own, and Josephine was pleased to be leaving it behind. She said goodnight to Julian and walked out into the evening air, scarcely knowing how to feel but longing to talk to Marta. There was a telephone box in Regent Street and she gave the operator the number for Holly Place. As she looked back, the white stone of Broadcasting House shone gloriously against the moon, a lighthouse of sorts amid the sea of London traffic, and she wondered how much of its magic was down to her mood. She waited impatiently for Marta's voice on the line but there was no answer, so she decided to go back to the Cowdray Club and try again from there.

The peace of Cavendish Square was a welcome contrast to Oxford Street, where crowds still flocked to see the coronation lights, and she headed gratefully for the sanctuary of number 20. 'Josephine?' The voice was hesitant and came from across the street, where Marta stood in the shadows by the iron railings. 'You're back early. I'd settled in for a longer wait.'

'I had a call to make, but she wasn't in.' Marta smiled, and Josephine walked over to join her. 'This isn't the first time I've found you waiting out here in the dark. A lot's happened since.'

'I know it has, but it feels just like the first time. I wasn't quite sure of my welcome then, either.'

'You're very welcome. I've wanted you from the moment I left you.'

'Good.' She held out her hand, and Josephine took the flower that was offered, a single briar rose with deep-pink petals. 'It's called Mary Queen of Scots. I've been growing it for you. I thought all this bloody rain would kill it, but it seems to have survived. I hope that's a good sign.'

'It's beautiful. No one's ever grown flowers for me before.'

'It's supposed to dissolve feuds, apparently, but I didn't know quite how relevant that would be when I planted it.'

'There is no feud,' Josephine said gently. 'How can there be? You're planting roses for me.' She paused and took Marta's hand. 'You're selling your house for me.'

'Ah, Lydia told you.'

'Yes, but you don't have to do that. You love that house. Don't do something you'll regret on the spur of the moment just because I've had a tantrum.'

'It's not on the spur of the moment. I'd already decided to do it, but you didn't give me the chance to tell you.'

'I'm sorry.'

'Don't be. You were right, and there'll be other houses to love. Anyway, that's not important. You are.' Josephine held her close, feeling an irresistible mixture of relief and desire in their embrace. 'Will you come back with me now? We could try and have the evening we were supposed to have yesterday.'

'I'd love to, but only if you're offering cold cuts for supper. You'll never sell if you keep cooking. The kitchen simply won't withstand it.'

'Nothing more ambitious than an omelette, I promise.' She laughed softly in the darkness and Josephine shivered as she felt

Marta's hand move down her back. 'Come on – let's find a cab.'

'I'll call one from the club. It'll be quicker.'

They went inside and ordered a taxi to Hampstead. 'He'll be five minutes,' the receptionist promised, 'and there's a note for you.'

Josephine thanked her and took the envelope. 'What is it?' Marta asked, seeing the look on her face as she opened it.

'It's from Archie,' Josephine said. 'Vivienne Beresford wants to see me.'

6

By Friday morning, Penrose felt like a naughty child for whom harmless distractions had to be found. The royal visit to the suburbs had kept him busy for most of Thursday afternoon, as Londoners eagerly reprised the celebrations of the day before, their appetite for the new reign apparently nowhere near as jaded as his own. Once again, roads were impassable, but this time without the formality and resources of coronation day itself: perspiring police struggled to clear the way, while small boys jumped on the running board and people stared in disbelief at the sight of their king and queen in ordinary residential streets, admiring the decorations that had been raised in their honour. Later that night, the massed drums and pipers of the Brigade of Guards beat the Tattoo in Horse Guard's Parade, and thousands gathered to witness the moving, floodlit spectacle. Penrose's presence was still mysteriously vital to the royal couple, so much so that he was beginning to feel that he knew them personally. And now, just when his bosses were running out of ideas and royal occasions, someone had obliged them by finding a woman's body in the cellar of an Islington furniture store. Rygate had sounded almost jubilant at the prospect of an engrossing murder that had nothing to do with the BBC, and with Vivienne Beresford due to make her first appearance in court at any minute, things were almost back to normal.

'What do we know about this one?' Penrose asked as Fallowfield drove them through Clerkenwell.

'She was found this morning by the manager – Mr Pollock – and one of his employees. The shop's closed for the coronation holiday, so no one's been around for a few days. The victim's in her forties, and we think she's a local woman called Rosina Field – she lived round the corner from the shop in Duncan Terrace.'

'Someone's identified her?'

'Not officially, no, but the local bobby recognised her. She was a familiar face on the streets and in the pubs, and lots of men round there knew her *very* well.' Fallowfield didn't have to be any more specific for Penrose to guess at the sort of crime that awaited them, and it was the sort that depressed him most, not least because it was so common. He had no idea how many murdered prostitutes he had seen in his career, but he never became immune to the senseless, squalid nature of their deaths, born naturally out of areas such as this with highly populated slums and dreary streets, areas that cried out for open spaces between the shabby blocks of buildings. 'Spilsbury's already there, sir,' Fallowfield added, and Penrose nodded.

Harding's Furniture Manufacturers occupied a large premises on Islington Green, and the windows on the ground floor revealed a confused mixture of shop and warehouse space. A small group of people had gathered on the pavement outside, and after the fuss over Beresford's murder, Penrose was gratified to know that the death of an ordinary person could also draw a crowd. He opened the door, conscious of the faces peering over his shoulder, and the shop bell rang needlessly to mark his arrival. Three people – two men and a woman – sat at one of the firm's dining-room tables, the centrepiece of its showroom. In different circumstances, they might have been a happy family group, proof of the domestic bliss which Harding's furniture no doubt guaranteed; today, they looked absurdly out of place. Penrose introduced himself and refused the offer of tea. 'What brought you all here today if the shop was meant to be closed?' he asked, addressing his questions to the manager.

'It was Stan. He got this note, see, so we came straight away to see what it meant.'

Penrose turned to the younger man, who cleared his throat nervously. 'Who are you, sir?'

'Stanley Witon. I'm one of the salesmen.'

The last word was spoken with pride, and Penrose guessed that Stanley was new to the firm. He held out his hand in an awkwardly formal gesture; the skin was clammy, the grip weak, and Penrose had to resist the temptation to wipe his hand on his trousers. 'Can I see the note?' Stanley looked at his boss, and Pollock slid a piece of paper across the table. The handwriting was poor, and Penrose looked curiously down at a single, bold declaration: *I don't know anything about this woman getting into the cellar.* 'How did you get this?' he asked.

'Fred gave it to me in the pub last night.'

'Last night? Why did you wait until this morning to do something about it?'

Stanley flushed and looked uncomfortable. 'I was a bit worse for wear, sir, and I didn't want Mr Pollock to think I made a habit of it.'

'Nothing wrong with a drink for the King, lad,' Pollock said reassuringly.

'Anyway, I thought it was a joke at first, but I told Mr Pollock this morning and he said we'd better check.'

'And who is Fred?'

Pollock stepped in again. 'Frederick Murphy. He's the odd-job man – cleaning, deliveries, that sort of thing.'

'Is this his writing?' Pollock and Witon nodded in unison. 'There's been no sign of him today, I suppose?'

'No, but I can give you an address for him. He lives in Colebrooke Row.'

'What number, sir?' Fallowfield asked.

'Fifty-seven.'

The sergeant thanked him and left the shop, taking one of the uniformed constables with him. Penrose turned back to Pollock. 'Tell me what happened when you got here today.'

197

'We went straight down to the cellar. We couldn't see anything at first, and we were just about to give up when Stan found her.'

'She was hidden, you see,' Stan said, growing in confidence now and keen not to have his moment of glory snatched from under him. 'Even then we weren't sure. It was hard to tell what we were looking at.'

'What do you mean?'

'Someone had wrapped her up in paper.'

'Paper?' Penrose repeated, finding it hard to believe what he had heard.

'Yes. We use it for deliveries.'

The paper's usual function hadn't been the issue, but Penrose moved on. 'Did you touch the body?'

Stanley hesitated. 'Not really.'

'Yes or no? It's important.'

'Well, we pulled the paper back from her face, just enough to know we couldn't help. Then Mr Pollock told me to go and find a policeman while he stayed with her.'

'Thank you,' Penrose said, standing up. 'Now, perhaps one of you could show me the cellar? I believe my colleague's already here.'

Pollock did as he was asked and Penrose made his way downstairs. The basement was bigger than he had expected, but low ceilings and feeble lighting made it cramped and claustrophobic. Part workshop, part storeroom, it smelt of freshly sawn wood. A police photographer had finished his initial work and stood patiently to one side while Spilsbury knelt awkwardly in the far corner of the room. He was a tall man – well over six feet – and his presence gave the space a strange, lilliputian air. 'You won't have seen one like this before, Archie,' he said without looking up. 'It's not often we're presented with a body that's been gift-wrapped.' Penrose could see nothing from where he stood and he moved closer, listening to the soft rustle of wood shavings underfoot, the sound of a forest in autumn. Rosina Field's body had been hidden behind a large tin trunk, squashed into a tiny space between the trunk and the wall, and all but obscured by a pile of wood. As Witon had described, she was wrapped tightly in thick brown paper torn from one of the rolls that leant against the wall – mummified, Penrose might have said, were it not for the complete absence of dignity and respect. Spilsbury had cut more of the paper away now and Penrose looked down at the dead woman's bruised and swollen face, at the scattering of blue-and-purple fingermarks on her neck. 'She's been dead less than forty-eight hours,' the pathologist said. 'She was strangled, obviously, but not before she'd taken a hell of a beating.'

Dark bloodstains on the collar and lapels of Rosina Field's blue wool coat underlined his words. 'Can you say if she was killed here?' Penrose asked.

'Almost certainly yes. There's blood on the floor and wall over there which would be consistent with the injuries.'

Fleetingly, Penrose closed his eyes, allowing the last horrific moments of the woman's life to play themselves out in his imagination. 'What a waste,' he said quietly, speaking as much to her as to his colleague. He watched the pathologist work for a while, wondering if the care and respect with which he handled her body was something that Rosina Field had ever known in life. The paper and the attempt to conceal the corpse jarred with the peculiar note that Witon had been given; why would Murphy draw attention to the body if he had gone to such lengths to hide it? Perhaps he had simply found Rosina Field and written the note as a defence against any accusations that might come his way. He explained the situation to Spilsbury, knowing that any thoughts he had would be interesting.

'Frederick Murphy, you say?'

'Yes, why?'

'Do you remember Katherine Peck?'

The name was familiar to Penrose, but he wasn't surprised that Spilsbury's encyclopaedic memory had him at a disadvantage. 'Remind me.'

'It was 1929, found in Flint Street with her throat cut,' the pathologist said, reeling the details off as if he were reading them straight from his record cards. 'A chap called Frederick Murphy had been seen drinking with her, and later that night he told two men that he'd killed her, but he denied it to the police when they reported him. He was charged, but one of the men subsequently disappeared and there was insufficient evidence for conviction in the one remaining testimony, so he got away with it.'

Penrose recalled the case, although it had not been one of his. 'It's not necessarily the same man,' he said cautiously. 'Murphy's a common enough name, and people don't usually cut a throat one day and strangle the next.'

'That's true, but there's no rule book,' Spilsbury pointed out, using the same measured, non-judgemental tone that made him such a devastating expert witness. 'I wouldn't be at all surprised if this *did* turn out to be him, Archie. Men like Murphy prey on women. They use them when they're alive, and they're not too fussy how they get rid of them.'

'You don't doubt he did it, then? The first murder, I mean.'

'Of course he did it.' Spilsbury paused in his work for a moment and looked up at Penrose with a steely smile. 'I hope it *is* the same man. I'd rather like a second chance at him.'

'It's not like you to take a case so personally,' Penrose said. Spilsbury was known for his fair-mindedness and his absolute devotion to the scientific facts, and he rarely allowed his own opinions to blur any conversation.

'You know as well as I do, Archie – glamorous cases like Anthony Beresford get the headlines, but our work is mostly this. They might not get the public outrage, but it's nice when they get justice.'

'Speaking of Anthony Beresford, are you absolutely sure about the time of death for Millicent Gray?' The pathologist gave Penrose a wry smile. 'What's that for?'

'I've been warned not to indulge you, Archie.'

'No prizes for guessing by whom. But I don't think Vivienne Beresford killed her, Bernard.' He returned the smile in kind. 'So you'd be indulging justice, not me.'

'Either way, I'm afraid I can't help. There's nothing to complicate the time of death, and I haven't seen anything to suggest that Vivienne Beresford *couldn't* have done it. Whether she did or not is a different matter, I agree. Can I ask why you're so convinced?'

'She doesn't strike me as a liar,' Penrose said. 'It's as simple as that. She's been absolutely honest about how and why she killed her husband, and I don't see why she'd behave differently with Millicent Gray. The evidence is largely circumstantial, and it won't be that which convicts her anyway. It'll be all the stuff in the papers – you can rely on the press to paint it blacker than it is. Beresford was a saint in most people's eyes, and his infidelity won't do him any harm. The men will cheer him on and the women will simply wish they'd been the one who tempted him to stray.'

'What a cynical view you have of the world,' Spilsbury said, standing up to allow the photographer a different angle on the body. 'I can't think why.'

'And if that isn't enough, they're dredging up all the scandals associated with her sister when she had nothing whatsoever to do with those.'

'That isn't strictly true,' Spilsbury said, and Penrose looked at him in surprise. 'She worked at the Golden Hat for a while. Didn't you know?'

'No, I didn't. Are you sure?'

'Positive. There was some trouble over a girl who died after leaving the club one night. Her fiancé broke it off, so she went home to her flat, drank cocaine in water, and died of convulsions shortly afterwards. There was no direct link to the Golden Hat other than her being there, and Vivienne Beresford – or Hanlon, as she was then – gave evidence to that effect at the inquest. Thinking about it, it must have been before your time – or shortly after you joined the force, anyway.'

'Nobody mentioned that when Olivia Hanlon died. Beresford led me to believe that his wife had nothing to do with it.'

'Yes, I expect he did. But if you recall, there wasn't much mention of *anything* when Olivia Hanlon died.'

'You weren't involved, were you?'

'Not officially, no, but I've cleaned up plenty of Miss Hanlon's messes in my time – hers, and others like her. Those clubs were a breeding ground for pimps and drug-peddlers, and it's women like Miss Field here who pay the price eventually.'

Again, Spilsbury's strident tone was uncharacteristic and it surprised Penrose. 'There's an element of that,' he said, 'but you could also argue that people like Olivia Hanlon and Kate Meyrick kept the girls off the streets by giving them somewhere safe to do what they would have done anyway.'

'You could argue that, but I choose not to. Freda Kempton, Nora Upchurch, Beatrice Sutton, Dora Lloyd, Katherine Peck – need I go on? It's like every other profession, Archie. The hard ones survive. The rest do what they can, and end up with people like Frederick Murphy.'

As if in response, Fallowfield appeared at the top of the cellar steps. 'Any luck?' Penrose asked.

'I'm afraid not, sir. The woman he lives with hasn't seen him since last night. She knew about the body, though. Murphy told her the same story – said he'd found it, but he didn't kill her.'

'All right. I want a full search of the pubs and coffee stalls tonight – as far afield as you can get the manpower for. Did you get a good description?'

'Better than that, sir. She gave me this, and I got the impression that she wouldn't be sorry to see the back of him.'

Penrose took the photograph and looked down at the ravaged face of a man in his fifties, thickset and unattractive. He showed the picture to Spilsbury. 'Is that your Frederick Murphy?'

'Oh yes,' the pathologist said instantly. 'Do find him quickly, Archie. I'll look forward to seeing him again.'

7

The court appearance was over so quickly that Vivienne half-believed she had dreamt it. There was very little that she remembered clearly, just a series of fleeting impressions. The sudden shaft of light as she emerged from a dark passage into the courtroom. The cool, polished wood which steadied her as she stood in front of the magistrate. The buzz of conversation from the public gallery, and – as she was led away – the woman who screamed at her for what she had done. It seemed wrong that a stranger could care so much for Anthony, when she – his wife for ten years – felt so little; it made her wonder what sort of person she was, and that was a question to which she had no answer.

She rubbed her ankle where she had twisted it, stumbling as she climbed the steps to the dark-blue prison van. They were loaded on like cattle, she and the other women, and the vehicle was cramped and awkward inside – five locked compartments on either side of a central corridor, each scarcely big enough to hold a prisoner and her shame, with a police matron watching for trouble from a seat at the end. Vivienne's shoulders bumped against the walls whenever the van lurched to left or right, and she had to put a hand flat to the door to prevent herself from being flung forward as it braked. Above her, through a small grille, she could see a single, inadequate ventilation shaft; the fan went round whenever the vehicle was moving but still there was no air, and the stuffiness made her feel sick and dizzy. She breathed deeply, trying to get some sense of the distance they had travelled or the direction in which they were moving, but it was impossible; without windows, and coloured by the uncertainty of what lay ahead, the journey was bewildering.

The punishment had begun even before they reached Holloway, she thought. There would be no final glimpse of freedom, no brief connection with an ordinary London day.

The Black Maria slowed down again, and this time she heard voices and the sound of gates being opened and closed. The van swung sharply to the right, then drew to a halt, and the engine fell silent. As soon as the doors were unlocked, it was obvious that some of the women were already familiar with prison routine; they led the way confidently to a small waiting room signposted reception, leaving Vivienne and the other first-timers to trail along behind. A policeman handed a pile of paperwork to the woman behind the desk, and Vivienne took a good look at her fellow inmates while they waited for instructions, guessing at the stories that had brought them here. She was surprised by how unremarkable they seemed – different ages and different classes, some with harder lives than others, but the sort of group that might be seen at any bus stop or in any post-office queue.

'C of E?'

The voice came again and Vivienne realised that the woman behind the desk was addressing her. 'I'm sorry?'

'I need your religion. Are you Church of England?'

Vivienne couldn't think of a time when religion had seemed less relevant, but the option she had been offered was as good as any and she nodded. In return, she was handed a white identity card, and she noticed that there were only two other options – red for Catholicism and blue for the Jewish faith. Prison life obviously had no room for subtleties, and she wondered what would have happened if she'd been a Moslem or a Christian Scientist.

'Date of birth?'

'Ninth of October, 1899.'

'And next of kin?'

She paused, genuinely at a loss for an answer. 'I'm sorry,' she said eventually. 'I don't have anyone.'

'You should have thought of that before you killed him.' Vivienne heard the comment clearly, as she had been meant to. She looked round, but the other prisoners simply stared back at her and it was impossible to say who had spoken. Shaken, she answered the rest of the questions as quietly as possible and allowed herself to be led upstairs to a larger room with a glass roof and a number of small cubicles. Each had a wooden seat and a couple of hooks for clothes, like the changing rooms at a swimming baths, except here the locks were on the outside. She was given a torn old copy of an illustrated weekly to read, and told to wait. The walls were as thin as the paper in her hand, and she could hear every sound around her – the cheerful singing of the drunk next door, the tears of a young girl who had stolen a dress in a moment of madness and didn't understand that a promise to return it was no longer enough. One hour passed, then two, and just as she thought they had forgotten her, the cubicle door was unlocked.

They took her to an office and told her to remove all her jewellery except her wedding ring. When she discarded that, too, and slid it across the desk with her necklace and earrings, they looked at her curiously but said nothing. Her handbag was emptied in front of her, tipped roughly upside down so that the contents spilled out onto the table: lipstick and perfume, loose coins, handkerchief, stamps, pen and paper – a universal language among women. A nurse inspected her for headlice, then she was made to stand behind a three-leaf screen and remove her clothes, item by item, while a prison officer watched her. She closed her eyes while they examined her again, defenceless and exposed as a stranger's hands explored her body, then she was weighed and measured and given a shapeless grey dressing gown, rough like a shroud, and a pair of felt slippers which were far too big and made her shuffle like an old woman. They took her to the bathroom, and the wave of nausea came again as she saw the small, cracked bar of soap and imagined whose hands it had touched; she washed without it, but still it felt as though she were rubbing the dirt *into* her skin, and she wondered if she would ever feel clean again.

They let her keep her own clothes, then took her to the hospital wing, which made no sense because she wasn't ill. The ward had half a dozen beds in it, placed so close together that there was barely room for a small wooden cupboard next to each. At one end, obscuring most of a depressing brown linoleum floor, stood a long scrubbed table, obviously for communal eating, and Vivienne realised that the lack of privacy she had experienced so far was nothing compared to this. From now on, she would never be alone. She sat down on the bed she was given, trying not to meet anybody's eye, aware that the other women were staring at her with a mixture of curiosity and contempt. In the distance, she heard a baby's cry, alien and unsettling in these surroundings, and it shocked her to realise that a child could be born into a place like this.

She drank some tea, dark and unbearably strong, but refused the bread and margarine which was served to her at the table. A doctor bombarded her with questions and she gave him the answers she thought he wanted, then she was escorted to the lavatory and made to change into her night things, ready for bed. All evening, she did as she was told, despising her own meekness. No one had bossed her around since Olivia died, not even Anthony, and all the resentment of youth came flooding back to her. Now, like then, she was trapped, and later – when she closed her eyes and tried to sleep – it was her sister's face, not Anthony's, that she saw, goading her again just as she had when she was alive, taunting her with the memory of what she had done, and reminding her that it was never too late to pay.

Part Five

The Wild Party

Josephine lay in bed and listened to the rain, brave enough with Marta beside her to consider what Vivienne Beresford might want. They had only met twice, and although the second conversation had been frank and confiding, she didn't understand how she could be of any use to Vivienne now. In the normal scheme of things, they might have become friends; after what had happened, she doubted they would be given the chance.

'Is there any point in my telling you to be careful?' Marta murmured sleepily into her hair.

'I didn't know you were awake.'

'I'm not.' Josephine smiled and hooked her foot round Marta's, bringing them closer together. 'When will you go to see her?'

'I'm still deciding whether or not I should go at all. What do you think?'

'Selfishly, I'd rather you didn't, because I know it will upset you. But I also know that you'll never forgive yourself if you don't, just in case you could have helped.'

'I don't see how I *can* help. I don't even know what she wants.'

'Then that's reason in itself to go. You'll always be wondering if you don't.' Marta sat up and reached over to the chair by the bed for a dressing gown. 'And I've been in her position, so I can guess what she wants – someone to talk to who isn't going to judge her, someone she doesn't know very well so she can say what she likes, and – most importantly – someone who isn't part of that system.' She thought for a moment, then added: 'It's hard to explain, but the minute you step into a prison . . . actually, even before that – the minute you're charged with something, you lose sight of who you are. You're no longer a human being, because you're defined by what you've done, not by how you feel. There's no room for emotion in that system, even though emotion is what put you there – for most people, anyway. Everything is about the process of justice, and everyone you meet is tied up with that on one side or the other – police, lawyers, prison officers, doctors. It's relentless and you just want it to stop, but it never does, so the best you can hope for is that someone will occasionally remind you of who you were before the nightmare started.'

'I wish I'd been there for you,' Josephine said quietly, taking her hand.

'You tried, but I wouldn't let you.'

'I know, and I never quite understood why.'

'Because I couldn't let you in. Things were bad enough, but to leave this world loving you would have been unbearable.' Gently, she wiped away a tear from Josephine's cheek. 'Go and see her, but promise me you'll try not to get too involved – there's only one way that this can end, and I don't want you destroyed by it.'

'I won't let that happen, I promise.'

'Do you want me to come with you?'

'No,' Josephine said, knowing how much courage it had taken for Marta even to make the offer, and loving her all the more for it. 'You don't have to do that. Just be here when I come back.'

2

Josephine had been to Holloway once before while researching a book, but the personal nature of this visit made the prison's peculiar atmosphere of order and despair even more oppressive than she remembered it. She waited nervously in the deputy governor's comfortable, book-lined sitting room, pleased at least that there would be one familiar face to greet her: Mary Size was a fellow member of the Cowdray Club, and Josephine had been grateful in the past for her wisdom and understanding. She was a compassionate woman, dedicated to reform in all areas of prison life, and if any of the women in her care could be said to be lucky, their fortune lay in the woman who governed their days.

'Josephine! I'm so sorry to have kept you waiting.'

'Please don't worry,' Josephine said, kissing the deputy governor on both cheeks and brushing aside the apology. 'I appreciate your finding the time to see me at all. I know how busy you are.'

'Oh, it's always a pleasure, and in this particular case I was glad to get your call. Mrs Beresford needs a friend and I'm sure you'll do her the power of good. But first things first – how are you?'

She sat down on the sofa, every inch the favourite aunt, and Josephine marvelled again that this kind, softly spoken woman should have earned herself such a formidable reputation, the scourge of the Home Office and of anyone else who resisted progress. 'I'm fine, thank you. Recovering from the Coronation like the rest of the country.'

'Wasn't it marvellous? And how is Marta?'

The soft Irish inflection in her voice gave the name an extra warmth. 'Very well. She's working for the Hitchcocks at the moment, and thoroughly enjoying it.'

'Ah, that must be glamorous.'

'I'm not so sure about that. She loves the scriptwriting, but there's a lot of mucking in involved. I believe one of her most recent tasks was to fetch more fish from Newlyn for some particularly un-obliging seagulls.'

Mary Size threw back her head and laughed. 'Oh well, no job is perfect. Give her my best when you see her.'

'I will.'

'Now, you probably have some questions before we take you along to the hospital wing.'

'The hospital wing? Has something happened?'

'No, no, nothing like that. It's confusing to an outsider, but every woman on remand for murder is sent to the hospital wing for observation, no matter how sane or well she is. In Beresford's case, it's as well that we keep an eye on her. Her story comes with a certain amount of notoriety, obviously, but the strength of feeling against her surprises me, I have to say. The other women are usually kinder to newcomers, but they've given her a particularly difficult time from the moment she arrived.'

'And how is she coping with that?'

'To be honest, not very well. I think it bewilders her.'

It would be nothing compared to the hostility she would ex-perience in court, Josephine thought. The newspapers had already made a martyr of her husband; when they named the woman charged with his murder, Vivienne Beresford could wave goodbye to any chance of sympathy or even justice. 'I have no idea why she wants to see me,' Josephine admitted. 'We've only met twice.'

'And yet you came. Perhaps that answers your question. Mutual respect counts for a lot, especially in prison.'

Josephine nodded. 'Yes, I imagine it does. Has she seen anyone else?'

'Only her solicitor. I've arranged for you to have a private room just off the ward. Technically speaking, you should be an official prison visitor to enjoy a privilege like that.' She smiled, and there was a twinkle in her eye as she added: 'But I haven't given up hope of persuading you to devote some of your time to prison reform. Think of this as a trial run.'

Josephine's heart sank at the thought of spending time at Holloway voluntarily, but she tried not to let it show 'Thank you, Mary. I'll give it some thought.' She stood up, keen now to get on with an experience she was dreading. 'How long can we have?'

'An hour. But you're welcome to come back another day. Remand visiting is at six, and I don't envisage a queue for Beresford – not for the right reasons, anyway. I'll get someone to take you over there now, but if there's anything else you need from me, Josephine, please ask.'

The warder summoned to escort her was young and full of energy, and Josephine wondered what had attracted her to such a desperate vocation, but there was no time to ask. The hospital complex was on the ground floor, quickly reached down a wide stone passage, and Josephine noticed that the smell of the building changed as soon as they left the main wings behind – disinfectant masked the mixture of sweat and hopelessness, but did not entirely hide it. Unsettled by a glimpse of padded cells and a lavatory marked with a red cross, she tried not to look to left or right but focused instead on her guide. They walked up some steps and past a large room which looked to all intents and purposes like a normal hospital ward – except that the nurses' uniforms were interspersed here and there with those of prison officers – before arriving at the room that Mary Size had allocated.

It was hard to regard it as a privilege. The space was tiny, barely larger than a cupboard, and furnished with two upright chairs and a scuffed wooden table. There was a small window high up in the wall, but it seemed stubbornly reluctant to let any light in, and Josephine sat down as invited on the chair that faced the door, trying to think of another room that had depressed her as much as this one. She waited a long time – at least, that was how it felt – but eventually there was a noise in the corridor outside and Vivienne Beresford appeared without announcement or ceremony in the doorway. She was wearing her own clothes, but that only served to emphasise how much she had changed in just a few days. It wasn't simply the loss of weight or the shadows under her eyes; she looked haunted, detached somehow from the present moment, and isolated by fear and grief; her expression – or rather the lack of it – was familiar to Josephine but she had never seen it in a woman before, only in a man returned from war. Images of Vivienne as she had been ran through her head – teasing Julian in the BBC canteen, walking out through the foyer with her husband, her head held high in spite of the embarrassment to which she had just been subjected – and she realised now what a strong impression Vivienne had made on her. Marta had been right to warn her, but the damage was done; she already felt involved.

The warder left them alone but her face appeared immediately at the square opening cut into the door. 'She won't go,' Vivienne said, following Josephine's eyes. 'There's always someone watching. I lie in bed at night, longing for the lights to go out, but they never do – not completely.' She sat down and gave Josephine an awkward half-smile. 'Thank you for coming. I wasn't sure if you would.'

'Neither was I at first. How are you?'

She ignored the question, perhaps because she wasn't listening, perhaps because the answer was so painfully obvious. 'Did you know there are children in here?' Josephine shook her head, un-settled by the disjointed conversation. 'They play in the garden when it's fine and we all know their names. Sometimes a woman walks down the corridor with a toddler in a pink romper suit, and they all cluck and coo like they would in the street.' Her words were distant and distracted, almost as if it were Josephine who had called for the meeting, and she was simply waiting for her to get to the point. 'Strange, isn't it? Just for a moment, they can block out the ugliness and pretend that this is normal.' Her voice cracked on the final word and Josephine waited for her to compose herself. 'I don't seem to be able to manage that yet. I wonder if that makes me stronger or weaker than they are?'

'I'm not sure you should be judging yourself in that way. Aren't there enough people doing that already?' Josephine took a cigarette case out of her bag and slid it across the table, where it sat untouched. 'It's easy to lose all sense of who you are when someone else decides your every move. I imagine you wonder who she is, this woman walking round in your body.' There was a flicker of surprise in Vivienne's eyes, followed swiftly by gratitude for a small moment of understanding, and Josephine could see how significant Marta's words had been.

'I think I'm going mad, Josephine. And my God, you were right – it's so much worse to be accused of something you haven't done. I knew I'd pay for what I did to Anthony, and it's right that I should – but not this as well.' She hesitated, then looked directly at Josephine for the first time. 'I didn't kill her. Do you believe me?'

Even now, she couldn't bring herself to speak the actress's name. 'Yes,' Josephine said quietly. 'I believe you.' The question had been a test, but it was Vivienne who seemed relieved that she had passed. She took a cigarette from the case and Josephine lit it for her. 'What does your solicitor say?'

'That I should plead guilty to everything and throw myself on the mercy of the jury in the hope that they'll ask for leniency. He's a fool, obviously.' She pulled back the sleeve of her blouse, and Josephine looked in horror at the ring of purple bruises around her wrist. 'The woman who did that is serving six years for beating her toddler within an inch of his life, but she was a big fan of my husband's. What hope do I stand with a jury of decent people if someone like that feels morally superior?' She re-buttoned the sleeve, wincing at the tenderness of the skin. 'If we were in France

I'd be sent flowers, but the English hate a *crime passionnel* – look at Edith Thompson. They didn't waste much time here in showing me her grave.'

'Is that what it was? A crime of passion? Forgive me if I'm speaking out of turn, but there didn't seem to be much of that involved in your marriage.'

'No, that's what my lawyer said. He seemed very disappointed that Anthony didn't hit me, or at least that I won't pretend he did. The best advice he could give was to prepare for a long haul. Murder trials can go on for some time, apparently, and I doubt this one will be short of coverage.' She stubbed the cigarette out and took another, acknowledging the action with a wry smile. 'I don't even smoke, but obviously that other woman does. They always used to tease me about it in the office. My puritanical streak, they called it.' The ordinariness of the memory stopped her in her tracks for a moment. 'It's funny, Josephine, but I feel so let down by the Corporation. I think that hurts even more than Anthony's betrayals – I'd got used to those over the years. I should have known they'd turn against me and take his side, I suppose, but it still hurts.'

'Not everyone's the same. Julian still believes in you.'

'That's sweet of him, but I meant the organisation. We all feel it, you know – that sense of pride in being part of something truly extraordinary. We bitch about the way it's run and the vanity of the broadcasters and the aloofness of the controllers, but we wouldn't have a word said against the BBC by anyone on the outside. And that's where I am now – on the outside. I miss it already. A sense of pride in one's work is quite unusual in my family. I suppose someone's told you by now what my maiden name was.'

'Yes,' Josephine admitted. 'Several people. In fact, one of them reminded me only the other night that I have your sister to thank for one of my most – or least – memorable birthdays.'

'Oh, Olivia certainly knew how to throw a party.' It was hard to say if the edge in her voice was scorn or bitterness. 'That's where

I met Anthony, you know. I was working in one of her clubs – off the Strand, not the Golden Hat. He used to come in with some friends after work. Eventually, he suggested that I went for a secretarial job at Savoy Hill. He knew I wasn't happy at the club, so he put a good word in for me. Neither of us realised how much I'd love it. It rather backfired on him, I suppose – he thought he was giving me respectability until we married, and instead he gave me a career that I wasn't prepared to sacrifice, for him or for anybody else.'

The idea of Anthony Beresford setting himself up as broadcasting's very own Henry Higgins hardly endeared him to Josephine. 'It's good to know that respectability was so important to him,' she said. 'At least on the surface.'

Vivienne smiled. 'It never really worked. The friends he wanted to impress – the ones who were happy to drink with me in the club – never accepted me, even after we were married. But it was different with people who didn't know what I'd done before. I never found it hard to earn their respect, not until now.'

'Did you love him?'

'Always. I loved him so much that it was very easy to hate him when the time came.'

Her words echoed Julian's, and Josephine wondered how soon in the marriage the transition had been made. 'When did you find out that he was having an affair?' she asked.

'The first time? Almost immediately. We'd only been married a few weeks.'

'Did he know?'

'Oh yes, I couldn't hide that sort of anger. When you first find out, it feels as though someone has kicked you in the stomach. You worry about the most ridiculous things – do they talk about me in bed? Are they laughing behind my back? But that passes, and what you're left with is doubt. You don't trust anyone from that moment on. No one is who they say they are, and the only thing you have to hold onto is that no one will ever hurt you like that again.'

'But he did.'

She thought about it. 'No, not really. Not in that extreme, all-consuming way. He was never faithful, but I stopped expecting him to be, and our marriage became merely dull rather than painful. I doubt we were unique in that.'

'Something must have changed, though. What you've done now might not be unique, but it *is* extreme. How long had you been planning it?'

Again, she considered the question. 'There isn't an easy answer to that. The when and the how was quite recent, but I don't think I can say when an inclination to do it became an intention. It crept up on me gradually, I suppose. I used to find myself imagining life without Anthony – I'd picture myself alone in the house, or in a different house that he'd never known, and eventually I was brave enough to admit that I'd prefer it that way. I'd fantasise about his having an accident – something quick, I never wanted him to suffer – and I realised how little grief I'd feel. Then guilt would get the better of me and I'd picture him as an old man, as if that could outweigh all the wicked thoughts. But that image of us together in ten years or twenty – well, it became less convincing each time.'

'There must have been a catalyst, though.'

'I discovered that he was going to leave me. He'd resigned from the BBC, and they were going to Canada. They must have been planning it for weeks, and I didn't have the faintest idea.' Already, Josephine had a hundred questions, but she wanted to let Vivienne finish her story before interrupting again. 'It was so strange, that moment. I felt as if I were standing outside myself, watching, while Anthony was shot. It was like a film, and there was nothing I could do to stop it. Even now, it doesn't seem real.'

'Did you ask Anthony about his plans?'

'No. I couldn't bear the lies.'

'But you're sure he was going away with Millicent Gray?'

'Of course I am. Why?'

'It's just that she was engaged on several different productions over the coming months. She was making plans, and that doesn't sound to me like a woman who was about to head out for a new life in Canada.'

'I found the tickets, Josephine. What are you trying to say? That one of them wasn't for her?'

Her voice was angry and insistent now, and for a moment Josephine's faith was shaken; if Vivienne *had* killed Millicent, the thought that she had done so unnecessarily would naturally horrify her. 'Was Anthony away from home much?'

'Yes, quite often. He'd disappear for two or three days at a time, usually at weekends, but not always.'

'There was no trace of him in that flat, Vivienne. If he'd spent that much time there, surely he'd have left something behind?'

'How do you know there was nothing?'

'I found Millicent's body. Julian asked me to go and see her to talk about the play.'

Vivienne stared at her, genuinely shocked. 'I'm sorry. I had no idea. That must have been terrible for you.'

'It was. I'm not supposed to discuss it, and especially not with you, but I will tell you this – if I didn't know already, I would never have guessed from her flat that there was anything serious between Millicent and your husband, and the girl who lives upstairs told me that he was hardly ever there.' She hesitated, reluctant to deal another blow to a woman who could surely not take much more. 'She also said that Millicent thought she was being made a fool of. Is there a chance that Anthony might have met somebody else?' Before Vivienne could say anything, they heard the sound of keys in the door and the warder appeared again. 'Five minutes, ladies.' Josephine nodded, keen to dismiss her and make the most of their remaining time. 'Well?' she asked, her impatience getting the better of her. 'You said there was something different about him, a sense of resolution. Could it have been that?'

'I don't know, Josephine. I have no idea what to think anymore. What does it matter, anyway? It's too late now to put things right.'

'Who do you think killed Millicent? Could it have been Anthony?'

'Why would he do that?'

'Perhaps she was causing trouble for him. Perhaps Millicent wasn't as keen to let the affair go as he was.'

For the first time, a flicker of something like hope transformed Vivienne's face. 'Maybe that's why she wanted to see me.'

'What?'

'Millicent Gray. She left me a note at the BBC, asking me to visit her on Wednesday morning. I assumed that she was going to tell me what she and Anthony were planning, but perhaps she was actually going to tell me that someone had replaced us both. She would have had nothing left to lose, after all – if Anthony had betrayed her, why shouldn't she hurt him and me at the same time?'

'Was Anthony capable of murder?'

She thought for a long time, and Josephine looked anxiously towards the door, willing it not to open. 'I would never have said so before. He could be vain and self-centred, and he always put his own feelings first, but he was never violent – in thought or in deed. Looking back, I'm not sure I could honestly say that I ever heard him raise his voice, and that used to infuriate me.' In Josephine's experience, vanity and selfishness were just as indicative of a capacity to kill as a propensity for violence, and nothing she had heard convinced her that Anthony Beresford was out of the frame for his mistress's murder; if that were the case, a jury might be persuaded to take a very different view of his death – but she was getting ahead of herself, and Marta's words of warning sounded again in her head. 'But I really don't see how he had time to do it,' Vivienne continued. 'It was the most important day of his career, and pride would never have allowed him to risk that.' She sighed heavily, the hope fading already. 'Maybe they were just careful, Josephine.

Maybe that's why there was nothing of him in that flat. It's not as if he hadn't had plenty of practice at adultery.'

'So who did kill her, if it wasn't you and it wasn't Anthony? Can you think of anyone?' Vivienne shook her head. 'And it's not just the flat. It's something Millicent said to me about never being enough for the person you love.'

'I didn't know you knew her that well.'

'I didn't. It was just a collision of unfortunate circumstances.'

Vivienne looked at her curiously. 'Your glass house?'

'I really must learn not say anything to you if I want it forgotten.'

'Yours wouldn't be the only secret I'll take to my grave, and it's becoming an increasingly safe bet.' The attempt at a joke fell flat, and she spoke again, more seriously this time. 'Tell me about him. We've spent an hour turning my marriage inside out, and I can't help feeling at a disadvantage. Who is he?' Misunderstanding Josephine's hesitation, she added: 'I'm not in a position to be indiscreet, even if I wanted to be.' The door opened behind her, and she gave Josephine a wry smile. 'Saved by the bell.'

'Time's up,' the warder said, taking Vivienne by the arm. She flinched, but resisted a move towards the door and looked pleadingly at her visitor. 'Tell me next time. Please, Josephine – promise me you'll come back. It's helped so much to talk to you.'

Trying not to think about what Marta would say when she found out, and knowing how foolish she was being, Josephine nodded. 'Yes, I promise. Is there anything else you need?'

'Only some time to think about what you've told me, and that's something I seem to have plenty of at the moment.'

3

Hampstead was quiet on Sunday morning, its countrified peace contributing to a sense that London was finally getting back to normal. Even the weather seemed to have relaxed now that the pressure of the Coronation was over, and the tense grey skies of recent days were replaced by a powder-blue wash and feather-brushed clouds that refused to hurry. Josephine left Holly Place early, having no desire to be there when Lydia 'popped round to collect a few things'. The sound of bells filled the air, calling people to mass at St Mary's, and, as she passed the church's distinctive white facade, nestled among a row of Georgian houses, she realised that the crippling sense of panic which normally gripped her whenever she walked away from Marta was entirely absent. For the first time in the three years that they had known each other, she felt confident of their relationship, unrationed and unrestricted. For the first time, she felt normal.

Their evening had been all the more precious for coming so soon after her visit to Holloway. Despite Josephine's concerns, Marta seemed to understand her reluctance to abandon Vivienne Beresford to her fate; if anything, she understood it better than Josephine did herself. Compassion and a belief in justice only offered half an explanation, and in some strange way, Josephine's urge to help was connected to the situation she found herself in with Lydia – penance, perhaps, to one wronged woman for the guilt she felt over another. She found a taxi quickly in Hampstead High Street, and on the spur of the moment asked the driver to drop her in Wigmore Street rather than Cavendish Square. The chances of finding Effie and her friends at home on a Sunday were good, and she wanted to find out if they could remember anything else about Millicent's relationship with Anthony now that the immediate shock of her death had passed. By the time she visited Vivienne again, she hoped to have more to tell her.

The quadrangle was quiet, except for the strains of a violin which drifted down from the top floor of one of the other houses. Josephine glanced through the railings of number 4 and saw that the basement apartment appeared exactly as it had on Thursday, except that someone had left a bunch of tulips outside. She rang the bell and looked up, hoping that Effie might appear at the first-floor window, but this time the door was opened by another girl – dark-haired and slightly older, wearing an oriental dressing gown and brandishing a slice of toast. 'I'm sorry to disturb you on a Sunday,' Josephine said, 'but I was hoping to speak to Effie. I was here the other day, and . . .'

'Oh, was it you who found Millie?'

'Yes, it was.'

'Super! Come in. I'm Lou, and Effie's upstairs – we were just having breakfast and reading the papers. Isn't it extraordinary? Come up and have some coffee.'

Slightly overwhelmed by the welcome, Josephine followed Lou up the wide staircase to the first-floor landing, trying to remember if she was the girl who worked at Heal's or the untidy one with rich parents. When Effie saw who her visitor was, she greeted her as if they had known each other for years. 'We were just talking about you!' she said, after introducing Josephine to Vi. 'I wanted to get in touch, but I suddenly realised I had absolutely no idea of how to get hold of you. Sit down. I'll fetch another cup.'

Josephine took the one remaining chair, thinking of how much the flat reminded her of her own days in shared lodgings and boarding houses around the country. She was amused to see that the seat next to hers – the most comfortable one in the room – was now occupied by Millicent Gray's cat, who had made an elaborate nest for herself among discarded coronation bunting. The cat glared at her, as if daring her to change the seating arrangements, and Josephine leaned over to reassure her. 'I see someone's fallen on her feet,' she said.

'Betty? Yes, we had to take her in,' Vi said. 'She's missing Millie dreadfully, but we're trying to make it up to her.'

'You seem to be doing all right,' Josephine observed, looking at the piece of bacon on Betty's blanket. 'She doesn't look too traumatised.'

'I wish we could all get over it so quickly.' Effie put a tray of coffee and toast in front of Josephine and sat down on the floor. 'Her parents came the other day and it was just awful. They were devastated – her mother didn't stop crying the whole time they were here. She said the worst thing was having to break the news to Millie's brother. He had an accident a few years back and he nearly died. It was Millie who helped him pull through. But I'm rambling – you must know all that.'

'I can't believe that woman could kill them both,' Vi said with feeling. 'What had Millie ever done to her? Something must have been wrong at home if the bloke went sniffing round elsewhere, and that was hardly Millie's fault.'

'Some women are spiteful like that, though. They just hate other people to be happy. We've got plenty of them at work – miserable at home, so they take it out on everyone who isn't.' Lou gestured to the pile of papers on the floor, satisfied that the news bore out her shop-bought wisdom. 'It was obvious what was going to happen when you read it all in black and white. Millie just didn't know what she'd got herself into.'

Josephine looked down at the headlines, horrified. She had known that it wouldn't be long before Vivienne was named in the press, but even she could not have predicted the raft of vitriol that covered the front pages with varying degrees of subtlety. In most papers, the story of Anthony Beresford's murder ran over several columns, and many contrasted his glittering career at the BBC with his wife's 'scandal-ridden' past, focusing with delicious irrelevance on her family connection to the disgraced nightclub hostess who had died in mysterious circumstances. Josephine looked with interest at the photograph of Paradise House, Olivia Hanlon's home; it was a substantial, rambling farmhouse near Harrow, ironically named, and captioned somewhat predictably by the press as 'Paradise Lost'.

'You can take that if you like,' Effie said despondently. 'I can't bear to read them anymore. Just think – I saw that woman on the day she killed Millie. I could have stopped her. If I'd done something, Millie might still be alive, but we were late for the bloody Coronation.' She glared at Vi, and Josephine guessed that there had been some harsh recriminations between the two of them. 'And it's not even as if we saw much.'

'It hasn't been proven that Vivienne Beresford killed Millie,' Josephine said tentatively.

All three turned to look at her in surprise, and she suddenly knew how Goldilocks must have felt. 'Do you know something we don't?' Effie demanded. 'Of course! That policeman who came here the other day – you knew him. What did he tell you?'

'Nothing,' Josephine said hurriedly, wondering how to encourage a little more circumspection on Vivienne's behalf without fanning the flames of rumour any further. 'I just meant that she's denied it, which is strange when she so readily pleads guilty to her husband's murder. Perhaps she's telling the truth.'

'So the person who did this to Millie might still be out there somewhere?'

Surprisingly, that thought hadn't actually occurred to Josephine, so caught up was she in the idea that Anthony Beresford might have killed his lover before he died. Vi looked horrified at the prospect of a murderer working his way gradually up the house, and Josephine felt obliged to reassure her. 'I think Millie's death was very personal,' she said. 'I'm sure there's nothing for you to worry about, and perhaps I'm being overcautious about the accusations.'

'Fancy Millie being involved with him, though,' Effie said. 'You hear him all the time, don't you, but I'd never have matched the face to the voice. I always thought Anthony Beresford was tall and dark.'

'And younger. Much younger. My mum wouldn't have it when I told her. As good as called me a liar, she did. I can't believe we'll never hear his voice again.'

There was a long silence as they all stared down at the headlines, and Josephine could imagine similar conversations taking place across family tables all around the country. She glanced through another of the papers, stopping when she saw the picture of Millicent Gray that Gerard Leaman had taken at the read-through, melodramatically captioned 'the last photograph of the dead woman'. The paper had no idea of the photograph's true significance, she thought – the moment when Vivienne Beresford was humiliated beyond all endurance. She scanned the columns around the picture and noticed that Leaman had a lot to say on Millicent, whom he had known personally, as well as plenty of gossip on Vivienne, whom he obviously didn't – although he claimed to have been a confidante of her sister's. It was an excellent advertisement for his business, which stopped short only at putting a contact number for bookings, and she both admired and despised his opportunistic flair. If he was so keen to talk, perhaps it was time she booked a portrait session; any glimpse into the past might be helpful, even if it was heavily based on gossip. 'I don't suppose you've thought of anything else that Millie said about Anthony, have you?' she asked, remembering suddenly why she was there.

'No, sorry. Only what I told you the other day.'

Josephine finished her coffee and refused the offer of another, disappointed that there was nothing more to learn. 'Have you still got the key to Millie's flat?' she asked.

Effie nodded. 'Yes. The police gave it back to the landlord when they'd finished, but Millie's stuff's got to be cleared out so he asked us to hang onto it and let them in.'

'Could I borrow it for a moment? I think I left my glasses there the other day, and it seemed such a trivial thing to bother about after what happened, but it would be so convenient to pop down and get them now.'

'Of course you can have it.' Effie fetched the key, still on its ribbon, and handed it to Josephine. 'Do you want me to come with you? It's not nice to be on your own down there. The police gave it a right good going over, but it still gives me the creeps. All I can see is her lying there.'

'No, don't worry. I'll be all right, and there's no need for you to put yourself through it. I'll bring the key straight back.'

She left them to their breakfast and their scandal and went down to the basement, feeling every bit as much the intruder now as she had the first time she had used the key dishonestly. She wasn't quite sure what she hoped to find, and she tried not to imagine Archie's face if he ever found out that she was poking round in a dead woman's flat like Miss Marple; they had only spoken briefly over the weekend, but his fury at being so comprehensively removed from the case was still raw, and the last thing he needed was for her to cause him more trouble by interfering. She opened the door and was greeted instantly by a row of boxes lined up in the hallway, presumably awaiting collection by Millicent's family. Their randomness was unbearably moving – ornaments held safe by clothes or old newspapers, pictures mixed with letters – and Josephine stared down at them, thinking how sad it was that everyone's life, no matter how full and how vibrant, was inevitably reduced to this jumble sale of grief. She hesitated, unsure of whether she could actually bring herself to rifle uninvited through a dead woman's belongings, then lifted the top layer of clothes from the nearest box, feeling like a thief at the church bazaar. She looked quickly through each carton in turn, but found nothing of interest except a file of contracts from the BBC, which confirmed what Julian had said about Millicent's extensive engagements for the next few months. After her performance in *Queen of Scots* on Thursday, Lydia could look forward to a busy time; if Josephine didn't know her better, she might find herself wondering if the actress had an alibi for Wednesday morning.

As Effie had observed, the police had left their mark on the flat in the aftermath of Josephine's horrific discovery. Much of the furniture had been moved, and a thin layer of dust covered all the surfaces, left over from the search for fingerprints. She forced herself to go through to the bedroom, but a quick glance round told her that there was no need to linger: the drawers were open and empty, and if there had ever been anything of interest in them, it was long gone. The sitting room, too, had been packed away except for the larger items of furniture and the gramophone. Only the kitchen seemed largely unchanged from the last time Josephine had been there, probably because it was the least personalised room to begin with.

She paused in the hallway, struck again by how desolate it seemed, then turned to go, but one of the boxes suddenly caught her eye. In her distaste at the task, she had looked quickly through the contents of each without paying any attention to the newspaper that everything was wrapped in, but she realised now that she had missed something important. One of the pages was annotated in blue ink, and she thought at first that it was the newspaper that she had used to make a note of Millicent's address, the one that she had brought with her, but the handwriting was not hers and the paper was dated two weeks earlier. The page was in the classified section of *The Times*, and someone – presumably Millicent – had circled one of the houses for sale and written a date and a time in the margin: 'Friday, 3 p.m.' There was no name and no photograph in the listing, but the house was in Harrow and described as an extensive seventeenth-century farmhouse; was she jumping to conclusions to guess that it was Paradise House? As quickly and as carefully as she could, Josephine lifted some of the other items onto the floor and looked more closely at the paper which lined the boxes. Some of it, she noticed, was much older than the rest and she was drawn to those faded, yellowed pages. In two minutes, she had pulled out enough to know that Millicent Gray had what amounted to an archive of press cuttings on Olivia Hanlon's death. What had she discovered, Josephine wondered, and was that the real reason she had asked to see Vivienne?

Conscious that no one took this long to find a pair of glasses, even with the handicap implied by the search, Josephine collected the pages that interested her, stuffed them into her handbag and re-packed the boxes. She had left the main front door on the latch and went back upstairs to the girls' flat, too excited almost to be civil. 'Any luck?' Effie asked.

'Yes, thank you.' She smiled and held up the reading glasses which had never left her side. 'I must go now, but why did you want to see me? You said you needed to get in touch.'

'Oh, it was about Millie's funeral. Her parents are going to let us know the arrangements, and they've asked us to tell all her closest friends. I wanted to send you the details.'

'That would be very kind,' Josephine said, feeling more fraudulent than ever. Before anyone could ask exactly how well she did know Millicent Gray, she jotted the Cowdray Club's address down on a piece of paper and said goodbye.

4

73a Belgrave Road was above a dentist's surgery and sandwiched between a butcher's and an ironmonger's shop. Despite being only a short distance as the crow flies from the grandeur of Eaton Square and Belgravia, its immediate surroundings were shabby and tired, and Josephine wondered how many of Gerard Leaman's potential clients were put off altogether by their first impressions of his premises. The flat was hardly Bond Street, but a plaque at the door brazened it out well, boasting a florid script and a simple statement of intent which cried out to be read in a dubious French accent: *'Photography by Gerard'*. She rang the bell, feeling like Mary Stuart on the last morning at Fotheringay, and resigned herself to the ordeal ahead, hoping to get away with a few straightforward poses and a good deal of chat.

The door was answered by a pleasant-faced elderly woman who introduced herself as Miss Tuff, Mr Gerard's assistant. Josephine followed her upstairs to the first floor and sat, as instructed, in a spacious waiting area, although the ease with which her appointment had been made suggested that the number of chairs available was a little optimistic. The room hovered uneasily between fashionable and clinical, with white walls, white carpets and a white sofa, and on the table in front of her – prominently positioned and lit by an art-deco lamp – was a trio of identical photograph albums. Josephine picked up the one closest to her, opening it at a photograph of Edith Evans looking unusually wistful, and flicked through the pages; some were head-shots, others full-length portraits, and many were pictures that had appeared in the *Sketch* or *Tatler*, but they all had in common a preference for subdued lighting, soft-focus and skilful retouching, and Josephine could see why Gerard had become a favourite with actresses of a certain age. The tonal values and finish were superb, and there was no doubting the technical skill of the photographer, but the pictures lacked the warmth that characterised images by Angus McBean or Hugh Cecil. The women looked bored and the men seemed uncomfortable, and Josephine suspected that none of his sitters really liked Gerard Leaman.

Miss Tuff brought her a cup of surprisingly good coffee and a plate of petit beurre, and Josephine amused herself with the second album, which concentrated on theatrical shots. After what she guessed was a carefully judged period of anticipation, Gerard made his entrance, dressed in flannels and a collarless shirt, all given the faintest hint of formality by a waistcoat. 'Miss Tey – Josephine, if I may? The camera is much more forgiving if we start as friends.'

'Yes, of course,' Josephine said, tempted to ask what he had already seen in her face that required allowances. 'It was good of you to see me so quickly. My publisher always asks me for publicity material at the last minute, so I'm very grateful.'

'Not at all. Come through to the studio, and we'll see what we can do.'

To her relief, his manner was completely different from the first time they had met. On his own territory – with nothing to prove and Miss Tuff to pander to his ego – there was obviously no need for the arrogant swagger that she had found so loathsome at Broadcasting House. The studio was a large room, cleverly divided into different areas to fulfil a number of functions. Miss Tuff sat in one corner, slightly screened from the rest of the space, and the area behind her functioned as a store room for rolled-up backdrops, props for set pieces – all contained in a gilded birdcage – and a trunk overflowing with wigs, clothes and theatrical masks. The working space itself was small but functional: in the far corner, a fireplace had been ripped out and boarded over, and Gerard had painted the walls a bluish white and fixed an arc light to shine onto them, compensating for the inadequate electric globes in the middle of the room. His photographic equipment was straightforward and obviously well-used – a quarter-plate camera that seemed too heavy for its stand, an old Liberty umbrella recovered in white cloth to function as a reflector – and Josephine wondered if that was a matter of choice or economic necessity. The carpet was dark, complementing the only other piece of furniture in the room – a vast black-glass table that carried just a single photograph: Millicent Gray, beautifully framed in silver.

Gerard placed Josephine in position on the sitter's upright chair and checked to make sure that she was comfortable. 'Now – tell me what you're looking for,' he said, unsettling her by giving her face a long, deep scrutiny. 'Other than to look beautiful, of course – we all want that.'

Josephine smiled, although there was no obvious hint of irony in the phrase. Like dentists with bad teeth and doctors prone to head colds, fate had played a cruel trick on Gerard Leaman when it came to his choice of profession; he was quite possibly the least photogenic person she had ever seen. 'Oh, just a nice, straight picture to go in a new book,' she said. 'It's for the American edition. The English don't give a damn about that sort of thing, thank God, but the American method is to tell the world how the author likes his bacon, how many gold fillings he has and what his grandfather said to Gladstone in eighty-two. It's a biography, so the picture should probably be quite serious – I don't want people dismissing the book out of hand before they've read a word.' Gerard's face fell as the commission was outlined to him, and Josephine realised that she was falling rapidly into the category of 'ordinary sitter'. 'I have got a film coming out later in the year, though, so perhaps something a little more glamorous for the publicity around that?' The photographer looked more interested but stared doubtfully at her smart suit, as if to say that he could not be expected to perform miracles. 'I've brought a change of clothes,' she added hurriedly, as his eyes began to stray to the costume chest.

There was a heavy sigh. 'Oh well, let's start with the dull one and see where we get to.'

Josephine didn't remember conflating serious with dull, but as Leaman's lack of tact was what had brought her here in the first place, she didn't argue. He began the usual round of ploys to get his sitter to relax, launching into a flow of what he obviously considered to be amusing and interesting chatter, and Josephine smiled and played along, waiting for a natural moment to introduce the subject that had brought her here. Once the session was underway, Gerard worked quickly and methodically, issuing instructions that were as clipped and as crisp as the sound of the shutter. After a few minutes, during which time he seemed to have taken enough photographs to cover this book and any number she was likely to write in the future, he paused and smiled at her. 'I could go on posing you all day.' At first, Josephine put the comment down to the photographer's usual desire to say something that he thinks will flatter, and privately thought it a pity that he hadn't saved his efforts for someone with a prettier face and less scepticism, but then she noticed that he genuinely seemed to be enjoying himself. 'You know, there is something of the Sitwells about you,' he observed, quite without warning.

'Not Edith!' Josephine said hastily before she could stop herself. 'I don't mind being Sasha, or even Osbert at a pinch, but I draw the line at Edith!'

Gerard said nothing, but continued to observe her in a sort of rapture. 'Epstein would love to do you!' he said eventually.

That was the last straw. Before she could offend him by laughing out loud, Josephine gestured to the picture of Millicent Gray. 'Such a tragedy,' she said, hoping that her voice struck the right balance between sympathy and curiosity. 'I read your tribute in the papers, and that's a very truthful photograph. You've really captured that sense of . . . well, that sense of fragility, I suppose. It's almost as if you had a glimpse of the future. You must have known her well to gain her trust like that.'

She could see instantly that the approach was a winning one. Whether it was a strength or a weakness, Gerard was clearly as susceptible to flattery as any of the models who posed for him. He bristled with pleasure at the compliment, like a cat stroked in sunshine, and gazed fondly at the picture. 'Millie was such a joy to work with,' he said, and Josephine could tell that he was as keen to talk as she was to listen. He paused for dramatic effect, then shook his head. 'I really can't believe that she'll never walk through those doors again, you know.'

'She came here often?'

'Oh yes, many times. We hit it off straightaway, you see. She often used to come to me for advice or to get things off her chest.'

If Gerard felt any remorse for his careless words at Broadcasting House – words which had had such a dramatic effect on three people's lives – he didn't show it. 'What sort of advice?' Josephine asked, finding it hard to believe that Millicent Gray had asked for anything of the sort from the photographer. 'Her performances were always so confident – it's hard to believe that she had doubts about anything.'

'Oh, you'd be surprised,' he said vaguely. 'Such an innocent child, really. She had no idea what she was caught up in.'

'What do you mean?' Josephine asked, trying not to sound too antagonistic. 'Surely she must have known that involving herself with a married man was dangerous?'

'It wasn't just any married man, though, was it? You don't cross a Hanlon. Lots of people learned that the hard way with Olivia.'

'So I gather. I went to the Golden Hat a few times, but I don't think I ever met her.'

He squinted at her with half-closed eyes, trying to predict what the photographic plate would do to the visual image. 'You wouldn't have done. Olivia kept herself to herself, very much in the backroom. Hers wasn't the sort of business that could be run in the limelight. Now – one more shot like that, then turn the chair round the other way and look back at me.'

Josephine did as she was told, and Gerard resumed his work, making little flattering noises and more ludicrous comparisons under his breath. 'What sort of business was it?' she asked innocently.

'Pleasure, and like any woman, pleasure has a thousand and one faces.'

He smiled, and Josephine wondered how many times he had used the phrase. 'So how did you get to know her?'

'She hired me to photograph her girls – to show them off at their best, if you know what I mean. She knew they'd be perfectly safe with me. I had no interest in touching the goods, and she paid me well. I was just starting out at the time, and the money more or less set me up.'

He looked at Josephine, as if gauging how much more to trust her with, and she wracked her brains for something that would get him on side once and for all. 'I feel such a fool,' she said confidingly. 'That day when we were both at the BBC for the read-through – I was so sorry for Vivienne. I honestly thought she was a good woman. First impressions can be so deceptive, can't they?'

He grinned, and left his camera for a moment to go over to a filing cabinet by Miss Tuff's desk. 'Here,' he said, taking out a photograph and passing it to Josephine. 'I wasn't particularly proud of the work at the time, but it'll make me a very rich man now if I can find someone brave enough to print it.'

She looked down at the picture of a woman – semi-nude, her hair partially covering her breasts, her face heavily made up. There was obviously a strong family resemblance between the two sisters: the eyes that looked out from the photograph were very like Vivienne Beresford's, the mouth had the same strong determination. 'So that's Olivia Hanlon,' she said, interested to see the woman she had heard so much about.

'Oh no – look again. That's Viv.' Shocked, Josephine did as she was asked, and saw that he was telling the truth. She had sat in front of this face for an hour only the day before yesterday, but she would never have recognised it in this context. It was hard to believe that a woman would put her own sister in this position, and she wondered again about the relationship between them. Whatever it had been, the existence of this photograph was damning; if Gerard did manage to sell it, he would be made for life and Vivienne might as well walk straight to the gallows. 'That was when Viv was in the family firm, before she turned respectable and married Anthony,' he added. 'Olivia never really forgave her for that, and you didn't cross Olivia.'

'You sound as if you're not quite sure whether that's to be admired or feared,' Josephine said, and Gerard smiled. 'What was she like, the Olivia you knew?'

'Remember Queenie in *The Wild Party?* I always think of Olivia when I read that poem.' He saw that the reference meant nothing to Josephine, and obliged her with a more prosaic description. 'Olivia was a fascinating woman if you didn't get too close. She was charming, vivacious, beautiful and warm, and if you imagine Viv without the streak of ice running through her, you'll be on the right track. But Olivia had a streak of something else, something much more dangerous. I once saw her beat a man with the heel of her shoe until his lips went blue, but usually she didn't have to go that far.'

'No,' Josephine said dryly, 'I can imagine that a gun was even more persuasive.'

'Oh, she never had to use that,' Gerard said seriously. 'She had this way of dealing with anyone who said or did something she didn't like. She'd just look at them – narrow her eyes and set her jaw until her silence made them start to babble. There was something in that stare that could bring the hardest men to their knees. In the end, they were eating out of her hand. There was no sentiment in her, no forgiveness.'

'No wonder Vivienne wanted to get out of that life.' Gerard just smiled. 'Do you really believe she killed Millicent?'

'Without a shadow of a doubt. It's in the blood.'

Josephine remained silent, and it wasn't simply her desire to keep Gerard sweet that prevented her from arguing; she realised now that believing Vivienne *hadn't* killed Millicent wasn't the same thing as believing her incapable of it. She had, after all, shot her husband in cold blood. 'Were you at the party when Olivia died?' she asked.

'My dear, *everyone* was there. Paradise House was the centre of the universe back then, and if you weren't invited, you were no one. There were no cameras allowed, obviously, but you could have whatever else you wanted there – that's why Olivia called it that, and she had an unerring instinct for who to trust, so it was utterly safe. Drink, drugs, girls – or boys, if that was more to your taste. The cocaine used to arrive from France by homing pigeon, brought in a gram at a time. Sometimes, for the really special occasions, when larger quantities were required, she'd risk paying a girl to bring it in.'

'And I'm assuming that this party *was* one of the special occasions?'

'Oh yes.'

'What was it like?'

'Wild, like the poem.' Gerard abandoned the camera, and if he suspected now that Josephine's portrait session had simply been an excuse to talk, he didn't seem to care. He pulled up another chair and sat down next to her. 'All the rooms were lit by candles,' he said. 'I remember the shadows on the ceiling, dark figures in corners as people found their pleasure for the night, the smell of incense. And there was music, always music. Olivia was luminous that night, on fire. You could smell it on her. I remember thinking afterwards that it was almost as if she knew the night was all she had, and she had to make the most of it.'

'Do you mean she was planning to commit suicide? I know that was one of the theories about her death.'

'I've never believed that. Olivia was far too selfish to kill herself deliberately. But perhaps she knew she'd pushed her luck once too often, and that time was running out.' He paused, reliving the night again, and Josephine waited for him to continue. 'She moved from room to room with a tray, always the perfect hostess. Sometimes it would be champagne, sometimes cocaine, sometimes sex – if the tray came through with photographs, you could choose who you wanted. People hovered round her, as if they could soak up some of that light for themselves. Men wanted her, women wanted to *be* her – with the occasional variation on that theme, obviously – but we were all just cheap imitations. Less glamorous, less daring, less reckless – but Olivia made you believe for a while that you could be refashioned in her image. The drugs helped, of course. Everyone was wrecked.'

'Was Vivienne there?'

'Yes.'

'And was she in the same state as everyone else?'

He considered the question for a moment. 'She joined in at first – drink, not drugs – but then she stopped. I remember there was a moment when she came back into the room from somewhere and just sat down on the divan. She didn't move, she didn't speak – she just stared at a shadow on the wall in front of her. Someone put his hand on her arm, trying his luck, even though she left all that behind when she married, but she didn't seem to notice. She just shivered, then got up and walked over to the tray of drinks that Olivia had left on the side and drank a glass straight down.'

'Then what?'

'I don't know. It was summer and all the windows were open, and a breeze caught the curtain and knocked a vase off the window-sill. It smashed, and that distracted me. When I looked back, Viv had gone.'

'And Olivia?'

'She'd decided to go for a swim. People tried to talk her out of it because she'd had too much of everything, but she wouldn't listen. She just told everyone to leave her alone and went out to the pool. That was the last time anybody saw her. The next thing I knew, there was a terrible scream from outside – I'll never forget it. It was Viv who found her, face down in the water. After that, it was like rats leaving a sinking ship.'

'You mean everyone left?'

He looked at her, as if finding it hard to believe that she could be so naive. 'Of course everyone left. The police were obviously going to be called, and no one wanted to be there when they arrived. Even the Prince of Wales was rumoured to be on his way that night, but he was quickly diverted when the hostess stopped breathing. Can you imagine the scandal?' He shook his head in disbelief. 'It's astonishing how quickly you can sober up when necessary. Someone put the lights on and everything that had been mysterious and magical was suddenly squalid and depressing. Smeared glasses, candle wax and cigarette stubs on the carpet, bottles everywhere and underwear draped over the furniture. It was suddenly all so lurid and vulgar, like coming face to face with every one of your demons at once. I had to go upstairs to fetch something I'd left in one of the bedrooms, and it was even worse up there because the panic hadn't quite reached the first floor. Tangled sheets and tangled bodies, in every possible combination. I remember finding it strange that naked flesh could be suddenly so disgusting.'

'Anthony didn't leave, did he?' Josephine said, remembering what Archie had told her.

'No. He cleared everyone else out and stayed behind to tidy up and talk to the police. That was brave of him, I always thought. His reputation was on the line, after all. And he must have done a damned good job. There were rumours and speculation, but no one could prove the scale of the party. The police didn't stand a prayer of getting anyone to talk – not that they tried very hard. Some of them spent more time at the Golden Hat than they did at the Yard, and Olivia had been bribing one of them for years to turn a blind eye. We all had something to lose.'

'Did Viv stay behind with him?'

'No. She was hysterical, and he didn't want her to have to deal with the police or with the press when they got wind of it. Billy drove her away. I'm not sure where, but he made sure she was safe.'

'Billy?'

'Billy Whiting. He works for the BBC now as a driver, but he was always close to Olivia. He cleared up her messes – and this was one hell of a mess.'

Josephine found it strange that Gerard could recall the details of that night so readily, and she wondered if his account could be trusted or if it was something he had prepared especially for the newspapers. 'You obviously remember it very well,' she said carefully. 'It must have made quite an impression on you.'

'Yes, it did – although it helps that you're the third person who's asked me about it in a couple of weeks. Things keep coming back to me now. That happens, I suppose, when your past resurfaces – you mull it over.'

'Did Millicent ask you about the party?'

He looked at her in surprise. 'Yes, she did.'

And Josephine could guess the questions she had asked. From what he had said so far, she doubted that Gerard knew enough to give Millicent the answers she wanted about Olivia Hanlon's death, but she asked him anyway, cautious in her phrasing. 'Do you think anyone else was involved in Olivia's death? Could it have been murder?'

She expected him to compare the enquiry to Millicent's again, but he didn't. 'I genuinely don't know,' he said, with a sudden air of finality.

'And you wouldn't tell me if you did?'

'Probably not. Still, I hope I'll get a research credit in your book for everything else I've told you.'

'My book?'

'Yes, the one you're obviously planning to write on the Hanlon family. I'm sure it will make a fascinating read.' It was a logical assumption, much more convincing than the excuse she had actually come here with, and Josephine wondered why she hadn't thought of it herself. 'In the meantime, I hope your publisher will be pleased with the photographs.' He gave her a knowing smile. 'Where would you like me to send them?'

'To my club,' Josephine said. 'I'll give Miss Tuff the address on my way out.'

5

Josephine spent a pleasant couple of hours with the Motleys, fulfilling her promise to keep them up to date with news of Marta, whilst keeping one ear on the stairs for Archie's return. He arrived earlier than she expected, and beamed at her when she went out to meet him. 'This is a nice surprise. Can I tempt you away from my cousins with a bottle?'

'Don't tell them, but it's actually you I came to see. I wasn't sure when you'd be back, though. I've been reading about your new case in the papers. Bodies in brown paper parcels? My God, if I put that into a novel, everyone would think I'd gone mad.'

'Oh, it gets better,' Archie said, leading the way upstairs to the top flat. 'What the press doesn't know yet is that Frederick Murphy has just walked into Poplar police station and given himself up. He still claims he's innocent, but at least we've got him for questioning now.'

'Do you believe him?'

'No, not at all. He did exactly the same thing eight years ago. If we're careful, we'll make the charge stick this time and he'll pay for what he's done. It's a shame that some other poor woman had to die in the meantime, though.' He opened the door and stood aside to let her through. 'Make yourself at home.'

'Thank you.' She hung up her coat and sat down in the chair she always favoured, opposite Bridget's exquisite painting of light over the Dwyryd Estuary at Portmeirion, an image of which she never tired.

'Have you had a good day?'

'I've had an *interesting* day. I've been having my photograph taken.' Archie looked at her curiously. 'There was method in it, I promise. And you'd have laughed – in the space of one hour, the photographer told me I was like Edith Sitwell, Gwen Farrar and Greta Garbo. I've spent some considerable time since wondering which one I'd prefer, but I dare say when the photographs arrive there'll be one of each and I'll be proved a chameleon.'

Archie laughed. 'Look on the bright side. If Hitchcock destroys your writing career, you can ask him for a job as a double.'

'Is that supposed to make me feel better?' She waited until he had shed his coat, then said: 'Talking of tall stories, I've got one myself and I need you to tell me if I really am insane this time.'

'Always a pleasure. Do you want a drink *with* the diagnosis, or afterwards?'

'Oh, as soon as possible. As I said, it's been that sort of day.'

He smiled and fetched some glasses. 'Mrs Snipe has left supper, too, if you're interested. Bacon-and-egg pie, new potatoes and salad, and there's enough for an army.'

'That would be lovely.' She waited while he poured two glasses of wine, then settled back in her chair. 'I'd better start right at the beginning. You know I went to see Vivienne in prison?'

'Yes. I thought that was very courageous of you.'

'It was more out of curiosity, if I'm honest.' She paused and decided to come straight to the point. 'I don't think she killed Millicent Gray.'

'No, neither do I.' His frankness threw her for a moment and she hesitated. 'I didn't want to charge her, Josephine. The evidence is largely circumstantial, and – like you – I think she's telling the truth. She doesn't strike me as a liar or a coward, and I like her – not that that's necessarily relevant to justice. But people higher up the chain – and at the BBC, of course – want this to go away as quickly as possible, and the easiest way of ensuring that is to throw the book at a woman we know has killed once. I'm just praying she'll have a half-decent barrister.'

'So who do you think *did* kill Millicent?'

He shrugged his shoulders, making it clear how frustrated he was. 'I don't know, and that's why I was so angry the other day. I've absolutely no chance of finding out because I've been taken off the case and Rygate's watching me like a hawk. If I as much as breathe in the direction of the Beresfords, I'll be up on a disciplinary and probably suspended.' He smiled and took out a cigarette. 'I have a feeling you're about to share a theory with me. Is this the insane part?'

'Probably. Is there any chance at all that it could have been Anthony Beresford?'

Archie thought for a moment. 'It's doubtful. He has an alibi for most of that morning, and even though there are a couple of times when it might have been technically possible for him to get to her flat and back, the crowds and the sheer significance of what he was doing on that day make it unlikely.' He explained the timings carefully to her, then asked: 'Even if you put the practicalities to one side, though, why would Beresford want to kill his lover?'

'I think she'd become more trouble to him than she was worth,' Josephine said. 'For a start, I don't think it was Millicent Gray that Beresford was leaving Vivienne for. I think he'd met someone else.'

'Why do you say that?'

'Millicent was contracted for lots of work at the BBC over the next few months, and didn't you think it was odd that there was nothing of Beresford in her flat?'

'Yes, but I put that down to discretion.'

'She was single, Archie, and that was her private space – why did she need to be discreet about it?' Still he looked doubtful, and Josephine didn't really blame him. 'There's more to it than that, though. She said something odd to me. I didn't take much notice at the time because my mind was on other things, but in hindsight it seems significant.'

'What did she say?'

'She overheard me arguing with Lydia about Marta...'

'Arguing with Lydia?'

'Yes. It's a long story and you were far too busy with the Coronation for me to bother you with it. I'll tell you over supper. But Millicent Gray obviously thought that we were allies. I can't remember her exact words, but she said something like "you put up with the pain because you think you'll be enough for them one day, but you never are". I think she'd realised that her affair with Anthony meant far more to her than it ever had to him.'

'Did you ask Vivienne about other women?'

'Yes. She didn't know of anybody, but I think she's coming to terms with the fact that there was a lot about her husband that she didn't know.'

'All right, you've convinced me that it's possible, but I still don't understand why he would kill Millicent because of that. Wouldn't he just leave her and pick up with the next woman along? I'm told it's what he's done before.'

'There's more, though,' Josephine said, and Archie gave her a look that said he had known somehow that there would be. 'Millicent Gray had found something out about Olivia Hanlon's death – I'm sure of that. And I genuinely believe that's why she asked to see Vivienne – she was going to tell her what had happened to her sister.'

'What? You really are going to have to explain why you've jumped to that conclusion – and what it's got to do with Anthony Beresford.'

'All right, but you must promise not to be angry.'

'Why would I be angry?'

'Just promise.'

'Cross my heart. Now tell me.'

Josephine heard her own excitement reflected in his voice, and thought carefully before she spoke, wanting to make the story as clear and as convincing as possible. 'After I saw Vivienne, I went back to Millicent Gray's flat to speak to her neighbours upstairs. I thought they might remember something else about her affair with Anthony. They didn't, but they still had the key to her flat, so I thought I'd have another look round.'

'Have you ever thought of swapping Suffolk for St Mary Mead?' he asked, amused.

Josephine ignored him and took the newspapers out of her bag. 'I found these.'

Archie glanced through them and there was no need for Josephine to explain any further. The smile left his face, and he looked furious. 'You found these in Millicent Gray's flat?' he demanded.

'Yes. Her parents had used them to wrap her things in. You promised not to be cross, Archie. I know I probably shouldn't have gone back in, but ...'

'I'm not cross with you. I'm cross with the person I put in charge of searching that bloody flat. These newspapers weren't wrapped round an ornament then, were they?' She shook her head and waited while he read through the pages more carefully. 'Have you telephoned this number?' he asked, pointing to the house advertisement.

'No, not yet.'

'I'll do it in the morning. We need to confirm that the property for sale *is* Paradise House, but that's easily checked – and I think it's a fair assumption. So Millicent Gray went there a couple of weeks ago?'

'It looks like it, and I know she's been asking questions about Olivia Hanlon's party since then.'

'Do you?'

She was beginning to enjoy the expression on Archie's face, hovering as it did somewhere between pride and bewilderment. 'You remember that photographer I told you about? Gerard Leaman – the one who opened his mouth at the wrong time during the read-through?' Archie nodded. 'Well, he's the photographer I went to see. He's been giving interviews in the press to anyone who'll listen, and I read that he claims to have known Olivia. I thought he might be exaggerating to get the publicity, but it's true. He was at that party.'

She repeated everything she could remember from Leaman's account, and Archie listened, fascinated. 'It was a very different picture by the time I got there,' he said when she had finished.

'Tell me about it.' Josephine refilled their glasses and leaned back in her chair. Archie was a good storyteller – his job had only improved a talent he already had – and his voice was rich and warm. She closed her eyes, trying to picture the scene he was recalling.

'The call came through in the early hours of the morning, and obviously it took a while to get there. The roads were very narrow, I remember, and the lane was closely hung with trees, so there was no help from the moon. We'd been told to look out for a small, octagonal lodge house on the road – the turning to Paradise House was shortly afterwards. Eventually we found it and the headlights picked out a small wooden sign. I remember wondering then how long the name had been so wholly inappropriate'

'What was the house like?'

'Lovely. One of those old, rambling redbrick affairs – a typical English country farmhouse, and very private. She'd chosen well, I think – no one would have disturbed her there. The trees cleared suddenly, and my first sight of the place was under a clean, white moon. All the lights were on – well, most of them. It was like looking at an ocean liner, but it was quiet, far too quiet. The ambulance had already arrived, and the front door was open, but no one came when we called so we waited a moment and then went in.'

'What sort of state was everything in?'

'Well, there was certainly no evidence of the chaos you've described. The sitting room was interesting, I remember that – lots of books and paintings, and decorated in very strong colours. But it was tidy. The only things out of place were a wrap draped casually across a chaise longue and a pair of shoes left abandoned in the middle of the room. I thought that was poignant at the time, but I was quite naive. Now, I suspect they'd been carefully placed.'

Josephine smiled at the image of Archie as an eager but inexperienced detective, the professional mirror image of the earnest younger man she had known. 'Were you still a detective constable?' she asked.

He glanced at the date on the old newspapers. 'June 1927. No, I was a sergeant then, but only by a few weeks. I was with a chief inspector called Jim Townsend at the time – he was a very good policeman, and he taught me a lot.'

'I don't suppose he was a regular at the Golden Hat, was he?'

'Not to my knowledge. Why?'

'Oh, just something Gerard said. Go on.'

'There was still no sign of anyone, so we went through to the back garden. The swimming pool was down some steps, a little way away from the house.'

'Was Olivia's body still in the water?'

'No, she was lying by the side at the deep end, partially covered with a towel. Beresford was with her, and the two ambulance men stood further back on a strip of grass, looking awkward and redundant like they always do when they get there too late.'

'What was Beresford like back then? Did you know who he was?'

'Not really. He hadn't made a name for himself at the BBC, so I only knew what I'd been told. He was very polite – almost too polite – and very obliging. You couldn't wish for a more co-operative witness – not that he claimed to have seen much. His story was a little polished, but he was a professional storyteller, so perhaps that's a bit harsh.'

'And what was the story?'

'That he and Vivienne had been there for dinner with a few other friends, but everyone else had left earlier in the evening. Later on, Olivia announced that she was going for a swim. Vivienne asked her if that was a good idea – she'd had a lot to drink, apparently – but she wouldn't be told and she went upstairs to change.'

'That part tallies, at least.'

'Yes. Beresford told me that he and Vivienne were newly married. He admitted that they'd gone back into the house and were too wrapped up in each other to think much about Olivia. After a while, Vivienne went out to check on her sister and the next thing he knew, she was screaming and calling his name and he rushed back outside.'

'He definitely said she was calling his name?'

'I think so. I'd have to check the statement because it was a long time ago, but I'm sure that's what he said. Olivia was lying face down in the water, obviously in trouble. Beresford says he dived in and managed to get her out, but it was too late. He blamed it on an asthma attack while she was in the water. There was a half-empty packet of Potter's Asthma Cigarettes by the pool.'

'You don't sound convinced by any of that.'

'There was a lot that didn't ring true. The length of time he'd waited to call the police, for a start, although you've explained that now – there must have been an awful lot of tidying up to do. Then there was this diving in business. He said he'd changed out of his wet clothes when he went inside to call us, but I couldn't find any wet clothes in the house.'

'Did you look in the laundry bin?'

He smiled again and Josephine had the decency to look embarrassed. 'Yes, Miss Marple, I did. It was in the bathroom, and it was empty.'

'Anything else?'

'I thought it was strange that he'd let Vivienne go. If I'd been in his position and she was that upset, I'd have wanted to stay with her to make sure she was all right. Beresford said he was concerned, but he didn't act it.'

'He'd never have won spouse of the year, though, would he?'

'No, I suppose not. And I remember how he watched me. I went over to look at the body while he was answering Jim's questions, and he never took his eyes off me.'

'What about the body? I'm assuming there were no signs of anything suspicious.'

'No, none at all. No telltale bruising, nothing to contradict Beresford's explanation of her death – just a small plume of froth on her lips, which would have been consistent with drowning.' He closed his eyes, and Josephine wished she could picture the scene as clearly as he obviously still could. 'She was on her back with her face turned towards the pool, and strands of dark blonde hair drying across her cheek. It's funny, but it's the bathing costume I re-member. It was bright red and her skin was so pale – it seemed such a sudden shock of colour. Someone had thrown a towel across her body and even that seemed a half-hearted act – it didn't give her any dignity in death, and she was long past taking any purposeful comfort from it.'

'What was she like? I was so pleased earlier when I thought I'd seen a picture of her, but she eluded me.'

'And she still does. That's one of the things I find so difficult about going to a body – it's always impossible to imagine what that person was like in life. Even when they've died peacefully in their beds or in a chair by the fireside, too much has already been lost. It's the best argument for the existence of a soul that I know of. And it was the same that night – Olivia Hanlon looked like she'd just fallen asleep, but the woman she had been was long gone.' He stubbed his cigarette out thoughtfully. 'Have you asked Vivienne about her?'

'No, not really. She came up briefly in conversation, but there was no real reason then to push the subject. I will now, though. I'd like her version of that night.'

'You're going to see her again?'

'I promised I would.' Archie nodded but didn't offer an opinion, and Josephine was grateful. 'Is that everything you remember?'

'Not quite, no. When I'd had a quick look round inside, Jim sent me down to the lodge house to see who lived there and if they could tell us anything.' He smiled to himself and slipped easily into a convincing Yorkshire accent. '"It's a bit too bloody neat for my liking, lad." I can still hear him saying it. "Nip down to that funny house at the gate and see if they know anything. All hell'll break loose when the papers get wind o' this, so we might as well have their story now before people start paying 'em to make it up."'

'I'm starting to like your inspector. Is he still in the force?'

'No, he retired a couple of years back, but we still keep in touch. He's living in Bournemouth now, near his grandchildren, and growing prizewinning tomatoes.'

'Something to look forward to, I suppose.'

'The tomatoes, perhaps. I've left it a bit late for the grandchildren. Anyway, I fetched a torch and walked down to the lodge. There were no lights on and no one answered when I knocked, but I walked round the back and caught a woman looking out of the window. She came to the door when she knew she'd been seen, wearing a dressing gown and looking frightened. She was Olivia Hanlon's housekeeper.'

'Gerard didn't mention a housekeeper.'

'Why would he? She certainly wasn't at any of those parties, so he'd probably never set eyes on her. But it stands to reason that you'd want someone to look after the place. Anyway, she let me in and she seemed upset, as if she knew bad news was coming. She kept finding things to distract me from speaking it aloud – washing cups, offering me tea. Then eventually she asked me if something awful had happened to Miss Hanlon.'

'She knew why you were there, then?' He nodded. 'And she liked Olivia?'

'She certainly seemed to. She'd been there ever since Olivia bought the house in the early twenties.'

'And could she tell you anything about that night?'

'No, not really. She did admit that Miss Hanlon often had lots of people to stay at weekends. It used to take her all day to clear up on Mondays, apparently. But she claimed that nothing untoward ever went on, and that this weekend was no different.'

'Was she surprised at the way Olivia died?'

'She told me she often swam at night. Apparently, Olivia always said that a pool was a ridiculous thing to have in England for nine months of the year, so she liked to make the most of it. And she was a good swimmer, even with her asthma.' He poured the last of the wine into their glasses and got up to fetch another bottle. 'It's been good to hear a more honest version of what went on that night – I've always wondered. But I'm not sure where any of it gets us. There's nothing in Gerard's account to implicate Beresford, any more than there is in mine.'

'Ah, you spotted the flaw.'

'If you're right about Millicent Gray, she must have discovered something else.'

'Gerard told me that Olivia never forgave Viv for marrying and turning over a new leaf. I suppose she felt betrayed. What if she'd been trying to persuade Viv to come back to the clubs and Anthony intervened and went too far?'

Archie looked sceptical. 'It's a bit speculative, and I'm not sure how you'd ever prove it now that they're both dead. You'll have to see what you can get out of Vivienne, but I can't help feeling that if she knew anything, she'd have mentioned it long before now.'

'I know. I'm probably clutching at straws. But like you, I just feel that Beresford managed that night a bit too well – clearing people out, getting Billy to drive Vivienne away somewhere . . .'

'Billy? Billy Whiting?'

'That's right. Did you question him at the time?'

'No, I had no idea he was even there. Again, I'd have to check the statement, but I'm sure Beresford just said at the time that a friend of his had come to collect Vivienne because she was so distressed by Olivia's death. I know Whiting from the current investigation. He's Beresford's driver at the BBC, and he found the body.'

'Gerard told me that he cleared up Olivia's messes.' She hesitated. 'I wonder if it would be more accurate to say that he cleared up Anthony's?' Archie said nothing, but Josephine suspected that they were thinking along the same lines. 'The timings you went through for Beresford's whereabouts – do any of them depend solely on Billy's word? Would he lie for him, do you think?'

Archie thought about it. 'He seemed very loyal, certainly. But the timings are fairly solid, even without Whiting's testimony – there were meetings and briefings and engineer checks. Unless . . .'

'Unless what?'

'The other possibility is that Billy killed Millicent Gray on Beresford's behalf. I haven't checked his whereabouts for that morning. There was no reason to. I have no idea where he went after he dropped the Beresfords off at Broadcasting House. If he was working for Beresford and loyal to him for all those years, if he had helped Beresford cover up Olivia's death, it's not too incredible that he would go to Millicent's flat and put an end to the threat once and for all, knowing all the time that Beresford had a cast-iron alibi for the whole day. He wasn't to know that Vivienne Beresford was going to throw everything out by choosing that day to shoot her husband.'

'That might explain how Vivienne's compact got there, too. It could easily have slipped out of her bag in the car – what if Billy kept it and used it to incriminate her?' They were both quiet for a moment, and Josephine waited anxiously for Archie to spot a problem that was invisible to her, but he didn't. In the end, she dared ask the question that had been preying on her mind for some time. 'If – and I know it's a big if – if this turns out to be true and we can prove it, will it have any mitigation on the murder that Vivienne *did* commit? Will she still hang?'

He didn't answer straight away, and Josephine wondered if he was considering the question or working out how best to protect her from something she didn't want to hear. 'That's hard to say,' he admitted eventually. 'From her point of view, the two things don't seem to be connected. She planned to kill her husband and she did it coldly and methodically. It wasn't in the heat of the moment, he wasn't violent towards her, and she can hardly argue that she was protecting herself. If she could go back now and say she did it because she found out that Beresford had murdered her sister, that might make a difference – but she can't. She's been very clear about why she killed him, and if anything her honesty will hang her. Her attitude won't go down well with a jury, even without the huge weight of public opinion against her.' Josephine was quiet, and Archie looked at her in concern. 'This is really troubling you, isn't it?'

'Yes, it is. Marta warned me not to get too involved, and that's exactly what I've done. What you've just said brings it all back into perspective. You and I can sit here all night speculating and playing at being detectives – no offence meant – but it's very real, isn't it? It's life and death for Vivienne, and that suddenly makes everything we've said sound stupid and naive. We've got absolutely no idea what happened – on coronation morning or ten years ago – and there's no way of finding out.'

'Don't give up just yet,' Archie said. 'I think I'll pay a little visit to Mr Whiting tomorrow morning.' He grinned, and she forced a smile in return. 'If you're happy to leave that line of questioning to me?'

'Of course I am. It's about time you did something.'

'Good. And in return, I'd like you to ask Vivienne Beresford why she left Paradise House so quickly that night. If it were my sister, I'm not sure I'd be so keen to go. I'll be interested to know if it was her decision or her husband's.'

'All right. Will you let me know how you get on with Billy?'

'As soon as I get back. Where will I find you?'

'I'm back at the club for a couple of days.' She was touched by how concerned he looked, and quickly explained. 'There's nothing wrong – not now, anyway. Just the opposite, in fact. Marta's gone to Cambridge to look at houses.'

'Marta's moving to Cambridge?'

'She's thinking about it. She asked me to go with her, but I know she needs time on her own to come to terms with the place again. She was so happy there, and so desperately unhappy. Only she can decide which one will prove more lasting.'

'And how would you feel about her moving out of London?'

Josephine shrugged. 'I don't mind where she lives, as long as she's happy and as long as we can be together. I've always got the club if I need to be in town, and Cambridge isn't far.'

'No, it isn't. We can travel up together if Bridget ever invites me. Now – how about some supper?'

She drained her glass and followed him through to the kitchen. 'Is it safe for you to question Billy? What if your boss finds out?'

'Do you know, Josephine, I'm not sure I care. After what you showed me in those newspapers and the case we're starting to build, I have a feeling that *I'm* the one who'll be knocking on *his* door – and nothing will give me greater pleasure.'

6

Penrose left Scotland Yard early on Tuesday morning, hoping to catch Billy Whiting before he set off for work. He left Fallowfield with a list of excuses to choose from if anyone asked where he was, and headed out towards the Notting Hill address that Whiting had given in his statement, relieved not to have been obliged to ask anyone at the BBC for the information. In his pocket, he carried the keys that he had found in Anthony Beresford's office drawer; it was strictly against the rules to 'borrow' evidence in this way, but he got on well with the sergeant in charge of its safekeeping, and he had a compelling hunch that he was on his way to see the man who would be able to tell him exactly what those keys were for.

The morning was beautiful, dry and warmer than it had been for several days, and this handsome quarter of town – with its elegant interlacing of broad streets, fine squares and unusual crescents – did wonders for Penrose's mood. But as much as he admired the spacious mid-Victorian houses in Ladbroke Grove, with their stucco fronts and grand porticoed balconies, he knew that the lifting of his spirits had a deeper explanation, and he was truly grateful to Josephine – for the specific piece of information which had brought him here, and for giving him a renewed sense of purpose. It wasn't the first time that bureaucracy and protocol had stood in his way, and he usually found a more creative way around them; he wasn't the type to abandon his principles so easily, and this morning he was pleased to feel a little of the old belligerence returning.

Dunworth Mews was off Westbourne Park Road – a pretty, cobbled street with a row of small terraced houses on either side, built in the traditional mews style with garages below and living quarters above. The lane was a dead end, and the address that he wanted was about halfway down. Billy Whiting's house was plainer than those on either side, which were variously adorned by flower pots, window boxes and a large wisteria, but it was tidy and well-kept, and Penrose wondered if he lived alone. Like most cottages of its kind, built to serve as stabling and staff quarters for the grander town houses, the property enjoyed an enviable location, central and convenient but tucked away from the hustle and bustle of the main street. And for a man of Billy's profession, it had the added advantage of somewhere safe to keep a car.

There was a door next to the garage, painted in the same cheerful red, and Penrose knocked loudly, hoping to be heard from the living area on the first floor. When there was no response, he tried again, but the result was the same and he was forced to concede defeat. Disappointed, he knocked at the house next door. When neighbours lived in such close proximity, the community spirit was bound to be strong – and prized or hated according to your personality; with a bit of luck, he would find someone who could help him. The woman who answered seemed surprised and a little wary at first – but she was also of the age that succumbed most easily to Penrose's good looks and pleasant voice. 'I'm sorry to trouble you,' he said, 'but I'm looking for Billy Whiting. Do you happen to know if he's already left for work?'

The woman smiled up at him, happy to oblige. 'I think Billy must be away,' she said, and there was the faintest hint of a Welsh accent in her voice, light and distant, as if it were the one thing left over from her childhood. 'I haven't seen him for a couple of days, and he said he had some leave due to him after the Coronation.'

Penrose's heart sank. 'Can you remember exactly when you last saw him? It is quite important.' He took out his warrant card, confident that the woman belonged in the half of the world which was more likely to help a police officer than obstruct one. 'It's about what happened last week on Constitution Hill. You may or may not know, but Mr Whiting was an important witness.'

'Yes, he told me. Very cut up about it, he was. That poor man. What sort of woman takes a gun to her husband, just like that? I said to my Harry, you don't know how lucky you are.' She put a hand conspiratorially on Penrose's arm and winked. 'Mind you, he's been ever so good to me since, so it's not all bad, is it?'

Penrose smiled, and wondered at the logic which could make Vivienne Beresford simultaneously a figure of hatred and a role model for downtrodden wives all over the country. 'And Mr Whiting? You were going to tell me when you last saw him.'

'Oh yes. It must have been Saturday or Sunday. Sunday, probably. He was putting the rubbish out, and they come on Monday.'

'Thank you, Mrs ... ?'

'Hughes. Bronwen Hughes.'

'Thank you, Mrs Hughes. When Mr Whiting comes back, would you ask him to contact me at Scotland Yard?' Penrose couldn't help feeling that it would have been more accurate to say 'if' rather than 'when', but there was no point in alarming her. 'My name is Detective Chief Inspector Penrose. Shall I write that down for you?'

'No, there's no need. I'll remember you,' she promised, and Penrose believed her. Furious with himself for the wasted time that had allowed Billy to slip through his fingers, he waited for Mrs Hughes to go back upstairs, then peered through the windows of the garage, but the glass was crackled and it was impossible to see anything. The door had a padlock on it, and he felt the weight of the keys in his pocket. Ignoring a voice in his head which was politely enquiring what he might do when he left the police force, Penrose took them out and chose the most likely candidate. The key fitted, as he had somehow known it would, and the padlock fell away. Quickly and quietly, he slipped inside.

The garage smelt of oil and leather, and it took a moment for his eyes to accustom themselves to the half-light. He saw the car in silhouette first, enough to know that it was a classic sports model, and just as he was debating whether or not it was safe to look for a light switch, the sun obliged him by emerging from behind a cloud to reveal the Bugatti in all its glory. Penrose stared in admiration at the sleek, torpedo shape of the bodywork, with its elegant flying fenders and the distinctive pear-shaped radiator and split wind-screen. The car was a work of art, deep blue with a magnolia leather interior, dating back, he guessed, to the 1920s, but immaculately kept. It wasn't inconceivable that Billy should own such a vehicle, or that he looked after cars for other people as a sideline to his main job, and Penrose tried to keep an open mind – but he knew in his heart that the Bugatti belonged to Anthony Beresford. He got into the driver's seat, not entirely immune to the strange law of nature which turns a man into a boy at such moments, and tried a key in the ignition. The engine started first time, smooth and low and inviting, and he turned it off before the temptation to drive be-came too much. Kensington, where Beresford lived, was just a few minutes away through Holland Park, and the keys had been found in his desk; surely there was only one conclusion to draw, but why was the car such a secret?

The answer suggested itself as soon as he searched the interior. There was a pocket on the inside of the passenger door, and he took out a pair of women's sunglasses, a hairbrush – she was a blonde woman, obviously – and a chiffon scarf, heavily scented with Nar-cisse Blanc, the same perfume that Bridget sometimes wore. The car was one of the models which had a small additional seat in the back, and as Penrose rummaged around on the floor, his hand fell on a book, a copy of Oscar Wilde's *The Happy Prince*, translated into French. He remembered the child's tin soldier which he had found with the car keys, and understood suddenly that what he was seeing here was a window into Anthony Beresford's other life – a life which had nothing to do with his wife or with Millicent Gray, a life which, in some way that he couldn't yet fathom, had killed two people. He used the last key to open the boot, and found a small suitcase with a single change of clothes – flannel trousers, an open-necked shirt and a sleeveless pullover, all very different to the standard BBC 'uniform' of suit and tie. Who did Anthony Beresford become, he wondered, when he left this garage?

Conscious that he had been away from Scotland Yard for far too long already, Penrose locked the garage securely and knocked once again on Mrs Hughes's door. 'I'm sorry, but there's one other thing I forgot to ask. Do you know if Mr Whiting went away in his car?'

'Yes, he did. At least, I know he was planning to.'

'So it's not still in his garage?'

For the first time, it seemed to dawn on Mrs Hughes that the questions were a little irregular, but her respect for his title won Penrose the day. 'He never used the garage,' she said, 'so no, his car isn't there. He rented the garage to a friend to make a bit of extra cash on the side. Billy always parked on the street.'

'Did you ever meet his friend?'

She shook her head. 'No, but I used to see him when he came to collect the car. I can't help you much there, though – there was nothing very memorable about him.'

Except his voice, thought Penrose. He thanked her and drove back to the Yard, deep in thought. From his office, he telephoned Broadcasting House, hoping that his enquiry would be one that could be dealt with by reception. When a woman answered, he chose not to give his name and asked if Mr Whiting was working today. The answer was all too predictable: Mr Whiting had called in sick on Monday morning. No one knew when to expect him back.

7

Cambridge thrived on its past, and how Marta had ever thought that she could leave hers behind here was a mystery to her now. She had forgotten how disarmingly beautiful the city was in May, when its natural talent for languid pleasures fused with the hope and urgency of a new summer, and she wandered the pavements for hours, relieved to find that a place she once loved had changed far less in her absence than she had. It charmed her now as much as ever, but she found it hard to gauge how happy her present-day self might be when all the time a girl sat like a ghost at her shoulder, annotating every building and stretch of river with a different memory. When it was time for her to leave, she had made no decisions about her future, but the ice, at least, was broken.

Her route to the station was mapped according to the streets she most loved: the jumbled collection of buildings on King's Parade, whose variety was a perfect foil to the single-minded grandeur of the chapel on the other side of the street; the secluded corners of St Edward's Passage, where a theatre now stood next to the church, mirror-images of worship in their own way; a glance down to the tiny cottages in Little St Mary's Lane which had always intrigued her, then past the Fitzwilliam Museum and through the Botanic Gardens to the outskirts of the town. The long approach to the station opened up in front of her, culminating in the familiar yellow brick and handsome arched frontage of the railway buildings, and she remembered how relieved she had been to walk down this road twenty years ago and wave her husband off to war. After so long, the intensity of the memory shocked her, and she was only thankful that she had not known then how much grief lay in store for her. Sometimes, ignorance was bliss, and perhaps that was the spirit she should adopt here: it was pointless to speculate about where she might be most content – far better simply to rent a house she liked and see what happened.

She was a little early, the train a little late, so she decided to pass the time in the station's buffet. Sunlight streamed through the frosted windows and she queued patiently at the counter, where glass cases piled high with sandwiches and cakes were flanked by small armies of lemonade and soda bottles, all arranged with military precision. A wireless was on in the background but it was no match for the woman behind the counter, whose cheerful commentary on the day's events was only interrupted by the gushing of a vast tea urn. Marta ordered coffee, chocolate and a packet of cigarettes, then looked round for somewhere to sit. There was an empty table by the window, but she was distracted by a familiar face in the corner, playing idly with a teacup and absorbed in a book. 'Bridget! How nice to see you,' she said. Bridget looked up and the expression on her face was hard to read, but Marta thought it was more than the usual surprise at meeting someone out of context. 'Are you going back to London? Archie will be pleased to see you.'

'No, I'm here until tomorrow. I've just been seeing someone off.'

The question of who hovered over the two empty cups and plates, but Marta didn't know Bridget well enough to pry. 'Do you mind if I join you?' she asked instead.

'No, of course not.' Bridget gestured to the chair opposite, but refused the offer of another cup of tea. 'Is Josephine with you?'

'No, I'm on my own.' The answer seemed to come as a relief, and Marta supposed it was only natural that there should be some friction between Bridget and Josephine. Josephine's friendship with Archie was unique and unshakeable, straying untidily into love and formerly – on his side at least – into desire, and Marta had found it very daunting herself in the early days. 'I'm thinking of taking a house here, so I wanted to spend a bit of time looking round,' she explained.

'A house in Cambridge? That's a bit sudden, isn't it?'

'Not really,' Marta said, trying not to resent the idea that where she chose to live was anybody's business but her own. 'I spent several years here when I was younger. My father and my husband were both academics.'

'Oh, I didn't realise that.'

'No, it's not something I talk about very much.' She had no intention of talking about it now, either, and was about to change the subject when the door opened behind them. Bridget glanced across the room and Marta was surprised by the look of panic that crossed her face. Hurriedly, she stood up to prevent the newcomer from reaching their table, but the young woman was too quick for her. She was tall and attractive, not much older than twenty, and Marta looked at her with interest.

'I forgot to take the key,' she said, trying to catch her breath. 'I'm sorry – I've just run the whole length of the platform and it wasn't a very graceful entrance. I didn't mean to interrupt.'

'Don't worry – we were only chatting.'

'Phyllis, this is Marta,' Bridget said. 'She's a friend of mine from London – we met at Portmeirion last year.'

'Not the most restful of holidays, I gather,' Phyllis said, and Marta was struck by the familiarity in that wry, engaging smile. A guard put his head round the door to give the final call for the Birmingham train, and Phyllis looked at Bridget in exasperation. 'Oh, please hurry up, Mother! If I miss this, I'll have to wait ages for another one.' Bridget found what she was looking for and handed it over, her face impassive. 'It was lovely to meet you,' her daughter said, oblivious to the awkwardness that she had caused. 'I'm sorry it's been such a rush. Perhaps next time we'll have longer to talk.'

She kissed Bridget on the cheek and hurried back out to the

trains, and Marta waited for the door to close behind her. 'Does Archie know you have a daughter?' she asked quietly.

'No, I haven't told him yet.'

'Why on earth not?'

'I just haven't found the right moment.'

'In nearly a year?' Marta stared at her in disbelief.

'I'm not sure this is any of your concern.'

The words were aggressive but they were spoken half-heartedly, and Marta sensed that they prefaced a conversation which Bridget both feared and longed for. 'Perhaps not,' she said, trying to sound less judgemental. 'But I don't understand why you'd keep something like that from Archie if you genuinely care for him. Surely you don't think it would make any difference to how *he* feels?' Bridget said nothing, and her silence gave free rein to Marta's imagination. 'Unless, of course, there's another complication. Are you still with Phyllis's father, Bridget? Is that what you don't want Archie to find out? That you have a completely separate life here, one that he doesn't fit into?'

'It's complicated.'

'Life *is*, when you keep secrets. I should know.'

'I love her father. I love him very much.'

Her sadness seemed to come from nowhere, sudden and all-consuming, and it was a much more effective line of defence than the hostility she had shown up to now. Marta had never expected to see such vulnerability in Archie's wilful, spirited lover; she had always found Bridget's independence deeply attractive, but now she seemed lost. 'I'm sorry, but I don't understand,' she said gently.

'Don't you? I hoped you might guess and make it easy for me. That way, I wouldn't have to say it. She's his, Marta. Phyllis is Archie's daughter, and he doesn't even know she exists.' Marta stared across the table, trying to make sense of what she had just heard, and Bridget's fear and frustration got the better of her. 'So do you understand now? Every moment I spend with Archie is a lie, and I don't know how to make that right. I *can't* make it right. It's too late.'

'Why didn't you tell him at the time?' Marta asked. 'Were things really so bad between you?'

'No, they weren't bad at all – it was just over. What we had was lovely, but neither of us intended it to be for life. He went back to war and I went back to the Slade, and we parted before we grew tired of each other – that's one of the things that made it so special. Then I found out I was pregnant, and I didn't know what to do. I was terrified.'

'Because you didn't think he'd stand by you? Archie's not like that.'

'No, it wasn't that – I was scared because I knew he would. I knew he'd marry me and we'd raise our child, then other children after that, and I didn't want that life. I know it was selfish, but I wanted my freedom and I've never really regretted that.'

'Until now?'

Bridget nodded. 'I never dreamt I'd see Archie again,' she admitted. 'Even when we bumped into each other at Portmeirion after all those years, I thought it would be a fleeting thing. I never imagined that either of us would feel so strongly – more now than we ever did. I thought it was young love, but it's turned out to be something rather more. Just shows how wrong you can be, doesn't it? It would be funny if it weren't so fucking tragic.'

'What does Phyllis know?'

'She thinks her father died in the war. That's what everyone thinks. It was such an easy lie to tell.' For Bridget and for hundreds like her, Marta thought, but that didn't make the consequences any less harsh. 'So you see I can't tell him – not now. It's not just Archie who would never forgive me. Phyllis sees things in black and white, and for twenty years I've denied her a father and a different sort of life. How could she even begin to understand? I'd lose them both, and I can't allow that to happen. Like I said, it's too late.'

'I had a daughter, Bridget. She was illegitimate, and when my husband found out, he had me locked up and he gave my daughter away to another family. I never knew her.'

'I'm sorry, I . . .'

'Don't be. I'm not telling you this for sympathy.' Marta opened the packet of cigarettes, wondering if she had the strength to finish what she had started. 'She died when she was a little bit younger than Phyllis is now, and I never had the chance to find out who she was – or who I might have been, if I'd been allowed to be her mother. That really *is* too late. There's nothing I can do now except torment myself with wondering. But you *can* do something. Archie can be part of Phyllis's life if you let him – and part of your life.'

'No.' She shook her head, as much in fear as in certainty. 'That's the stuff of fairytales. Archie could never forgive me, even if he wanted to.' In her heart, Marta suspected that she was right, and she said nothing. 'And that's my punishment, I suppose,' Bridget added. 'Knowing that I could have had his love all those years. I'll never forgive myself for that. At least what Phyllis and Archie don't know can't hurt them.'

'But how long do you really think you can go on like this? The way I see it, you have two choices. You take the risk and tell him, or you break it off with him now and lose him anyway.'

'At least my daughter wouldn't hate me.'

'No, she wouldn't. But how would you feel about yourself? And could you live with that?' Bridget was silent. Out of the window, Marta saw the London train pull in, announcing its arrival with a flounce of steam and a lengthy groan of brakes. 'I have to go,' she said, standing up, 'but think about what I've said.'

Bridget caught her hand. 'Please don't tell Josephine.'

'You can't ask me to keep something like that from her. You know how much she cares about Archie.'

'Exactly. She'll tell him straight away, and if he's going to find out, it has to be from me.'

Marta hesitated, reluctant to allow anything else to come

between her and Josephine when they were finally making sense of what they meant to each other. 'I won't keep it from her indefinitely,' she said, determined not to gamble Josephine's trust on someone else's secret, 'but I'll give you some time to make a decision. Just don't wait too long.'

8

'No one ever tells you where you're going in prison.' Vivienne sat down opposite Josephine, looking less strained than the last time they had met. 'Someone comes in and tells you to collect your things, then they take you somewhere which is marginally more frightful than the horror you've just got used to.' She smiled, and placed a packet of cigarettes on the table between them. 'I'm pleased this time it was different. I wasn't really sure you'd keep your promise. I suppose I should have more faith.'

'Yes, you should, if only in the lure of such irresistible surroundings.' She nodded to the cigarettes. 'Perks already? You must be settling in.'

'Oh, I've got quite a routine. We make our beds before breakfast, then clean the ward and the lavatories – the lavatories are the long straw, because there's invariably a fight going on in the ward. Then we sit by our beds, waiting to be asked if we're all right by the sister, the doctor and the matron in turn. The answer is always yes, by the way – it's so drilled into us that one poor girl has started saying it before she's even asked the question. Oh, and the big news – I've learned to play whist since you were last here. It's a peculiar game, but it passes the time between morning rounds and lunch.' Josephine smiled and offered her a light for the cigarette. 'These are from Julian,' Vivienne added. 'I hadn't realised that remand prisoners can have things sent in. We get newspapers, too, but they cut out anything relevant to your case before they hand them over.'

'Is there anything left in yours to read?' Josephine asked. Since Vivienne's name appeared in the papers for the first time on Sunday, the press had gone to town, covering everything from her background and her family connections to a rather lurid recon-struction of the murder. Some were cautious and speculative, others personal and vitriolic, but all were damning. It was probably just as well that she hadn't seen them.

'It's funny you should say that, but there's barely enough paper left to hold the pages together. I'm very grateful for the sports sec-tion. Most people's have something missing, but mine is like one of those paper chains you cut out to amuse small children. Our parents used to do them for us on long journeys. My father was al-ways particularly good with elephants. He promised to teach me one day, but he never did.'

It was the first time that Josephine had ever heard Vivienne refer to her wider family. 'Are both your parents dead?' she asked.

'Yes, they died in the Salisbury rail crash when I was six. Their train derailed and collided with a milk train on a sharp bend. Twenty-eight people were killed that day. I'll never forget it.'

'I'm sorry,' Josephine said. 'That's a very young age to have your whole world turned upside down.'

'Yes, I suppose it is, but at least they never lived to see my shame – or Olivia's.'

'Who looked after you when they died?'

'We moved round a few aunts and uncles, but it was Olivia who really brought me up. She was nine years older, and our parents' death hit her hard. I think she decided then and there that she was going to control the world and not the other way round, and she did it well, at least for a while. And she gave me what she thought was a good life. It wasn't her fault that I hated it, I suppose. She never forgave me for throwing it back in her face – as she saw it – when I met Anthony. And she loathed the fact that she could no longer control *me*, although she never gave up trying.' Josephine was about to ask how those efforts had been made, but Vivienne didn't give her the chance. 'Anyway, we said we'd talk about you this time. Who was the affair with?'

The directness of the question took Josephine by surprise. Talking about Marta was the last thing she wanted to do when she was only just beginning to resolve her own guilt, and she had no intention of showing any sort of vulnerability in front of a woman she hardly knew. 'It wasn't an affair, exactly,' she said, hoping to deflect the conversation before it started.

'It never is when you're the latecomer.'

'I suppose that's one way of putting it, but we don't have much time today and your life feels rather more urgent than mine at the moment. There are things we need to talk about. Have you thought any more about what I asked you last time?'

Vivienne gave her a wry smile. 'I've thought of very little else,' she admitted, 'and you're right – it's entirely possible that Anthony *had* moved onto someone different and left Millicent Gray behind. That would explain what she said to you, and his absence from her flat. But I really don't think he killed her just because she was causing trouble with a new life he wanted to make for himself. He wasn't that petty, Josephine, or that cruel. He didn't need to be. He used people, casually and on a whim. For the most part, they were happy to be used and I turned a blind eye to it all just to keep him – in some sense of the word. We were all complicit in the situation, now I think about it, and when I look back over those years with the sort of detachment that prison gives you, I realise that none of us were very nice people. I'm not sure that anything we did was actually about love.' She sighed and stubbed her cigarette out, barely touched. 'And surely murder *is* about love, isn't it? Not merely convenience.'

Josephine was tempted to point out that Vivienne would know more about that than she did, but she resisted. Instead, she thought about her conversation with Archie and all that the contents of that car implied. Nothing had been proved yet, but it was entirely possible that Vivienne was wrong and that her husband *had* known love – the love of another woman, perhaps even of a child. A love worth killing to protect. And if that were true, somebody, somewhere, was mourning Anthony Beresford's death far more than Vivienne ever had. She still had no idea how she was going to break that particular revelation to the woman in front of her, but she wanted first to give Vivienne a glimmer of hope for her own future, a hope of proving the innocence that meant so much to her. 'Would Anthony kill to protect a secret from his past, do you think?'

Her answer was an expression of incredulity. 'A secret? What sort of secret?'

'That he'd killed before.'

'Josephine, don't be ludicrous. Who on earth do you think he's killed?'

'Your sister.'

Vivienne gave a short, sharp laugh, but the smile soon left her face. 'My God, you're serious,' she said. 'I have absolutely no idea how you arrived at that ridiculous conclusion, but Anthony didn't kill Olivia. He really didn't.'

'I know it's a shock, but just listen for a moment. Did you know that Paradise House is for sale?'

'No, but why would I? I haven't had any connection to that place for ten years. And what's Paradise House got to do with Millicent Gray?'

'She made an appointment to go there just before she died.'

Vivienne hesitated. 'How do you know?'

'I went to her flat after we last spoke, and I found the details written down. She'd also been digging into Olivia's death – collecting press cuttings from the time, asking Gerard Leaman questions about what happened that night. Other people as well, for all I know. Why would she do that, unless it was to find something that she could use against Anthony?' She waited for a reason to be offered, but none was forthcoming. 'And I think she *did* find something – enough to make her believe that Anthony had killed

Olivia. That could explain why she asked you round – to expose him.'

'That woman's death has got nothing to do with Olivia's,' Vivienne said in a tone that left no room for argument.

'You don't know that.'

'And you don't know that it *has*. What you've come here with is all speculation, isn't it? You haven't got any proof. You haven't stumbled across this mythical piece of information that came as such a revelation to Millicent Gray.'

Perhaps naively, Josephine had not expected such antagonism from a woman she was trying to help, but she had reckoned without the complexity of Vivienne's feelings for her husband; even at the expense of her own life, she stubbornly refused to see him as a murderer. 'All right, I can't prove anything yet, but I was hoping that you might tell me something about that night . . .'

'Anyway, why would Anthony possibly want to kill Olivia?'

It was spoken as a challenge, but there was a telltale note of fear in her voice now. In spite of Vivienne's protestations, Josephine suspected that something she had said had hit a nerve, and she hammered home her point as best she could. 'You told me yourself that Olivia resented your marriage and that she tried to control you. Anthony can't have been happy about the way she treated you, or about the scandal that he had married into. The Golden Hat hardly sits well with a meteoric rise at the BBC, at least as far as the public is concerned. Olivia was a threat to both of you. Perhaps he tried to do something about her lifestyle, and perhaps he went too far.'

To her astonishment, Vivienne began to laugh. The tears ran down her face, and Josephine – offended at first by the easy dismissal of all she had said – suddenly realised that they were not tears of mirth. She waited for Vivienne to compose herself, feeling completely out of her depth. She had come to Holloway certain of her theory and confident of its reception; now, all she could do was wait for the other woman to offer some sort of direction. 'Oh, that he were so protective,' Vivienne said eventually. 'Believe me, Josephine, you couldn't be further from the truth.' Her behaviour was drawing curious glances now from the warder on the other side of the door, and she lowered her voice to ensure that no one else would be able to hear. 'I killed Olivia, Josephine. It's not something that I ever wanted to admit to, especially now that the only other person who knew is dead, but I can't let you go off on a wild goose chase that won't help me and that might get you hurt. I didn't kill Millicent Gray, and I doubt that Anthony did, so in all probability her killer is still free. Perhaps you're right – perhaps she discovered what I'd done somehow, and was intending to blackmail me into letting Anthony go. Perhaps he even told her, for God's sake – it's not bad, as pillow talk goes. But none of that helps me. I don't want to sound ungrateful, but all the delving you've done on my behalf will only tighten the rope around my neck if it ever becomes public.' She waited while Josephine tried to come to terms with the shock of the confession. 'And will it become public? Will you feel the need to share what I've just told you with your policeman friend?'

'I don't know,' Josephine said truthfully, at a loss even to know how to feel, let alone what to do. In all the musing that she had done over the last few days, she had been certain of one thing – that Vivienne Beresford had, in some sense, been wronged. Suddenly, she was less sure. 'Before I make any promises, I need to understand why you did it,' she said.

'Because she was sleeping with my husband.' She saw the expression on Josephine's face, and added: 'That's right – the first of Anthony's sordid little affairs was with my own sister, for God's sake.'

'What happened?'

'It was at the party, obviously. I didn't really want to go, but Anthony said we should and I wasn't bothered enough to argue. After all, Olivia couldn't boss me around anymore because I'd left that life behind. Anthony and I had only been married for a few weeks – we weren't long back from our honeymoon – and I was so happy. I didn't think anything could touch me. Flaunting that in front of Olivia was tempting, so I agreed.'

'How did you find out?'

'I saw them together. The party was the usual affair – excess with no restraint, everything that the perfect hostess couldn't *quite* get away with in a club. I suppose we'd been there about an hour when Anthony went off somewhere. I waited for him to come back, but he didn't, so I went to look for him. He was nowhere in the house, so I went out to the garden, away from the crowd. I called his name but there was no answer, so I left the terrace and walked across the lawn to the shrubbery. There was a bench there, just beyond the reach of the lights from the house. That's where they were, and it was perfectly obvious that they weren't simply taking the air.'

'What did you do?'

'I didn't know what to do at first. I was so shocked and upset that I couldn't move and I couldn't say anything. I just watched. Then I turned and ran back into the house.'

'Did they know you'd seen them?'

'I don't know. I don't think so, although they must have heard my footsteps on the gravel. Certainly, if they did know, Olivia didn't show any sign of shame. I went back to the sitting room and sat down, and I was just numb, Josephine. It was as if no one else was there. Olivia came back inside a few minutes later, as blasé as ever, and Anthony followed shortly afterwards. She looked extraordinary, as if all the light in the room were concentrated on her, and on her alone. I remember watching her shadow on the wall, mesmerised by the way she moved, and I can still feel that searing, white hatred. I've never known anything like it, before or since. It was paralysing. Then the curtain knocked something off the windowsill, and it was as if something inside me had snapped.

It brought me to my senses, and I knew then that I would kill her that night.' Josephine said nothing, reluctant to reveal any sort of moral judgement, but it was becoming increasingly difficult to remain unbiased towards someone who had killed not once, but twice. 'My chance soon came,' Vivienne admitted. 'After a while, Olivia announced that she was going out to swim and she wanted to be alone, so I followed her. The deep end of the pool couldn't be seen from the house, so I knelt down by the side and waited for her to reach me, as if I were going to speak to her. It sounds strange now, but she looked at me as if she knew exactly what I was going to do, as if it was what she had wanted all along. I gave her time to say one last thing to me, then I put my hands on her shoulders and held her under. It was surprisingly easy.'

The story was being told in confidence and Josephine did her best to listen in the same spirit, but Vivienne's anger – and its consequences – had begun to frighten her. 'What *did* Olivia say to you?' she asked.

'That I would never make him happy. And she was right.'

In vain, Josephine tried to detach herself from the morality of what Vivienne had done and concentrate instead on how much it explained of all that had passed since. 'I understand now why you said Anthony's first betrayal was the one that really hurt you,' she said. 'But was there really no other way?'

She thought for a long time before answering. 'I loved Olivia, but I always hoped she'd be different. I suppose I loved the sister I wanted, not the sister I had. So what I did was about her as much as him. That night, she destroyed everything, simply because she could, and when I killed her, I killed my own chances of ever really believing in anyone. I don't know if there was another way. It didn't feel like it at the time.'

'How *did* it feel?'

'Sickening. I couldn't believe how easy it was. I remember thinking the same thing when I killed Anthony – just one shot, and that was it. I thought Olivia was stronger than that, but it was over so quickly. I was horrified by what I'd done, and I don't remember much of what happened afterwards. I know I was screaming and I couldn't control myself. Thank God Anthony got to me before anyone else.'

'Did he know what you'd done?'

'Yes, I told him. I wasn't thinking at the time, and I couldn't have lied even if I'd wanted to. He told me to go back into the house and make sure that no one else came outside while he got Olivia's body out and tried to resuscitate her. It was no good, though – I could see it in his face as soon as he came back in. He told everyone that there'd been an accident and asked them to leave, although they didn't need much encouragement. He was extraordinary, but then he was always good at saving his own skin and he simply applied those principles to mine.'

'That's why you left the party in such a hurry.'

She nodded. 'Anthony didn't trust me not to talk, so he got Billy to take me away. After what I'd seen, I thought he might take Olivia's side, but he didn't. He was so kind and so attentive. It's ironic, but I think it brought us closer together for a while.'

It wasn't the most convincing solution to marital unhappiness that Josephine had ever heard, and she couldn't help but question some of the assumptions that Vivienne seemed to have made. 'Didn't you want to make sure of what you'd seen?' she asked. 'If everyone was in such a state, how could you be sure that it wasn't just a moment of madness on their part, a mistake that they'd regret in the morning?'

'It wasn't a mistake. I saw how they looked at each other.'

'But you were upset. Did you ask ever ask Anthony what had gone on between them?'

She shook her head. 'Never. I didn't want to know. We barely spoke of Olivia again.'

'Where did you go when you left the party?' Josephine asked, changing the subject to something that Vivienne wouldn't need to feel so defensive about.

'Billy took me back to Anthony's parents at first, just until the initial crisis was over. Anthony stayed with Olivia's body and handled all the formalities with the police, but there wasn't much of an investigation. One of the policemen was tenacious, but someone higher up didn't want any close investigation of the Golden Hat – it was all far too close to home – so he smoothed things over and transferred that policeman to other duties. I was never even questioned.' How history repeated itself, Josephine thought. 'The verdict was death by misadventure, and the fire in the press soon died down.'

'What happened to the house?'

'We sold it not long after the funeral. Anthony took care of all that. It had quite a reputation by then, and we didn't get much for it. The money went to pay off some of the debts that Olivia left behind.'

'Were they bad?'

'Horrendous. All the clubs had already gone except for the Golden Hat, and she was clinging on to that with white knuckles. There were people after her from all over the place, and that rather played into my hands. It made it easy for everyone to believe that she would choose oblivion rather than face her problems.'

'Is that why you stayed with Anthony? Because he knew what you'd done? I've always wondered why you put up with the way he treated you.'

'In the end, yes. At first I thought his affair with Olivia was a one-off – infatuation, perhaps, or a reaction to being tied down, all those excuses that you fool yourself with. But when I realised that it was always going to be that way, I knew I was trapped. That marriage – that stale, passionless marriage – was my punishment for what I did to Olivia. The only escape was death – his or mine, and I chose his.'

'Would you have killed him if you hadn't killed before, do you think?'

The question seemed to stop her in her tracks. 'No,' she said eventually. 'I don't think I would. Once you've crossed that line, you never think of yourself in the same way again. Since that day, I've always known that I'm capable of taking the life of someone I love, and doing it for the second time is easier than doing it for the first.' She took another cigarette and stood to stretch her legs. 'I'm sorry, Josephine. I know you thought you were helping me but there's nothing in any of that to save me. *Will* you tell Penrose?'

'There's something else we need to talk about first,' Josephine said, wondering how long she could keep avoiding the question. 'The police have found a car – Anthony's car.'

'He didn't have a car. I've already told them that.'

'Yes he did. He kept it at Billy Whiting's house, and the keys were found in his drawer at Broadcasting House.'

'The police showed them to me, but he . . .'

Josephine put a hand on Vivienne's shoulder and encouraged her to sit down again. 'We haven't got much time left today, so don't argue with me. I want to help you, and the only reason I'm telling you this is because you need to know – not to trick you or to hurt you.'

The fear returned to her eyes, worse even than before. 'Why would that hurt me? It's just a car.'

'No it isn't. There were things in it – a hairbrush, a woman's scarf, a suitcase with a change of clothes. Men's clothes, in Anthony's size.'

'Stop it. Please stop it.'

Her voice was low and even, but Josephine knew that she was on the verge of hysteria. 'There was a book on the back seat . . .'

'I don't want to know, Josephine.'

'You have to know. It was a child's book and it was in French. You told me once that Anthony spent time abroad. Was it in France?'

'A child?' She looked up in disbelief, begging Josephine to take the words back, and the pain in her eyes was unbearable. 'That toy soldier in his desk . . . I thought they were being stupid when they asked me about it.'

'I know it seemed strange, but now it looks like . . .'

'I know what it looks like. But those women meant nothing, Josephine – nothing. Jesus Christ, that's the only way I've coped with his infidelity for all these years. You can't come in here now and destroy the one piece of sanity I've got left. Anthony had other women, but his life was with *me*. Leave me that, for God's sake.' She broke down in tears – raw, violent sobs that shook her body – and Josephine tried to comfort her but she was pushed away. 'Get out!' Vivienne screamed. 'I don't want to hear any more. Get out!'

The warder was by her side instantly, and comfort was the last thing on her mind. She pulled Vivienne roughly back into her chair and held her there, pinning her arms tightly behind her back. 'Are you all right, miss?' she asked Josephine.

'Yes, I'm fine. Please don't hurt her. It's my fault – I've just given her some terrible news.'

'Even so, I'm going to have to ask you to leave now while we quieten her down.'

Josephine could only imagine what sort of methods were used in Holloway to 'quieten someone down', and she stood her ground. 'Five minutes more,' she begged, looking at Vivienne. 'If you're to stand any chance at all, you need my help. Do you really want to hang for Anthony's death after what you've just heard?' The words sobered Vivienne, and she shook her head. 'I'll take full responsibility,' Josephine said to the warder. 'If anything else happens, I'll explain to Miss Size that you did all you could.'

The woman looked doubtful, but nodded her agreement. 'I'm not leaving the room again, though. You can have five minutes, but I'm staying here.'

'Thank you.' Josephine turned back to Vivienne, conscious now of having to choose her words more carefully. 'Billy knew about the car,' she said. 'Could he have helped Anthony in other ways, do you think?'

She waited, and when there was still no response, repeated the question, but Vivienne was no longer listening. She seemed distracted now, and Josephine wracked her brains for a way of getting through. 'Tell me again what was in the car,' Vivienne said before she had thought of anything, and Josephine repeated the list of items, adding the type of perfume and the name of the book. 'And the car? What was it?'

'A royal blue Bugatti.' She stared at Vivienne, but her eyes were impossible to read. 'You've thought of something, haven't you? Something suddenly makes sense to you. What is it?'

'Will you do something for me?' Vivienne asked, ignoring her questions. 'I know I have no right to expect you to help me after what I've told you, but it's the last thing I'll ask of you, I promise.'

'I'll do it if I can.'

'Go to Paradise House, then come back here and tell me what you've seen.'

The thought of a trip to Paradise House had already crossed Josephine's mind. She longed to see the place that she had heard so much about, particularly after the latest revelation. 'All right, but what am I looking for?'

'I can't tell you that yet. I need to be sure first. Will you still go?'

'Yes, as soon as I can.'

'Thank you. I won't forget this.'

She clasped Josephine's hand, but the warder separated them and led Josephine to the door. 'I'll see you tomorrow,' she said, turning back.

'All right. But promise me one more thing?'

'What?'

'Be sure to take someone with you.'

Part Six

The End of the Affair

Harrow Weald was about ten miles out of London, a straight-forward drive of an hour or so through the city's north-western suburbs. Josephine toyed with the idea of phoning ahead to make an appointment but decided against it, just in case Paradise House had already been sold; far better to turn up unannounced and at least get as far as the front door.

'I still can't believe I've let you talk me into doing this,' Marta said, as they left the old brick houses and shady elms of Hampstead behind. 'It wasn't quite the sort of house hunting I had in mind.'

'Think of it as a day out. The village is supposed to be very pretty.'

'And I bet the murder site is absolutely lovely at this time of year.' She pulled up at a set of traffic lights by the new Gaumont State Cinema and gave Josephine a weary smile. 'Seriously, though, you should have spoken to Archie first. He'll be furious when he finds out what we've done.'

'It's not as if I haven't tried,' Josephine said, a little too defensively because she knew that Marta was right. 'He was out last night and I left a message with Ronnie, but he never responded. I'll try him again as soon as we get back. By then, we might have a better idea of what Vivienne thinks she knows.'

'All right,' Marta said reluctantly, 'but I'm not letting you do anything ridiculous. The more I hear about this woman the less I trust her. That business about taking someone with you and not even telling you what you're looking for – she could be deliberately setting a trap for you. You've already unearthed one truth she'd rather have kept hidden.'

'What, you think she's manipulating me from the confines of Holloway's hospital wing?' Josephine looked at Marta in surprise. 'It's not like you to be quite so Edgar Wallace about something – that's far more my style.'

'But she *is* manipulating you – and you know she is.' A horn sounded behind, alerting them to the green light, and Marta turned right onto the main road. 'The slightest sign of anything not quite right about that house and we don't go in – agreed?'

'Yes, of course.' In actual fact, Josephine was more than happy to meet Marta's conditions: she had no real wish to delve much deeper into Vivienne Beresford's soul. The day before had had a profound effect on her, and she had walked away from Holloway feeling dirty, confused, and a little foolish, knowing in her heart that she was being used. Marta's return from Cambridge could not have been more welcome, and she brought with her a much-needed reminder of light and normality in a world which had, for Josephine, become twisted and coloured by the events of the last week. She had allowed her own life to become far too entwined with someone else's darkness, but one night with Marta had helped her to regain the perspective she had lost. Curiosity wouldn't let her walk away without completing this final task, but after that she was determined to let justice take its course. 'It's funny, you know – I thought I was doing this for Vivienne, but I realised after we talked that I'm actually doing it for Millicent Gray. I feel I owe it to her. Does that sound ridiculous?'

'No, not at all. You found her body, for God's sake, and you're still in shock.' The high-class shops of Cricklewood Broadway gave way to a line of dreary factories, disfiguring the landscape on either side of the Edgware Road, and Josephine marvelled at how rapidly the city had spread in this direction; only a few years ago, they would have been in open countryside by now, with scarcely a house to be seen. 'Do you still believe that Vivienne's innocent – of that, at least?'

'Yes, I do. Not because she wasn't capable of it – I'm beginning to think she's capable of pretty much anything – but because she didn't feel the need to. Millicent simply wasn't important – it was Anthony she hated.'

'That logic didn't work with her sister, though, did it? Vivienne killed her, not Anthony.'

'I rather got the impression that was the result of years of resentment.' She recalled with a shiver how unnerved she had been by the quiet, calm way in which Vivienne had talked about the murder. 'God, she frightened me, Marta. I can sympathise with her position – of course I can. It must have been terrible to be trapped in that marriage for all those years, having to put up with every new humiliation that Beresford chose to inflict on her, and I can imagine what the shock must have done to her when she found out that both he and Olivia had betrayed her. But other than the immediate horror of what she'd done and the fear of getting caught, there's no regret – that's what I can't come to terms with. She still thinks that what she did was justified. Gerard Leaman said she had a streak of ice running through her, and I'm beginning to think that he was right. It's a bit like having sympathy for the Devil.'

'Why do you sound so surprised?' Marta asked. 'Look at what she did on coronation day – that must have taken nerves of steel. Is it the next left?'

Josephine unfolded the map and looked at the route they had planned. 'No, the one after that. London Road.' She sighed, and tried to answer the more difficult question. 'I don't know why I'm surprised. I suppose it's because I thought I liked her, and I don't want to have been so wrong.'

'You're not wrong, you've just seen another side to her. You met the Vivienne Beresford who belongs at the BBC, who thrives in a world you're familiar with, who gets on with people you admire – people like Julian Terry. In Holloway, you saw the woman who's been raised in her sister's image, the woman with a heart of stone. I know she made such a big thing about getting away from the club scene, but she's probably very grateful for that background now – it'll serve her much better in prison that the respectable life she left it for.' She slowed the car according to Josephine's instructions, and turned into London Road. 'Vivienne Beresford is a chameleon, like we all are.'

Marta looked pointedly at her, and Josephine chose to ignore the implication. 'As colour-changes go, though, hers are rather extreme,' she said.

'Yes, I agree with you there. Isn't it funny when you meet people out of context? I bumped into Bridget while I was away, and believe me – she was *very* different.'

'You haven't said much about Cambridge since you got back.'

'No, I know.' She smiled. 'I've been a bit preoccupied with running errands for a double murderer.'

'So how was it?'

'It was strangely unsettling and comfortingly familiar, all at the same time. I still can't decide how I feel about it.'

'There's no hurry, though, is there?'

'No, I don't suppose there is.'

'It's an important decision, Marta – take your time. Go and stay at the cottage if you feel like it – it might help to be somewhere more neutral while you're thinking about it. And Cambridge isn't far from there – we could even go together if you'd like some company next time.'

'Yes, I would.'

'Good,' Josephine said, and added out of devilment: 'In the meantime, you might fall in love with the house we're about to see.'

'If I do, we're having the pool filled in. Do you have any idea what Vivienne expects us to find when we get there?'

'Proof of Anthony's other life, I think. I've been mulling it over, and my bet would be that *he* bought the house when Olivia died. I think he lived there with a woman he met in France, and I think they have a child.' They were getting close now, and Josephine consulted the map again. 'We're a couple of miles away. Old Redding is just through Stanmore and before Harrow Weald Common. I hadn't realised that it was quite so close to Grim's Dyke.'

'Sounds lovely,' muttered Marta. 'Should that mean something to me?'

'It was W. S. Gilbert's house. He drowned in the lake there.'

'It must be something they put in the water round here. I don't suppose Vivienne Beresford was spotted running from the scene, was she?'

Josephine laughed, relieved at last to be able to distance herself from the subject. 'No. Gilbert's death was quite tragic, actually. He'd invited two girls to swim in the lake and one of them got into trouble, so he dived in to save her and had a heart attack. Everyone was so upset when it happened. I'm surprised you don't remember it. It was in the news again recently when his wife died.'

'I'd never wish any harm on the man personally, but I can't help feeling that the girl who got into trouble did us all a great service. There's enough light opera in the world to last me a lifetime.' Before Josephine could argue, they passed the village sign for Old Redding. As she had predicted, it was quiet and picturesque, an enticing combination of gentle, rolling meadows and lush green woodland. 'Is there anything more specific to help us find the house?' Marta asked.

'I know it's down a private drive, and Archie mentioned a lodge. The village can't be that big, though – if we go slowly, we should be able to spot it.'

It soon became evident that the suggestion was better in theory than in practice. They reached the other side of Old Redding without finding what they were looking for, and a couple of forays down side roads only told them that Olivia Hanlon could not have chosen a better setting for her purposes: Paradise House was even more secluded and elusive than they had been led to believe, and the village seemed to collude in the conspiracy, keeping it safely hidden from view, while presenting a picture of tranquil respectability to anyone who passed. 'This is hopeless,' Marta said eventually. 'We could be driving round all day. I'll stop and ask someone.'

'Be careful,' Josephine warned. 'We don't want to draw too much attention to ourselves.'

'Why should we? I'm looking for a house and you've come to give me a second opinion – there's nothing suspicious in that.' She grinned. '*We* know we're poking about in someone else's business, but there's no reason for anyone else to guess. Anyway, we might pick up some gossip.' She drew up outside a pretty Victorian pub on the main through-road, painted white and decorated with an enormous number of carefully tended tubs and hanging baskets. 'Someone obviously likes petunias,' Marta said wryly, looking at the profusion of red, white and indigo flowers which seemed determined to make the royal celebrations last the whole summer. 'I won't be a minute.'

Josephine watched her go inside, amused to see that – in spite of all her warnings – Marta was now the one surging ahead with the scheme, and confident of her ability to sweet-talk information out of any publican, particularly if he was a man. True to form, she returned a few minutes later, clutching a piece of paper and looking smug. 'What have you found out?' Josephine asked.

'Well, this is how we get there,' Marta said, handing her a hastily scribbled map with directions. 'And you were right. Paradise House is owned by a French family. He works away and isn't here all the time – we all know why that is – and she's a charming woman who loves her garden. They have a little boy, Christophe, and they've been here for seven or eight years.'

Josephine nodded. 'Yes, that fits. Vivienne told me that they came back from France at the end of the twenties. It sounds like he moved his lover in shortly afterwards.'

'And now they're selling up to go abroad. They're popular in the village, if only because they live quietly and keep themselves to themselves – unlike the previous occupant. Everyone seems very sorry that they're leaving.'

Josephine shook her head in admiration. 'That really is quite brilliant.'

'What is?'

'Well, I always wondered how Beresford got away with being someone else. It's very easy to change your appearance. If we're right about all this, I imagine that the celebrity who left London in a suit was virtually unrecognisable as the carefree family man who arrived here in a Bugatti and an open-necked shirt, and no one really knew what he looked like anyway. But his voice was something else altogether – he gave himself away every time he opened his mouth. A French accent would make him sound very different.'

Marta turned the car round and headed back in the direction from which they had come. 'Do you think she knows he's married, or has he been leading them both on?'

A double deception was something that Josephine hadn't actually considered. 'She'd have to be party to it, surely? His behaviour would seem a bit peculiar if she weren't, but who's to say? He's obviously very convincing. And if she *doesn't* know, I get the impression that Vivienne is very keen for her illusions to be shattered as soon as possible. She'd probably kill to do it personally – and that's not a pun.' She thought for a moment, then said more seriously: 'Whoever she is, she's bound to be devastated. How must that feel? To lose the person you love and not be able to mourn him publicly – perhaps even to discover for the first time through the newspapers that he was married. I'm not sure she'll be answering the door to anyone, let alone a couple of casual house hunters. We're probably wasting our time.'

'Or we could just discover a perfectly happy French family who are packing up to move to a new life and have never heard of Anthony Beresford. There's only one way to find out.'

The narrow, tree-hung lane was so overgrown that they nearly missed the turning that had been noted down for them. Swearing under her breath, Marta pulled down hard on the steering wheel and the car made a graceless but effective lurch to the left. She learned her lesson and dropped her speed, humouring the sharp bends in the road, and after another half a mile or so they saw the small, octagonal lodge which Archie had described. It marked the entrance to a gravelled driveway, and Marta slowed the car still more.

'This must be it,' Josephine said, feeling suddenly excited. 'Look, there's the name.' The sign was discreet and all but buried in a tangle of laurel and rhododendron bushes, but enough of the lettering was visible to confirm that they were in the right place. They had found Paradise House. What else it would reveal remained to be seen.

2

'You lot are all the same. You've had enough tries at framing me for murder, and I suppose you think you've got me for this one?' The voice was rough and coarse, and there was no trace of the Irish descent that the name proclaimed. 'Well, we'll see about that. You couldn't make it stick last time, and you won't now. I didn't kill her, and none of your filthy tricks can prove that I did.'

Penrose looked across the table at Frederick George Murphy and made no attempt to hide his dislike. Usually, he avoided relating a man's actions to his appearance, but in this case the cliché happened to be true: Murphy did have the look of a hardened criminal – a stocky, red-faced bully with a pug-nose and a blank stare, not to mention five previous prison sentences for assault, burglary and pimping. So far in the course of this murder investigation, no one had been prepared to testify favourably to the defendant's character, not even the woman he lived with, and Penrose was confident of a successful result in court. Resisting the temptation to engage with the accusation of corruption, he charged Frederick George Murphy with the murder of Rosina Field at Islington Green on the twelfth of May, and left the room.

A clerk was waiting for him in the corridor outside. 'Telephone call for you, sir. It's the Deputy Governor of Holloway, and she says it's urgent.'

Penrose nodded and walked over to the desk, wondering what Mary Size wanted. He liked and respected the prison governor, but they sat at opposite ends of the legal system and their paths rarely crossed; his work was invariably over when hers was just beginning. 'Miss Size, what can I do for you?'

She came straight to the point. 'It's about Vivienne Beresford, Chief Inspector.'

'I'm afraid I'm no longer working on that case.'

'But she's asking to speak to you.'

Penrose sighed, intrigued by the request and frustrated at his inability to accept it. 'As much as I sympathise with Mrs Beresford's position, my hands are tied. You of all people must understand that?'

'Oh, I do indeed,' she said with feeling. Like Penrose, Mary Size had had her fair share of battles over bureaucracy and protocol, and the two were natural allies. 'But things have just become rather more complicated, Chief Inspector. This involves Miss Tey.'

'Josephine?' he asked, taken completely by surprise. 'What do you mean?'

'You know that she's been visiting Mrs Beresford?'

'Yes, she told me.'

'Then let me be brief, because time is of the essence. Beresford asked to see me first thing this morning. She told me that she hadn't slept all night because she was worried about having inadvertently said something to Miss Tey which might put her in danger.'

The concerns about Josephine's safety which had been playing in Penrose's mind over the last few days suddenly surfaced with a devastating sense of reality. 'What did she say?' he asked, gripping the receiver and trying not to panic.

'She would only tell me that it concerned the murder of Millicent Gray. Beresford is convinced that she knows who did it, and she thinks that Miss Tey might have set out to prove it. She has a proposal for you.'

'I'm not sure she's in a bargaining position.'

'Normally, I would agreed with you. In this particular case, though, we might want to listen.'

'All right. What's the proposal?'

'Beresford will tell you where Miss Tey has gone, prove to you once and for all that she wasn't responsible for Millicent Gray's death, and tell you who was. She has also said that she will give you enough evidence to convict her sister's murderer.'

'Olivia Hanlon was murdered?'

'Yes, she says she has proof.'

'And do you believe her?'

'She's very convincing.'

'So what are her conditions?'

'There's only one. She asks that you take her with you when you go after Miss Tey.'

'But that's impossible. My superiors would never agree to that, and surely the Home Office would take a dim view of something so unorthodox.'

'Unorthodox, yes, but not unprecedented. There are rare occasions when a prisoner is allowed out in the interests of justice – handcuffed to a warder at all times, of course, and with a police escort. Beresford is still on remand, and in a case with a lower profile she might easily have been granted bail while she awaited her trial.'

'But you've just said it yourself – this is such a high-profile case. The press would have a field day if they got wind of it. I'll happily go and see Rygate now, but he'll laugh me out of his office.'

'Then let me give you one more thing to consider which might sway things your way. If we don't agree to what she suggests, Beresford has made it clear that there will be consequences. She tells me that she has significant evidence of police negligence with regard to her sister's death – negligence bordering on corruption. She has also made it clear that what she knows about Millicent Gray's death will do considerable damage to the reputation of the BBC.'

'Has she spoken to her solicitor?' Penrose asked hopefully.

'This morning, on the telephone. I needn't tell you that he is stressing her right to prove her innocence, as well as the destructive nature of what might emerge in court at her trial. Does that help?'

'Very much.' Penrose recalled his conversations with Josephine and tried to follow the logic of what she was thinking. 'Did Mrs Beresford mention Paradise House?' he asked. 'Is that where she wants to go?'

'Perhaps that's what she meant, but she wouldn't be specific. She's an intelligent woman, as you know.'

Penrose thought about it. If the worst came to the worst, he would go independently to Paradise House, but there was a chance that he was wrong and the most reliable way of ensuring Josephine's safety was to give Vivienne Beresford what she wanted. 'Let me have a few minutes to see what I can do,' he said.

'I'll wait by my telephone.'

Penrose ended the call and immediately telephoned Holly Place, reluctant to believe that Josephine would play with fire like this without speaking to him first. There was no answer, so he tried the Cowdray Club, only to be told that Josephine hadn't been seen since the previous afternoon. As a last resort, he called Ronnie and Lettice at their studio. 'Is Josephine with you?' he demanded as soon as Ronnie answered.

'And good morning to you, too, Archie.'

'Don't mess me about. Have you seen her?'

'No, she telephoned last night, but—'

'She telephoned? Why didn't you tell me?'

'Because you weren't here to tell,' Ronnie said, with not unreasonable indignation.

'Did she leave a message?'

'Only to call her when you got the chance. Why, Archie? Is something wrong?'

Penrose slammed the receiver down without an explanation, imagining all sorts of horrors, most of which had a starring role for Billy Whiting. Somehow, he managed to stay calm while he mentally gathered every scrap of ammunition that he could think of before making his next move. When he was ready, he telephoned

Bill Murray at Broadcasting House and left a very clear message for the Director General; next, he climbed the stairs to the fourth floor and had a frank conversation with the Assistant Commissioner, reminding Rygate of his position at the time of Olivia Hanlon's death; and finally, sooner than even he had dared to hope, he called Mary Size and asked her to make sure that Vivienne Beresford was ready and waiting.

3

Marta parked the Morris in the lane, a few yards short of the five-bar gate that marked the entrance to Paradise House. The approach was still exactly as Archie had described it – a narrow track, enclosed by the exuberant growth of an early summer which had seen rain and sun in equal measure, giving way abruptly to open sky – and Josephine wondered if the rest of the property was as little-changed by the passing of a decade. She got out of the car and walked over to the gate to take a closer look at the house she had heard so much about. It was attractive and elegant in a haphazard sort of way, built of red brick and dating back to the seventeenth century. Its front walls were covered in ivy and wisteria, and the uneven positioning of the windows suggested a house with many landings and staircases – one that had, perhaps, originally been made up of several smaller dwellings. The driveway split in two to form a circular area immediately in front of the property, bordered by mixed hedging, but there were no vehicles parked outside. In fact, the whole house felt lonely and remote, distanced from the life of the village and with the woodland acting as a buffer between the grounds and the main road. All she could hear was the trickle of water from a stream somewhere over to her left. Everything else was disarmingly quiet.

Marta joined her by the gate. 'The place looks deserted,' she said, staring up at the windows, some of which had their curtains tightly drawn. 'It's a dull day – I'd have expected a light on somewhere if there were anyone at home.'

'At least if it's empty we can have a good look round without being disturbed, but I doubt we'll find whatever it is we're looking for without going in.' Josephine sighed, disappointed at the thought of coming so far only to be thwarted by a locked door. 'Still, I suppose you can learn quite a lot from looking through a window or two.'

'Yes, but we'd better make sure we're right first. It doesn't look good to be caught with your nose pressed to the glass.' She opened the gate and led the way to the front door, which was flanked by rose beds on either side. The thud of the heavy iron knocker sounded unnaturally loud in the stillness, but it brought no response and Marta tried again. 'Well, we're obviously not going to be invited in,' she said after a decent interval. 'Looks like we'll have to show ourselves around.'

Josephine was already ahead of her, peering through the nearest set of windows into the dining room – tastefully decorated in an Arts and Crafts style, with apple-green walls, boldly painted furniture and a large vase of flowers. The house had obviously clung tenaciously to its history, proudly proclaiming its age with exposed timbers and beams and a beautiful polished brick floor, but the flowers had fared less well; once striking, the display was now wilting and badly in need of attention. 'I'm not sure anyone's been here for a few days,' she said. 'Either that, or they've been too preoccupied to worry about the flower arrangements.'

She turned in the direction of a path which led round to the back of the house, but Marta caught her arm. 'What if you're right, Josephine?' she asked. 'What if there's a woman in there grieving for someone she loved? Of course she's not going to answer the door. Lying our way over the threshold is one thing, but poking round uninvited suddenly feels a bit shabby – particularly if we're only doing it to satisfy Vivienne Beresford's curiosity. She killed him, after all – our coming here on her behalf isn't exactly tactful.'

Josephine hesitated, knowing that Marta was right but reluctant to abandon the promise she had made. 'I understand what you're saying and I agree with you, but I realised yesterday when I was talking to Vivienne that there's no easy right or wrong to any of this. Millicent Gray should have known better than to get involved with another woman's husband, but she didn't deserve to die. Vivienne has killed twice, and yet I can sympathise with her position. This woman – whoever she is – might be destroyed by her grief now, but if she was party to the deception, you could argue that she brought it on herself. I've stopped trying to rationalise it now. I just want the answers.'

Marta nodded, either convinced by her argument or too partial to object any further, and they walked round to the back of the house together. The extensive grounds were south-facing, and – in better weather – would have enjoyed sunshine for most of the day; even under slate-grey skies, they formed a stunning backdrop to the house, offering privacy and seclusion to anyone lucky enough to live there. The area immediately by the house was the most formal part of the garden – terraced, with an ornamental fishpond and a rose-clad pergola that gave views over four carefully manicured tiers of lawn, all linked by stone steps. In one direction, a pathway with clipped yew trees led to a substantial kitchen garden and a small apple orchard, and in the other, a sweeping expanse of lawn sloped gently down to the southern boundary, marked by a line of graceful weeping willows. Just visible from where they stood, but with a troubling presence which dominated Josephine's first impressions of the grounds, was the corner of a swimming pool.

'Gosh, this is beautiful,' Marta said, distracted for a moment from their purpose, and Josephine smiled at her enthusiasm.

'It's a shame you don't have an audience. For a moment there, you sounded every inch the prospective buyer.'

'In my dreams. I'd love a house like this, but I doubt I could afford it. Did the advertisement say how much they were asking?'

'Not that I recall.' She watched as Marta crouched down to smell a clump of verbena in the small herb garden just outside the back door, pinching a sprig of the plant between her thumb and forefinger. 'You're serious, aren't you? Doesn't what happened here put you off?'

Marta laughed. 'I can't believe you're asking me that without the slightest whiff of irony. The cottage couldn't have a darker past, but think of how beautiful it is now and how much we love it there.' She stood up, brushing soil off her clothes, and spoke more seriously, to herself as much as to Josephine. 'And unlike Cambridge, these aren't my ghosts.'

Josephine took Marta's hand and kissed it, smelling the faintest trace of lemon on her skin. 'It's not always weakness to turn your back on ghosts,' she said. 'You don't have to vanquish them all.'

'I know, and I'm learning which ones to ignore, I promise.'

'Good.' Josephine followed Marta's eyes across the lawn to a dark bank of trees on the eastern side. 'Actually, I think a couple of acres would suit you.'

Marta smiled. 'Yes, so do I. Do you want to look at the pool before we do a circuit of the house?'

'I suppose we might as well get it over with.' An old dovecot marked the opening to a winding stone path which led through shrubs and past statues to the poolside. There was a diving board at one end, and the chequered pattern of the pool's black-and-white tiles was made abstract by a light summer rain on the surface of the water, but all Josephine could see was the image of that night, etched into her imagination by other people's memories of it: Vivienne Beresford's hands on her sister's shoulders, holding her under until she no longer struggled; Olivia's body, lifeless and pale by the side of the pool. She glanced back at the house, unsettled now by her thoughts and by Marta's suggestion that someone might be at home after all, but most of the building was obscured by a soft white powdering of apple blossom.

'Either they don't know there was a death here or they're not bothered,' Marta said, nodding to a sheltered arbour along one side of the pool which housed a dining table, a motley collection of chairs, and various other trappings of summer living. 'It doesn't seem to have stopped them having fun here.'

'I imagine Anthony Beresford raised a toast to that night every day of his life,' Josephine said. 'Vivienne played right into his hands by giving him something like that to hold over her. He struck me as the sort of man who would have done exactly what he wanted anyway, but what she did gave her no recourse whatsoever.'

There was a small wooden building behind the pool area which seemed to function partly as a summer house and partly as a shed, and Marta opened the door to look inside. 'Why the hell didn't he just leave her?' she asked, glancing round at the paraphernalia of family life – the croquet set and tennis racquets, the three bicycles stacked neatly along a side wall, one of them a child's. 'Just look at this stuff – his whole world was obviously here, so why didn't he embrace it? Everything could have been so different.'

Josephine didn't answer; it was one of the things which puzzled her most about the theory of Beresford's double life, and his much talked-of concern with respectability didn't seem an entirely satisfactory explanation. 'I don't know,' she said. 'I can see why he wouldn't end his marriage for the sort of affair we thought he was having with Millicent, but this is very different.' She looked round again, willing the pieces of the puzzle to fall into place, but inspiration still eluded her. 'Anyway, one step at a time. We haven't even proved he was here yet. Let's go back to the house.'

The kitchen seemed to be the most recent addition to the property, connected at right angles to the main building and forming a pleasant, L-shaped courtyard. Josephine peered through the window and noticed that – apart from some clutter by the back door, where a stand of umbrellas and walking sticks had spilled over onto the floor – the room was neat and orderly; if meals had been prepared there recently, someone had cleared up very thoroughly afterwards. Her eyes swept the room again, and this time she noticed a small, pale face looking back at her. The child stood framed in the doorway, a boy of nine or ten with a shock of blonde hair, clutching an empty glass. It was hard to say which of them was more surprised, but before Josephine had the chance to say anything, the boy turned and ran back into the house. 'We'd better get our story straight,' she said quietly to Marta. 'I have a feeling we're about to need it.'

They heard the boy's voice calling out for someone, speaking quickly in French, and he reappeared a few seconds later with a stocky, broad-shouldered man who held his hand protectively. 'If he's the Frenchman, that's our moral high ground gone,' Marta said. 'We'd better be bloody convincing.'

'Just remember how much you love the house. And smile,' Josephine added, hoping that hers looked more sincere than it felt.

The man unlocked the back door and immediately disillusioned them of the idea that he might be anything other than English. 'Can I help you?' he asked warily in a heavy London accent, looking at each of them in turn.

'This must seem terribly rude,' Marta said, her embarrassment judged to perfection, 'but we were hoping to see the house.'

'The house?'

'That's right. We did knock but there was no answer, and everything was so . . .' She paused, and Josephine waited as eagerly for the lie as the man for whom it was intended. 'Well, everything was just so beautiful that we couldn't resist coming a bit further in. I'm sorry, but I suppose you could say that the house led us astray. It *is* still for sale, isn't it? I've been abroad, but I read the notice in the paper when I got back, and the name intrigued me. I knew we were meant for each other.'

Josephine held her breath. Marta's speech had been perfectly pitched until the final claim, but she wasn't to know that the words 'Paradise House' hadn't actually been mentioned in the advertisement. To her relief, the man seemed to have forgotten the details, if he had ever known them, and he simply shook his head. 'I'm sorry,' he said. 'You've had a wasted trip.'

He went to close the door but Marta wasn't prepared to give in quite so easily. '*Is* the house sold?' she asked.

'No, not exactly,' he admitted, 'but things have changed since the notice went in and the owner hasn't made up her mind whether to sell or not.'

'So could we at least have a look round?' Marta pleaded. 'Then if she does decide to go ahead with the sale, I would at least be in a position to make an offer.' The man looked at her, as if trying to gauge how serious she was. 'We have come rather a long way,' Marta lied, 'and my friend has to go back to Scotland tomorrow. You know what we women are like – I can't do a thing without a second opinion. We won't keep you long, and I'd be so grateful. Could you at least ask the owner for me?'

The man bent down and whispered to the little boy, who went obediently out into the garden to play. 'All right,' he said. 'Come in for a minute and I'll speak to her.'

It was unclear whether he meant by telephone or in person, but Marta winked triumphantly at Josephine and they followed their guide through to a long, low sitting room, with windows to three aspects and an enormous inglenook fireplace built into the other wall. It was a beautiful space, decorated with sumptuous informality in the colours of a winter sunset – red walls, flame-orange curtains and sofas piled high with tasselled cushions in black and gold. One side of the fireplace was taken up with a bookshelf which stretched from floor to ceiling; the rest of the walls were bare except for an extraordinary angular portrait of two women, instantly recognisable as the work of Tamara de Lempicka and precisely placed to be reflected by a large Venetian mirror. A gramophone and a pile of records sat on a table near to where Josephine was standing, and she noticed that the needle was pulled to one side, as if the music – a Fats Waller tune – had been interrupted. She was fascinated to stand in the room that both Gerard Leaman and Vivienne had described on the night of the party, but one glance round told her that anything more personal still eluded her – there were no photographs, no letters lying about, nothing that could prove – or disprove – that Anthony Beresford had ever lived here.

'Wait here,' their host instructed. 'I won't be long.'

'Thank you, Mr . . . ?' Marta said, but her question – unheard or ignored – went unacknowledged. 'There isn't much sign of packing, is there?' she added when he had left the room.

'No, there isn't.' After a couple of minutes, they heard footsteps moving about on the floor above and Josephine stood up. 'I'm going to have a look round while he's gone,' she said, and Marta looked at her as if she were mad.

'What if he catches you poking about?' she asked. 'He'll know we're lying straight away.'

'And what if he comes back and says the house is off the market? We'll be escorted politely to the front door, and that will be that. This might be our only chance to find something.'

'All right, but I'm coming with you.'

'Don't be silly – we can't both go. At least if he comes back while I'm gone you can tell him I'm looking for the cloakroom.'

She left the room before Marta could argue any further, knowing that her time was limited. There were three doors off the sitting room, and she chose the one that went out into the hall. She had already seen enough of the dining room to know that it was unlikely to help her, so she passed straight through to the room next door – a small oak-panelled study, overlooking the courtyard. A desk with a typewriter stood by the window, and next to the typewriter was a photograph, turned face down. Eagerly, Josephine picked it up. The glass in the small oval frame had been broken, but the photograph itself was undamaged. It had been taken in the garden, next to a beautiful, ornate sundial, and it pictured the little boy they had just met, younger and sitting on a man's lap, laughing into the camera. The man was dressed casually in clothes meant for gardening, and Josephine was moved by the love and pride with which he looked down at his son. Had she not been seeking Anthony Beresford, she would never have recognised him: the transformation was extraordinary, and its agent was not so much the different clothes or the change of surroundings, but his obvious happiness. She looked with interest at the only face in the picture that she had never seen before: the woman wore no make up and was by no means conventionally pretty, but there was an amusement in her eyes and a wry worldliness about her smile that seemed more memorable than pleasant features would have been; it was, she thought, the face of a woman whose company would never be dull.

Josephine heard footsteps in the hall and hurriedly returned the photograph to the desk where she had found it, but she had not been quick enough. The man stood in the doorway, watching her, and she could not decide if the expression on his face was fury or simply panic. 'Who are you?' he asked, 'and why are you really here?'

4

Vivienne sat in the back of the police car, trying to cope with the outside world. She had been at Holloway for less than a week, but already London felt strange and disorienting, and she understood now why people who had known an institutional life for any length of time found it difficult to readjust to anything else. Beside her, the prison warder stared straight ahead, calm and impassive, and Vivienne wondered why – when she had always been shackled to someone – this temporary humiliation should matter so much? The cold steel of the handcuff around her wrist made her suddenly claustrophobic and she tried to subdue the panic by concentrating on the sliver of sky above the city's streets, grey and depressing, an ungracious welcome for the swallows who had flown so far to announce summer. Wilde's story came back to her, unwelcome and uninvited, and she thought again of the book in Anthony's car, the book that she had always found so sad as a child. 'Could I have some air?' she asked, and Penrose – sitting in the passenger seat – wound down his window.

It was strange how quickly the journey came flooding back to her as soon as familiar landmarks began to appear – the fields that marked the end of city life, the buildings on the outskirts of the village, and most familiar of all, the small knot of hatred that grew tighter in her stomach as they drew close to Paradise House. She scarcely knew how to contain her rage at the depth of Anthony's deception. Another life, another lover, a child – and with them, no doubt, he was another man, the one she had always looked for but never found. For the sake of her own sanity, Vivienne steered her thoughts away from Anthony to other things. She thought about the years she had spent in Olivia's clubs, perched on a stool and wearing a mechanical smile, watching as her sister dealt ruthlessly with anyone who crossed her. She thought back to the night at Paradise House when her whole life had changed, and remembered how surprised she had been to discover a similar violence deep within herself. But most of all, she thought about the question that Josephine had asked: would she have killed Anthony if she had not killed Olivia? The answer haunted her now with the knowledge that she had wasted her life, and she wondered how she could ever have been so stupid.

5

'Well?'

Josephine hesitated, unable to think of a single excuse which would justify her behaviour. When she failed to speak, the man walked over to her and took her gently but firmly by the arm. 'I think it's time for you and your friend to leave.'

She shook him off, just as Marta appeared in the doorway. 'What's going on?' she asked.

'I don't know who you are or what you're after, but I want you both out of here now. The house isn't for sale.' Josephine shook her head discreetly, warning Marta not to argue. His manner was still civil, but she could not forget the expression in his eyes when he had first seen her looking at the photograph, and fear had eclipsed her initial embarrassment at having been caught. Her recklessness had put them both in danger, and she would be pleased now when they were safely off the premises. To her relief, Marta seemed as eager to leave as she was, and they allowed themselves to be escorted to the front door and out into the driveway without any further objection. 'I'll see you to your car.'

'There's really no need,' Josephine protested.

'I think there is.' He ushered them forward, but was distracted by the sound of another car approaching down the lane, obviously moving at speed. As they watched, a black Daimler appeared at the open gate, and Josephine recognised Bill Fallowfield at the wheel. The car slowed, and Archie jumped out. 'Mr Whiting,' he said, subtly moving the man to one side, away from Marta and Josephine, 'how nice to see you again. I've been hoping to catch up with you. There are a few questions I'd like to ask you, but perhaps you'd care to tell me what's going on here first?'

Josephine looked again at the man who had let them into the house, realising now who he was and how close she and Marta had been to the main suspect for Millicent Gray's murder. The agony of the actress's death returned to her in a series of vivid and horrific images, and she understood how foolish she had been. Whiting recovered quickly from his surprise, and his answer to Archie's question was calm and composed. 'These ladies came to look at the house, but it's off the market. I was just making sure they got safely on their way.'

Archie looked at Josephine and she could see that fury had replaced his initial relief at seeing her safe and well. 'Are you all right?'

The enquiry was brusque, the tone clinical, and she knew she would have a lot of explaining to do. 'Yes, we're fine.' She gave him an embarrassed half-smile, hoping that some of his coldness was an attempt to disguise the connection between them, but he had already turned away.

'Why is the house your concern, Mr Whiting?' he asked. 'What are you doing here?' This time it was Billy Whiting's turn to have no ready answer. He stared first at Josephine and then at Archie, and she could see him trying to work out if he had imagined a familiarity. 'You're very quiet all of a sudden,' Archie continued sarcastically, 'but if you're doing guided tours, perhaps we could all have a look round? I've brought someone with me who'd very much like to see Paradise House again.'

He turned back to the car and nodded to Fallowfield. Josephine watched Billy Whiting's face as Vivienne Beresford got out of the back seat, handcuffed to a prison warder, and saw his disbelief turn swiftly to horror. 'Where is she, Billy?' Vivienne demanded. 'Where are you hiding my sister?'

Whiting said nothing but glanced instinctively back at the house, and the movement – though fleeting – was enough to tell

Vivienne all she needed to know. Josephine followed her gaze up to the first floor and saw a woman standing at the window immediately above the front door; her face was indistinct in the unlit room, but there was no doubt in Josephine's mind that she was looking at the woman in the photograph – Anthony Beresford's lover, and the mother of his child. She was still trying to match the realisation to the words she had just heard when Vivienne gave a choked sob of recognition. For a moment, Josephine thought she was going to break down, but she made a visible effort to hold herself together. She tried to move towards the door, but the warder held her back.

'What do you mean, Mrs Beresford?' Archie asked, looking at her in astonishment. 'Your sister is dead. How can she be here?'

Vivienne ignored him and stared at Billy until he could no longer meet her eye. 'You knew, didn't you? And all this time you've been helping them – keeping his car in your garage, making sure that no one got too close, propping up our charade of a marriage. You've spent years driving us round, listening to us squabble, asking me how he is and what we're doing together at the weekend, and all the time you knew it was a sham.' She shook her head in disbelief. 'And you were so kind to me that night. You drove me away and made me feel safe, but you weren't protecting me at all, were you? You were protecting Anthony and Olivia and their filthy little secret.' She moved a couple of steps closer to Whiting and Josephine noticed how uneasy her presence made him, but she couldn't decide whether it was out of guilt or genuine fear. 'So how far did it go, Billy? Did you kill for them? Did Millicent Gray get a little too close to the truth?'

The accusation tempted him out of his silence. 'I had nothing to do with that woman's death,' he said desperately. 'I'm not a killer. You know I'm not.'

'And neither was I, it seems – not until recently, anyway.' Her tone was becoming increasingly aggressive, and Josephine wondered if and when Archie would step in. 'So you just cleared up the mess, as usual?' she asked, pressing him for an answer. 'Well, you can't clear this one up for her, Billy. This is beyond even you.'

Whiting looked at Archie. 'I didn't kill anyone,' he repeated. 'You have to believe me.'

'Forgive me if I don't take anybody's word entirely at face value just yet,' Archie said. 'Put Mr Whiting in the car, Sergeant, and call for back-up. I'm going to take Mrs Beresford inside and find out what the hell *is* going on here.'

'There's a child around somewhere,' Marta warned. 'I think he's in the garden. Shall we go and find him?'

Josephine tried and failed to remember the last time she had seen such an unforgiving expression on Archie's face. 'I think you've both done quite enough for one day,' he said, 'and you're certainly not going to start wandering off round the garden. Sergeant, when the other car gets here, ask them to stay with Whiting while you look for the boy. I don't want him frightened by uniforms. In the meantime, make sure everyone else stays exactly where they are. Is that clear?'

'Yes, sir,' Fallowfield said, glancing apologetically at Marta and Josephine.

'Good.' He turned away, and Josephine watched as he took Vivienne and her escort back into Paradise House. She glanced up at the window again, but Olivia Hanlon – if that was who she was – had disappeared.

*

Penrose watched Vivienne Beresford glance round curiously as soon as she was over the threshold, but she seemed certain of where she was going and he let her lead the way upstairs, waiting in vain for the other woman to show herself. After the strong colours in the rest of the house, the main bedroom – with walls distempered a dull white – seemed daring and radical; the shade had been deliberately chosen to show two bright abstract paintings off to their best advantage, and it combined with unusually high ceilings to give the room a spacious, airy feel. There was a sycamore tree outside the window, and a breeze blew its branches against the glass as Penrose looked at the woman sitting on the bed with her head bowed, conscious of intruding where he did not belong. She lifted her face when she heard them come in, and he saw that her eyes were swollen from crying and her face was pale and drawn; she had aged, but he recognised her instantly from his last visit, and he wondered how many of the lines around her face and eyes had been added by the shock and the grief of the week she had just lived through. On the bedside table, easily within her reach, there was a gun.

Vivienne stumbled in the doorway, as if she hadn't entirely believed – or wanted to believe – her own theory. The reality of coming face to face with her worst suspicions threatened to be too much for her, and the warder had to steady her. Slowly, languidly, Olivia Hanlon picked up the gun and nursed it in her lap, and Penrose saw in her demeanour the desperation of someone who was lost beyond all hope of return. The warder seemed to recognise it, too, and Penrose guessed that she had witnessed it many times in the women in her charge. Her fear was obvious and justified, and his conscience wouldn't let him keep her there. 'Give me the key,' he said, and then, when she hesitated, 'I'll take full responsibility for anything that happens.' Relieved, she did as he asked and Penrose released her from the handcuffs and sent her downstairs, confident that Mary Size's expectations of her staff would not include acting as a sitting target for a woman with nothing left to lose. Vivienne rubbed her wrist absent-mindedly but barely seemed to notice that she had lost her shadow, so transfixed was she by her sister. For both women, the world had shrunk to include just the two of them, and Penrose realised that he was merely a silent observer.

It was Olivia who spoke first. 'How dare you come here after what you've done?' she said.

'What *I've* done?' Vivienne looked at her in astonishment. 'You made me think that I'd killed you, then lived with my husband for ten years behind my back – and you challenge me about what *I've* done?'

Penrose interrupted, hoping to distract the women from their mutual hatred by straightforward questions. 'Is this true?' he asked. 'Are you Olivia Hanlon? Forgive me if I'm confused, but the last time we met you told me you were her housekeeper.'

The woman looked directly at him for the first time, and he remembered how convincing she had been back then; not for a moment had he suspected that she wasn't who she said she was, and he wondered how far he should trust her word now. 'Yes, I was Olivia Hanlon, but she died to me ten years ago.'

'So whose body was lying by the pool that night? Who have we buried as you?'

'Her name was Colette Haas. She worked for me as a prostitute in Paris, and then in London.'

Penrose glanced at Vivienne, but the name obviously meant nothing to her; the details of the deception she had guessed at were as new to her as they were to him. 'And how did Colette Haas die?'

She gave a hollow laugh. 'More obligingly than Olivia Hanlon.'

'Tell me, Miss Hanlon,' Penrose said, and there was an edge to his voice now which matched hers; it wasn't only Vivienne Beresford who felt cheated of the truth.

'As I said, she'd worked for me in Paris and in London. Every now and again, we needed more cocaine than we could get via the usual methods, and I asked people to bring it in for me. She was one of the girls who volunteered. It was dangerous, but I paid her well and she always needed money because she was rather too fond of the stuff herself. The delivery was scheduled for that night. Billy collected her from the station and brought her up to the house. It

314

was a good party, and Colette was looking for oblivion. I suppose you could say that I helped her find it.'

'So she died of an overdose?'

'Does it matter how she died?'

'Yes, it matters very much.' Penrose managed to keep his voice even, but only just. Olivia Hanlon's detached recollection of the girl she had used disgusted him. He had not been able to forget the sadness of Rosina Field's death, her body dumped so callously in that cellar, her life dismissed so easily. The assumption that women of a certain type were dispensable was one of the things he hated most about his job, and he saw it both in the men he arrested and – occasionally – among his colleagues. He expected it from someone like Frederick Murphy, but somehow he had never believed that a woman would treat a member of her own sex in the same way, and he cursed himself for his own naivety.

'No, she didn't die of an overdose,' Olivia admitted. 'She drowned. After everyone else had fled to save their own skins before the police arrived, there was one person left who was too out of control to go anywhere.'

'And you drowned her.' It wasn't a question; by now, Penrose was all too certain of what had happened that night and how he and Townsend had been fooled.

'Did Anthony know what you were doing?' Vivienne asked, and then, when she received no response, 'For Christ's sake, Olivia, tell me if my husband was a killer.'

She took a couple of steps closer to the bed and Olivia picked up the gun which had lain forgotten in her lap. 'Your husband? How easily you use that word. Anthony loved me, Vivienne. He would have done anything for me, so what do *you* think he knew?' Penrose took Vivienne's arm and tried to pull her gently away, but she resisted. 'You made it all so easy, Viv. I goaded you all night, and I knew exactly how you'd react when you saw me with Anthony. I'd seen you in those clubs, remember – my little sister, hard as nails.

Nothing ever got to you, did it? There was no passion in you, only anger, and anger is so easy to manipulate. Did you really think you could kill me so easily, Viv? A few seconds under the water and out of your life for good? Remember who taught you everything you know.' She raised the gun and Penrose moved forward, but to his astonishment she simply held it out to Vivienne. 'Here – take it. It's all over now, so finish what you started. I won't stop you this time.'

'Put the gun down, Miss Hanlon,' Penrose said urgently.

'Why? She can't take anything more from me than she already has.' She stared challengingly at her sister, goading her now as she had all those years ago. 'Take the gun, Viv.' It was an order, and Vivienne did as she was asked, holding the weapon with a familiarity that told Penrose that the single shot to Anthony Beresford's head had not been a lucky accident.

'So you waited until Anthony had got rid of everyone, then you killed Colette Haas and put her body where yours should have been?'

'Yes.'

Olivia Hanlon's willingness to admit to everything suggested that she no longer wished to live, and she seemed oblivious to the gun and the danger she was in, but Penrose wondered if she had considered the positive effect that her implication of Anthony Beresford might have on Vivienne's chances in front of a jury? Unwittingly, she could be helping her sister to live, but only if there was no further bloodshed. 'Then you went to the lodge and played housekeeper?' he said, hoping that Vivienne would have the sense to realise that the more Olivia was allowed to say, the more reasons she had not to pull the trigger.

'Yes, although that was never part of the plan. I just went there to get out of the way. Stupidly, I didn't expect anyone to come looking, but you saw me and I had to let you in. It was the best story I could think of at the time.'

'You let me think that I'd taken a life,' Vivienne said. 'Do you have any idea how that changes everything you've ever believed about yourself?'

'Of course I do. I know exactly how it feels.'

'And that's why Anthony was so tender towards me afterwards, isn't it? It had nothing to do with genuine love, or even regret – it was expediency. He needed me on side, so he did what Anthony always did best – he took control.'

Olivia shrugged. 'Perhaps that was the Anthony you knew. Mine was very different.'

It was a simple observation, but perhaps the most inflammatory thing she had said yet. Penrose did his best to divert Vivienne from a conversation which would only throw up more damaging comparisons between the two relationships, but he knew that there was no such thing as safe territory. 'What did you do after that night?' he asked Olivia.

'We waited for things to die down, then I left the country as Colette Haas. I stayed in France while Anthony was working in Europe, and we saw each other when we could.'

'You were with him there as well?' Vivienne asked, stunned, and the pain in her voice as she saw the lies torn down one by one was almost unbearable.

'Yes. We came back to this country shortly after you did, and moved straight in here.'

'We?' Penrose queried, and immediately regretted it.

'Yes. By then we had a child. Can you imagine a more idyllic place to raise a little boy, Viv? And Anthony was such a good father. Christophe worshipped him.' At the thought of her son, her own pain seemed finally to eclipse her desire to hurt her sister. 'Do you have any idea what that little boy has lost, thanks to you?' she demanded.

'It didn't have to be that way. Why didn't you just take Anthony from me, Olivia? If you loved each other that much, why put me through all those bleak, empty years? I might have been happy with someone else, for God's sake. What had I ever really done to either of you to deserve that?'

In her distress, Vivienne had relaxed her grip on the gun and Penrose edged a little closer to her. 'Answer the question, Miss Hanlon,' he said, deliberately allying himself with the bigger threat in the room. 'A lot of lives might have been saved by a straightforward divorce.'

She glared at both of them, but obliged him with an answer. 'Olivia Hanlon needed to die,' she said. 'It was as simple as that. I had debts – big debts, and they weren't going to go away. The house was at risk and other things had caught up with me. My friendly policeman couldn't protect me anymore, not after the scandal of Goddard and Mrs Meyrick, and there were people who wanted me dead. Even Colette Haas had started to cause trouble by threatening to expose what really went on at the Golden Hat if I didn't pay her more money, and I couldn't afford to do that. So I could never have lived openly with Anthony, even if he wasn't married. At best, I would have ended up in prison; at worst, someone on the outside would have caught up with me. This was the only way.'

'Which policeman was protecting you, Miss Hanlon?' Penrose asked, scarcely wanting to hear the answer.

'Jim Townsend, but I'm sure you've worked that out already. How is he these days? I must have paid for that bungalow over the years, so I hope Bournemouth suits him.'

It would have been hard for Penrose to rationalise the sense of betrayal which he felt at that moment, and he responded in the only way he could. 'Mr Whiting has implied that you murdered Millicent Gray,' he asked, determined now to bridge the years between the crimes with truth, no matter who was hurt in the process. 'Is he right?'

Whiting's disloyalty came as a painful shock to Olivia Hanlon, as he had known it would, but she had no choice but to believe it. 'She found out about us somehow. I think she followed Anthony one day, then she made an appointment to see the house and bided her time until she'd worked out who his lover was. She sent me a note. I think you got one, too?' Vivienne nodded. 'She was going to confront us with each other, but I couldn't allow that to happen, so I got there first.'

'Did you kill her?' Penrose asked again, wanting no misunderstandings later – if they were ever lucky enough to get out of the house and into a courtroom.

'Yes. I knew Anthony would never be a suspect on a day like that, so I took my chances. She was already dead by the time you arrived, Viv. I heard you coming down the steps, and you have no idea how tempted I was to answer the door. I watched you leave, and it was so strange to see you again after all those years.'

'Did Mr Beresford know what you were going to do?' Penrose asked.

'No, not this time. I was going to tell him later – we didn't have any secrets – but of course I never got the chance.'

'And you were going to let me take the blame for that, as well,' Vivienne said, scarcely able to believe what she was hearing.

'Not deliberately, no. You really weren't that important to me, Viv. When I found out that Anthony was dead, I stopped caring what happened to anyone else, especially myself.'

Penrose tried to imagine what that moment had been like for her, receiving the news from Billy or switching on the wireless to hear her lover's voice, only to discover that he had been killed. 'What about your son, Miss Hanlon? Surely you must care about him?'

She thought for a long time before answering, and Penrose wondered if she was going to ignore the question altogether. 'I love my son,' she said eventually, 'but I love him because he's part of Anthony and our life together. Now that life is gone, I have no idea how I feel. At the moment, I can't even bear to look at him.'

Vivienne had been listening intently, sensing a vulnerability

319

that she was determined to exploit. 'It's an idyllic picture, Olivia, but it must have been hard on you to realise that it still wasn't enough for him.'

'What do you mean?'

'Anthony and all those other women. He always needed something more, didn't he?'

'What?' She laughed scornfully. 'They were a cover, Viv – that's all. They gave him the excuse to be with me when he wasn't with you. As long as everyone thought he was a serial philanderer, nobody would guess the truth. But they meant nothing to him. He never even touched them.'

'You're sure about that, are you? You never thought about how attractive Millicent Gray was when you went to see her? How young? All that energy and vitality and adoration – could Anthony resist that, do you think?' For the first time, a flicker of doubt crossed Olivia Hanlon's face. Penrose had no idea if there was any truth in what her sister was saying, or if Vivienne was simply trying to get her own back, but whatever she was doing gave her the upper hand. Olivia seemed distracted and short of breath, and he suddenly remembered that she suffered from asthma. 'Isn't that why you killed her?' Vivienne suggested. 'Because she reminded you of how you used to feel? I wouldn't be quite so sure of what you had, Olivia. Millicent threw some very intimate details in my face to hurt me, and I don't doubt that she would have shared them with you if she'd lived long enough. Perhaps you and Anthony had more secrets than you realised.'

'We were going to have a new life,' Olivia insisted. 'The three of us, together as a family at last.' She just managed to get the words out before a fit of coughing overtook her. Penrose went to get her some water from the sink in the corner, but Vivienne used the gun as an effective deterrent and Olivia seemed to find the strength to bring the attack under control. 'This is where we made love, Vivienne,' she said, clutching the sheets with both hands. 'Here – you can still smell him. It's where we played with our child. Those are Anthony's books on the shelf, and we chose those paintings together. His clothes are in those drawers. His life is in this house. He was mine, and nobody else's.'

The effort that such a speech required proved almost too much for her. She stopped talking and her breathing took on a hollow, rasping sound, but her sister showed no mercy. 'Anthony was *my* husband!' she shouted, slamming her free hand down on the bed.

'But he loved *me*.' Olivia clutched her chest, only capable now of short, broken phrases. 'You had . . . the broadcaster, Viv . . . the respectability . . . that was . . . what you wanted . . . You had . . . the career, because . . . because you wouldn't . . . have . . . the child . . . but you were . . . just . . . another woman . . . at the office.'

Olivia collapsed on the bed, gasping for breath. Desperately she tried to reach the cupboard in her bedside table, and Penrose guessed it was where she kept her respirator, but she no longer had the strength and he made a move to fetch it for her. 'Don't touch it!' Vivienne shouted, and he heard the click of the gun being cocked. 'Don't you dare help her. I would never have killed Anthony if she hadn't fooled me all those years ago. His blood is on her hands. She doesn't deserve to live.'

'You can't just let her die like this,' Penrose argued. 'You're not stupid. Think about all she's said and how it helps your case. If you let her die now when you could have saved her, you'll be right back to where you started and you won't stand a chance.'

'Do you think I care about that now? Too much has happened, and this is worth more to me than my life.'

There was no decision to make. Penrose went for the cupboard, incapable of standing by while someone was dying, and he heard the shot long before he registered its impact. Vivienne had aimed only to wound him, but the pain in his back was excruciating and he fell to the floor, unable to do anything but watch as Olivia Hanlon fought for her life. He closed his eyes for a moment in a vain struggle not to lose consciousness; when he opened them again, he was dimly aware of Josephine bending over him and Fallowfield standing in the doorway. 'Marta's waiting for the ambulance,' she said, her voice deliberately calm and reassuring. 'They'll be here any minute. Just hang on and lie still. You're losing a lot of blood.' Penrose nodded and bit his lip hard, trying to control the wave of dizziness and nausea that washed over him when he saw the crimson stain spreading quickly across the rug. Josephine took his hand and held it tight, focused only on the danger to him, even in the chaos that surrounded them; he squeezed it gratefully, trying desperately to do the same, but a sudden movement to the right caught his eye and he looked up to see a small child standing in the doorway. The boy stared at his mother, outstretched on the bed, and before Penrose could even shout a warning, the child ran across the room to the bedside table, oblivious to the danger he was in. Startled by his arrival, Vivienne raised the gun again and pointed it straight at him, reacting instinctively now to any new threat, regardless of how innocent it might be. 'Vivienne, no!' Josephine screamed in horror. 'For God's sake, don't do it. He's only a child.' Vivienne hesitated as the nephew and stepson she had never known calmly removed the respirator and handed it to his mother. 'This isn't the way to make anything right,' Josephine said quietly. 'You're better than that, and you know it.'

To Penrose's relief, Vivienne lowered the gun and allowed Fallowfield to take it from her. 'You were right,' she said to Josephine as the sergeant led her from the room. 'There *is* always a choice. I just wish I hadn't waited until now to make the right one.'

6

The cold, grey ash of dawn spread itself over a world which refused to look any different, despite all that had happened in the last twenty-four hours. Josephine turned away from the window and nodded again to the nurse as she passed, feeling by now that they were almost old friends. Overnight, she had been offered every form of practical comfort as she waited for news of Archie – endless cups of tea, reassuring words, a softer chair to sleep in – and she had been grateful for all of it; now, the nurse had exhausted every weapon in her armoury except for a simple smile of solidarity, but Josephine was surprised by how effective even that could be.

'I'll try Bridget again,' Marta said, putting down a cup of coffee which was just as full now as when she had picked it up. 'Where the fuck can she be? She told me she was coming back to London yesterday.'

'Perhaps something came up.'

'Or perhaps she's just avoiding it.'

Josephine looked at her in surprise. 'Why would she do that?'

'Oh, I don't know. Ignore me. I'm just tired.' She stood up and stretched. 'I don't suppose you have a number for her in Cambridge, do you?'

'No, I wouldn't know where to start.'

'All right. I won't be long. Is there anything else you need?'

'You could give Lettice and Ronnie a quick ring. I know they're as worried about Archie as we are, but it was such a relief when they went home. If we keep them up to date, they might stay there, at least for a bit.' Marta smiled. 'Is that churlish of me?'

'Not unreasonably so, no. I'll do my best to keep them at bay.'

'Thank you. And good luck with Bridget.' She watched as Marta walked down the corridor to the telephone, wondering why she seemed so irritated by Bridget's absence, then turned back to the mismatched collection of reproductions on the waiting-room wall which she had come to know so well. Archie had been lucky, there was no doubt of that: the bullet had entered his right shoulder, narrowly avoiding his lungs, but the blood-loss had been extensive and she had only had to take one look at the expression on the ambulance driver's face to realise how serious his condition was. Even now, no one would go as far as to say that he was out of the woods. During the past few hours, Josephine had revisited all the complex, untidy memories that coloured her history with Archie, adding guilt to an already lengthy list of emotions: it was her recklessness that had put him in danger in the first place; if he died, she would never forgive herself.

The longer she waited the slower time seemed to pass, and she wondered where Marta had got to. She was about to count Monet's water lilies for the fourth time in half an hour when the nurse approached again, this time with a greater sense of purpose. 'Mr Penrose is stable at last,' she said, finally allowing her smile to give hope as well as reassurance. 'The doctor says you can see him in a little while if you'd like to, just for a few minutes.'

*

Marta slammed the receiver down harder than she meant to, drawing a look of disapproval from the matron at the desk. She knew that her anger at Bridget's disappearance was irrational, fuelled in equal measure by exhaustion, shock and her concern for Archie, but sitting round doing nothing wasn't making her mood any better, and her conscience nagged at her to avert the crisis that she had unwittingly set in motion by discovering Bridget's secret. On a whim, she went downstairs and hailed a cab; if she couldn't speak to Bridget in person, she could at least leave a note at her digs, so that when and if she decided to return to London to confront her dilemma head-on, she would know immediately what had happened.

The streets were quiet at this time of the morning and the taxi got her to Hampstead in a matter of minutes. The Vale of Health Hotel nestled in a restful hollow on the edge of the heath, not far from Holly Place; it was quiet and secluded, with an old-fashioned air which would not have been out of place in an Edwardian novel, but its name was misleading and the building was actually divided into a number of artists' studios. Bridget rented the ground floor and, as the taxi drew up outside, Marta was surprised to see the lights on. She asked the driver to wait and hammered loudly on the front door, caring little now who else she woke in the process; when Bridget answered, she pushed past her without pausing for the formality of an invitation.

'Jesus, Marta, what in hell's name are you doing here at this time of the morning?'

'I've been telephoning you all night. Why didn't you answer?'

'I was working. I always take the phone off when I need to concentrate. It stops me being bothered.' She emphasised the final word, and Marta looked down at the telephone wire which had indeed been removed from the wall. She glanced round the room, sparsely decorated and devoted to a single purpose, and her attention was taken by a half-worked canvas on an easel by the window, obviously the painting which had demanded Bridget's undivided attention. It was a portrait of Archie, unsettling in its intimacy, and if Marta had ever doubted the artist's feelings for her subject, she didn't any longer. His face stared back at her, and the expression in his eyes was something that no one would ever want to see in the person they loved – anger, disbelief, betrayal; all the demons that Bridget had been trying to exorcise through her work. 'You promised you'd give me some time,' she said, looking intently at Marta and speaking more calmly. 'I have to do this my way.'

'I know and I'm not here to bully you, but there *is* no time. Archie's been hurt – that's why I was phoning. You need to come to the hospital.'

The colour drained from Bridget's face and she stared at Marta in disbelief. 'Hurt? What do you mean? Is he all right?'

'They've made him as comfortable as they can but it's a serious gunshot wound to the shoulder.'

'Oh God, no. I've dreaded this, Marta – every time he does something dangerous in this fucking job of his. I've only just found him again. I can't lose him – not now.'

She stood in the middle of the room, suddenly as helpless as a child, and Marta took a coat off the hook by the door and handed it to her. 'Come on – there's a taxi outside.'

They were silent for most of the journey back, and Marta was relieved that Bridget seemed too shocked to ask how or why Archie had been hurt. 'You have to tell him,' she said eventually, when the hospital's handsome red-brick facade came into view. 'Not now, obviously, but when he's strong enough to hear what you have to say. Let something good come out of this. If you don't, you'll always regret it.'

*

Josephine shut the door quietly behind her and sat down next to the bed. Archie's eyes were closed and his face was pale in the room's cool, soothing half-light, but the pain which had frightened her so much had been replaced by something more peaceful, at least for now. Reluctant to wake him, she put her hand gently on the sheet, as close to his as she dared without actually touching him, and finally allowed herself to cry.

'Josephine, don't – there's no need.' His fingers brushed hers, more reassuring than his words. 'I'm all right.'

'But you might not have been. I'm so sorry, Archie. I don't know how I could have been so stupid.'

'Don't blame yourself. You saved that child's life.'

'Perhaps, but only because I put it at risk in the first place. And you weren't quite so forgiving at the time. I've never seen you as furious as you were when you first got there.'

He tried to smile, but a wave of pain damned the effort. 'What happened after I blacked out?' he asked when it had passed. 'Did Olivia . . .'

'Yes, she pulled through. But don't worry about any of that now. Just save your strength.'

'Where's Bridget?'

'We haven't been able to contact her yet. Marta's trying again now. She'll be here soon, I'm sure.'

'And she'll probably finish the job that Vivienne Beresford started. She's always telling me not to take risks.' He frowned, irritated that his body wouldn't let him speak as freely as he wanted to. 'I thought I was never going to see her again, Josephine. All I could think about as I lay there was how much time we'd wasted.'

'Then you must tell her that. Stop worrying about how she'll react and just be honest with her.'

'That sounds ominous.' Bridget stood in the doorway, uncertain of her welcome, and Josephine would have found it hard to explain the muddle of emotions that she felt when she saw the joy in Archie's eyes.

'I don't think you've got too much to worry about,' she said, getting up to go. 'I'd better leave you to it.'

Acknowledgements

I'm forever grateful to Josephine Tey (Elizabeth MacKintosh), who continues to be such a rich inspiration for this series – and to her readers, who love those eight precious detective novels as much as I do, and who have embraced these books because of it.

Many writers have helped to shape and inform *London Rain*. The book began with another crime novel, *Death at Broadcasting House* by Val Gielgud and Holt Marvell (long overdue a reprint), and with the subsequent 1934 film version, much of which was shot at BH. Val Gielgud's various memoirs inspired the character of Julian Terry, and fans of today's radio drama owe a great deal to his pioneering spirit, a legacy every bit as lasting and important as his brother's to the stage. I'm indebted to the *BBC Yearbook*, and to *The Story of Broadcasting House: Home of the BBC* by Mark Hines, whose beautiful descriptions and photographs are the next best thing to walking through that iconic building in the 1930s; to memoirs by SW Smithers, Maurice Gorham, and Sydney Moseley, all of which gave valuable insights into the early days of the Corporation; and to *The Radio Times Story* by Tony Currie, which – together with that very special Coronation issue – documents a British institution.

Many of the deaths that take place during *London Rain's* Coronation are real, and more information on them can be found in newspaper accounts of the day, which also do a splendid job of recreating the atmosphere on the city's streets.

Olivia Hanlon's life was inspired by Kate Meyrick's memoir,

Secrets of the 43 Club; her death, by the speculation surrounding Brian Jones's final days at Cotchford Farm in 1969. A rock star isn't an obvious reference for period crime fiction, but in many respects the 1960s hold a mirror to the 1920s, and eagle-eyed readers will have noticed an occasional nod to the Rolling Stones. In a similar vein, *Fine Day for a Hanging: the Ruth Ellis Story* by Carol Ann Lee helped me to understand the motives of my own killer.

Love and thanks to everyone at Faber & Faber, David Higham Associates, HarperCollins and Fletcher & Company for the care they take with the series; to Mick Wiggins for yet another beautiful cover; to Richard Reynolds and Heffers Bookshop for making writing *and* reading such a pleasure; and especially to my family and friends, who support each novel so fabulously, and who will all know why a new year and a new book mean even more this time. And to Mandy, whose love and insight make each book more joyful, more satisfying, and just plain better – thank you. Two authors in the house now – that's a bit special.

There are some people you never want to speak of in the past tense. PD James was a part of this series from the very beginning, and she greeted each new book with warmth and excitement – as generous and original in her reading as in her writing. Phyllis was a great friend to Mandy and to me for many years, and we miss her. I would much rather be taking her a copy of *London Rain* than dedicating it to her, but the novel – like the ones before it and the ones still to come – has been cheered on by her words, the finest advice any writer can have: 'Make it the best book you can, dear.'